# *A Wizard's Spell*

## The Dragon Roost Bed & Breakfast Series:

## Book 3

### Betsy J. Bennett

Ahead of the Press Publishing
St. Louis, Missouri

**Library of Congress Cataloguing-in-Publication Data**

A Wizard's Spell
The Dragon's Roost Bed and Breakfast Series: Book 3
Betsy J. Bennett / author


ISBN     Paperback        978-1-950392-16-2
ISBN     KINDLE           978-1-950392-17-9

Ahead of The Press Publishing
St. Louis, Missouri

# TABLE OF CONTENTS

SUMMARY of Previous
DRAGON'S ROOST BED AND BREAKFAST SERIES
BOOK 1
:

## A Dragon's Tea

**Nothing made sense...**

To hide from her ex-boyfriend Lori Lawrick runs to
her Aunt Jan. Jan runs a bed and breakfast, and Lori
decides that might be what she needs to put her life
back in order. She will help her Aunt cook and plant
vegetables while she decides what to do with her
life.

**He said he was born to make tea...**

At her Aunt's B&B, Lori meets Byron, a handsome jeweler who creates
incredible works of art in gold and precious stones, but he says it is his
duty to make tea. While the tea served in a fancy dragon-shaped teapot is
excellent, it is not what she would consider putting him to his best
use. She dreams of him, and when he kisses her, she wants to chop into a
tree the statement "It happened here" explaining the magnitude of the
effect the kiss had on her.

**The B&B stands at a nexus of several different worlds...**

Lori comes to realize nothing is what it seems at the B&B. There is a witch
who threatens Byron's life when she asks for tea. Plants grow overnight
when watered by the tea, and then there is Byron himself who infuriates
her and at the same time makes her pulse throb who is never around
when the tea is served. When Lori discovers a real dragon who terrifies
her, she must find the strength to save Byron, the B&B and maybe the
entire planet from evil sneaking in from a portal from another world.

SUMMARY of

DRAGON'S ROOST BED AND BREAKFAST SERIES

### A Gargoyle's Vow
### Book 2

Brenda thought her Aunt's Bed and Breakfast a house of horrors

As an eight-year-old child Brenda was bitten by a monster chained in the basement. Now 17 years later she returns to face her fears.

He looks like a monster
With claws at his hands and feet, broad wings, horns and a massive snout, Milton terrifies Brenda.
Centuries ago, before the Earth was even formed, Milton committed the worst sin imaginable and as payment for this sin, he is forced to look like an evil gargoyle.

Now she needs his help
Milton offers to help Brenda's infant nephew, but only if Brenda agrees to marry him. While she agonizes over her decision, Brenda learns that he is not evil as he appears. But she also realizes if she marries him, she will not be first in his life. He must complete his quest, even if it means sacrificing her.

How can her growing love survive under those conditions?

-

# CHAPTER 1

Magic cackled in the air around him. Iridescent powerstrands swirled around his ankles, sinuous and snake-like energy which he and other wizards like him could manipulate into anything animate or inanimate. But not here. He was too exposed and vulnerable.

Lethargic thunder rumbled overhead in a long, drawn out moan, a precursor of the cold front arriving from the west. Feeling the pressure to hurry, Pierce Billova climbed the back stairs two at a time toward his attic lair.

No visitor to his exclusive Boston home had ever come upon the staircase unexpectedly. It was hidden by more than the door in the kitchen which blended so carefully into the wall as to be considered invisible.

Both were concealed by magic.

The sun had set less than an hour before, and the moon, a powerful force for magicians, waxed full. Outside, black nimbus clouds hung heavy, throbbing, as if desperate to release their revenge on the city. The storm, when it came, wouldn't be anything for the history books. Not a hurricane or enough to raise flood waters, just a good, soaking October shower, the kind his Midwestern grandfather had called a frog-drowner.

With his trained inner eye, Pierce could visualize the extent of the front. It wasn't only the people of Massachusetts who would be grabbing their umbrellas in a few minutes. There would be windshield wipers working furiously as far away as Tallahassee. When he was in the mood, or when the need was great, he could control the weather with a wave of his hand and a firmly spoken command.

Weather sense was one of his stronger abilities. Yet he had not originated this storm. Someone else was dabbling where he or she shouldn't, creating a massive imbalance and this storm was a consequence. If it wasn't controlled or contained, the external manifestations would only grow worse.

Pierce felt the small hairs on his arms raise and his blood surged in response to the violence outside. Lightning flashed. A spare two seconds later, thunder rattled the windows, strong enough he could feel it in the soles of his feet. His anticipation grew. The storm's arrival only heightened his urgency to practice his arcane art.

There was an ugly, festering unbalance in the forces he studied. Energy could not be created or destroyed, that much physicists got right, but it could be manipulated. Huge chunks of powerstrands, magical energy, were disappearing, a void far too massive to be the result of anything but evil corruption.

His path was almost pitch black, except for the glow of powerstrands that lapped at his feet. They shimmered in brilliant colors, as if in another lifetime they had been neon lights advertising a wide selection of beer brands. It had taken five years of apprenticeship before he was able to see his first. Now, as much as they were tools, they were also companions.

When he reached the door to his attic lair he held his right hand out, fingers splayed over the knob, feeling with his heightened senses the warding spells he had set. They were undisturbed. Still the hint of something insidious, something evil that shouldn't be there invaded his consciousness. Lightning flashed again, as if telling him to heed this disruption. There was nothing sedate about the thunder now. It cracked in a loud explosion directly above.

The powerstrands at his feet were unconcerned; a few, the yellow ones, frolicked like puppies. A sharp stench of evil reached his nose, a scent of something burning, or a conglomeration of things rotting. The trace vanished quickly, leaving him to think he had imagined it, or it came from the storm, or more likely he brought the disturbance with him. As much as he looked forward to plying his art, this was no pleasant task he set himself.

His palm tingled in anticipation and his pulse raced. When overcome by rare fits of whimsy, Pierce could easily imagine the wards on the doorknob welcomed his return to his secret base. He could almost believe the energy itself was sentient, recognized in him a master, one of the very few on this planet they could communicate with.

Silently and with a minimum of movement—broad, crass actions were indicative of amateurs—he twisted his hand near the knob without actually touching it. The powerstrands sidled, one over another, releasing their knot. On well-oiled hinges, the door slid open.

He stood on the threshold, breathing deeply. If he were ever asked, he might say this was his favorite part of his career, the anticipatory moment before he curled his first powerstrand, before he changed matter and energy. His lungs filled slowly. He held the air, savoring the trace hints of herbs and magic, and since he was an indifferent housekeeper, more than a little dust.

Then, feeding the rush of desperation which brought him here in the first place, Pierce methodically stripped off his clothing, leaving shirt, pants, socks and jockeys in a heap on the floor, and slipped, naked, into the silky, long black robe he wore as a master wizard.

Dressed, he turned and reset his wards, his mind locked on his upcoming investigation, ignoring the tick against the back of his neck that something wasn't right, and perhaps he wasn't as thorough as he could have been in maintaining his privacy. He was too anxious to start, and he had been safe here for years.

The powerstrands curled at his feet in over a dozen iridescent colors: blood red to pale blushing rose, midnight blue through turquoise, five distinct shades of green. Each had their own strengths, their own uses. They twined around his knees and up to his hip, almost purring. They tickled and caused a low level non-sexual arousal. He bent down, stroked them, as he would a familiar cat, pleased anew with his own whimsy as he imagined they purred in response to his touch. The powerstrands came because they were called, and although the more powerful came reluctantly, they came.

That was the ability of a master wizard.

Wasting no additional time, Pierce straightened. He wiggled his fingers, and power crackled exactly like the lightning directly above him, but a type of energy which had nothing to do with electricity. A shimmering lime-green powerstrand crawled up his legs, wrapped itself around his forearm, and bent itself to his will.

He would ride it, as witches rode brooms, as Wardens rode dragons, as legend stated Demetrius had once ridden the sun. He slid easily into the procedure, holding his body rigid, which was the first lesson he had learned as an apprentice, how to hold absolutely still.

Methodically and instinctively, Pierce separated his body from his soul. He anticipated, and felt, a pulling, a reluctance psychological more than physical, as if his soul wasn't willing to go wandering the universe without his heart and lungs. He continued, slowly, like getting out of a diving suit a size too small, until he experienced a subtle pop and his consciousness was free to float above the restraints of his physical body.

His heart beat, his lungs filled with air, blood traveled the endless route through long, interconnecting veins, only he wasn't there while any of that was happening. Empty of his soul, his body was only a husk, living, yet vegetative. Any neurosurgeon sneaking in now with an EEG would call him brain dead—and be wrong. He wasn't dead, just, for all practical purposes, not home.

In astral form, he rode his powerstrand, slipping through walls and space instantly, looking for the evil he sought. Physical laws of magic had been broken, not the temporal, manmade laws of Congress or local governments. Other master wizards across the continents were looking for this contamination as well, but Pierce, through luck and hard work, had a lead, and the pollution was almost within his grasp.

He sailed through the night. While he always hungered for additional power, it was a fine line he traveled, for evil was persuasive. Still, Pierce had been trained well. He feared his own corruption more than death.

He traveled north by northwest, leaving Boston, heading for upstate New York. The night aged, the storm moved east. When the powerstrand he rode faded, he pulled a fresh one.

Then another.

And another.

He made mental notes of what he discovered, for below him distortion appeared clearly in the forces he worshiped. He could see the ugly corruption of power. This information was vital, but still wasn't the irrefutable proof he sought.

Pierce looked back quickly, almost over his shoulder, except at the moment he had no shoulder, sensing a disturbance but oddly, no danger. Something shifted beside him and he recognized it, fleetingly, as friend. He continued his astral journey, satisfied with his safety, halting only when a sharp sting of bullets entered the body he had left behind.

# CHAPTER 2

"I think we're losing him—"

"Blood pressure dropping—"

"I need a type and crossmatch, stat!"

Within the orchestrated cacophony, the emergency room staff danced, pumping drugs, taking samples, making silent, experienced analysis of the patient's condition, while their audience of one remained unresponsive to their machinations.

Time passed, measured by a dozen beeping monitors, the dripping of clear fluids, and the frustrations of their failure. An operating room was prepared. X-Rays were taken. Next of kin notified. The intensity of their efforts heightened. This staff was used to winning, but perhaps they would not this time.

A policeman marched back and forth outside the glass-enclosed examination room, blood on his uniform, furiously scribbling notes. He had arrived first on the scene, minutes before the paramedics. If the patient survived, it would be in large part due to disaster classes he'd renewed every two years, and from the numerous times he'd had to put that knowledge into practice. His precinct would receive the bullets when they were retrieved, three he'd thought he'd heard the paramedics comment. Three. Lord help the guy. They would study the victim's clothing, his wallet, any trace they could recover from nails, skin, hair. They would also search the alley, although it would be determined later that had been a dump site. The shooting had taken place elsewhere.

Beside the policeman, the ambulance staff stripped the bloodied linen from their stretcher, remade it with stiffly-starched white sheets. They were oddly silent, this group of two who kept their sanity on rough calls with lighthearted banter. As a pair, they looked toward the examination room, where they see the battle being fought. They shook their heads, as if to clear the image. A moment later, they drove off to their next call under the flare of flashing red lights, the driver laughing when the punchline was revealed to a joke started over an hour before, when it looked like their shift would be relatively slow.

The trauma team worked on.

"Shot with a .38—"

"It's this one in the lung I'm worried about—"

"OR's ready."

"If he lives—"

Pierce Billova watched with an unattached fascination. From his perspective, high above the room, he could see everything, the technicians, the doctors, and their increasing desperation as they worked on the all-but-lifeless form on the stretcher. Below him, standing in a corner, Pierce noticed his friend and partner Daniel Rayock, looking pale. Daniel muttered under his breath, twining his hands with the harnessing of their power, which to the uninitiated medical staff, would only look like idle movements of frustration.

*What in hell is bothering him now?* Pierce thought, but then decided he must be fairly slow on the uptake himself. Rayock must know the victim.

Being a rational man, Pierce Billova wanted to review what he suspected about Pasco Minelli, at the moment the top of his most-likely-to-have-done-this list, when he realized something oddly disconcerting, something which should have been more readily apparent than it was.

He knew the victim too.

The body the doctors worked over so frantically was his own.

No. That wasn't possible. The body on the gurney couldn't be his. A twin perhaps, a doppelganger. Given the nature of his work, the possibly increased dramatically. Not a biological double, but one formed by the hidden arts to infiltrate his power circle, to steal his secrets.

Perhaps he should warn Daniel.

An electric jolt passed through him but it felt disembodied, as if it were far more psychological than physical.

It had to be magic. He often traveled astrally, leaving his body behind. In his line of work, there were meetings he needed to witness without his body's presence being an issue, places where he couldn't appear.

Astral-travel usually felt like a surveillance camera, watching the action in real-time without having to participate. Although this time was different. And with that thought, he came to the shocked realization of how it was different: he was no longer tied to his body by an invisible umbilical cord. The stranger that he could not attach the pronoun 'me' to, was himself. Once he bit into the theory, he tried to be satisfied with it.

*So this was what being dead was like.*

Maybe he should tell the doctors it was already too late for what they were doing. Pack your bags. Call it a night. Then again, maybe not...

Rayock moved his hands, harnessing magic and dominion, using subtle movements Pierce recognized and he experienced, strongly, the pull back. Yet this…condition…was too fascinating to answer even the commands of another major wizard.

He had known then the duality of both release from a physical body and the grounding of a spirit-lifeline back to his form. Of course his heart had beat then. Besides the fact that there was no grounding, no body to return to, this wasn't a whole lot different. Suddenly, abruptly, it felt like holiday. Unexpected, serendipitous freedom.

He couldn't quite see, there were too many people in the way, but then, inexplicably they parted, and he looked down at himself again, barely recognizing the face which had stared back at him from the mirror for thirty-two years. His eyes were open, a half-mast stare of blankness, his lips were still. There were none of the little twitches of eyelashes or pulse tripping that always accompanied a living form, no matter how deeply asleep. He had difficulty recognizing himself because of the lack of animation.

His shirt had been torn open, and blood, drying now, covered most of his chest, starting from three tiny points-of-entry. His crystal, on the silver chain around his neck, looked pale, lifeless. That stunned him almost as much as the sight of his body.

He was used to the crystal responding, purring like a kitten or roaring like a lion. Even when it was dormant, it was—for want of a better word— sentient. Now it was nothing more than semi-precious stone, badly cut, worn smooth from exposure to his body.

Wouldn't his senator father and society-matron mother be shocked to know their do-no-wrong son wore crystals? That he was, allowing for no misplaced modesty, one of the greatest wizards ever to practice the art? That would certainly give them something to talk about during Washington cocktail parties.

Although, considering the circumstances, perhaps the fact he'd been murdered would give them enough fodder to feed the herd of gossip columnists and political analysts who followed them everywhere. They could easily overlook one lifeless crystal, not that it mattered. Rayock would tend to any details involving questionable possessions should the matter arise. Such was their friendship and the oaths they took to ensure the secrecy of their art.

Pierce tried to take a deep breath, an automatic sigh of resignation, found he couldn't. Under the conditions he felt that was to be expected, and he would have laughed had the panoramic scene not been so absurd. There was a span of events he couldn't quite remember, between the shocked instant he first felt the bullets enter his chest, and just about a moment ago. What had he been doing that he had left his body so completely vulnerable? How had his shields been so easily broached?

The doctors would have to hurry up and finish so he could get on with his life. *On with his life.* His sense of ridiculous increased as possibilities arranged themselves in his warp-speed mind. Would he have to change all his verb tenses? I was, instead of I am, when he met people? Was there an action verb that still applied to him? Ran, laughed, breathed? Probably not. That would take some getting used to.

And he wasn't going to hang around here either. Hospitals were never Pierce Billova's idea of a fun Saturday evening. Until he saw an elevator going up, until some guy wearing choir robes pointed him in another direction, he saw no particular need to watch. It was, all things considered, morbid. It might even ruin his entire day.

Now there was a comforting thought. But he was dead, clearly dead, and so rules that normally applied to people no longer had any bearing, did they? Maybe, maybe not. But then again, considering his secret profession, the social niceties and the legislative enacted laws rarely applied to him anyway.

Concentrating, and not looking down at the stretcher and the technology beeping away and the blood pooling on the floor, Pierce found it possible to walk. A type of walk, easier, when he didn't study his feet, a good three inches from the floor. The waiting room was jammed. Heavy night at the emergency room. Should the trauma team back there just give up on him, they'd have a chance to do something about the backlog.

"Hang on a little longer," he told them as he slipped through a wall.
\*\*\*

The street pulsed with activity. A chilled rain drained from pewter clouds with an intensity Noah would recognize, and Pierce wondered why these people didn't have enough sense to go home, find a warm fire or barring that a toasty radiator or the camaraderie of a barstool, but the streets were packed. Theater goers, concert groupies, late night shoppers, those who haunted the peep shows and the night shadows, the smoke filled taverns. Those with places to go, those who just hung out.

Pierce emerged into the night, leaving the hospital—and a rather significant part of himself—behind. He experienced odd, curious sensations which only seemed to grow more incredible the further away he wandered. He didn't feel the rain or the cold, for that matter he wasn't certain he could feel his fingers, but his feet worked, allowing him to make his way through a part of the city he wasn't familiar with. This was not an old stomping ground.

Everything looked real, causing him to run out of the path of a delirious taxi, whether or not there was any possibility of additional personal damage. Holograms. Virtual reality without the goggles and the gloves. He did not feel his power.

Far more unexpected, he did not miss it.

The rain crashed down harder. Senses returned. He was not certain before this instant that he had been able to hear anything beyond his own inner chaotic voice. Now, distinctly, he could hear the splash of the fat, insistent drops as they exploded on the ground, hear the growl from engines, the squeal of tires as cars maneuvered through puddles large enough to qualify as independent bodies of water on a Rand-McNally Road Atlas.

He liked the sounds. They were somehow more real than anything else around him. He grinned, or tried to, uncertain whether he succeeded, when he heard forced laughter of an overly-made-up prostitute bartering with two well-dressed businessmen each old enough to be her father. "How about I take both of you. Your hotel room. You won't regret it..." He continued on, before the negotiations grew more serious.

Yes, he could hear the raindrops, but he couldn't feel them. Couldn't smell them. Couldn't, when he stuck his tongue out, taste them. He was left with two of five senses. Not a high percentage. He was a sensual man. Although he devoted a large amount of time to analyzing inner emotions, he found touch, taste, and smell made the world an interesting place. He was curiously reluctant to try his finely honed sixth-sense, but then he knew why. Magic, like making love, required a body.

He didn't see her at first. What he felt instead was a steady, yet inexorable pull to the left, and having nothing better to do, made a conscious decision to follow. Pierce had ignored three such pulls already, exploring on his own rather than going where he was lead, wherever that was to be. This directional-assistance was no stronger than the previous occurrences, but perhaps his curiosity was more intense.

He wasn't certain at first how he knew it was a woman, but he was. She was dressed rather androgynously in a black raincoat which hid any hint of her figure, and the shoes on her feet, the only other part he could see with any clarity, were flats, and could belong to a man as a woman. Her hair, in this light he had no idea what color it was, was plastered to her head, and fell down to her neck in tight ringlets, which might have been the result of a beautician's art, but more likely was the expected consequence of large amounts of moisture. He moved closer.

She was leaning over the open window of a sleek Jaguar, which Pierce rather thought was silver, although given the lighting conditions and his rather bizarre sensory input could have been any color at all. The bastard inside the car kept the engine running. He was not getting wet at all.

Pierce squatted beside her, close enough to kiss the tip of her nose if it pleased him. She took no notice. She reeked of desperation, making it impossible for Pierce to decide if she were pretty. Besides, he was more interested in eavesdropping than determining if she belonged on the cover of Vogue. She had no bearing on his current life—if he had one—and being dead he doubted he could have much effect on her either. He would, for the moment, play the voyeur and give into a delicious, secret lust which in the past had been firmly controlled by the tenets of his art.

"Please," she said, gripping the rim of the half-open window with fingers that had to be colder than Pierce's. "Please, you've got to listen."

"Baby, you're old news."

Pierce tried unsuccessfully to see the man behind the steering wheel.

"Harry, I'm pregnant."

Pierce looked at her again. It wasn't quite what he expected her to say.

The bastard, sitting on dry leather, smiled, slowly, slickly, showing not so much an evil glance as an uncaring one. "Then I suppose you know what to do about it."

Her fingers were white against the windowsill, bloodless. There didn't seem to be much color in her cheeks or her neck either. Her eyes were hooded, thickly lashed. Pierce had no conception if they were bloodshot.

She moved possessively, one hand over the raincoat which showed no appreciable swell. "Don't you care about your child?"

He laughed, shook his head 'no' without putting much effort into the maneuver. She was an annoyance, but a minor one, a mosquito buzzing his ears, rather than, for example a flat tire, something he'd have to deal with. "And here I thought you were sophisticated, baby," biting out the word sophisticated as if it were a medical degree and he discovered she'd barely eked by with a GED.

Her left hand joined the right on the windowsill, curled around the raised lip of smoky shatter-proof glass. "This is important."

Pierce could tell she thought so, and tried to determine if it would be important to him, if some former lover told him of approaching fatherhood. His was a life filled with momentary pleasures, seeking the latest in excitements without any long term goals which didn't involve being footloose and fancy free to practice his alchemy in the privacy of his hidden rooms.

He came to no decision before the woman spoke again. If the man had responded to her plea he'd missed it, but Pierce, knowing something of self-preservation arrogance, rather doubted the man had made any comment at all.

"I don't have many options." Her lips quivered. Dispassionately, and unexpectedly, he noticed how full they were, how expressive. He'd bet, under other circumstances, she'd have a killer smile.

The creep behind the steering wheel made no move to pry her fingers off the window of his precious car, but revved the engine a few times, enough to indicate he'd been stalled long enough. "You don't need many options, only one, and if you think you're getting money out of me for it, you're mistaken. Now be a good girl and run along. You're old news, honey."

The Jaguar drove off, the woman crouched in the reforming puddles, alone, except for her tears and a fetus she'd have to "deal with". She cursed him then, her former lover, but Pierce didn't hear, for he was feeling another pull, this one far stronger, and he felt himself being reunited with something important he'd left behind.

Still, he wanted to stop, offer comfort, even when he knew he had none to give. Before he returned to his own pain, he felt hers. He thought he needed to save the life of that child, and maybe offer what comfort he could to the woman.

Before he could formulate an action plan, he was back in the ER, filling his lungs with air, and fighting a blood red powerstrand trying to wrap itself around his neck.

# CHAPTER 3

"Mr. Billova--"

He'd been lost somewhere in a nightmare, where a woman had asked, "Don't you even care about your son or daughter?" as if that were the most important thing in the universe, more important than if the stars were going to appear, or the sun to rise. A child. A pregnancy. Since returning to his body, her pain had been far more real than any of his own.

"Mr. Billova--"

Pierce turned around slowly from where he stood, staring through the window of the Boston high-rise, and faced his secretary. *So we're back to Mr. Billova* he thought. They'd passed those boundaries years before.

He'd been idly scratching the healing wounds from chest surgery. The pain was manageable, but the scars annoyed him because he hadn't quite gotten used to his marred chest. He'd been assured they would fade, yet would never completely disappear.

It would take only a second of his time to erase them, an easy spell, but he hadn't bothered, for two distinct yet separate reasons. The first was the scars reminded him he had unfinished business. Someone shot him. Someone would have to be dealt with very soon. He couldn't let his guard down until he found the answers he was looking for.

The second explanation was a little less sharply defined. The scars made him feel human. Pierce had spent the better part of his life trying to understand, then ignore his "humanness;" now, he found, in a slight, almost perverse way, he embraced it. He didn't understand his own motivations, but he knew since witnessing the woman kneeling in the rain, being human wasn't necessarily a bad thing.

"Mr. Billova?"

"Yes, Candy?"

Another indication of the change in their relationship was that she didn't simply sweep into his office, drop that sheaf of papers on his desk, and expect him to treat her with that comfortable camaraderie which was common in the long-term relationships between bosses and executive assistants.

"The Boroni deposition was just delivered by messenger, and I've got the Zane file here you were looking for." She approached his desk, but not before giving him a long, hard look. His jacket was slung over an oak coat rack that in all the years had never held a coat, and his tie was loosened, the top two buttons of his shirt undone. Before this incident, he'd never once been less than immaculate. Nine o'clock in the morning, or nine o'clock at night, not a button out of place or a wrinkle.

Could that be what was bothering her, the fact he had altered in superficial manners, or had his actions become so unpredictable he no longer hid behind the familiar facade? He scratched again at the scar and wondered if he were becoming more human, or less.

He spared a glance at the file, made no move to accept it. He couldn't actually remember its importance, although judging from her statement, he'd been waiting for it.

"Thank you."

There wasn't a trace of gratitude in the remark. He was indifferent, but properly raised. A token was the best he could manage.

Pierce returned to the window, rested his hand on the glass, touching it, savoring the sensation now that his full range of senses had returned. "You know, in all the years I've had this office, I don't think I've looked out this window once."

"Sir?"

He made a broad sweeping motion. "Have all these buildings been here all along?"

Her face purposely grew blank, as if, while she watched he had sprouted a single horn in his forehead and she was under military orders not to notice.

"You've been awfully busy." She made it sound like an excuse, but also, inexplicably, like an apology, as if it were partly her fault.

Pierce shut his eyes tight, pulled in a deep breath until his damaged lungs protested. He recognized he was acting strangely. One of the strongest tenets of his vocation was that in his public life he must act 'normal' at all times, and there couldn't be the slightest indication of anything unusual. With that thought firmly in mind, he took a single step toward the desk and the paperwork she delivered before he stopped. "Leave them on the desk. I'm taking off early today."

"I beg your pardon?" She looked at him as if he'd just committed a cardinal sin, and here in the august offices of Mies, Malizia and Igrisan.

"There's nothing pressing there, is there?" he asked, just for the perverse pleasure of watching her blanch. Considering his secretary's skin color was very dark, she was losing tone at an alarming rate.

"Nothing pressing?"

"I'm going away for the weekend," he said, although he hadn't decided on that course of action until he spoke. In fact, he had no idea where the sentence had come from, but it caught his fancy. A few days on the coast were exactly what he needed.

"Your mother will be pleased." His mother had already left four messages since he decided, quite arbitrarily, he wasn't speaking to her anymore. Candy wasn't used to being an intermediary.

"I'm not going to the cabin." Cabin. Renowned summer home on the New Jersey shoreline, opulent enough for entertaining visiting royalty, whether it be European, or the more American version, a president or two. It had been called a cabin since his grandfather built the drafty monstrosity almost fifty years before.

"No?" she asked. She probably wouldn't have been much more startled if he'd mentioned he wanted to dance naked in the fountain at Rockefeller Center on St. Patrick's Day.

"You won't be able to reach me."

"Mr. Billova—" Then in an unprecedented act of courage she reached out, touched his silk shirt sleeve. "Won't you consider seeing that doctor your mother recommended?"

He easily could have taken offense, perhaps as early as yesterday he would have. Instead he recognized in her something which he never suspected: her concern for him, which at the moment was overriding her desire for job security. He'd thrown enough fits, tantrums was perhaps the better word, over this very subject over the last four days, that she had to know with a look he could return her to the typing pool, if in this day and age of word processors there was such a thing.

She backed away, her black eyes wide, expecting immediate reprisal for her boldness. Like any good executive assistant, she often told him candidly what she thought, except she knew, and he knew she knew, this subject was strictly off limits. He wasn't about to see the psychologist his mother and the partners recommended. And he wasn't going crazy, or at least he didn't think so.

For a moment it occurred to him he might owe her an apology or some kind of reassurance that he wasn't about to have her publicly flogged, but he didn't have the words. A lifetime of concentrating on himself left him bereft of offering her any benevolent acknowledgement. Their relationship had always been professional.

With one touch she had taken it a bit further, had tried, apparently, to break through his pain. She cared. It was a revelation he couldn't deal with, even as he wondered if she'd offered that type of support before. Had she, and he been too frozen to notice?

He tried to smile, found the action awkward, instead returned his lips to their normal sneer and nodded, an indication he had noticed, even though he had no idea what to do about it. If Candy stood very still, it was similar only the doe in the headlights paralysis which often ended in road-kill.

Odd, he'd never considered himself a monster, especially considering the types of power he wielded in his secret life. He suddenly got a glimmer of how she might see him, with no time to wonder if she'd always been afraid of him, or if this had happened since those bullets had found a resting place in his chest.

"Can you hold the fort while I'm gone?"

"Of course." Her answer was wary, as if she expected to be shot at any minute. He decided to experiment, add a trace of reciprocal warmth. "If anyone gives you any grief about rescheduling appointments—"

"I can handle it." Her spine stiffened, but she avoided his glance, returning instead to protecting herself from the ice of his indifference. His experiment had been a failure.

"Yes, I know you can." He made a mental note to give her a raise. More money he could handle. An honest emotional response was still beyond him, even as he realized for the first time a fatter paycheck was not what she craved. With sudden instinct, he knew she would have preferred him to treat her with more respect, notice her, even once, not as a woman, but as someone more than fingers on a keyboard or a voice on the telephone.

He gripped his suit coat, without bothering to put it on. Though he'd been staring out the window, he couldn't remember if it was December or August, March or June. He'd have to pay better attention.

Pierce reached the door she'd left open, turning to find she hadn't moved from beside his desk. "Candy—"

"Yes, Mr. Billova?"

"For everything you've done, thank you."

"Mr. Billova?"

He wanted to touch her then, place a simple hand on her arm, non-sexual, non-threatening, to let her know how much he appreciated her, but he didn't know how. He wasn't certain how she would take any physical approach, so he stood there, more than half-confused.

"I'm all right, or rather, I think I will be. I simply need some time to heal." If she thought he meant his body, so much the better.

He struggled to find words. Oddly, a clear rope of magical power rubbed against his socks, he felt it, knew if he lowered his eyes to his feet, he'd be able to see it, but for the first time he realized magic might not be the solution to every problem besetting him. He met her glance with a straight, direct glaze, something else which had been missing since he took three bullets. He hadn't been able to meet anyone's eyes. "I know the work you do is excellent. I do appreciate you. I don't always have the opportunity—"

"Mr. Billova, that's not necessary—"

"Actually, it is. I…um…hate to sound morbid, or revert to generalities, but since the…accident…"

A spark of life flashed in her eyes, appearing, then vanishing so quickly, he almost felt he imagined it. "You've had a lot on your mind. You should still be in a hospital bed."

"There's always that. I want you to know…" then words failed him, and he cleared his throat, if only to stall. "I don't know when I'll be back."

She flashed a smile, showing glistening white teeth. When she first took to guarding his desk she had worn braces, a luxury she missed as a child, but something which had been a priority high enough to demand a good portion of her early paychecks. "That's fine. I'll reschedule the appointments, make the excuses."

He found it frightening that a large part of her job description now involved making excuses for him. He scratched idly at his chest again. "I've got to go."

Turning the key in the ignition of the small, haughty Porsche, Pierce wondered if he should stop at the police station. He had been ordered to keep in touch, as detectives hit solid walls in their search for suspects in the who-dun-it. He doubted they had any leads. He hadn't been forthcoming when the officers had haunted his ICU bed.

"I have no enemies," he'd said, plastic tubes crisscrossing every inch of his body. Right. Well, it was correct as far as that went. He had no enemies the police could find.

"Is there anyone who would want you dead, Mr. Billova?"

How could he start the list? Wizards on the whole were solitary. One master, a fellow practitioner or two, friendships formed during apprenticeship, anything else transitory and shallow. Even marriage was frowned upon. Male and female wizards rarely trusted each other long enough to form a meaningful relationship, let alone a marriage. The magic they practiced was too esoteric, hindered, not helped, with assistance. And those wizards who practiced the dark arts, who dipped their sleeves into the sauces of evil, were often considered pillars of the community in their regular lives.

A random drive-by shooting, he had told the police, motiveless. He was a victim, wrong place, wrong time. He couldn't even answer their questions about what he was doing in Brooklyn at that hour. He was sure he had been somewhere else, but couldn't get his mind to focus long enough to narrow the possibilities. What self-respecting wizard would be caught in Brooklyn?

It was best he avoided the police for now, if for no other reason than to give himself time to develop a story he could stick with. I was in my lair, practicing my magic when I was shot.

That couldn't be right. He was found miles away, and no one could get past his wards.

No. He didn't remember where he was shot, so had to take the police at their word, and keep his secrets to himself.

He wasn't used to being home in the daylight, and it made him realize just how much time he spent at the office, especially since he went back to work directly following his escape from ICU. The foyer looked different, brighter, larger. The message light flashed on his answering machine. Even without his inherent power he didn't have to check. It was undoubtedly from his mother. He should be grateful she cared, but instead her interest felt intrusive.

He climbed the front stairs, annoyed one flight would have him out of breath; he wasn't recovering as quickly as he needed to.

At the master bedroom he stopped to pack a bag. He wasn't vain, but used to creature comforts. His own razor and toothbrush, the private cologne he favored. Clean socks. It was perhaps the only legacy remaining from his parents, the money-can-buy-everything mentality merged with a form of possessiveness. Some things you bought and replaced, some things you bought and held onto.

It didn't take more than ten minutes to stuff everything he might conceivably need into a flight bag, and he was half-way down the carpeted stairs before he realized he wasn't quite ready to leave. There was one thing he needed to check, that he hadn't had the time—the courage, if he were being honest—to investigate yet.

Pierce dropped the bag, then moved silently through the empty house to the kitchen. With a flash from his hands, powerstrands separated, revealing the hidden door which silently swung open. It would be wise not to leave a sanctuary or a routine until he knew if his special abilities had survived his change-of-life experience.

He stood, poised, yet strangely reluctant to continue as he looked up the staircase to the attic. His pulse tripped and he refused to accept his twinges of fear.

Instead he wiggled his fingers experimentally, watched as red, butterscotch and violet strands recognized him before they started undulating down the steps toward him. He could protect himself. If there were clues here, he needed to find them.

Once decided, he wasn't a man to procrastinate. Five steps from the locked door, something smelled wrong. The sensation came not from his nose, but his secret talent. Pierce knelt, rubbing sensitive fingers along the step, the walls and wainscoting. The powerstrands now coiling around his ankles and legs had huddled here, and he needed to decide if they had been pointing the blemish out, or hiding it.

There, on the stair, was a single brown blotch, larger than a pinhead, smaller than a dime. A drop of blood? Something itched at the back of his skull, flashing him back to the shooting. Pierce remembered nothing about that night. Nothing.

The police theorized it had been an attempted robbery, but odds were good his attack wasn't done by some drug addict, some petty street thief, regardless of what Brooklyn's finest thought. He was too powerful in his field for this to have been a random crime.

He bent down, touched the brown stain again. The house was over a hundred years old. The stain could have been there for decades. Why then did he think of the shooting? He had spells which he could use to determine exactly what it was, but at the moment, he had other pressing concerns. Pierce ran his hands over the knob and the door jam. Tingling. Very light, and perhaps a residual from his own experiments, but something was just a bit...too clean...he thought, if he had to come up with an image. Something had been wiped here, like a car thief erasing fingerprints from the steering wheel. Even his own signature was gone.

He shook his head, made a mental note to check again, when he felt stronger. Divesting himself of clothing, Pierce locked himself inside his workshop.

Using conventional means, he lit six fat candles. The light they provided was unnecessary. Although no electricity flowed through this part of the house, the powerstrands provided him with enough ambient light.

He shifted six pale orange powerstrands off his black floor-length robe where it looked like they were nesting, then pulled it on over his naked body. The robe fit just as easily over clothing, however, Pierce liked the sensual decadence of nakedness while he worked. He'd grown used to the feel of the rough textured fabric rubbing against his flesh. He smiled, almost laughed. Here, in the lab, more than any time since leaving the hospital, he had come home.

The air was pungent, filled with the assorted scents of unguents and herbs. When he waltzed into another wizard's lair, he could tell with some degree of accuracy exactly what that other magician had been up to, based on smell alone. Pierce filled his lungs, stretching muscles against his bruised chest, ignoring the increase in pain. The candles added the aroma of tallow and warmth, which had a smell of its own, in addition to the leaves he had blended with the wax himself.

Part of his apprenticeship had been to identify and collect the plants of his profession, dry them, and set them in wax and in clearly labeled jars. After earning his robe he could buy the ingredients he needed, since he rarely had the time or the inclination to search hillsides or shadowed vales for whatever herb he was low on.

He could even hear the echoes of his old master's bellow when he'd said "Rosemary, that's for remembrance," when identifying that spice, and the old man had stormed, "if you aspire to the stage, I suggest you go now and leave the ignorant imbecile you are. Now, if you intend to learn its true magical properties, you'd best keep your mouth shut and your mind open."

All the apprentices had been berated almost constantly. Magic was not an easily learned trade. When he thought back, he remembered those days with pleasure. Odd, since a lot of the time he had been tired, hungry, cold, confused and miserable. But magic awaited him.

Mysteries and majesties.

Power.

He reset the wards, weaving different strands together, liking the pattern the distinct canary yellow hues made against the doorknob. They were not sentient, no matter how many times he imagined them to be, but this time they clearly seemed eager to be set to work, as if they had some significant lapse to atone for. He believed powerstrands had placement memory; they had been knotted before and recalled the action, so would more easily be bound again, but this current agreement seemed deeper, more intense.

Perhaps fifty different strands undulated around the slate floor, silently slipping or wrapping around each other in a snake-like dance of raw energy. He wondered if there were more than usual, and rather than following through with that thought, Pierce ignored them and initiated his routine.

He stood straight, unmoving, taking the time to clear his mind, to steady his pulse and his breathing.

For a moment, a split second, he panicked, as if he felt the sharp sting of the bullets again. He scanned the corners and the walls, the dark, shadowed places where even powerstrands refused to visit, but the attic workshop remained empty, undisturbed. Yet the flash of bullets, the pain, was stronger here than any time since he'd left the hospital.

Even if it had been Pasco's finger on the trigger and he had proof, Pierce would keep the information to himself until he could deal with it in his own manner. Blaming Pasco was starting to make even less sense than it had when he hovered disembodied above an emergency room gurney. Pasco had been a friend once, before he made choices which put earning his robe forever out of his reach.

No, something else was bothering him. Had he been here, in his lair, walking tethered on the astral plane when the attack occurred? Pierce scanned the tiles he had laid himself, and found not the slightest trace of blood. That didn't make sense.

He was safe here. Besides, he had been fully dressed when he had been shot, not wearing this arcane robe. He had been found in an alley, behind a bar, by two drunks out to stretch their legs around closing time.

If only there was a spell he could use to go back and see the past. But that was forbidden, which meant it wasn't necessarily impossible, but he knew enough about the forbidden magicks to stay away. Seeing the future was discouraged, a shade different from forbidden. He tried that once, only to be certain he could, then never again. He preferred to leave his future unwritten, his past unexplored.

Power tingled at his fingertips, as if it had been anxious for him to reappear. He straightened his spine, pulled a fresh breath of air into his lungs, felt, for a fleeting second, that hint of wrongness he'd experienced on the stairs. Pierce decided to ignore it. Often that was the best course. He would hold that investigation until all the clues came together.

He shivered, felt the cold of the stone flooring against his bare feet. The candles flickered, as if warning him to get a grip. Pierce tried to clear his head again. Intelligent candles. He really was losing his mind. Perhaps he should leave. This obviously wasn't working. It was too soon. His body was still too weak from surgery to put it through the rigors of intense concentration.

This was unlike him. Usually, when he prepared to call his power, his mind remained focused. The room was large, cavernous, occupied the entire top floor of his house. The rules stated no plastic, no electricity, nothing mechanical. In addition to the slate floors, he had mortared the walls with rounded river stones. The ceiling was comprised of rough-hewn black walnut. An acoustical nightmare, it was just as well magic, as a profession, was performed in almost total silence. Except for the occasional crackle of power, the low muttered chant, there was never any noise.

A small brazier stood in one corner, for times when he studied up here during the winter and needed heat. He'd had to brace the walls on the lower floors to support the additional weight, reroute telephone wires, the electric boxes, the ceiling fan. He kept almost no furniture here beyond several sturdy bookshelves to hold his volumes of spells. The ledgers of his own experimentation, his successes and failures were written in the secret code he'd been taught and then altered, words that would mean nothing if they fell into the wrong hands. A work table was stacked high with curious items: stones, runes, half-finished icons and the jars of herbs.

Beyond that, a massive table took up almost one entire side of the house. He used as a desk for experimentation. He wrote with a quill and ink he distilled himself. The candles stood braced on candleholders three feet high.

And there was the taxadermically preserved moose head. "Still here, are you?" he asked the moose head. It often accused him, with its silent stare, but today there was nothing lingering, no blame, regret, or even dust.

What to do? His spell book rested open on a work counter, magicks he had mastered, those he still experimented with. Even more important were the projects he had left unfinished, his work where, in comic-book-language, he fought the battle of good against evil.

Pasco Minelli. If he were to get back in the swing of things, his first order of business would be to determine what manner of devilment that creep had been up to. Yet, at the moment, Pasco held no interest for him. Pierce rubbed itching scar tissue and tried to analyze why, since hunting Minelli had been his number one interest for several months. Had three bullets destroyed his drive? He decided not. When a sorcerer killed, he often used a minion to do the dirty work, but rarely used bullets—not when there were so many other esoteric devices that could never be traced back to him—by the police anyway.

Still, there was a perverse type of logic. Had the assassin used powerstrands, those who would revenge Pierce's death would narrow the search immediately and take appropriate counter-measures. With that backward-reasoning, he should keep Pasco at the top of his list.

Also there was a wer-wizard named Andrew he had been warned about by a gargoyle of all things. Every few weeks he tried to follow that lead, with no success.

And there was the inner vision of a woman, pleading in the rain for the life of an innocent.

He could find her. He had the power at his disposal.

How? He didn't know her name, no idea what she looked like, and if previous experience were any gage, he had no particular affinity for pregnant women.

He wasn't even sure the event he had witnessed had taken place within walking distance of the hospital. Things had been weird then. He easily could have been traveling vast distances, and he had been, apparently, out a long time.

Still, he was a master wizard whose curiosity was aroused. Power throbbed all around him, within him. He felt, oddly enough, pleasure, wrapped in anticipation, but pleasure nonetheless. He demanded the power respond, then started chanting, his hands moving in ancient patterns knotting the waves of authority to his own control. He felt himself growing lighter, slipping from his body, traveling along the astral plane. If there were a way, he would find her.

# CHAPTER 4

Pierce popped back into his body with the instinctive awareness he was not alone. He raised his hands defensively, ready to blast any attacker to kingdom-come when a familiar face popped into view.

"Whoa! Hold up."

"Daniel."

Daniel Rayock had been his friend and fellow apprentice, since they both started exploring the realms of magic twenty years before. Daniel was a short man, thirty pounds heavier than he should be, with an appreciation for good food. He owned a small restaurant on the east side, which ran to pastas and steaks, although the desserts were something to die for, and it was said by more than one reviewer, that his tiramisu and cheese cakes were so fabulous they could only have been created by magic.

"I meant to say welcome back when I saw you at the hospital, but you disappeared almost immediately," Pierce greeted.

Daniel shrugged, and continued wandering around the lair. "I was in the area."

"Brooklyn?"

He shrugged, made no comment.

"You've lost weight."

"The new me. Do you like it?"

"It fits. How did your trip go? You were gone most of a year."

"Annoying. I almost had what I wanted. I've regrouped. I'm coming at it from a new angle."

"Did that involve blasting through my wards?"

"Well," Daniel could ooze charm when he wanted. He rarely tried, unless for a pretty woman, and even then he found it a game since most women would have nothing to do with him, and had no idea of the power he controlled. "I have to keep my hand in, don't I?"

"Not in my lair you don't. I most specifically locked the door." Pierce swiped at his forehead. After the exertion of astral-travel, he always suspected his body should be sweating. It never did, but then all the work was done by the spirit.

Rayock grinned, looked boyish. "I know your charms. I had no difficulty with them."

Pierce lowered his brows, concentrated in the direction of the stairway, picking up the markers left by another practitioner. It reeked, stank of the invasion. Nothing subtle.

"Well, a bit of difficulty with the last one," Rayock muttered with his infectious charisma.

"You made enough noise to attract every ear on the planet."

It wasn't exactly noise, at least not the kind picked up by CIA technicians with their audio recording devices. The noise he referred to dealt with disrupting the forces controlled by wizards.

Pierce wrapped a small red powerstrand around his wrist, savored the momentary image of turning Daniel into pulp. Instead he went to the door, set about repairing the damage. "You were sloppy. There's no excuse. You've marked my lair to anyone sensitive."

Rayock straightened the collar of his striped shirt. "Anyone who is sensitive already knows where your lair is. Besides, I thought you were in trouble. It wouldn't have been the first time."

Pierce growled. Any black bear, facing any intruder, would have sounded exactly the same. "Did it occur to you I might have been working? That is what this laboratory is for, isn't it?"

"Did it occur to you that someone has tried to kill you once this month, and it's not inconceivable for him or her to try again?"

"Here?" Pierce raised a disbelieving eyebrow. "At my power base?"

Rayock paused, smiled slowly with a cat-with-canary grin which curved the edges of his lips upwards. "Why not? Tell me, have you garnered any more information on Minelli?"

He was tired. Magic, even magic which took no physical exertion, was draining. Pierce rubbed his eyelids, his eyebrows, his forehead, tried very hard not to touch the healing scar. "No."

"Location?"

Tension knotted in his shoulders, heightened because of the strain from the wound in his chest. It hurt simply to take a deep breath. "Nothing."

"Then your journey was a failure?"

Pierce kept his face poker-controlled, so easy to do it was second nature, even around friends. "I wasn't looking for Minelli. I have another concern."

Daniel smiled, as if sharing a secret. "Has Master given you another assignment then?"

Rayock moved idly around the room, touching things which although not necessarily private, were personal. Pierce wanted to slap his hands.

"No. This project is mine, and none of your business." He closed the spell book, moved his hand, palm down, over the soft ancient leather. His temples throbbed, a headache had taken refuge behind his eyes. Exhaustion sheeted through his body, leaving him more tired than usual.

"When you're almost killed, you make it my business." Daniel, who was four years younger, smiled again, this time with youthful exuberance. "By the way, you never thanked me for saving your miserable hide in the emergency room."

"Did it ever occur to you I wasn't ready to return?"

"Weren't ready?" Manicured eyebrows raised in unabashed curiosity. "What did you experience?"

"Nothing that concerns you."

"Whatever it is must be big."

"Confusing more than important. I don't like when things don't add up."

"Minelli getting into more trouble? Did you find his trace?"

"I told you, this has nothing to do with Minelli." Pierce sat on an ancient, scared bench, retrieved his socks, started putting them on the old fashioned way, one foot at a time. The movement added pressure to his temples. Pierce would not give into temptation, especially not in front of Daniel, and rub them again.

"What are you working on? Does Master know?"

"It doesn't concern Master, and it doesn't concern you." He slipped jockeys on under the robe, pulled his pants up next.

"Listen, Bogart—"

"I told you not to call me that." The snap was guttural. The nickname was too close to his name of power, and in properly naming something you gained control over it.

"I'm leaving." Pierce removed the black robe, dropping it heedlessly on the slate floor. He picked up his slightly crumpled shirt, fit it over his broad shoulders. The orange powerstrands which had earlier been nesting on his robe had taken root on the shirt. "I'm taking the weekend off."

"Fine. I'll go with you."

"Sorry, this time I go alone. I don't need a babysitter." He tucked his shirt in, fastened the button at the waist of his pants, then tightened his belt.

"Rules are—"

"Hang the rules."

"There's something else you don't know."

"What?"

"Batty Belinda is missing."

"Missing? Why do you say that?"

Rayock shrugged. "She hasn't been heard from in a while. Master went looking. There's no trace of her."

"How the hell did that happen?"

"I don't know."

Pierce watched as the six orange powerstrands gave Daniel wide berth. "Dead?"

"Or controlled, or blocked. Master wants us all to try to locate her."

Pierce dug his hand into his pocket, felt the comforting domestic presence of car keys. The missing witch would have to wait. There were others to search for her, and she was not powerless. If she were in trouble, she would leave a trail wide enough for a blind man to find.

At the moment he had other priorities, ones he wasn't going to share with Daniel Rayock. He hadn't been able to find her, this woman who still had no name, no face, and no specific place in his life, but there had been a pull, and he would start his search in that direction. His interest was intense enough that he would not allow himself to be diverted.

"Are you going to do anything about Wurle?"

Pierce opened the laboratory door, whispered and the flames on six candles blew out simultaneously. Their dying breath wafted up in a thin, white stream toward the ceiling, undulating, like a belly dancer. Pierce breathed deeply, inhaling the rich scent of herbs and tallow. Candles were comforting. He supposed that was one of the main reasons they figured so prominently in seductions. In candlelight many truths could be hidden, yet a person could be comforted by their warmth, scent, and brightness.

He waited until Rayock preceded him through, then stopping at the small landing, he manually shut the door. With a deliberate sloppiness he didn't quite understand, reset his guards on the portal. "I'll put Wurle on my list. And Daniel, don't ever broach my wards again. You can consider this a friendly warning." His emphasis clearly lay on the final word.

# CHAPTER 5

Across the street stood an abortion clinic. A small, nondescript building, it huddled within a medical office complex, indistinguishable from the neurologist and rheumatologist offices around it. From the outside it gave the impression of stability, sedate red brick with neatly trimmed juniper bushes and marigolds and impatiens exploding in a well-behaved border.

A discrete sign stood sentry in front of the automatic door which CeeDee couldn't read from where she sat, but which she knew said Grassing Women's Center.

A woman's center. And what they did was...

It would be better, much better, if she didn't think about what they did there. If she just went in, made an appointment, and came back when they were expecting her to have that awful, yet most assuredly painless procedure done.

Painless. Now there was a term only someone insensitive could apply to an act which in her mind should be unconscionable.

Should be, but oddly wasn't. She had no husband. Not that she needed one, but it certainly would have made the decision easier if she'd had someone to talk it over with. She had a former lover, that much was obvious, but he hadn't bothered to tell her he was a creep, and he never mentioned he was married which she discovered quite unexpectedly when she went up to his door to share the glad tidings. He rushed her out of the house so fast her head spun, then made arrangements to have dinner with her the following night.

"So what if I'm married," he said with a look of total incredulity on his face. "It's an open arrangement. I have my interests, she has hers." Then he had the audacity to ask her to meet him the next evening at their rendezvous spot. His wife, it seemed, traveled, was gone three or four nights a week. He got lonely.

"Well, you won't have much time for loneliness now," CeeDee told him. "You're going to be a father."

He left her weeping as his Jaguar sped off in the pouring rain. The next day in the mail she received several hundred dollars in cash and a terse note that said essentially it was "her problem and she should take care of it herself." The implication was clear. She made a silent vow not to answer the phone for the next few days, but the decision was wasted because it didn't ring.

Last week on Sunday, when she knew the clinic wasn't open, when she knew there wouldn't be any threat, she wrapped herself in courage and actually got as far as the front door. It was a habit left over from an insecure childhood. Whatever major, important event was about to take place in her life, she had to make a dry-run, when the pressure wasn't on, go over her moves, as if physically approaching a doctors' office could give her the courage to actually go through with an abortion.

Cupping her hands against the plate glass door, she had looked into the lobby, discovering it clean, professional and modern if slightly impersonal. It was the kind of room she expected to find as a prelude to an obstetricians' office, although she doubted the magazines on the brass and glass tables were Working Mother and Parents.

She knew the phone number. She could have made the appointment impersonally, while sitting at her desk at work, or at home on any of her days off, but if she had, she wouldn't have been able to get inside the front door. This time, when she was only going to make the appointment, the pressure should be less. It was a small increment, but that's how she did things. One step at a time.

All she had to do was put one foot in front of the other, look both ways, walk across the street, up over the small, crumbling curb, and go for it. Before that, she just had to convince herself she was doing the right thing.

CeeDee sat back down. She wasn't ready. There were too many other things she needed to do, before she made any permanent changes to her life.

What she needed, she decided, was a little magic.

\*\*\*

Oh God, it was her. Pierce had been driving aimlessly for the past four hours, searching for the resurgence of that pull, meandering old country roads, going no place in particular, when he spotted her. He stepped on the brake so quickly he almost got himself rear-ended, and earned a well-deserved blast from the half ton pick-up behind him. It sounded very much like Ahh-ooo-ga.

Instead of blocking traffic on the tree-lined main street of whatever picturesque little town this was, he found a parking place in front of an old fashioned drug store and turned the engine off.

He wasn't certain how he knew it was the woman he met on his out-of-body sojourn, since considering lighting, the rain, and other conditions

over which he had no control, such as the fact at the time he was newly
dead, and he hadn't really seen her face, but he was absolutely certain it
was her. It wasn't, necessarily, magic. Magic usually felt quite different,
hitting him broadside, or electrocuting his senses. Then again, it might be a
different sort of magic. Even a master wizard never knew what to expect
from his craft from day to day.

He got out of the car, straightened his knees and spine to his full six
foot one height, jaywalked across the street until he got a better look at her.
She didn't notice him, which gave him a curious déjà vu feeling. Panicked,
without realizing what he felt was indeed panic, he took a deep breath,
filled his lungs with a verdant New England aroma thick with Atlantic
Ocean salt and the earthy, slightly pungent scent of maple leaves
decomposing. Not dead then. At least his senses were functioning.

She was older than he first inferred, a youthful twenty-five or so,
instead of a juvenile sixteen, and he was willing to accept in his first vision
of her he caught her at a bad time, since he hadn't exactly been having a
red letter day himself.

Pierce leaned against a broad trunked hickory, watched her without a
twinge of embarrassment. This was after all, a small town. People could
lean against a tree without getting mowed down by flood-water crowds. In
New York City, such behavior was unheard of.

She sat on a wooden bench, the kind with advertising on the back, this
one a three color ad for a podiatrist who catered to cowards. He scoffed,
wondering what kind of courage it took to have some man with a foot
fetish make plaster casts of your feet.

She wore all gray. Gray slacks in what looked like some kind of wool
blend, a lighter gray blouse, a darker gray blazer, as if there was no color in
her, like she was the shadow and her substance was put in safe-keeping in a
hat box in her closet. The ringlets were hidden. Her hair had been
imprisoned within a gray fluffy thing and hung defeated down her back.
He'd seen the look in her eyes before, the blank stare of death he had last
seen looking down at his own body.

She was waiting for someone. No. That wasn't it. She was just sitting,
in much the same manner he was just leaning. She didn't look like she
planned to move much before the Second Coming.

Instinctively he checked for sources of power, to see if this were an
elaborate trap, but there was nothing but the normal magical energy
humming around, conversing in colorful patterned waves, nothing specific
to either her or him. Because of what he was, those power waves were

already congregating in his direction, knotting, like embroidery floss, different colors, different strengths.

They were attracted to him. Idly Pierce waved his hand, setting them at ease. I recognize you. I respect your power, but at the moment I have no need of you. Only very inexperienced wizards, or those particularly desperate, allowed the power waves to bunch, attracting the attention of anyone sensitive.

It would be a simple manner to sit beside her. He practiced opening gambits, the king's-pawn-two movements of strangers brought together by scattered sunshine and splintery park benches that she could match by alerting her own pawns—or her knights and bishops. Yet he wasn't ready to introduce himself.

Pierce didn't understand his own reluctance, only recognized while he had to meet her, he couldn't barge in as was his usual modus operandi when dealing with members of the opposite sex. There was something far too fragile about her, something likely to shatter. He would give them both time. Too many of his own turbulent emotions needed to be understood, simply because too much of his power hinged on understanding his own internal combustion psyche.

He would not retreat so much as regroup. Pierce backtracked toward his car, but instead veered toward the corner drug store, needing distance to put into perspective what he was feeling, before he made a total fool of himself.

He hadn't been in a drugstore like this since he was a child, and even then, he wasn't certain he'd ever been in a building this old-fashioned, other than the hardwood-floored, cutesy tourist traps he loved while traveling Northern Vermont. Along the back wall was a small pharmacy, to his left a well-worn ice cream bar loaded with patrons, most of which appeared to be unshaven old men drinking black coffee and freshly scrubbed high school kids eating French fries and sipping chocolate malts.

The rest of the store was typical five and dime, a health and beauty aids section, housewares, domestics, hardware, plastic shoes. He even noticed a compact pet section, stuffed with green and blue parakeets chattering in overfilled cages, goldfish and guppies in green skinned tanks. He walked down the aisle slowly, discovered a bunch of unrecognizable lumps half-buried in cedar chips might have be hamsters, which he always considered the stupidest of pets for a kid since they were nocturnal and if disturbed from daytime slumber by a child who only wanted to play, were apt to bite.

It was, for all practical purposes, a general store, where nearly anything but high end groceries and clothing could be had for a reasonable price. Drapes, flower pots, nail polish, light bulbs and motor oil, all under one roof.

Blind to the other people surrounding him, lost in his own musings, Pierce eased his way toward the window at the soda fountain side of the store and watched the woman, sitting still enough Michelangelo could have sculpted her likeness in marble. He held his breath as a bus pulled up, realizing this was a contingency he hadn't anticipated, knowing he'd lost her for time and all eternity for not going up and introducing himself. He was about to curse, mash something into an unrecognizable pulp when the bus pulled away in a stream of black diesel smoke and he noticed she was still sitting there, unmolested.

"Can I help you?"

Startled, he noticed the waitress who met him eye to eye, a small plastic red poppy in her top button hole, with gray hair which complimented nicely the red of her uniform. She wore a pin with her name, Jan, and a small round button, the kind with sayings, and this one said "Dragons Make the Best Tea." He had no time to wonder what that meant.

She looked over at him and he was no longer certain he hadn't died when the three bullets crashed into his chest, for suddenly and completely he felt himself in an episode of the Twilight Zone. She radiated power in an understated way, but it was a type he had not come across before.

She held a small pad and a pencil, and it wouldn't have surprised him if she chewed Juicy Fruit. Since it looked like his prey wasn't about to move from her park bench any time in the near future he had time to regroup, develop a plan of attack. Besides, Pierce realized he probably hadn't eaten anything since yesterday because the thought of breakfast always made him nauseous and this morning he'd left work in such a flurry that he hadn't stopped to consider food.

He was suddenly starving. Besides, he could always drop money and run should another bus appear, this one going in this unknown woman's direction. Judging by the speed of the first, he'd have plenty of time to catch her.

Without thought, and keeping his eyes glued on the bench, he slipped into the booth he'd been hovering beside. He ordered a BLT, a cup of whatever soup she had simmering on a steam table and in a fit of personal defiance since he rarely did anything that veered from his routine, and suddenly he found himself doing many things differently, he ordered a strawberry milkshake.

He was far more used to a gin and tonic for lunch with a bunch of French food he never really cared for. He'd become too predictable.

The soup was black bean with curry which he never would have ordered in a million years but which was thick, hot, and delicious and he feasted as if he just discovered food that morning. The sandwich was immense, loaded with bacon, and the tomatoes were fresh, or at any rate couldn't have come out of any Boston green grocers for they had real, honest to goodness tomato flavor. And the milkshake, too thick to eat with anything but a spoon, had massive chunks of flavorful strawberries and was enough to slip him into ecstasy. For just one second he was glad he hadn't died on that emergency room gurney, and vowed silently to start a new appreciation of things that heretofore he had patently ignored.

"Can I get you anything else?" the waitress asked, nabbing a strand of hair and swiping it back behind her ear. She worked hard, manning the busy counter and four booths by herself.

"No," he smiled, looked at her for the first time. She was the type of service person he never noticed, always too busy, too important to acknowledge. "Wait, yes you can. Can you tell me what that building is over there?"

Pierce pointed to the red brick building that his woman stared at. She watched it as if she'd planted a bomb which should have exploded everything to kingdom come ten minutes before.

The waitress gave a short, clipped laugh. "See someone you know go in there?"

"No, I'm just curious."

"It's the abortion clinic."

And his heart thumped and bumped and almost stopped beating. Of course. What else? He thanked the waitress, left her a big tip because he was feeling suddenly generous, and was about to run out of the store and tell this woman he'd never met not to do anything foolish, when he realized how ridiculous that would be.

Heaven forbid he create some kind of scene and it got back to his mother and the firm's partners. He'd never live it down. He'd be spending every free minute for the rest of his life resting on a psychologist's couch. He couldn't be certain, really certain, it was her, the woman he saw once when he was dead. No, he needed a plan. An opening line. A haven't-I-seen-you-somewhere-before, that didn't quite involve long tunnels, white lights, and an overly efficient emergency and surgical room staff.

She liked men with money. That was obvious from the bastard in the Jaguar. He could put on his jacket and spread a little cash. Except that his jackets, and he had closets full of them, were one state away. He hadn't even bothered to pick up the one he wore into work that morning.

Pierce checked his wallet. All he saw was the remains of a twenty dollar bill he had used to buy his lunch and a stack of gold cards. Not that he suspected cash would help. He could hardly bring flowers, could he?

He caught the waitress' eye. "How long until the next bus comes through?" he asked, for he had a vision to recapture, an angel more alive than he was himself.

She didn't bother to check her watch. "Every thirty minutes from whenever the last one appeared." Which didn't give him much time.

"You look like you need a crossword puzzle book," the waitress said.

"I beg your pardon?" The words were so unexpected, they could have been spoken in Swahili.

"A crossword puzzle book. You know, like the New York Times?"

"I don't need a crossword puzzle book."

The waitress turned, pointed her finger at a pimply faced youth, spoke with the intensity of a SWAT officer yelling: "Put the gun down and get on your knees." "You," she said to the youth, "call your mother right now."

"I was going to, Jeesh," the boy said, although it seemed to Pierce both that he hadn't been, and he would.

The waitress turned back to Pierce. "And, if you need to run away, you might try a B&B"

B&B. It sounded alcoholic, a blue drink in a tall, fancy glass, perhaps, ordered in those trendy bars where women had names like Fifi and Mandy, and an evening of pleasure could be bought with a smile.

She was perceptive, or he had lowered his eyebrows, indicative of his confusion. "Bed and Breakfast."

"I'm not running away," he growled, but he was and he had. It seemed unlikely he would ever go back. Yes, he needed the grounding of a 'normal' career to hide his profession, but he'd had enough of his law practice. Maybe he could apprentice next as a plumber. But first he would check on the woman, who stared at the abortion clinic as if she wanted back something which had already been taken from her.

It shocked Pierce that he might be too late. That the "problem" might already have been taken care of. His heart started tripping as he stared out the window.

The woman hadn't moved. During his incredible lunch he had watched another bus come and go, and she still sat, waiting, her eyes fixated on the building across the street. It wasn't exactly true to say she hadn't moved at all. Every now and then her right hand would caress her still flat stomach, then about a minute or so after that she swiped at a tear that never quite seemed to overflow past her thick dark lashes.

The waitress had moved from Pierce's booth, and was now hassling a scruffy-bearded old man who sat with a piece of blueberry pie. "Have you ever been back?" she asked, "since the war? It might be healing to go back."

Pierce dropped the waitress from his mind, but he picked up the red and white starburst mint she had left beside his bill and popped it into his mouth. It seemed the perfect counterpoint to the strawberry milkshake.

Fat clouds hovered, gray and hulking, typical for October, and the breeze attacked knife sharp gusts. It arrived sporadically though, a wanderer off the ocean who wouldn't stay longer than to toss an errant piece of fast-food packaging into the air, before vanishing again.

Still, for all the grayness of the day, there was enough light to see the girl on the bench's features, enough to imprint her in his memory. She wore no lipstick, no eye make-up, and judging by the pale porcelain beauty of her white skin, none of the other type of camouflage, foundation, blush, shadow, whatever else women put on their faces these days which Pierce had no idea about other than to know when he took a date on a long weekend, the make-up had its own suitcase.

Her green eyes held shadows he shouldn't be able to read, but to which he put his own interpretation. The clinic across the street was reason enough. He wished, for the first time in his life, that he knew women, and had taken time out from all the ones he'd dated, the ones he'd been intimate with, to actually talk and discover what made them tick.

While he was often in the company of women, he seriously doubted he'd ever had a conversation with one that scratched below the surface of what made them both feel good. "Do you like that?" he'd ask, suckling a nipple, anticipating a breathless affirmative, without ever wondering what she really thought of all the important things in life: world peace, trips to the dry cleaners, parking tickets.

His lack of knowledge shocked him, for if asked even an hour ago he would have responded that he was the consummate lover, and knew everything about pleasing a woman. Never before had he realized that there were ways to please a woman beyond the sexual, more layers than the physical.

"Hi, you mind if I sit here?"

She looked up, startled, blinked, held her hand out automatically in invitation. She obviously hadn't heard him arrive.

"No, please, be my guest."

Her voice was rich, intoxicating, and it was the same one he had heard before, when there had been rain and he had been dead. The warm, firm words twirled around his insides, tickling him in all kinds of prickly places. If he had any doubt before that this was 'his' woman, those qualms had been laid to rest with the seductiveness of her speaking.

Pierce sat, carefully choosing his distance without trying to look like he did, close enough he could talk with her, not so close she'd feel like she was under attack. Charm came easily to him, but Pierce never realized until he stood in that drugstore that his charm was superficial; it only appeared when the outcome didn't matter. Now, bordering on desperation, he felt tongue-tied, inadequate.

He opened the crossword puzzle book he just bought, growling that the waitress had been right, that it was a good idea, although he had scoffed, had deliberately not bought the New York Times compilation. Casually, he turned past the index, the letters to the editor, to the first page. He ignored her for a good twenty, thirty seconds, before he put his ball in play. "I don't suppose you know an eight letter word for approval, do you?"

As he looked up, Pierce hoped he didn't look as pitiful as he felt. Pitiful, first because he didn't know the answer, and he had all kinds of academic degrees. She would probably laugh, think he was an ignoramus, someone escaped from a remedial program so far below the competency scale he'd never even make it to that alleged plumbing apprenticeship. Why couldn't it have been a law crossword puzzle book? Tort. Writ. Habeas corpus.

Then, when she didn't know, he could ah-ha! shout 'Eureka', and be brilliant.

Second, he planned to impress her. Of course, what kind of woman was impressed with a three dollar crossword puzzle book, he had no idea. Silently Pierce cursed the waitress. See if he would eat her black bean soup ever again.

Even if it were fabulous.

The woman in gray blinked again, looked at him guiltily. She had already dismissed him and had just started rubbing her belly. It occurred to Pierce that in all the time she'd been sitting, she hadn't once looked at her watch. If she were early for the appointment, it wasn't bothering her. Silently, he erased the bomb scenario. Maybe there was still hope for all three of them: him, her, and that unnamed, yet unfelt little presence.

# CHAPTER 6

"I do apologize," he said, hoped his grin was friendly but not too aggressive, hoped his tie was on straight but that he didn't appear too straight-laced.

She leaned forward, curled up the top corner of her upper lip. "Approval?" she asked.

His one fear was that she would dismiss him out of hand, tell him to mind his own business. This wasn't the city, but then it wasn't only in a metropolis where women needed to keep barriers around themselves.

She thought, counted letters on her fingers she didn't share with him, started again when whatever word she had chosen came up short. She looked at his book, laughed. "I don't suppose you have any clues, do you?"

"Let's see..." He was about ready to hum. Already they'd established a rapport. "Eee gads. This is worse than a thought. Greenish-blue beryl is the clue for 1 down, with about thirty-two letters. What in heaven's name is a beryl?"

She didn't hesitate, but spoke with the confidence of a museum curator. "A green mineral, includes the gems emerald and aquamarine."

Pierce ah-haed, said "aquamarine," to himself like a Peter Falk Columbo and fitted it into the small boxes of one down. He hoped she was paying attention to his bravery. He was doing the crossword in pen.

She wasn't looking at him, but then, she wasn't eye-locked across the street anymore either. Pierce took that as a positive step. But then, as he was self-congratulating himself, she continued, in a nonchalant voice, "Beryl is also the principle ore of beryllium."

He laughed, said, "What do you do, memorize dictionaries in your spare time?" with just the proper degree of grudging respect so she wouldn't think he was putting her down in a Neanderthal gesture of male-supremacy. There were an awful lot of extremely brilliant female lawyers. He hoped she wasn't one of those. His own ego couldn't take being bested in his own field.

"Scrabble player."

The wind kicked up, just a bit, and a troop of brown oak leaves pirouetted in dizzying arcs before leaving to seek a more appreciative audience. Pierce nodded, taking a while to remember exactly what

Scrabble was. It sounded like something made with scrambled eggs and lima beans.

"You're not a Scrabble player?"

He shook his head. "It's not that I don't play games, it's just I don't play friendly games, and board games usually fall in that category."

"Applause," she said, interrupting him.

He grinned, let a trace of laughter escape. "What? I haven't even told you my tennis ranking and you're already offering accolades?"

"No, your eight letter word. Applause. It does start with the A from aquamarine, doesn't it?" She scratched the tip of that curling lip. "Of course 'accolade' is also an eight-letter word that starts with A and could, I suppose, mean approval."

"Although not specifically," he said, pleased that he could display his vocabulary wasn't entirely primitive.

Distracted and momentarily off balance, Pierce checked his puzzle book, wrote applause, then in an effort not to appear too helpless, filled in some answers he knew. After all, this puzzle was, by some stroke of misfortune, labeled easy.

"I don't suppose you'd like to hear about my tennis ranking?" he asked, the top half of the puzzle filled in, and curse his luck, not a single question he could ask her without sounding like he hadn't finished the fourth grade. There was easy, then there was too easy. He'd sell his soul for another beryl question.

"No, I don't think so." Within seconds, she was back to staring at the brick building. Pierce thought it politic not to notice.

Photographer's need, capital of Canada, wild plum, wasn't there anything here he didn't know, or baring that, one he could pretend not to know? Scarlett's home, FDR's dog, rain sound.

He stretched his legs out, crossed them at the ankles. Too casual. Sat up, straighter, put his arm on the back rest of the bench. Too aggressive. Pulling himself together, Pierce decided the last time he was this nervous he was begging to be taken on as an apprentice to learn magic. "I used to do crossword puzzles all the time," he volunteered. "I started in high school, continued all through college."

"I see." What she did or didn't see was immaterial, for she didn't look at him.

He re-crossed his ankles. "I haven't done one in years."

"Hummm." This time she didn't even offer the barest of polite answers. So much for scintillating conversation. He knew beyond a doubt that another bus was due any minute, and if she didn't have an appointment she was bound to vanish into thin air, or at least as thin as the air on a commuter bus can be.

He grasped at straws, pulled one out of nowhere, an excuse which had no truth, and which was unexpected, for he usually dazzled women with his wealth.

"I had some trouble with the IRS."

This time she looked, took his measure, must have found him harmless. "What did you say?"

He set the puzzle on the bench between them, then rested his arm along the top, taking his time, spinning his fantasy. "I had some trouble with the IRS, got myself in a jam what with high-living, and nothing in the savings account. I was at the point where I was about to declare personal bankruptcy, when a friend talked me out of it. Seems it's the worst of all modern evils. He told me I'd be better off committing suicide then taking out a Chapter 11. He told me stories that curled my hair."

She didn't miss a beat. "Because of that you've taken up crossword puzzles."

He had to give her credit. She followed the conversation better than he did, and it was his fable to begin with.

"Exactly." He sighed, wondered if it were too late to change his story to one of family wealth and privilege. "I made myself a budget, one I could live with, not easily, but one which will get the debts paid in the shortest amount of time, without having to sell myself into prostitution."

She rolled her eyes, and for the first time, smiled.

"And your budget allows for crossword puzzle books?"

He sighed, looked terribly sincere. "That's about all it allows for. I never realized how many fair-weather friends I had. Once the money dried up, once I stopped buying drinks and theater tickets, everyone went away."

She seemed interested now, really interested.

"There's twenty dollars in my entertainment budget. Twenty dollars a week. Hell, I used to spend ten times that an hour on the weekend. And since it's not that much money, I spend it on Fridays, knowing I've got an entire week to get through if I blow it."

She turned a bit, crossing one slender ankle over another, resting an elbow on the back of the podiatrist-labeled bench. Her feet were small, but she did not look fragile. Instead she looked like she could pull a handcart across with Rocky Mountains whistling campfire songs, giving birth along the trail, without causing the company much inconvenience. Sturdy stock, he thought, and liked the image. It was not a thought he had spared for any woman he ever dated. Pierce tended toward leggy blonds, all angles, as if they were geodesic sculptures, defined by arc tangents.

"Something amusing?" she asked.

He must be more transparent than he thought. "Do you know what an arc tangent is?"

"Of course. It's—"

He held his hands out, stalling her. "No, no need to define it. I was just thinking—I doubt any woman I've ever dated knew what one is."

"Well, that's a relief," she said, dramatically wiping her palm across her forehead.

"What's a relief?"

"Now we don't have to date."

Pierce would have complained, wanted to, before he realized she had just made a joke. "I guess the pressure is off then."

With her statement they were both relieved, and a bit disappointed. He wondered what it would be like dating her, taking her out, spreading her dull, non-descript hair across his pillow, and he bet it would shine with glorious highlights. Silently, he liked the thought of her keeping all that magnificence hidden, that only he knew about it. It made it better for him, until he remembered, there was at least one other man who had seen her hair cascading over a pillow. One man who didn't appreciate her, which, the way he added up the total, worked in his favor.

Still, the equation included a fetus, an infant, a toddler, a child, a teenager, a commitment. He really was better off with the arc tangents.

Pierce was satisfied with his conclusion for a good twenty seconds, then noticed that her nose was turned up, at the end, just a bit, and it was small and elfin. She was actually, stunningly, incredibly lovely, and he wondered if that was why she wore gray, to downplay her beauty so it wasn't immediately apparent.

"So, what do you do?"

He hoped his look was blank, for he immediately thought of black silk sheets, and her hair tenting across his body as she knelt on hands and knees over him, their bodies locked together a bit lower in a passionate intimacy he could easily imagine. He was about to grab her, fuel the pressures which would have them both screaming in wild abandon.

"With your budget," she completed, making him profoundly grateful she could not read his mind.

Pierce finger combed his hair, rolled his eyes, took a moment to build a scenario as foreign to him as wizardry would be to his mother. "Well, this is only the third week, so I'm still experimenting. The first week I bought a book, rented a video."

She nodded approval.

"The second week I went to the movies, just to be around people, forgot myself and bought nachos, a drink, candy."

"Twenty dollars shot to bits, in one night." She was very sympathetic. Her lips curled. Color appeared on her cheeks. If the day started with a crisp blusteriness, it had suddenly warmed.

"A bit more than twenty dollars, but you're right, my entire week's entertainment budget shot to smithereens. It was the type of movie I always see: trains blowing up, and women wearing bikinis holding submachine guns while diffusing nuclear weapons. I didn't enjoy it. Even knowing it was a treat, I kept thinking of all the things I'd rather have."

"Darn. What a tragedy."

So much for sympathy. She actually giggled.

"It could have been worse. The movie could have had something to recommend it—like social significance."

"It did have social—" he said, then let the sentence, and his excuse drop off. He pouted, hoped he looked puppy-dog boyish. "Well, maybe it didn't."

"So, besides the crossword puzzle book, what did you do this week?"

He made a face, something he might have seen only on a Halloween pumpkin, or someone under the age of eight who had accidentally swallowed scrambled eggs and lima beans. "Another sore subject. I bought lunch out. I'm sick of my own cooking. Believe me, it was a treat."

"So you must not have a wife, children?"

"No. And my love life's been put on hold indefinitely. Once I get some of the bigger bills paid off, I'll redo the budget, keep paying off the IRS, but at least have a little breathing room. At the moment, I don't want a woman in my life. I can't afford one."

"No? There's plenty of things you can do that don't cost much money."

"Really? I checked into it. You know I can't even bring a date to the zoo for twenty dollars, not with the understanding that after a few hours of looking at tigers we'll need a soda at the very least."

"Picnics? Did you ever try one?"

"No."

"How about the library? They have videos now, many you can rent for free. Museums, parks. Tennis."

He forced his shoulders into an exaggerated slump. "I let the country club membership go."

She pointed a slender, un-ringed finger, topped with an unpolished fingernail. "There are free public courts you know."

He matched her enthusiasm. After all, it had been almost five minutes since she looked across the street.

"Listen, I've got to run. Things to do, places to go, people to see." He waited, hoping to catch her eyes, hoping he wasn't blowing it.

"Bye." She turned, removed her elbow from the bench, looking at the building across the street but some of the desperation in her glance had vanished.

"I'd like to see you again."

She cleared her throat, muttered, rubbed the heel of one shoe with the toe of another. "I don't know."

"Here, on this bench, this time tomorrow." She made no response. Nothing. "In broad daylight," Pierce added. "Thousands of people milling around. You could bring a guard dog. Or your mother. Would that make you feel better? Please? If you do, you'll probably save me from going to jail."

The smile was back, with an unexpected bonus, a twinkle in her eyes. "What are you talking about?"

"That if you don't meet me, I'll get lonely, go shopping, run up huge balances I can't afford to pay, and the government will send me to federal prison for tax evasion and it will be all your fault."

"My fault?"

"If you meet me I promise I won't buy so much as a single macadamia nut."

"You're the nut."

"Then is it a date?" Unsure, he started counting his chances, silently. One, two, three.

"It couldn't possibly be a date. I know what an arc tangent is, remember?"

"Alright, be picky. I didn't mean a date like dinner reservations and opening night theater tickets, I meant it in terms of your appointment calendar. A date, like meeting your oral surgeon for a root canal."

"Whew. Now I know what you think of me."

He showed teeth, pulling back his lips in a ferocious snarl.

She laughed, charmed. "Sure, why not? I'll pencil you in."

What do you know? He won the lottery. He hadn't been this excited since, well it had been a while. He left for his car the long way, so she wouldn't see he hadn't quite misplaced all the finer things in life. And he hummed a surprisingly appropriate "Ode to Joy", something he couldn't remember ever doing before.

***

The park bench stood empty when he arrived, which should not have bothered him since he was a good thirty minutes early, but Pierce grew certain she wasn't going to show. He stared across the street, as if he could infer whether she had slipped in and had a quick, out-patient procedure and was back home, drowning her sorrows in whatever intoxicant women drowned their sorrows in these days.

Pierce paced, sat on the bench, paced some more, wished he had caught the license plate of the Jaguar so he could knock that creep into next Tuesday without quite taking the time to realize he had treated women quite shabbily himself. Not that he'd ever been greeted with the prospect of fatherhood, but when he felt a relationship had run its course, it was over, regardless of what the other party thought or wanted. He maintained a never-look-back credo, very easy since on the whole he never gave much thought to relationships beyond the moment.

"I wasn't certain I was going to come," she said, slipping up beside him, looking neither nervous nor uncomfortable, yet far from enthusiastic. He got a warmer greeting from his dental hygienist.

"I'm glad you did." Sincerity was a new emotion for him, especially since he couldn't foresee getting anything out of their association. All he wanted...Pierce wasn't sure what he wanted, hadn't taken the time to give it any thought, beyond seeing her again, talking to her, finding out if she made the trip across the street in the hours they'd been apart.

"What have you got?" she asked.

He held out the book, purchased that morning after nearly an hour loitering in a bookstore. New England Weeds and Wild Flowers. Pierce had racked his brain trying to think of something they could do together which didn't take any money, and for that matter didn't involve driving for he could hardly claim poverty and take her for a ride in the Porsche.

Even though she mentioned free concerts and low cost county fairs, there were apparently none going on this weekend within an easy distance of this park bench.

"I bought it the first week," he said, making it a confession, trying to sound just a bit reluctant to part with the information. He wanted to sound like he was hard-up without being a hard case.

Two finely plucked eyebrows raised, showing eyes a brilliant kelly green.

"You bought a book on wild flowers?" She sounded incredulous, as if she'd been sharing insights with Candy.

Pierce bristled, felt possessive and oddly defensive. He hadn't felt quite this exposed since his mother caught him trying to buy occult books at the ripe old age of seven. He liked the book, even though, beyond belladonna and hemlock and a few even more obscure herbs—or on the other extreme, long-stemmed roses wrapped in green tissue paper—he rarely gave plants a second glance. "Sure, is there anything wrong with that?"

"No, but you hardly seem the type."

She had him pegged. He'd pull a string, see what he unraveled. This light conversation thing was fascinating. He wondered why he'd never tried it before. "What do you think I'd read?"

Yesterday's wind kicked up. He recognized the familiar scent of salt, seaweed, and things left to dry off the rocky coast of Rhode Island. The weatherman on his car radio had assured him it would be calm all day. Of course, how anything could be calm, while he sat beside her, Pierce had no idea. He watched while the breeze lightly played with her bangs, making them dance. His fingers tingled, wanting to do the exact same thing himself.

"Heaven forbid, I haven't got a clue. But not wild flowers."

"Why not?"

"It's a subject women are usually interested in."

Enjoying himself immensely, and for reasons he couldn't immediately fathom, Pierce crossed his arms against his chest, and puffed out a lower lip. "And you thought I'd read Mud, Muggings and Mayhem or a technical guide to changing the sound card on my PC, didn't you?"

She laughed, and neither of them felt offense, only surprisingly, stiletto-sharp attraction. "The thought had crossed my mind."

"So there, too," he said, battling an impulse to stick out his tongue. "It just so happens I already have the two books I mentioned."

Her eyes crinkled, and small laugh lines appeared at the corners, testifying to her vibrant health. "That I don't doubt."

Banter aside, he lowered his voice, tried to sound humble. "I knew this budget would last a long time. I wanted some kind of inexpensive reference book I could use over and over. I thought of coin collecting, but I gave it the old once-over in the bookstore and decided all the coins in my pocket were only worth face value."

"If that much," she said.

"If that much," Pierce agreed. "So that kinda left out coin collecting. The same with stamp collecting."

She grinned, showing perfect white teeth. "All the mail you get is metered and addressed To Occupant."

"No, most of the mail I get comes from the IRS or my tax lawyer, and neither are about to send me stamps in collector's condition from Borneo or Hertza Bolavania."

She laughed out loud. "True."

"Have you noticed how most hobbies, all the interesting ones anyway, cost a fortune?"

"No, but I suppose you're right."

"Take train collecting."

"Miniature or life-sized?"

He was about to slug her. "Miniature. Even the simple kind that goes around the base of a Christmas tree costs a fortune."

"I am beginning to appreciate the nature of the problem."

"I found a book on geo-caching for beginners that I got excited about. I even took it to the register. That's free, you get to go to all kinds of interesting parks, and it looked fun."

"I don't suppose you already own a GPS, do you?"

"You're fairly astute. You discovered the problem. I mean I've got a GPS in the car, and certainly my phone has the app for street names and such, but nothing portable I can take into parks looking for hidden caches. That left, after about two hours in a bookstore, identifying wild flowers or birds."

"Birds," she laughed. But he could see she thought, understood his dilemma.

"And I'm not exactly the bird watcher type."

"If you say so." This time she was particularly non-committal. Pierce wished he knew more about her. With his luck she worked for the Audubon society and was world renowned for identifying purple spotted winged gossets, or whatever the latest endangered species was.

"Watching birds," he said, "sounds like more effort than I'm willing to put forth. Climbing sheer cliffs to see eaglets, slogging through alligator swamps to view...whatever flies around swamps."

"Mosquitoes," she answered.

"You have experience with swamps as well as aquamarine beryls?"

"No, on both counts, but I suppose you're right. Bird watching does sound incredibly dangerous. Besides, you'd have to buy binoculars."

"I hadn't thought of that. But, I do have binoculars. I use them at the track."

Without an inch of censure, she said, "I'm beginning to see why the IRS is so interested in your tax returns."

Pleased, and unexpectedly charmed, Pierce grinned, decided this charade was the best thing he'd done in ages. ' So, what do you think this is, weed or wild flower," he asked pointing to something vibrant growing through the slots of the bench. It was not well used.

And she laughed, punched him in the arm, said "Goldenrod," and the day was off to a fine start.

They walked together probably for two hours, giving his purchase a fine work-over, and he found himself stunned at her knowledge. There wasn't a wild flower she didn't know, a seed she couldn't point out, a leaf she couldn't identify. It was beginning to look like he'd have to invest in a Scrabble game, whatever that was, in order to keep up with her.

The time vanished far too quickly, and their companionship grew. They never really touched, never discussed any subjects more profound than the weather, the merits of eating raw dandelions, the fact that twenty dollars didn't go very far these days. On the last he completely disagreed. Pierce had no idea when he'd had so much fun, no matter how much money he'd spent.

It was well past "getting dark" and into almost complete opacity when they separated, both reluctant to leave. Pierce was used to paying for his pleasures with a woman, even if it were dinner, Broadway tickets, and a cab home, yet he didn't feel constrained as he left her. The clinic across the street had closed an hour before. He could leave her with good conscience.

"Can I meet you again?" he asked. "Saturday, next week?" That would give her too much time to do things he could only pray she wouldn't, but he didn't want to appear too eager, and there were things he needed to accomplish.

She shuffled gravel around a crack in the sidewalk, the small stones which had undoubtedly been laid down by the road crews during some horrendous ice storm, or whenever the last glacier left Rhode Island. It was a reminder winter was coming, and with it changes. He could hardly take her looking for Queen Anne's Lace in December.

She paused again, thinking, and he was afraid even though he'd had a wonderful time, she couldn't wait to get away from him, and was busy developing plausible excuses why she didn't want to spend any more time with this broke fraud.

"I'd like to take you out to dinner. ." he said, and damn the budget.

"No, please, don't even think that. You've got to be good."

Good? That was absolutely the farthest thing from his mind.

"I'm used to showing a woman a better time..."

Apology. He hoped it was enough. He tight-roped a fine line between masculine prowess and friendly persuasion, capped by a limit of twenty dollars. Really, could the two of them eat at McDonalds for twenty dollars? He wasn't sure.

"You will not take me to dinner," she said firmly. "I won't let you. I will meet you though," she said suddenly, "if you do one thing for me."

"Anything." At this point he was willing to beg.

"Spend your twenty dollars before you meet me."

"Why would I do that, when together we could—" Could what? Ride the subway? Take a cab one way, for two blocks?

"I want to see what you buy," then, surprisingly, miraculously, she reached out, touched his sleeve. "I really do. Saturday will be fine." She retracted her hand, looked away, suddenly shy.

Pierce spread charm the best money in the country had bred into him. "I think we should we blow the twenty dollars together." Of course if they did, it was highly unlikely he'd stop at twenty.

She looked up at him with innocence, with something that shocked him because it might have been trust. He dated a lot of women, was intimate with most, yet doubted he'd ever met one who offered the kind of open, blind trust she was handing to him without his asking.

She thought, debated options. He'd bet she was the kind to nibble a fingernail, or worry a paperclip into modern art. She was a woman, he could see, who didn't think lightly, but instead gave things her complete attention, body and soul.

"No, please don't. I'd rather see what you've selected. I want to think about it all week, anticipate your selection. I want to be surprised when I find out how wrong I was."

He was a man who liked to kiss on first dates, as a prelude to other things he anticipated about first dates, and her lips were full, ripe, looked sweeter than June strawberries. There was no sign of her pregnancy, if it still existed, and her stomach was flat, firm, her breasts high and pert. His palms itched to attempt the buttons of her cotton blouse.

Pierce grasped, looking for the emergency brake on his imagination, and tugged at it with all his strength. Whoever she was, whatever she meant to him, he knew she was something he would have to discover slowly, brushing away impediments in delightful increments, like an archeologist or a homicide detective.

"All right, no problem. You've put the pressure on me, but I can manage to be creative and innovative, and still stay under my miserable limit. Now, can you get home from here? Can I walk you to your car?"

"No need, it's right here." So her idle wanderings had direction after all. She could have, he thought rather pragmatically, abandoned her car in the medical complex parking, but instead it was a good twenty minutes away in the lot of a small strip mall, all but deserted for this late on a Saturday night.

"And have a good time this week, will you?" Pierce asked in all sincerity. "I want to hear all about everything you did."

She nodded, as if not quite certain what she was agreeing to. Then they separated, both taking off in different directions, the abortion clinic forgotten.

As she left, it occurred to Pierce that he had met her three times now and he didn't even know her name.

# CHAPTER 7

It was still early when he got home, although Pierce doubted that would have mattered, for his blood hummed and he felt invigorated. Cloud nine, he supposed, and wondered why he had never found it before, wondered why he had never looked. Wild flowers served as an aphrodisiac, and he didn't even have to buy them, or for that matter, eat them, or whatever, traditionally you were supposed to do with aphrodisiacs. He slipped his key into the front door lock, reflectively checking the tell-tales he left guarding the door. Nothing had been disturbed in his absence.

Silence shrouded the house. In the hallway he tried to recall if he'd ever noticed the silence before, and determined he hadn't. His thoughts were generally too loud for him to concentrate on externals. Not a floorboard creaked, not a shutter banged against siding in the increasing wind.

Concentrating, he couldn't even hear the muted hum from the refrigerator. CD's were stacked by the sound system, his television and radio waited for only the push of a button, whether he turned them on magically or not. He could have noise any time he wanted, but this evening it wasn't sound he craved.

He wanted conversation. Perhaps he had left her too early. He should have stayed, found an excuse to buy her dinner, to sit with her in some dimly lit café over sushi and whispered confidences. He rubbed his chin, wondered if his near-death experience had done this, when he caught his expression in the gilded hall mirror.

Pierce stopped, startled, as if he faced a stranger. If he had lacked animation when he first observed himself in the emergency room, this evening his look was diametrically opposite. His dark eyes glistened, showed a depth of blue he had never witnessed before. They were bright, inquisitive. He was a master wizard, inquisitive by nature. Why now was that the word he associated with his own eyes?

A rough brush of late-evening beard had sprouted, coming in a shade darker than his hair. He hadn't shaved before he left for his afternoon appointment with the bench sitter, a first, since on his normal dates, he was always impeccably groomed. What had he been thinking that he hadn't stopped long enough to see to something so routine?

But he knew what he had been thinking. He'd been so desperate to be with her, concentrating so intently on what he would say, how he hoped she would respond, that he hadn't considered himself.

For a wizard, stepping from pre-established routines could be deadly, but, like the scar on his chest, he decided he liked the thought of becoming more spontaneous, more human. Perhaps he had been an automaton for far too long. Perhaps, only since he died was he learning what it meant to be alive. Morbid. But good or bad? Only time would tell. Time, and more afternoons spent with the woman.

He was a handsome man. Even baring any misplaced modesty, he had to say so. His body was hard, honed by hours spent at the gym he went to more to see and be seen, than because he needed the workout. Because he was a wizard, because too much of his life could be considered weird, he had to go places, do the things normal people did, so if anything unusual in his background turned up, in the press, or with the police, friends could say, "sure I know him. He's a normal guy. Always seemed fairly straight-laced to me."

Good breeding had given him the bone structure, the hale good health, the confidence and composure of the attractive. Best schools and proper tutors in social graces had given him entrance into his parents' world of Washington politics, or his own, of legal representation. And his master had taught him how to successfully hide anything that didn't fit his image.

The wheat blond hair he had as a child darkened with adulthood to what his mother called 'mousey brown.' She dyed hers, but his vanity took other forms. It was longer now than he normally kept it. He hadn't been to a barber since before the hospital stay. Now it was windblown, rakish. With a sharp grin he decided to postpone the barber appointment another week.

For a second he debated unbuttoning his shirt, so he could view the scars from a new perspective, then decided that was information he didn't need. He knew what they looked like as he stepped from the shower.

Just as quickly, he changed his mind. He did need to know. He removed his jacket, worked on the buttons, tried to see his body as she would. For she would see it. After today, that much was established. They would be intimate soon. She just didn't know it yet.

The scars were red, ugly, large. Idly Pierce scratched the edges, where the pink healing skin itched. They hadn't looked this bad when the bandages were first removed. Or perhaps they had, but he was thinking the scars were such a small price to pay for the privilege of remaining alive. He hadn't looked at them with a woman's sensitivity. He hoped she wouldn't be repelled, although if she was, he would repair the damage. It was as easy as that.

Deliberately turning his back on the mirror, he reworked the buttons, feeling an unaccustomed modesty. Pierce ignored the displacement he felt looking at his own reflection, and decided he could hardly wait for Saturday.

He was about to go kill a few hours in his lair, when he noticed the message light flashing. Not on his land line, but a small, almost invisible power strand, waiting, like a puppy cowering in a corner beside a wet spot on the carpet.

He sniffed around the house before he opened it. Message strands didn't come with return addresses, at least the unopened ones didn't, and if it were from some type of bad-guy, he would expose himself. He decided it didn't matter. If those who abused power sought him, at least he was at his power base where he was the least vulnerable. He flicked his fingers, and the message opened up to a single word.

"Come."

His master's command. No doubt. He could transfer there instantly, when the need was great, but judging from the message clue, he doubted it was urgent, so he pulled his car keys out, reset his locks, and drove the several blocks across town.

A high school janitor in his day-life, it pleased Bernard Drollard to be seen as a quiet, mild-mannered Clark Kent, when in real life, he was a Superman. His powers as a wizard were immense, but during the day he wore stained overalls, carried a hammer and a walkie-talkie, waxed floors with a buffer, and bought 10W40 by the case.

Still, his high school was a standard for order, no violence ever got out of hand, and things in the old, broken down building often found themselves fixed in a manner which could only be called miraculous.

Some of the early apprentices, almost all of whom didn't make it to graduation, had been annoyed when they discovered Drollard's modest occupation. They equated wizard power with personal power, and while that was often the case, it didn't have to be. It had never occurred to the younger Pierce to question. He was so pleased to have found a mentor, he would have learned magic from the village idiot, if he had spells to teach.

When the door to the house shut behind him, Pierce bowed deeply, the appropriate response of an apprentice to a teacher, no matter how long it had been since the younger had been under his instruction.

"Master."

From the outside, the quaint two story brick house looked rundown. Situated in an older part of town untouched by urban renewal, like those around it, it had slowly rusticated. It was just the kind of place a high school janitor could afford, and Drollard puttered around outside during summer weekends, putting in new windows, caulking leaks, threatening the invasive dandelion encroachment with a weed-puller and harsh words.

For all that, the inside was as comfortable as a master wizard could make it. A fire roared in the fireplace, and the books on the shelves were well thumbed. The chairs were comfortably mismatched, and sagged in the middle, enough to envelop him, like a hug.

There had been a wife once, judging from odd comments Drollard had dropped over the years, but her fate Pierce had never been able to determine. Early divorce due to neglect, or killed by forces beyond her control, he had no idea. An old basset hound, grayed and arthritic lay underfoot no matter which way he turned, quite a feat for a pet he'd rarely seen move. The dog was comforting. Pierce had not yet settled deep enough into his craft that comfort was a trait he sought.

Pierce always felt at home here, even during the early years when all he had received for his hours of concentration were verbal abuse and threats. Years before he had found himself unconsciously decorating his own home in the same hues, the same textures, until he realized what he was doing, and had struck out in a completely opposite direction, ending up with mostly glass and mirror, ultra-modern. No herringbone tweed and basset hounds for him.

"You got here quickly enough. I just sent the line. What were you doing, waiting for it?" Drollard asked as he motioned Pierce into the sitting room.

The room hadn't changed a dust mote in twenty years, probably longer. It was here he first understood magic, real magic, not sleight of hand was possible. It was here his first lesson started. Although most of his training had taken place in the basement, and it was not until he was nearly ready to take his final exams that he was admitted to Drollard's attic lair, Pierce's happiest thoughts derived from this room.

"I thought you'd be out for at least several more hours. Did the lady turn down your proposition?"

"Lady?" Pierce asked, concealing his shock, knowing that yes, his master still had a right to check into his private life. Since he had become a master, he assumed Drollard didn't bother. But then he realized it was not the woman at the abortion clinic Drollard was referring to, but to a woman in general. Pierce dated frantically on the weekends, and was always out every night until late, dancing, drinking, and often spending his sleeping hours at the woman's apartment.

"We parted on mutually agreeable terms," Pierce said, found himself scratching his chest where the healing skin itched. "For some reason, I wasn't willing to expose this," his wounds, "to candlelight, just yet."

"Don't worry, you will."

Pierce grinned, acknowledging the reassurance he didn't need. Masters to pupils were almost never supportive. They were dominant, aggressive and authoritative. This new facet of their relationship pleased Pierce, and he wondered if it had been there before, perhaps for years, and he hadn't noticed.

He felt the need to add something, an excuse perhaps, or an acknowledgement. "I don't like feeling so vulnerable." That wasn't what he meant to say.

Drollard leaned forward, hands on his knees, concerned. "Have there been any other attempts?"

Pierce idly waved him back down. "Nothing, not even a stray, inquisitive powerstrand. I didn't necessarily mean physically vulnerable. I misspoke."

"I don't think so. Of all my students, you were the one most certain of your diction."

Pierce laughed, bemused. "Vocabulary and grammar, both a gift from my mother, perhaps her only legacy to me."

"So, vulnerable how?"

"It's hard to explain. I wish I knew. I haven't quite worked it out myself. It's like," he struggled for images, wondered if a Scrabble game would help provide clues. "Like I have been working on a jigsaw puzzle for years, intricate and confusing, but still a puzzle. I wasn't certain I had all the pieces and I wasn't certain I knew what the picture was, but I knew if I tried really, really hard that I could eventually get it to make sense. And now I find it isn't a jigsaw puzzle at all, but it's three dimensional, and oddly enough, it's sentient, changing as I work on it. Pieces I'd put in earlier no longer fit. They've changed shape."

Dead asleep by the blast furnace of a fireplace, the basset hound tweaked a hind leg and snorted, undoubtedly a dream of youthful exuberance. Drollard moved toward the bar nestled securely in the bookcases, spoke with his back to Pierce. "Do you know what wisdom is?"

Physical response was sharp and immediate, wavering between pride and shock. He chose deliberately to respond with laughter. "Wisdom? I'm only a few years into a black robe."

"Regardless of what normal people think, wisdom is not necessarily only obtained with great age."

"I'll be flattered, later, I'm sure," he said, and knew he was flattered. Wisdom? What greater praise from one person to another was there? It had to transcend even love, for it was his experience a person couldn't always choose who they loved, or how they expressed it. Wisdom was like a gift, priceless and very desirable. "But I doubt it's wisdom. More likely confusion. Everyone else had the blueprints to this puzzle, and I'm only just figuring out that I lost my copy."

"Maturity, then?"

Pierce snorted. "I like that word even less. Don't grant me praise when I'm still bumbling around in the dark with my hands outstretched. I may occasionally run into something, but it's due to blind luck or stupidity, not wisdom, or heaven forbid, maturity."

"Power doesn't—"

At his master's movement, Pierce continued quickly. "Power doesn't come with a rule book, I know. I've heard it often enough. Now, let me add your comments to my confusing, ever changing puzzle."

"Daniel said you've got something else cooking?"

Ahh, so that was what this meeting was about. He should have known Daniel would run to master. He trusted this man with his life, had given him all the devotion an apprentice gives his instructor, but now found himself curiously reluctant to admit what he was doing. Too much was unsettled, too much unlikely, although considering their secret professions, unlikely was often the norm.

"I was searching for the shooter." A lie so quickly formed, it must have been huddling in the far reaches of his brain for just such an opportunity. Then, using that logic, not a true lie. Realistically, he should be hunting for the shooter.

He had no idea why he didn't admit to spending time with the woman. He was allowed to date, have a personal life beyond his private life, but he wasn't ready to share her yet. Two dates and one wild flower book were nothing to be ashamed of, deny or cover-up. He wouldn't even have to confess when he was first drawn to her. It would have been easy to fill in the blanks.

He'd needed a break from work, needed something besides his recovery to occupy his thoughts. So he'd been driving aimlessly through Rhode Island, stopped at a park bench to get his bearings, opened up a conversation which showed potential. Was it the potential he was hiding? No woman had ever meant anything to him before.

"Any leads on the shooter?"

"No, at least nothing I can run to ground."

Brandy appeared on the table in front of him, rich, expensive and intoxicating. Pierce found even the depth of the color pleasing.

"Can you?" Drollard asked, pointing to the alcohol. "Will it interfere with any pain medication you're taking?" He could, with the negligent flip of his wrist, turn it into anything else. Of course, as a wizard, he could as easily negate any deleterious effect of alcohol on medication.

Pierce picked up the snifter, swirled the contents, watching the warm liquid coat the sides, inhaling the bouquet, finding it inviting.

"This is fine. No need for anything else." He sipped, let the fire burn on his tongue for several long seconds before swallowing. Yes, he did have an added appreciation for taste since his near death experience. This brandy was the best of the best, still he found himself hungering for strawberry milkshake.

"What have you got?"

"Nothing. Images. Impressions." Perhaps he'd actually have more if he had been sniffing out the shooter. Perhaps he should concentrate more on bullet casings, less on gamine women he had no idea why he should want.

"What?"

"It had to be done by another practitioner."

"I was wondering how long it would take you to come to that conclusion."

"Then you know?" Pierce asked, sitting forward. "What have you got?"

"Probably nothing more than you have, considering impressions, maybe even significantly less. But we are looking for a wizard. Tell me what you think, where you're leaning."

"Not a lot has come back to me, nothing as a matter of fact, so I'm trying to go over in my mind what I was probably doing.

I don't think I was in my body when the shooting occurred. I can't remember, but I think I was out, looking for Minelli."

"Makes sense."

"I had wards set. If that were the case, of course I would have had wards set, and I would have been in my lair. No one should have been able to reach me."

"Are there signs your wards were tampered with?"

He swirled the brandy, found the action itself relaxing, more than the alcohol. It seemed to be imparting warmth to the palm of his hand, an electric blanket that worked through crystal. "Yes, and no. I haven't found a trace of anything, and the powerstrands, the ones hanging around, were unaffected. Nothing was disturbed, or out of place. But everything is too clean. I am not that clean when I work. I leave traces of what I'm doing in my own lair."

"And they were all gone? Curious."

He scratched his chest, this time deliberately. "This recovery has made me uncomfortable, and I have trouble concentrating. I'd been staying away from the lair the past week, regaining my strength, but when I went up yesterday afternoon, I couldn't force the concentration."

"You feel vulnerable?"

Pierce cleared his throat, using the pause to wonder at his own motivations. He trusted his master. He had to. Then why was he not only unwilling to speak the truth, he was outright lying? It was an impression, and he had to run with it. The last time he felt a pull this strongly, he came upon a woman, huddled in the rain beside an expensive car.

"I'm not so much vulnerable as weak. Not so much weak, as not ready. Emotionally, physically, whatever. Not ready."

"It will come back. I promise."

"I know." He felt a flood of guilt, weaving this lie so tightly, with thread so thin, to a man he trusted.

"Do you want me to send Daniel to you? To guard your back? If not Daniel, then any of the others."

Pierce shut his eyes, leaned back deeply into the chair, inhaled then exhaled slowly. "It's not a question of having my back guarded. I'm not ready yet to fall back down the rabbit hole. Don't get upset, I haven't lost any sensitivity, and I can still call and control the power when I need, but oddly enough, I'm not feeling the urgency."

"Minelli is still an issue. That white powder he's pumping on the street is causing a lot of deaths and the DEA is involved, since this is new stuff and they can't quite figure out what it is."

Minelli. One time fellow apprentice and friend. It hurt so much worse to be betrayed by an ally.

Drollard sipped, spoke again. "There's something else you might not have heard. Powerstrands are disappearing. It's not as bad as it was earlier in the year, and it might be a glitch, that they are not gone at all, but congregating somewhere. That's not the main thing I want to bring up. Belinda Wurle is missing and apparently has been for some months."

"Months? Daniel told me she was missing, but I got the impression it wasn't more than a day or two."

"That's what we thought. We don't keep tabs on her—on any of the witches, you know that, but when we started asking questions, it seems like no one has seen her since early spring."

"She's not a major player. Do you think someone took her out?"

Drollard leaned back, took another small sip of his brandy before he spoke. "They said she had a line on dragon fangs."

"I suppose that's why she's missing. I doubt dragon fangs are that easy to come by. Dragons don't readily give them up."

"True. I'd like to send you to New York, where there have been some random dragon sightings, to see if you can pick up anything."

"Tonight?"

"Not yet, probably not for a few weeks. There's still some lines I need to pull. I don't want to send you in blind if I do send you. And I'd like you to heal a bit more."

"I'm fine," Pierce hedged, but he knew as he said it he wasn't and he knew his master knew too.

"As you feel the need, keep searching for the shooter, and anything you can pull on Belinda but I doubt you can find more than we already have."

Pierce swirled the brandy, watching the way the liquid coated the expensive glass. "Sure. There is one other thing. I don't know why I didn't mention this a few months back—"

"What?"

"It might have nothing to do with what we're talking about, but mid-summer a gargoyle approached me."

"A real gargoyle?"

"Yeah. He had a mortal woman with him he claimed was his wife and an incomplete dragon."

"Incomplete dragon?"

"An infant, probably not more than two or three weeks old. Looked human. It was sickly, without a soul and without a chakra. They were searching for the chakra, said a wizard had taken it, and had latched onto me."

"But you—"

"I didn't know anything about it or the thief for that matter. He, the gargoyle, said he was searching for a wer-wizard called Andrew."

"Andrew. Doesn't ring any bells. Have you followed through with this?"

"Before the shooting I'd check about once a week or so, when nothing was pressuring me, but I never considered it my quest. The gargoyle was looking for a wizard and I was the first one he uncovered."

"This is interesting. I'll check the powerstrands, see what I can find. And Pierce, this puts Belinda's statement that she was looking for dragon fangs in a new light. This might be significant."

"I can leave for New York tomorrow, if you give me time to arrange a leave of absence from work."

"No, no, don't bother with her. It's the other I would rather you concentrate on. Belinda is a tough old bird and she can take care of herself. I just wanted you to be apprised of what's going on. You get shot, almost the same time, another of us turns up missing."

"With Belinda's reputation, can we be certain she's dead, or taken?"

"No, of course not. For all we know she could be hiding. She's certainly gone to ground before. She finds a new spell she thinks none of the rest of us have tried, and she hides herself in the mountains or off-world to practice in secret. I thought you should know. If there is a connection, you might be the most sensitive."

"I can't imagine Belinda as the shooter, if that's what you're implying."

"I know you like her. There're not many of us who do."

"Master, has Belinda ever taken an apprentice?"

"I don't believe so. She started long before my time, if you can believe it, but I never heard of her taking in a student."

"Well, if I ever get my strength up, I'll give it a look. And don't look at me like that. Think of this time off more as a prolonged recuperation, instead of a vacation. I'll be back to full strength soon enough. In the meantime—"

"No one will know you're vulnerable."

"Thanks. Is there anything else?"

"One thing."

Pierce sipped the liquor again, slowly, as if unaffected. "Yes?"

Drollard, who had been standing, leaned against a high backed chair. "I meant what I said before all this happened. You're ready to take on an apprentice. Just listen. You don't have to jump in with a dozen students. One might be enough. It might be a way for you to keep your hand in, while you pull your power base around you again."

"I'm not ready for the commitment."

"Perhaps not, but think about what I said. A teacher often learns more, far more, than the student. It might help you put things in perspective. To go back over the very basic tenets of our profession."

"Wait a minute, do you think I need that? A few moments ago you were using words like wisdom and maturity, and now you want me to go back to lesson one?"

"I am not insulting you, Pierce, nor am I belittling your accomplishments. Your ability is immense. None of your classmates have made master yet. Some I've taught, ten, fifteen years out of apprenticeship haven't made master. You've come far, and you've come fast. It might help you recognize some of your puzzle pieces, to go back to your analogy, if you started looking at them with a fresh eye."

"And you've got some students?"

"One or two. They're fine with me for the time being. There's no hurry for your decision. I just want you to consider it. Think too, of the advantages of having wizards in your debt. The easiest way to do that is to instruct."

"So, they hate me for fifteen years, then they're in my debt?"

"Yes, but looking at the long term picture, you'll need support then, too. We'll find something to tie to Minelli. He's not good enough to avoid us much longer. If he's behind this power loss, or your shooting, or even the reason Belinda is in hiding, it should be easy to put right."

"Do you think he's working alone?"

"Odd you should ask. The elves are all up in arms about something, hissing and biting and I have no idea what is annoying them, but they do think there's a new wizard, one they hadn't come across before. This new wizard might be working with Minelli. I wouldn't have thought Minelli clever enough to set up the marketing for the drug by himself."

"Fine. Another wizard."

"That's all I've got, upset elves."

"They've been known to go ballistic over an early frost and don't get them started on the emerald ash bore."

"This is something else. I haven't looked into it myself because you're right, it's probably nothing, and I wouldn't have mentioned it except it might fit in with all the rest."

"Missing witch. Missing powerstrands. Upset elves. Minelli and his hallucinogenic drug. And perhaps a new wizard. I'll add that to the search for my shooter."

"You do that. And don't forget the gargoyle and the dragon fangs," he added with a grin. Then you'll need something to keep your hand in.

Teaching is exacting and exhausting, I don't deny it, but I think it will help you, especially now, when you might be, should I use the word, 'hesitant' to try any of the more powerful spells at your command."

"I'll think about it." He set the snifter on the coffee table. "Is there anything else?"

"No. You're free to go. What are your plans?"

"For the weekend?"

"Yes."

"I'm going to see my parents. It seems like the normal thing to do. Mom will certainly be reassured to see me."

"It will leave you vulnerable."

"Perhaps. But I don't want to be seen holed up in my lair. If someone is watching me, I want to give them something to watch."

"You have countermeasures?"

"Always. I hope because you had to ask that they're good?"

"They probably are. You always were the best of my students, but I haven't looked. And I won't, unless you ask it. I will grant you that much dignity."

Pierce stood, bowed deeply. "Master." And took the words of praise home with him, where it kept him warm all night. "*You always were the best of my students.*"

\*\*\*

CeeDee Radling unlocked the front door of her small condo, slipped out of her shoes and slouched into a boneless heap on the couch.

"Maggie," she said, "I am a lot more tired than I should be."

She yawned, stretched languidly like a kitten preparing for a long winter's nap, and melted deeper into the cushions. She was alone, not another living soul in the apartment, not a lover, a dog, or even a houseplant.

She was alone, except for a three foot rather obese teddy bear she had bought two weeks before when she first discovered her pregnancy. She named the saucy-grinned toy Maggie on the spot, because she needed something to share her happiness with. Maggie hugged. Maggie listened. Maggie was there in the night when memories of an awful rainy night intruded.

"So how did your day go?" CeeDee asked, closing her eyes, speaking not so much to the bear, but to a child whose life she had not yet felt. "My day wasn't so bad. The doctor did say I was to take it easy."

He also said she was able to go about her normal routine, which was laughable, for how could she have a normal routine and be pregnant too?

Maggie had been chosen, selected, born, in one of those make a Teddy shops which had proliferated in every mall in the country. CeeDee'd gone shopping, not so much to buy something, not even to compare prices and make decisions, yellow outfits? Pink? but to avoid making a decision at all.

Since then, Maggie had been her best friend, her only friend, actually, since Maggie was the only one who knew of her predicament. She reached out, stretching, until she grabbed the soft bear. She had stuffed it herself, chosen the wardrobe, fallen in love with it immediately, even when she suspected Maggie might be the only thing she would keep out of this entire debacle. The bear wasn't for the baby. There wasn't likely to be a baby much longer. The bear was for her, when her heart broke, when her arms and her womb were empty, when she needed something to be there for her.

"You don't understand, do you, Maggie?" How could Maggie possibly understand, when CeeDee herself didn't. She wanted a baby more than she wanted to breathe. There were even times when she thought she could swing it.

She had benefits, including maternity leave. There were decent daycares and preschools. She worked at a major university after all, one with an associated medical school and primary education program.

Needs could be met. But she honestly and completely felt every child needed two-parents, at least at the start. It was too hard raising a baby on your own. And she would let no child of hers be neglected, even if the state didn't consider it neglect, if he or she were left forty hours a week at a child center.

A baby needed to imprint. A baby needed a momma there to wipe tears and put Band-Aids on skinned knees, and to sing lullabies. No, "let the infant cry itself to sleep" on her watch. No, better to end it now, than to ruin a perfect child.

She rubbed her stomach. She had not even a single moment of morning sickness. It was as if this baby was meant for her, as if it was trying to make itself so accommodating, so completely invisible, that she could forget about it long enough to make the decision for her. But she knew it was there. Even though she hadn't yet felt the first butterfly flutter of movement, she knew it was there, by the way her body had changed. Not just the absence of her period or the plus sign on the at-home test.

She suspected long before that facet appeared to her. Her breasts were tender, and her nipples darker. She felt clumsy and dropped things, although there was no big belly getting in her way, no altered center of gravity to make getting out of deep chairs any more difficult. Her fingernails were harder, and her complexion better on the plus side, and she had long stretches of time when she couldn't get enough sleep or enough chocolate covered peppermint patties on the negative.

With Maggie firmly under her arm, CeeDee migrated into the kitchen and poured herself a glass of milk. She wasn't by nature a milk drinker, but decided she loved it and would keep the habit long after…well, long after. She pealed the paper off half a dozen mint patties before she ate the first one. CeeDee knew once she got started, she wouldn't be able to rip the wrappers off fast enough. Ahh, whatever this baby was, it was going to be sweet.

She couldn't keep it. She had no savings, was still paying off her college loans, and her car was on its last legs. It wasn't nearly safe enough for a baby. She doubted it would make it another six months before it died for good, or needed serious intervention. She had bills, not a lot, certainly nothing like that guy at the bus stop, but there was a balance on her credit card, and with winter coming, her heating and electric bills would be high again. She couldn't afford car seats and high chairs and three hundred thousand disposable diapers.

She went to the bathroom and started the bathwater running. She thought best in the bath. If she sat, she read, if she laid down she slept, and she couldn't mull over her problems in either of those situations, so bath it was. The bubbles were new, bought on impulse yesterday after meeting the crossword puzzle maniac. After she left him she'd felt decidedly lonely with no idea why, and wanted to pamper herself. So she'd gone to the mall, bought another outfit for Maggie, this one with lace, and scented bubble bath for herself.

She lived in a massive old home subdivided into three condos, and her section contained one of the original bedrooms and the original bath. The tub was deep, wide, claw-footed, almost large enough to swim laps. Steam swarmed around her, as did the fresh, sensual scent of roses. She pulled her hair up, off her shoulders, out of the water, and sank, melting into pure pleasure letting the heat slowly sate her into pleasant lassitude.

Up to her neck in bubbles, she decided she needed music to make this interlude perfect, but wasn't about to trail soap bubbles over worn carpet, so shut her eyes and concentrated on imagining the sounds of the powerful, pulsing jazz she loved. Her imagination was so good she heard the throaty sax, the throbbing piano. She must have put the CD on as she headed toward the kitchen. Such things were always happening. Tiny things she was always forgetting she'd done. Still, she enjoyed the music. Let it relax her. She allowed it to take her somewhere her problems were not so overwhelming.

With her eyes closed, she thought of the wildflowers. It had been fun this afternoon. Why couldn't she meet a nice guy like that when she was actually in the market for a nice guy, not when she had a decision to make that wasn't at all conducive a new romance?

Still, it was pleasant thinking about him, how the day had flown by, and how he seemed so sensitive, so hopeful. Yes, hopeful. Not devastated by his situation, nor angry, but hopeful he had a plan which would work out.

Charmed, she laughed, and couldn't wait to see what he would have to show for his twenty dollars. Who would have thought she could have so much fun with twenty dollars she didn't even have to spend?

Her bath water had grown cold, and she was preparing to get out, when she wished it were just a tad warmer, so she could soak ten minutes longer, and she must have convinced herself it was, because it actually felt warmer. She closed her eyes, rubbed her stomach. Yes, the swelling was visible now. She had to wear a pin in her pants since they wouldn't easily button, and if she didn't make a decision very soon, she'd have to get serious about a maternity wardrobe.

She had to go through with her plans. The baby's father was a creepazoid. That should have made the decision easier. Except it didn't. It only mattered that the baby be born healthy.

Or not born at all.

# CHAPTER 8

Pierce entered the monstrosity of a house and wondered why it never felt like home. Even as a child this place had given him the creeps, made him feel like he had slipped into a museum after hours and would be caught by some security guard if he wandered around unescorted.

He had been raised in a "Don't touch that, it's priceless," home. Also, his parents frequently entertained, and their philosophy was "Children should be neither seen nor heard" when some influential person was around. It was still partially in effect. Politicians hoping to get reelected still arrived with some regularity. Lobbyists and legislators requiring support on a bill stopped by to see an old master for advice. Generally there were two or three casual acquaintances invited over when his father needed extra votes for some bill he was pushing.

Pierce could stand none of them, so generally made himself scarce from the old family homestead. With that thought, he was about to turn on his heel and head for the hills, but he began his escape a moment too late.

"Pierce, it's so good to see you." His mother gave him an air kiss more for show, even though at the moment they were the only two in the open, two floor foyer, the room lit by a chandelier which cost more than his car. She was dressed in a finely tailored silk suit, the color of the cornflowers he had identified earlier that day, and it pleased him immensely when he made the connection. Only twenty-four hours before he'd have seen her outfit as some kind of blue, without attaching any emotional significance to it, probably without even noticing.

It was eleven o'clock at night, for he had driven straight through after he left his master, and his mother looked polished enough to meet the 60 Minutes news team head on, or grace the cover of Time. Both of which she had done, and she wasn't the politician in the family: or more specifically, she wasn't the elected politician.

She reached up, cupping his chin in her palms, as if she were looking for something, or as if she were about to confess some long buried family secret only he could hear. But after a moment she dropped her hands, and the opportunity for whispers passed, and she slipped back into being more than slightly distant. "I'm glad you caught us in. We're leaving for Washington in the morning."

Without conscious thought, Pierce waved down a powerstrand starting to crawl up his leg, looking for attention. Some of them, the ones he unrealistically called "the juvenile ones" sought attention, almost as if they craved it. Almost all the rest had to be called to heel, ordered, with a high powered magical summons, but these little ones, particularly in the home of a master wizard, were always underfoot, waiting for him to scratch its head before he sent it on its way.

"You're leaving?"

"You didn't know? I was sure I sent you my schedule."

"You probably did. Things have been a little crazy in my life lately."

She shivered, then righted herself, coming back with her million dollar smile. It was almost as if she had forgotten what had happened to him, as if it hadn't registered why she had spent a significant part of last month in a Brooklyn hospital at his bedside. She recovered quickly enough, taking his hand as she rarely had when he was young enough to need it, and directed him into the parlor, where she poured herself a drink. It was late enough for one. Any time after noon qualified.

"Can I get you anything?"

"Herbal tea, but don't bother to ring for it. I'll go hunt some up myself in a few minutes."

She looked at him strangely, as if this were a symptom of some other encroaching catastrophe, but she went herself, instead of ringing, as he suspected she would. Pierce needed a moment or two to come to terms with being back home. It always took that long to fight down the nausea.

"Do the police have any leads?" his mother asked five minutes later as Pierce poured chamomile tea into fine boned china mug which held less than a single good sized gulp.

"Nothing they're willing to share with me." He supposed one of these days he should start looking.

"We do have some of the best detectives on the case," she said, waving her hand, as if this were some major concession on her part. "It could have been done to get your father's attention, you know. Force him to—"

He dropped the cup. It settled with a loud crash of glass on glass, but did not break. "Did you ever think the killer might have been after me, and me alone?" he asked, raising his voice. He'd worked very hard over his entire life not to display a single emotion in her presence. She jumped back, psychologically more than physically, her multi-ringed hand to her chest.

"Not everything in this world revolves directly around my father."

Margaret smiled, tried to bring the conversation back down to more civilized tones. "I'd hate to have to tell him that. But yes, you're right. William does think it was a random act of violence, and the…assault…" she said, struggling for a word, "had nothing to do with him."

Pierce poured himself another dribble of tea, discovered he'd lost the taste for it, so abandoned it. "I'm off to bed then," he said. "Will I see you in the morning?"

"I'll make certain of it. Your father said—"

"What?" he asked when it appeared she wouldn't finish the thought.

"That you have the ability to keep yourself safe, and you should be more careful."

He tried to digest that, found nothing more there than what appeared on the surface. "He's right. I'll be more careful. Good night, mother."

Oddly enough, the first time he'd seen a powerstrand was in this house, on the second floor as he was heading up toward his bedroom. It had been past midnight and he'd been out, wandering the grounds, forcing himself to memorize long chants his master had assigned. Pierce was a kinetic learner, so he needed to be in motion to have anything solidify in his gray matter. When exhausted, he stumbled back into the house and found a fat neon green powerstrand disappearing into the ceiling over a linen closet.

After that he'd been able to see them everywhere, any time he looked, but that was his first. He'd been searching during the long years of his early apprenticeship, and he was one of the last in his class of six to discover them.

The covers on his bed had already been pulled back. He stripped off his clothing, and put on a pair of pajama bottoms for modesty, then spied the obsidian bowl which was really the only thing of a personal nature in the room. He'd discovered it in his father's den years before and asked to borrow it. It had stayed here ever since.

Without waiting for the guilt which he knew would be a by-product, Pierce quickly filled the bowl with tap water, then sought and captured a small bronze colored powerstrand, and twined it around the bowl. These strands dealt only with the present, but frequently left a tell-tale that linked directly back to the sender, so he never could use them to hunt out another wizard. And he rarely had interest in spying on mortals, that on the whole he left this particular talent alone.

"Show me the woman from the bus stop."

The strand pulsed, changing colors, from the bronze, to a richer mahogany, and while that was happening, the water in the bowl grew turbulent, as if he stirred it. Then suddenly, all was clear. Pierce felt as if he looked in her window, not two feet from her.

She slept on her side, clutching a teddy bear, the stuffed animal wearing peach-colored footed pajamas. She wore something which looked like soft-brushed flannel, in twirling shades of green, and he thought of wildflowers again and was pleased. Her deep rich auburn hair was fanned out on her pillow, and looked far longer in this vision than it had in life. She was close enough his fingers ached with the desire to run through the long strands and feel their intoxicating softness. With that thought, his body sprang to life, hard and pulsing, and he savored the discomfort.

She was sound asleep, her eyelids moving softly as if in dream, and there was firm color of health on her cheeks. Her lips were turned up, as if her dreams were pleasant. The bed was probably a queen, judging by the amount of space beside her, and it pleased him to no small extent to notice that except for the wide-eyed, grinning bear, she was alone.

With a single subtle swish of his hand, the vision vanished, and the bronze strand unknotted. It did something peculiar then. It stood straight up, about eighteen inches in length, and bowed, as if pleased to be of service.

Pierce cleared his throat, resisted the impulse to scratch it on its "head" and nodded in response. "Thank you for your effort. You can go now." He felt more than a little foolish talking to a powerstrand, but somehow felt this particular one deserved it.

Without waiting, the strand vanished, sliding through the wall soundlessly. Pierce almost regretted not telling it to keep his location secret, but then felt foolish for the impulse. He could certainly order powerstrands, but this was the first time he ever wanted to beg an innocent request from one.

Pleased his nameless woman was sleeping peacefully, Pierce emptied and dried his bowl, turned the lights off, and slid into the bed. Until it completely faded on its own, he enjoyed the sexual arousal thinking of her brought him.

The dream didn't quite form. Images swirled around in his brain, but it was as if they were on fast forward, walking through a fog. Something was wrong, something he felt he vitally needed to discover, but he couldn't sort the images out. Every time he tried, his brain superimposed images of a car in the rain and a woman kneeling.

For a second a stab of rationality intruded into the dream. He wondered if he had seen the future when he had taken his post-death walkabout, and the woman had yet to be turned down by her callus lover. But he refused to believe that. The abortion clinic was too prevalent in her current life. It was not a conclusion she could have drawn on her own, not before all other options had been analyzed.

Suddenly he couldn't breathe. His lungs burned, and he gasped, trying to pull oxygen into them, but without effect. His throat tightened, and he was choking or suffocating, he had no idea which, only if he didn't break whatever hold this was on him, he'd be dead soon.

Pierce struggled to pull himself from the dream, and found there was no need. He was already awake, and his situation was growing more desperate. He couldn't breathe. Black spots brought about by asphyxia danced behind his eyelids.

No powerstrands loitered within easy grasp to use as a weapon against whatever assaulted him. He brought his hands to his throat, and found something there, something tightening, but he couldn't loosen it, and he found no one holding the noose. He had no target.

He felt himself growing weaker, his struggles useless. He kicked his legs, waved his arms, all ineffective as deep within his chest, his lungs starved for oxygen. Numbness spread. Three minutes was a long time without oxygen, but he was powerless.

He could speak no spell, twist no powerstrand. He would die here, perhaps the victim of the same assassin who had tried to kill him with three .38 caliber bullets. He slumped back on the bed, spent, the last of his strength gone.

Then he gasped, and gasped again, as his airway cleared and life-giving oxygen rushing in. He breathed heavily, feeling the tingling in his hands and feet, the heavy numbness receding. He sat up in bed and found his father in the doorway, twirling his hands together, but at what he couldn't see, for his vision remained unreliable. Still, Pierce was a trained wizard, and knew he had been under assault. He raised his own hands, in preparation for a counterattack, before his mother burst in beside his father.

"For heaven's sake, Pierce, what's the matter?"

Light flooded in from the hallway, but the bedroom remained dark. Quickly she raced to his bedside and flipped on the table lamp.

He coughed, struggled again to get air in, found his throat burning. His senses were on high alert, and he watched his father, who now stood motionless.

"What?" his throat raspy. He really could use a tall glass of water and twenty minutes to put his larynx back in working order.

"You called out. You've been calling out. It had to have been a nightmare." She sat on the side of his bed, while his father hadn't made more than a single step into the oversized room. "Were you remembering something from the assault?"

"No, I don't think so." He rubbed his eyes, then followed the movement to its logical conclusion and rubbed his throat. Perhaps she was right. Perhaps he had been screaming, but it hardly seemed likely. Around him, his vision recovering, he noticed small pink powerstrands separated from where they had gathered at the far edge of his king sized bed, and then they vanished, slipping through the walls, down into the plush carpeting, becoming invisible. He watched for a few more seconds, until his mother physically turned his head, both her palms cupping his chin.

"If it's important, it will come back to you. The doctor did say you should start to remember more of what happened. The images are trying to break through into your consciousness. Give them enough time and you'll remember clear enough." Her touch on his chin changed, became gentler, in this woman who had never been more than tangentially maternal.

"I'm all right. Really. Thank you both for coming. I don't know what it was. I don't remember. Mom, I hope this means my memory is starting to come back." While he said that, he looked to his father, as if offering a threat, or a warning.

"Is there anything else we can do before we leave you?"

"No, no of course not. Wait, Mom, Dad. There is one thing." He rubbed his throat, thought of how he wanted to word this. "It's kind of off-beat, and has nothing to do with the accident." Funny, why would he call three .38 slugs in his chest an accident? "I need a gift for a woman. I want it to cost twenty dollars without going so much as a penny over."

"Pierce, is this a joke? It's three o'clock in the morning."

"What do you need it for, son?"

"Think of it as a grab bag gift. I don't even know her name, so I have no idea of her likes and dislikes. I want it to lean toward whimsical, but if possible I'd like it to have some depth as well."

"Give her a gift certificate. They're appropriate for any situation. If you're not sure where, have your secretary choose the store, so this nameless woman can get herself something frilly."

"That won't work, Mom. It has to be a gift. I want to enchant her." Funny, pleasing her seemed the most important thing in his life.

"A gift certificate will always work, Pierce. Really, you think just like a man. Now, I'm going off to bed. If you remember anything worth taking to the police, please let us know in the morning, over coffee."

"Sorry to have disturbed you, Mom, Dad."

"I can't think of anything either, although you know flowers are always appropriate."

He rubbed his throat. It felt bruised on the inside as well as outside. "That's probably what I'll go with. Thanks Dad." And he was glad they couldn't think of anything, because he saw this as a test. Something he had to do himself. He had completely forgotten about the pink power strands. Pink, which always tended toward life-forces. They could be used to heal. Or they could be used to kill. If one or more had managed to wrap themselves around his throat, he could easily be strangled.

The rest of the week vanished. Following his pattern, Pierce dated every night, women he'd spent time with before the shooting, women who hadn't been able to touch him in any way that mattered, yet hoping in his frenzy he could put his life back into perspective, return to the emotionless void that was normal for him. He almost found it. With an attractive woman on his arm, in his bed, he didn't feel anything, not even curiosity as to what their week was like.

Then Saturday morning dawned. Because he generally worked through the weekends, he'd arranged to take the day off. He woke early, and headed for his lair before he even showered. His first thought was to look for the woman, to check her bedroom, or the clinic, but although he owed her nothing, he could grant her privacy. And, being honest with himself, Pierce knew it was more than that. He was desperate to see her, so he disciplined himself to stay away.

Instead he prepared to look for Belinda. Batty Belinda. She wasn't a wizard, although there were female wizards. She was a witch, a totally different career path. But in every profession there was some degree of crossovers, people who trained for one profession and frequented the edges of another.

She couldn't manipulate powerstrands, but she could see them, and more importantly could call them, so she earned her living hanging around the less powerful wizards, providing powerstrands for their work. She was more than a little eccentric even for a witch, and while she frequently edged toward the blacker arts it was felt she hadn't crossed any irreparable lines into evil.

Still, once she had been nice to him. When he was barely twelve, Pierce had been all but killing himself trying to find magic. His blood sang with it, and his mind knew it had to exist beyond showmanship but he had no idea how to pursue the talent he recognized in himself. Then one day he had been walking home from the bus stop when she stopped him.

"You're mage born," she whispered.

"What?" More than a little put off by her ratty clothing and her smell, he contemplated running the opposite direction, but he'd read enough science fiction and fantasy to know what mage born meant. With one sentence it made the ancient, gray-haired crone beautiful in his eyes.

"Mage born," she said again. "You're a wizard."

"I'm not a wizard," Pierce replied, although it was his fondest wish, so secret and so deep, that he wouldn't have even dared write it in a journal, if he ever did something that personal.

She was a woman who easily would have been hung as a witch a little more than a century ago, and people wouldn't have been far off if they thought that still. Even then, knowing nothing, he could tell she was a little weird. His initial impulse was to run, but he held himself rigid, desperate for anything she had to tell him.

"You are, boy. You've got the mark."

"The mark?"

"There on your wrist. Most of us try to hide it," and she lifted the sleeve from her right wrist to reveal a birthmark exactly the same as his.

"How can I learn to be a wizard?" he asked, for Pierce had figured out magic wasn't something which was just going to come to him. He needed instruction.

"You find a mentor you will call Master."

He didn't have to think of his response. "If he—or she—would teach me magic, I'd be willing to call them Master. Will you do it?"

"Not I. But there are others."

"How will I find one?" Although he was nearly a teenager, he couldn't go up to every stranger he saw and check the right wrist.

She grinned a near toothless, ambiguous grin. "You'll know by smell."

"Smell? What smell?" If his master were to smell like her, he'd be fighting nausea every second he learned the craft.

"He will smell like magic."

She started to walk away, surprisingly quickly, for so old and bent an old woman. "What smell? What does magic smell like?"

"It will smell like magic. I can see you don't understand. Stand still. No, don't fidget, don't even blink. Stand still. That's the first lesson. Now concentrate on me, my smell, beyond the body odor, beyond the lack of hygiene. Use your nose, boy, and your senses."

And then, after about two minutes of standing rigid, barely daring to breathe, he smelled it, or rather felt it, that tingling in his nose. She knew when he got it, for she grinned again, this time a bit more sincerely. "Find someone who smells like that and ask him to take you on as apprentice. It won't be cheap."

"I can pay."

She cackled, for it was a joke, and he had provided her punch-line. "If you find a Master, you will pay boy, with your heart, soul, mind, and your blood. It is an expensive calling, lad, one which will take all you have to give and more."

She vanished then, so quickly he didn't see her leave, and he hunted, and not two weeks later he smelled the man who was to become his teacher.

He had spoken with her only one other time. A few years back, while he was still an apprentice, and starting to find his stride as a wizard, she had approached him at a wizardly gathering, and he remembered her, wanted to tell her 'thanks' for sending him in the right direction, but she stopped him short by muttering something to the effect that she knew a particularly nasty secret about him he wouldn't want shared. He had no idea at the time what it could be, so he ignored it and he didn't think about it again, until this moment.

She might know something about someone else, or, more likely, told someone she knew his deepest, darkest secret, and that had led to her death. It wouldn't surprise him. But if there were wizards around who were murdering witches, he should look into it.

He set his wards, and as he slipped into his robe, he scratched the pink, puckered scar on his chest. It looked worse this morning than it had, but Pierce was willing to believe that was perceptional only, because he was seeing his mystery woman, and not because the scar itself was any more disfiguring.

As he slipped from his body, he was startled from his memory and turned quickly, looking over his shoulder, but the lair was empty. There was nothing there. There had been nothing there, or had there been? That evening when he was shot, he had been here. Pierce was sure of it now. And something else. He had been following a lead on Pasco Minelli, and had been so keen to release from his body perhaps he wasn't as careful as he should have been.

Upstate New York. His mind tingled. That's where he had been heading that night. People used to New York City considered anything north of Yonkers upstate, but this was beyond that. Traveling astrally, he passed Albany, then kept going north, towns with picturesque names, Half Moon and Saratoga Springs and Glens Falls, heading towards Plattsburg.

The memory flooded, clear, sharp. There had been a great loss of powerstrands, a significant depletion of them, and beyond looking for Pasco, whom he suspected was behind the theft, he was trying to find out where the power was going. For power cannot be destroyed. That was one of the unbreakable laws of his profession.

Power can be moved, and it can be transformed, but it cannot be destroyed. So it was imperative he find out where it was going. A power outlay that huge had to mean something significant was going down.

Astrally, Pierce had reached a small town named Au Sable Forks, a one traffic light tourist town with trendy upscale clothing stores catering to the ski trade, thick sweaters and thin parkas, boots, gloves, Christmas ornaments. His skin tingled. He had been here before. He had gotten this close when he was forced away.

He left the town, knowing it required more exploration, and headed out over the winding roads of the Adirondack Mountains. The path he followed was slippery, appearing and disappearing, but again, something serious had happened here. Between the forested mountains, there were broad flatlands with trails beaten down in the grass, as if armies had passed by, and there was the sour after-smell of magic used, but he couldn't determine by what or how.

A headache blinded him, and Pierce shut his eyes, hoping the memory would return. It did, but it was unclear and contradictory. He witnessed the past. Not specifically the past from the night he was shot, but the past from a few months before. What made it confusing was it was this same past vision he witnessed the night he had been shot.

He saw a dragon. No, he had seen a dragon, a huge copper colored fighting beast attacking three people. One had been a wizard, one a soldier of some kind, and the third had been Belinda.

Astrally, Pierce breathed a sigh of relief. This is what he had been doing when he had been shot—viewing the past, a scene so significant he had witnessed it twice now. Either the residuals had not faded on their own, or some magic-practitioner made sure anyone looking in this direction would find this image, concealing anything else.

He could not rub his temples, although he wanted to. He remained without a body. There had been a dragon, but he had never seen one before, had no idea they still existed.

A dragon had killed Belinda. Speaking to the powerstrand, Pierce lowered his altitude, and scoured the forest, looking for tell-tales. He found the soldier's body first, crumpled in a heap in a clearing, left to rot, from some three months earlier, he would guess.

There wasn't much left of the carcass, nothing which he could use to determine the identity of the killer, which meant no powerstrands at all. Even those few scavenger strands who pull remaining energy from a dead body had long since disappeared.

Without an autopsy or a more complete investigation, he knew any analysis would be inconclusive, but he detected long gashes in the soldier's bones. Dragon talons. Pierce wouldn't have drawn that conclusion otherwise, but he had seen a one, he was certain. He tried to remember if that necessarily meant evil and had to table that investigation for later.

For he had discovered Belinda's body. She was laying in a heap, head down, hips and legs high, tossed aside from a great distance. She had a broken neck. Her skull was smashed, not merely cracked. Some great force had thrust her away, and she had died instantly.

No sign of wizard fire, but that was inconclusive. If the wizard had been fighting the dragon…no, he needed more research into dragons before he could determine what happened here.

It looked like there was a trip to upstate New York in his future.

Pierce popped back into his body, shivering as he realized how cold the lair had gotten. Quickly he dressed. The trees would be past their prime this October, and of course, in September, there would have been more wild flowers.

# CHAPTER 9

"Hi."

"Hi, yourself."

She beat him to the bench this time which pleased him, although he apologized for keeping her waiting. His one fear as he kept to the far left lane of the highway patrol monitored Massachusetts Turnpike was that she would get tired of waiting, would be gone long before he could reach her. He'd been caught 'traveling' away from his body far later than he had wanted to be.

She was bundled up, for the wind had a bite to it, bitter and invasive. She wore a hooded sweatshirt with the logo of a major university, but it was pink and bright, and Pierce thought of cotton candy and summers by the coast. He felt warmer just looking at her. He wondered if this flash of color was something that simply showed up sporadically in her wardrobe, or if it pre-dated the gray and blackness of her current attire. Her jeans and her hiking boots were black. He was pleased that although the clouds were low and rain was due in an hour or two, the sweatshirt was not what she wore when she had pleaded for her child's life with the guy in the Jag. Pierce wanted nothing to remind him of that night. He expected he would be seeing a lot more of her, and he had vowed that he would see her smile.

As he approached, he tried to analyze her posture, the way she held her head, the slope of her shoulders, the position of her ankles, to determine if anything was different, if during the week they had been apart she'd made a decision.

With a woman, something that catastrophic had to be visible. Even if she were used to lying, even if she were a consummate actress, there would be haunted shadows visible in her eyes, a hole somewhere in her responses he should be able to determine.

He breathed a sigh of relief as he discovered nothing overt. Her color was better, the wind off the ocean had brought a slight blush to her cheeks, and, although she was dressed casually, she wore carefully applied make-up on her eyelids and lashes. Her eyes were clear, met his in open anticipation, holding nothing back, no secrets, no trace of pain she had not yet managed to compartmentalize.

In addition there was a trace of scent on her skin which wrapped his senses and made him ache to touch her. He thought of lilacs in the spring, roses in the deep summer, and carefully tended fires of winter. He vowed he would see her dressed in nothing but the warmth from a hearth fire and the glow of his loving.

Then she smiled when she saw him and his heart almost broke the sound barrier.

It surprised him to unexpectedly realize she was far more attractive dressed casually than any of the high-fashioned women he'd squired around all week.

"How did your week go?"

Pierce blew out a long stream of air, ruffled his bangs in exaggerated desperation, looking about as dangerous, he hoped, as your average retired basset hound. He slumped onto the bench beside her, made no move to encroach on her territory. For the moment, being with her was enough.

"Monsters," he said, surprising himself by using that word first. He felt the need to enlarge his statement, both to enchant her and to hide the fact he had been viewing the results of a nefarious being's actions only a few hours before. "I've been fighting demons with long bloody fangs. I had to fight them off with all my might." He swung his arms, as if he held a sword. Beside her, he had no trouble feeling heroic.

Sparkling, she laughed. "Tell me more."

It didn't take longer than a nanosecond to realize the hole he had dug, then fallen in. "You really don't want to hear about it. It's too frightening."

She leaned forward, closer, compassionate. "Sometimes the most frightening things need to be shared. Then they are not quite so overwhelming." She wasn't laughing anymore.

At that second, he felt a terrible aching pang for lying to her. She didn't deserve deception. Some other creep had lied to her, and look where that landed her, at a bus stop facing an abortion clinic. But he was not willing to tell her the truth. Too much of his life was based on trickery to change now.

"I'm sorry. I was exaggerating. It really wasn't that bad."

"No dragons?"

Mentally he backtracked. He had used the word monsters. "No dragons."

Her chin dropped. "I really would have preferred dragons."

With that look, he wanted to call the power strands around her, and create for her an illusion she'd never forget, a beast of gigantic proportions, with teeth long enough to be used as railroad spikes and scales harder than tungsten steel. One that breathed fire. Such was his magic, his power, he could even create a dragon. Change the power strands into living matter, give birth to the creature which he had seen just that morning.

Pierce reached out, didn't know why he felt this overwhelming need to take her hand, to offer her comfort. "No you don't. You really don't want to face a live dragon."

"You sound as if you've seen one." Her scent was fruity with traces of lime. He was used to all the subtle lures of feminine perfume, and annoyed with himself how deeply this one aroma twined itself deep into his psyche. How many facets did this jewel have? And would he ever get used to her quicksilver moods? He hoped not. He prayed she would keep him guessing long into his nineties.

He thought back to the parallel world where he sometimes traveled, where very few human rules applied. The creatures there were wyverns, not quite dragons, although what specifically made them not fit into Class Draconia, he had no idea. "Yes. I have battled a dragon. And I would do anything I could to protect you from one."

She nodded, leaned back against the podiatrist bench, more serious than she had been the second before. She brought a fingernail to her full, red lips, ran the pad of her finger over her bottom teeth, thinking seriously. "All right. I'll take your word for it. I never want to see a dragon. But if I do, I know you'll protect me, although I'll warn you, I'm a modern woman, used to defending myself."

"Ok, so maybe you'll have to defend me. I find that quite reassuring." He quirked his lips, realized how much he loved the idea of her doing so.

She giggled, almost as if she knew something too serious had happened and she needed to lighten the mood. "Now that you've got that silliness out, how about if you tell me how your week really went?"

Her hands were back in her lap, and boldly-and casually—an odd joining of emotions, he touched her, the back of her wrist, the length of her fingers. "Before I do, was your week happy? Could you tell me everything was magical this entire week, you won the lottery, or your favorite flavor of ice cream went buy-one-get-one-free?"

She leaned back against the bench, folded her hands over her stomach, making him hope, pray that there was a tiny swelling there, and everything was proceeding perfectly. "You know, it was a good week. Nothing magical happened, no leprechauns begging me to take their gold, no rainbows either for that matter, but everything just fit in right. Do you know what I'm talking about?"

He did, or at least he hoped so, but he wanted to hear her speak, listen to the cadence of her voice, the inflections she settled on her verbs. "Tell me everything."

"I wouldn't have thought of this, living through it I thought the week was just long, but on the whole it was a rabbit week."

"Rabbit week? I suppose you're going to explain?"

"Sure." She grinned, and the pleasure lit up her eyes, making them glisten. The day was a fabulous October day, with the salty scent from the Atlantic noticeable only because it permeated into every rough board, every paving stone. "When I was very little, rabbits were my good luck charm."

"Many people consider rabbit's feet good luck."

For the second she looked insulted, as if she would slap his hands, as if by his comment he deserved severe punishment, if not outright torture. She all but raised the hackles at her neck. Instead she put her fabulously straight teeth together, opened her lips wide, and growled, with the kind of ferocity which made him think of silk sheets, afternoons, sweat soaked exhaustion.

"Not rabbit's feet. Rabbits. I'll explain. Before I go any further, do you want the long version, or the twenty-seven cent version?"

He rattled his hands in his pants pocket, reaching keys and very little change. "Your twenty-seven cents, or mine?"

She laughed, she glowed. Enchantment flowed from her. "I keep forgetting. How thoughtless. I guess it will have to be mine."

"Then you better give me the long version. I have this newfound respect for money."

"When I was very little, my grandfather used to take me to the park where we would chase rabbits. I didn't see him often, so it was really a treat. He always spun this tale for me. He said he kept hundreds of rabbits in his garage as pets, and each time I arrived, he was so downcast, saying that he had just let them go."

"And you were heartbroken because you missed them."

"Absolutely."

"And you never realized there were no rabbit cages in your grandfather's garage, and it was unlikely coincidence that each time you arrived he had so thoughtlessly let them have their freedom just that morning."

"It really didn't seem that preposterous," she said, trying to defend herself. "And I was very young."

"Very gullible."

"Young," she insisted.

"I'm willing to bet each time he told you his story, your eyes were probably as wide as they are now." Funny, he could see her, windblown hair worn in shoulder length braids, perhaps a skinned knee, shattered, because she'd missed these rabbits.

"So we went to the park, and chased them. These rabbits were fairly used to tourists, but still, we never got close."

"It's always the chase that matters, anyway."

"I know that now, but I didn't then. I was always horribly disappointed I never could catch one. I gave it my best shot, running until I was exhausted. And I always had the best time with my grandfather. When I was tired, he would walk me back home, hand in hand, and we would sip hot chocolate together, or chocolate milk and Oreos, and everything would be perfect. Since then, every time something good happens, I consider it a rabbit day."

Pierce shut his eyes to the diffuse sunlight, and let her words bathe him in happiness.

"You don't win the lottery on a rabbit day, or even get accepted to Harvard Law. On a rabbit day you find a parking spot exactly where you need it, or the rain holds off until you unlock your front door. Your line at the toll booth is the one which moves the fastest, or you have correct change. The phone company might write and say they overcharged you one dollar and eleven cents. It's never anything big, but always a pleasant surprise. You know, those little things add up."

He grinned, loving the image, not having the courage to look at her. Too much was going right. He didn't want to spoil the moment with lies, or an agenda that a master wizard had to keep secret.

"I know just what you mean. Funny, isn't it, how important little things are?"

"Then you understand?"

"Of course. I'm going to start collecting rabbit days. I've had them myself."

"Good. Now tell me about a rabbit day of yours."

"I'll have to go back a while."

"That's ok. It's recognizing them that's important."

"Actually, it wasn't that long ago. Monday as a matter of fact. I was getting ready for court, and I was early for a change, which would make it a rabbit day all by itself. I found something I thought I'd lost. Nothing vital, just something silly I liked, and I'd been looking for for weeks. An old school friend showed up unexpectedly and we went out to lunch. Just a good day. Things went well, even the things that had a high potential for blowing up."

"Good," she said. "Now tell me about the rest of your week."

"Ahhh," he said, in mock exaggeration. "After Monday it was all downhill. A case I was feeling good about went to hell in a hand basket. It may take forever to get that mess untangled, and the big bosses were there to witness the whole thing shatter. They didn't say anything, offered raised eyebrows that meant, 'We Expected Better of You'. I got some letters from my lawyers about interest on the money I owe the IRS. I was relatively sure they put the decimal place in the wrong point and that the numbers to the left were randomly generated."

She laughed, appreciating his foolishness.

Pierce continued, feeling more alive than he had in ages. "At any rate, this thing may drag on a bit longer than I intended."

She nodded sympathetically. "But you're surviving?"

Simply put, he found her question touching. She didn't know him, and she cared. "Yeah." He nodded, pleased with the insight. "You know, I am surviving."

"I'm glad to hear that." She rubbed her hands together. The preliminaries of their meeting were taken care of, now she could get down to the reason they met. "So what did you spend this week's twenty dollars on?"

He'd given it a lot of thought simply because it took far more effort than he expected. Although he never wasted money, it was always something he treated casually. Price tags meant little. He wished now, quite sincerely, that he told her his entertainment budget was in the fifty dollar range, then at least he could start to show her a good time. There wasn't anything he could do with twenty dollars. Hell, parking the car took that much.

He wiggled eyebrows, seductive, taunting. "I thought you wanted to guess."

"Oh, believe me, I have. But I'm not telling. I refuse to be embarrassed, and by the same token, I refuse to give you any of my brilliant insights. You're on your own."

"Traitor. So, do you want to see?"

"Sure."

He had a bag, a fairly good sized one. And yes, he had spent over twenty dollars, but not by much. The idea came to him when he went home to visit his parents and stopped to talk with the gardener.

She accepted it with slender hands, nails neatly trimmed, not the long claws he was used to but a perfect complement to her otherwise well-trimmed body. Her wrists were slender, lightly tanned, and the left one was darker than the right. A mystery, he decided with his wizard intellect, until he inferred she drove with the window open.

The women he had dated this week were perfectly and evenly bronzed, with no tan lines anywhere. He had enough personal experience to know not all of that was due to expensive, tan-through swim wear. And she wore, thank goodness, no rings. None at all. He suspected the moose-like thing on the face of her watch was Bullwinkle, although he couldn't be sure. He hadn't thought of Bullwinkle in nearly thirty years.

"Go ahead, open it. It won't bite."

If it had been her birthday, she couldn't have looked more intrigued. She slowly, meticulously, unfolded the edges of the crinkled brown paper bag, then looked inside, incredulity turning to unabashed pleasure. "Bulbs?"

He grinned, a before-vanishing Cheshire Cat. "Tulips, daffodils, crocus, hyacinth, who knows what else."

She grinned, honestly, sincerely, positively delighted. "What in the world possessed you to buy bulbs?"

He shrugged, offered her a piece of cinnamon chewing gum he figured his artificial persona could afford. While she peeled back the metallic paper, while she chewed, he gave her his line, the one he'd been working on during the entire ride down. "The evenings are the hardest. I'm not used to staying home, and cruising downtown knowing I have to stick to this budget or die is about to kill me, and it doesn't look like it's getting much better. So I wanted something with long term benefits. Something that wasn't, for example, a twenty dollar bottle of wine I could drink in an evening. Something beautiful. You know, it isn't easy to come up with things like that."

She tilted her head, and her lips opened slightly, and her eyes grew fuzzy, and she listened, really listened to what he was saying. No other woman in his entire life had ever listened to him that intently before.

"Go on, don't stop now."

"I actually thought of buying a Scrabble game," and here she laughed, "but the only one I know to play it with is you, and I suspect you already have one—"

"Not to mention the deluxe edition costs more than twenty dollars," she said with a grin.

"Right. I figured if worse came to worse, you could let me borrow yours, of course, you'd have to play with me a game or two, just so I'm certain I've got the rules down."

"And then, you'd need a Scrabble dictionary."

"Stop it. Now you can appreciate how impossible this budget is. Besides, there's that game for cell phones that costs quite a bit less we could do without ever seeing each other face to face."

She nodded sagely, compassionately, with a face so straight, she might have been told he had just gotten the Texas death penalty. "Yes, when even the simple pleasures like Scrabble are out of reach you need to find pleasure where you can."

Pierce couldn't help it. He burst out laughing, and infectious, she joined him.

"That still doesn't explain the bulbs."

"Well, you can see my plight. There's absolutely nothing I can do to entertain myself for twenty dollars. Then I was reading the newspaper, found an advertisement, one hundred bulbs for twenty dollars."

"What a deal."

Her eyes sparkled.

His heart tripped.

He waited, biding his time, building anticipation. "I like them. I hope they all grow, but if even eighty percent of them come up, the yard will be pretty. And more than that, year after year they will be pretty. Planting bulbs you are touching the future."

"Yes, I suppose you are."

"In April or May, when these things start to make an appearance, I'm probably going to be desperate for something beautiful in my life, some enchantment. Right now, although I'm suffering, the budget isn't that bad. Oh, I complain, but it's new enough I haven't gotten frustrated."

"The novelty hasn't worn off," she said, understanding what he meant.

"Exactly. But in April—"

"In April you're going to be desperate and seeing these flowers, you hope to give yourself enough encouragement to keep going. Do you have a place to plant these?"

"Sure. I let my condo go, couldn't keep up the maintenance fees let alone the payments. I bought a house as an investment. Not a big house, or a fancy house, but the mortgage is a lot less than I was paying, which is good. I'm going to fix it up, slowly, maybe sell it eventually. I haven't been there long. It needs flowers."

Now was the time. He'd ask her, hope it wasn't too soon.

"You have a few minutes? Would you like to help me plant?"

It was the perfect opportunity for her to demur, for he knew with a honed instinct, in spite of her physical condition, she wasn't a woman who lightly accepted a man's invitation to his home, regardless of what the current version of seeing-my-etchings happened to be.

She thought, maybe two seconds, nodded decisively. "Sure, I'd like that."

He had found the house for sale Saturday after he left her, called the real estate agent from his car phone, bought it on the spot. It had been vacant a long time, so there wasn't anyone to move out. He shoved in some furniture in case she had to come in to use the bathroom or for a drink of water, but there weren't any clothes in the dressers and the closet was empty. His little illusion wouldn't hold up to close investigation. Although, all things considered, it wouldn't take much more than a few hand twists, a few well illustrated thoughts, to fill the place with either illusion or reality. Such was his gift.

Pierce reached his hand out. "Come on."

She looked like she would rather have tried to fashion pierced earrings onto the hood of a spitting cobra than take it, but her disgust or confusion was short lived. Her fingers wrapped round his in complete trust. "It's within walking distance?"

He shrugged, grinned, looked across the street to the medical center. "Not really, but do you have anything better to do?"

"No." Trust was starting to build between them, and maybe something stronger, like friendship.

After she got to her feet, she retrieved her hand, and feeling confused without quite knowing why, as if he had too many loose limbs going in too many directions, Pierce shoved his hands into his pockets. She carried the bulbs. Conversation felt stilted, difficult. Looking for blue cornflowers they'd laughed like they'd been best friends since kindergarten. Now they walked as if they'd seen this movie before and knew Darth Vader and a light saber waited for them in the alley.

"I got the tools from a rental place down the street." It wasn't so much that he needed to confess how clever he'd been, but that he'd put a lot of time and effort into his scheme, including buying a house he doubted he'd ever get his money out of, and someone should be patting him on the back.

"Borrowing money from next week's entertainment?"

"Actually, no. I've rationalized this one a bit. I do have a working budget, a maintenance budget. I'm not all that poor you know. I'm not starving, for example. The money for renting the tools came out of upkeep."

She believed it. It sounded logical, so why shouldn't she.

"Now if I'd bought tools, the top of the line ones I wanted that would be cheating."

"So, you spent part of the week in hardware stores?"

"Something to do. It was open late nights, kept me out of the bars, you know. I tried to rationalize the tools, any hoe for example would probably last me a lifetime and would be a good investment, but then I thought, that's the kind of idea that got me in trouble in the first place."

"Oh?"

"I buy the tools because they're a good investment, right?"

"Right."

"Then how about a suit? That's an investment, right?"

"I'm beginning to see your point."

"And a new, fancy computer system, when there's nothing really wrong with the old one, except it's a little slow."

"It's easy for things to get out of hand."

"And I'm really new to this budget business. Even with most of my credit cards shredded, I've still got a few I can get my hands on without much difficulty." In his world women were impressed with how much money you had, not the problems your tax lawyer faced across a desk from stern faced IRS auditors.

"So I rented the tools."

"Good idea."

"And when the bills are all paid off, I'm going to show you the best time you ever had."

She laughed, shook her head, and her nose crinkled, just the tiniest bit, which only made her look more appealing. "I don't think you've learned your lesson yet."

She kept walking beside him, and the mood between them mutated back to easy, companionable.

"Here." It was an ancient house, structurally sound, four surprisingly roomy bedrooms, freshly painted inside and out. The external shingles were painted federal blue that in Rhode Island weathered to a rough, old fashioned gray. There was an old, unattached garage with a dirt floor, and a trace smell of stale, dusty mold which unaccountably Pierce decided he loved, regardless that it made him sneeze. All the years growing up he'd never once encountered mold in any form, except perhaps, the cultured, well-mannered kind that made bleu cheese and penicillin.

"Do you mind getting your hands dirty?"

She shook her head, walked the parameter of the front and side yards. "Where do you want what?"

"I don't know. Left to my own devices, I would have hired a service."

She rolled her eyes heavenward, then opened the bag, spread his selection of bulbs out on the grass, separating them in some order he couldn't quite fathom, but which looked highly involved and technical.

She squatted, heels flat to the ground. "Do you like flowers?"

It was a question Pierce should have anticipated, been ready for.

"You know what? Before this I never gave them much thought. I bought roses when I needed to, orchids in corsages, FTD for Mother's Day, funerals, apologies, that kind of thing. Flowers were easy. They didn't require much planning. A phone call, a gold master card. This was different. Something I had to plan, work toward."

She didn't smile, didn't tighten her eyes as if she suspected he were feeding her a line, so Pierce continued.

"I love flowers, but more than that this week I realized I love the promise of flowers, the fact that perennials come up every year when the soil is warm, and winter has finally been defeated. I like adding color and beauty. I like them better than museums."

She rocked back on her heels, and the green of her eyes deepened. "I don't follow you."

"My mother was, is actually, a kind of culture freak," which was certainly true. "Growing up she dragged me to every museum on this continent and all the major ones in Europe. And it was all so bloody artificial. Perfect lighting, perfect pictures hung perfectly straight, with sizes and frames and who knows what else perfectly coordinated. It wasn't real, but I suppose it wasn't meant to be."

He let her chew on that for a while, respected her more as she waited for him to get to the point. "I think everyone should have the right to enjoy good artwork, and I won't deny museums have their place, like fifth grade field trips for example. But I'd rather see a riotous profusion of flowers in some effervescent summer garden as I'm driving by on the turnpike in New Jersey than view another oil painting done by some masochist two hundred years ago."

"I see."

"I've made a fool of myself."

"No, not at all."

The gardens around the house were desperately overgrown with thistles and other noxious weeds, which she wouldn't let him pull until he identified them from his wild flower book, so it was a relatively good thing he'd left it in his house. They played in the dirt for almost three hours while she lectured him on bone meal, ground cover, the ratios of nitrogen and potassium in fertilizer and the advantages of trays of bedding plants.

With the understanding he gained from digging roots and fungus in his wizard training, this was the first time he'd ever had dirt under his fingers and he liked the sensation. Pierce wondered what his parents would say if they saw him now. What his Master would think, then Pierce decided it didn't really matter.

"What are you thinking? You've got that faraway look in your eyes."

"Oh, just the usual, 'if only so-and-so could see me now.' I'm sure you know what I mean."

"Down on your knees, planting flowers?"

"Yeah. I wasn't lying when I mentioned I am the type who calls a landscaping service. This garden might not be spectacular, but I did it myself. I mean, we did it together," he corrected. "Every single April I'll remember this day, and what I felt about you."

"Pierce—"

"I meant, I'll thank you again for your help."

He wiped his hands on his jeans, then casually turned on the hose to water his bulbs. When he finished, he held the hose out so that she could wash her hands, allowed her to do the same for him.

"You've got a spot, right there, on your chin. Dirt."

He moved his thumb against the soft skin of her chin more of a caress than an effort to get her clean. With the action, he found his body reacting predictably. It struck him how powerfully he wanted her. He was not used to this kind of desperation, this lack of control.

Without thinking, he slowly lowered his lips to hers, taking his time, giving her the opportunity to back away, to slap his face. He forced himself to be gentle, to take the kiss slow, but that impulse vanished the second his lips touched hers.

Pierce kept his hands rigid at his sides, forming fists, for he knew if he touched her, their relationship would proceed faster than either one intended. It mattered to him that she'd been hurt. It mattered that she carried another man's son. And it mattered more than he could say that he finally kissed her. And he knew when he saw these tulips, hyacinths and daffodils he would always remember this instant frozen in time.

He kissed her a dozen small nipping kisses, friendship kisses, and they progressed to more. Her lips were soft, giving, responded to his caresses. She shut her eyes, her lashes thick, full, intoxicating and moved her hands gently to his shoulders, his back. He nuzzled her nose with his, nipped at her neck, felt a welcoming fullness in his sex that pleased him just knowing it was there. He didn't have to act on it. This wasn't yet about sex, but something deeper, more intimate.

He wanted her desperately, in his bed, where he could bring them both to heaven, but for the first time in his life he realized postponing the pleasure was far more pleasurable than acting immediately. Anticipation sky rocketed. His heart raced and his breathing quickened. She opened her mouth hesitantly and his tongue thrust inside, tasting her, teasing her, entering her as he so desperately wanted to fill her elsewhere.

His hands were restless, but by the same token, controlled. He avoided her breasts, although through the sweatshirt she wore he could imagine her pointed nipples, erect with growing arousal. He knew she would welcome his lips there, suckling against the pointed nubs, even if he had to seduce her to accept his attentions. But today, in the fading sunlight, after planting tulips to enjoy months from now, Pierce was satisfied with anticipation, with foreplay that did not have to lead directly to tangled sheets and morning-after explanations.

He wanted. He needed. He ached. And for the first time in his adult life, that was enough. He wouldn't be satisfied. No, not by a long shot, but he was not interested in rushing something better anticipated.

She purred softly, responsively and Pierce matched her in this non-verbal communication. He was enjoying himself as he wrapped his fingers around her firm buttocks and pulled her toward him, against his arousal. CeeDee fit him perfectly. She was his match in every way. And he would stop this, of his own volition.

In a minute.

There was no rush. He would put the brakes on. And his lips met hers again, merged, matched, mated. His feet shifted, moved, she followed, as if they were dancing, and they were, to the most primal dance begun at the beginning of time. She rubbed against him. He sidled against her.

CeeDee put her hands out, flush against his chest. He might not have noticed if she hadn't been putting pressure on a spot that not long ago had been the sight of a gunshot wound.

"I think," she said backing away, "that was more than I bargained for."

"I—" Then he swore. "I'm so sorry. I never meant it to go that far. I honestly intended to stop."

Her lips were full, moist, her eyes slightly unfocused, but that might have been his vision, not hers. Her hair was tangled, windblown or finger combed by his hands, looked far sexier to him than if she'd just escaped from having it professionally styled. She looked fully and completely kissed. It was a hint of what she would look like after a night of intimacy with him, when they allowed themselves to take this passion bubbling between them to the next level over and over through the secrets of the night.

"It?" she asked.

He wasn't thinking. His brain had slipped into neutral, or some such nonsense, and she was analyzing his sentences, coming up with pronouns she couldn't identify? He didn't even remember what he said, knew that perhaps he needed to apologize.

"I'm sorry. If I've taken too much, if you weren't willing to give—" he paused, ran his fingers through his hair to prevent himself from touching her again, kissing her again. "I really intended to stop. I don't want what you have every right to think I wanted."

"You don't?"

"God, yes, of course I do. But not now. I don't even know your name. I think of you at odd times during the week, giving myself—well, we won't get into what I give myself since I'm trying hard not to be crude, but I can't tell you how long I've wanted to kiss you. I think since the first time I saw you, when you went on and on about that beryl, which, by the way, I still have no concept of. I find you so incredibly beautiful. I know you think that's just a line, and I suppose you've heard it a million times before, but I'm embarrassingly sincere."

She stepped back, still held her hands palm out, although she was no longer touching him. "I think I'd better go. The flowers will be lovely in the spring. When I drive by, I'll remember this afternoon."

When I drive by… in other words, when we're through, and I don't see you any longer.

Panic surged through him. He looked, saw, a dozen powerstrands, slithering equally between them. He could, well not hold her so much as make it so she didn't want to leave. But he had never abused power like that before, and never would, especially when this relationship still had potential.

He had to believe it still had potential, that he hadn't ruined what might be his healing heart with his kisses.

"I really, really feel I need to apologize again, but what I'd really like to do is ask you in."

CHAPTER 10

"I think your apology lacks credibility."

"No, not in-in. To sit, talk. Get to know each other. Separate chairs. In the living room. We could invite your mother. I've got drinks. Well, water really. I'll um, keep my hands to myself."

She smiled, as if she found his bumbling enchanting. "I think from what I know of you you're a man who likes to give into temptation, who generally doesn't bother to put off momentary pleasures."

How would she know that? Ahh, the IRS problems of a man who lived in the moment, not prepping for tomorrow.

"In my defense, can I explain to you what your kisses did to me?"

"No thanks." CeeDee rubbed her own lips, as if reliving the experience herself. She looked around, toward the west, where the sun was setting in a brilliant display of fall colors, paining the undersides of those hulking cumulous clouds with all kinds of magical hues.

The wind picked up, sending sharp shards of October iciness through them both, destroying the potential ambiance for an *al fresco* evening. It was far too cold for standing outside.

Slowly she shook her head. "Really, not tonight."

His heart thumped so loudly he was certain she heard it. Regardless of his best intentions, Pierce wasn't willing to let the evening end just yet. "So, are you afraid?" Although the house wouldn't stand up to any degree of inspection, the mattress was new, and the sheets clean. He was a man who prepared for any eventuality.

Her eyes were sharp again, clear. Obviously she recovered far quicker from the tender assault than he did. "I don't think I'd better. This is, after all a first date."

"First date?"

He hadn't seen it that way. First opportunity, perhaps, but his dates were usually a bit more involved. She inched back a small, yet telling distance, wiping dirt against her jeans. Pierce decided he had been honest. He was attracted to her and more. This wasn't simple hormones gurgling. He doubted there was anything simple developing between them.

He liked the way she looked, especially now, with her lips looking full, thoroughly kissed. Additional color appeared on her cheeks, a red he hoped wouldn't turn into an autumn cold. For all it was October, the sun that afternoon had been plenty direct, and they had been playing in the damp soil for hours. She had found some type of rubber band in a back pocket, used it to tie her thousand-shades-of red-brown hair back, although it was fine, and now, more of it had escaped than remained prisoner. "I had a good time, really, but I think I'd better be going."

She turned. The jeans were not artfully molded to her derriere, not painted on to highlight. Instead they fit her comfortably, were dirty at the knees, and the pockets at her hip bones showed the slightest sign of wear. Pierce doubted there was even one woman of his acquaintance who bought pants from a rack, let alone would actually be seen in public wearing them.

She was undeniably beautiful. Her emerald eyes clear and alert, skin tone glowing—and he hoped that her pregnancy was still progressing normally, that she had done nothing precipitous. It was starting to bother him, a lot, that she'd been with another man.

Still, Pierce was reluctant to let her go without a promise to meet again. "I tell you what, how about going on a picnic with me next week."

"Picnic?" she asked. "The first weekend in November?"

"It might be cold, but the advantage is, there probably won't be a lot of crowds on the beach. We can dress warmly. Drink hot chocolate from a thermos."

She bit her bottom lip. He ached to do the same to her. "I'm not sure."

"I want to see you again, and short of taking you out on an official date, where I get to spend money, this is the most reasonable thing I can think of...that is if you won't come in."

"I'd love to go on a picnic."

"Saturday? I'll save my Friday splurge for twenty-four hours if you pick the park."

"Sure, I'll be glad to."

"I'll bring the food."

"On two conditions."

"What?"

"That you let me bring the dessert, something sinfully fattening."

"Can't argue with that."

"And that I bring the tennis rackets."

His chest was doing much better, which meant he could breathe now without being conscious of every single muscle expansion, but he wasn't quite approved for anything physical. "No tennis. I'm not quite up to it yet. Bring Scrabble or jacks or marbles or something less physical."

"It's a date."

"Then I'll meet you at our bus stop bench, Saturday at what time, noon?"

She nodded her agreement, turned, started to walk back toward the park bench.

"Don't go. I meant what I said. I don't even know your name."

She grinned, stepped back, held out her hand. "My name is CeeDee."

"Seedy?" It didn't sound like the name of anyone he'd ever been associated with before. As a matter of fact, it sounded, just a tad disreputable.

"Cynthia Diane. CeeDee."

It surprised him how much he wanted to merge his lips against hers to kiss her again and endlessly. Instead, he met her palm with a responding handshake. "Well, CeeDee, I'm Pierce, and you've got yourself a date."

\*\*\*

"Candy, you have a few minutes?"

She hadn't quite gotten as far as holding her keys in her hand, but she did have the computer turned off and had rinsed the coffee pot. It was after five. And more nights than he cared to remember, Pierce had kept her after, to do foolish things he'd felt were imperative, which could easily have waited a day or two. He'd made good on his self-promise, and her paycheck was considerably larger. He'd done it without telling her, and she'd come with stub in hand the week before, stating there had to be some mix-up which accounting hadn't been able to find. He hadn't expected her arrival, if he had, he would have been prepared, with his excuses ready. For a man who really was a wizard and kept half his life hidden, and a lawyer on top of that, and had been told on occasion he had something of a glib tongue, he wasn't often caught off guard, but this was one of those memorable times when he had no words at his disposal.

If anything he thought she'd accept the raise as her due, or not even notice. "Mr. Billova, there has to be a mistake."

"No mistake." He sought for rationale.

"But this isn't a merit review." Merit reviews were in April, and he had months to plan what he was going to say.

"No. Consider it hazardous duty pay. You've earned it."

"But this is more than—" She didn't finish her sentence, but there was no need for her to. More than the partner's secretaries made. That hadn't occurred to him either.

"The partners accepted it without question. They must realize what percentage of the work which comes out of this office is directly attributable to you."

It was as close as he'd ever gotten to giving her a compliment and she turned, stunned, still holding her paycheck, but now holding the remainder of her questions as well. He hoped she would think about it, accept his definition of hazard pay. It was, without a doubt, exactly that.

So now when he asked for her advice, she said "Sure, what's on your mind?" as if they'd been sharing confidences for years, even if he knew she suspected he only needed another report faxed, or another half-dozen people called.

"A personal question."

Her eyes glistened. She knew her boss fairly well, and this sounded like gossip to her. "Should I sit?"

"If you want. This won't take long." She didn't, instead towered over him. It sometimes stunned Pierce when he realized just how tall she was.

He dug his hands in his pockets, standard, facing a jury, delaying tactics. Again, these were words which didn't come easily to him.

"How do you ask a woman if she's had an abortion?"

"I think I'll sit." There was never a trace of black dialect in her speech, but every now and then when they were alone, Candy could lay on a Southern drawl thick enough to drive the alligators from the bayous. "Ohh, Mr. Billova, you gone and gotten some poor 'lil girl in trouble? Yoh poor daddy ain't gonna be none too pleased about it."

"Let's leave my father, and heaven forbid, my mother, out of this for the next few minutes, can we? I can't exactly ask her if she did, can I?"

It was a measure of their professional relationship that Candy didn't laugh out loud. Instead, barely disguising a smirk she said, "Not if you want to keep breathing."

The friendly sarcasm was lost on Pierce who in a fit of agitation, had his elbows rooted to the surface of the desk and was staring at it his fingernails as if he were about to develop a self-cannibalistic habit and bite them, and in so doing, ruin a perfectly good manicure.

"I don't know her well enough to give her a book of 2000 common baby names or a rattle in a neutral pastel color."

"You don't know her well enough?" One thin, finely shaped leg crossed over its mate. "It sounds to me like you know her fairly well if you're concerned about this subject. There's really no problem you know. If I were you, I'd wait it out. All you got to do is lay back, couple three, four months. If the lady's keeping any kind of secret, you'll know."

He looked up, met her eyes with a look of such raw desperation she'd only seen in people who'd already received a jury's guilty verdict and were standing about to hear just how bad the sentence was going to be.

"I don't want to wait. If she hasn't had the abortion yet, I want to make damn sure she doesn't. Even if I have to convince her to put the baby up for adoption."

"Well, there has been some precedent setting legal work done on this subject. You could get an injunction, forbidding the abortion until you work things out."

"I can just see the headlines now." But he wasn't thinking about the newspapers, or the expected response from his parents. He was delving through a mental Rolodex wondering who he knew professionally to help him with the injunction. He was a lawyer. He fought things through in a courtroom. The courts were a mess on this particular subject, but what the hell. His mind moved fairly fast, however, and all kinds of implications raced around his gray cells.

"If some guy tried to prevent you from having an abortion, what would be your immediate reaction?"

"After punching his lights out, you mean?"

Pierce nodded, somewhat reluctantly. He already knew where this was going to end up.

"I'd make damn sure I had the procedure done as soon as possible. No slack hipped, arrogant, cocky male is going to tell me what to do with my body."

The revelation came as no surprise. "Yeah, that's what I thought." There was a time or two when he wondered if she hadn't already had one, when his super-efficient secretary acted a little bit testy, a little bit worried, a little bit moody, which cleared up after a week's vacation. He never asked her. Didn't want to know, figured it was none of his business, but hopefully would have listened, would have been sympathetic—even if he knew it would be an artificial sympathy—if she'd broached the subject.

"We are talking about your baby, aren't we?"

"No, it's not my baby. Whatever put that in your mind? I'm always careful."

"True, except when it comes to stopping speeding bullets."

"That's another subject I wish we wouldn't discuss."

"Understood. Just how far along is this pregnancy?"

"Far enough she knew about it two months ago." Which put it right exactly on par with his extended hospital stay.

"And she told you?"

"No one told me. That's the problem. I'm not supposed to know. And, if at all possible, I want her to confide in me."

"So you got this woman pregnant and you're sure she won't tell you? It's been my experience that the daddy is the first to know, especially if he has a bank account."

He scowled, slowly hiked an eyebrow, and was just about to show his teeth. In his leisure hours he read Anne Rice.

"Right. It's not your baby."

"Right."

"Then there isn't a problem."

"No?"

"Of course not. All you've got to do is make love to the woman."

It was a fairly good thing Pierce was sitting, for he was almost knocked off his feet. "Make love to her?" His mouth had gone dry. It was nearly impossible to speak. For a man considered by most to be unflappable, his legendary cool had flown south for the winter.

"Really, sometimes I think you men haven't got a single working brain cell. You wine and dine her, set the seduction, whatever you prefer, hand her a certificate of health, and say you're allergic to condoms, or that you prefer making love in a more natural, unhindered manner. If the lady goes through with it, she's probably already pregnant."

Make love to CeeDee. Heaven's above, why hadn't he thought of that himself? Make love to CeeDee. He rubbed his palms on the soft material of his slacks. Sweaty palms? Maybe he did need to see his mother's psychologist.

"Pierce, Mr. Billova, are you all right?"

Heavens only knew what Candy saw. He pulled himself together, glad they had the desk between them, for just the thought of making love to CeeDee was enough to cause a rather immediate reaction in his body, a spontaneous form of combustion he'd never quite experienced this sharply, this suddenly.

He tried to swallow. If his palms were wet, it certainly wasn't a condition his tongue shared. "She could be on the pill or have an IUD."

"She could be, but it's unlikely if she had the abortion sometime in the past four to six weeks. The body needs time to heal."

Right then and there it occurred to him that a picnic this weekend might be the time and place to set such a seduction.

The lady was never going to know what hit her.

# CHAPTER 11

Deep in his astral traveling, Pierce followed Pasco Minelli. A two bit wizard, he'd been making a lot of noise fooling around with things he should have known better than to touch. For a while, Minelli had worked in Vegas as a showman, making things appear, disappear, all flash and drama, skirting the edges of lines never meant to be crossed.

Then two years ago Minelli had hung up the rhinestones and disappeared for a dozen months, and when he reappeared he had reinvented himself as a self-made millionaire smoking narrow, expensive cigars, and driving small, imported cars. It was rumored he'd become a hitman, and a string of bodies with no apparent cause of death seemed to back-up this hypothesis.

While that was breaking any number of rules and certainly cause enough to have his wings clipped in a permanent manner, Minelli started mining parallel worlds for things that did not and should not exist on this one. Should you want an actual live pixie to keep in a private museum, he was your man, were you able to meet the exorbitant price he demanded.

Then, when the powerstrands started disappearing, his name rose to the top of the list, simply because there were no other viable suspects. Really, if he wasn't responsible, then he probably offered his assistance to whoever was.

Today Pierce found Minelli dealing with a psychotropic drug found in another world, a soft white power that gave incredible hallucinations, but also had some rather significant side effects. It would keep the NYPD scratching their collective heads for components of this drug defied laboratory analysis. He brought the stuff back, then let his dealers sell it on the street. The dealers knew nothing, and no trail, beyond the one Pierce had found, would ever lead back to Minelli.

Although Pierce felt exhaustion ripple through him as he watched, he was not ready yet to call it a night. He released the powerstrand he held as he pulled another one. Minelli raised his pointed nose, sniffing in the direction Pierce watched invisibly, then reached out, grasped the spent lime green strand Pierce had just released.

"Whatever you want, why don't you make yourself visible and we can chat?" His voice was high, had a fingernails-on-blackboard screech Pierce found extremely disconcerting. Then he squeezed the strand, wrapping his hands around it, as if strangling the life from it. Pierce shivered. He had no idea if they could feel pain, but the strand writhed, and somehow looked as if it suffered.

"Stay then, enjoy yourself, you peeping tom. You won't find out anything more from me." He laughed, then releasing the strand, let it fall from his fingers, where it wobbled slowly until it was able to vanish by sliding through a wall.

When he was certain Minelli would be tied up for at least an hour with the two-bit hooker he kept on payroll as a computer analyst, Pierce executed a strategic retreat and headed for Minelli's lair. He didn't get close, instead counted the telltales and the wards, filing the information in his brain in case he ever needed to make an assault on the building. Some were far more sophisticated than he would have suspected Minelli able to create on his own.

Pierce would have liked to look inside, for an image was twirling around the back of his mind, a low-level itch that made him edgy, certain he was overlooking something serious, yet blatantly obvious. He looked again, then a second time, but nothing struck him. Other than the powerstrands used in his security, there was no excessive use of power, nothing obvious. Still, the problem was, there was a time when Pierce had called Pasco friend.

Pierce slipped back, into his own body, his own lair, and dropped into exhaustion. He had time only to wrap himself in a blanket he kept for that purpose and fall into deep dream-haunted sleep.

\*\*\*

"Master," the younger man bowed, then straightened.

"What do you think you're doing?" the voice roared through the lair, and although because of stone and clever spells it was soundproof, the echo reverberated "doing, doing, doing."

The younger wizard smiled. He'd been raised in poverty, making the rounds from one foster home to another, until he found someone to teach him magic. But he hadn't forgotten what it was to be hungry, overlooked, and the brunt of slight cruelties. "Making a one hundred percent profit. I've got no overhead. You want to see the money I've made?"

"Did I not tell you I've got an agenda and we have to keep a low profile?"

"Yes, world domination. Do you think I'm interested in your dreams of conquest?"

"You should be. This is the opportunity you've been waiting for. I'm going to destroy all the wizards who stand against me. Think which side you want to be on."

He had money. He had power. He had skill, although nothing approaching his new master's abilities. But he had never deliberately killed. "You'll never bring them down. There are too many."

"Ahh, but I've got a weapon. Against this they will be defenseless."

"A weapon?" he sounded intrigued in spite of himself. He had been thinking of breaking ties with his new master, for there were lines even he wouldn't cross, but he needed information.

"You know how all the dinosaurs disappeared without warning? Perhaps it wasn't a meteor. Perhaps it was a weapon forged by wizards."

"And you've got this weapon?"

"I do now. Oh, yes. I do."

\*\*\*

The decision was made, and really, when she considered it, there was no decision at all: CeeDee had just been fooling herself. No, not fooling herself, for that would involve some sort of macabre joke. She had been torturing herself into thinking she was capable of going through with the procedure, when she wanted more than anything to keep the baby.

She would keep it. If they starved, they would starve together, or rather, she would starve, then some social agency would take the infant, now an orphan, and place her with a good family where she would always have food. CeeDee liked thinking of the fetus as a daughter, although she knew enough to try to vary her pronouns, he: Monday, Wednesday and Friday, and she the remaining days, but she slipped up more often than not and decided to maintain the unproven theory of the baby as a little girl.

If she lost Pierce because of the pregnancy, then she lost him. Realistically she knew she could not expect him to be happy about her impending motherhood, not when their relationship was so fragile and new, and they were not yet past the awkward part of getting to know each other. Right now Rose Aurora, the name she had chosen, needed her more. Besides, Pierce didn't need any additional financial drains, and a baby was nothing if not a huge expense, in time, money, and emotional aggravation.

The decision made, she found an obstetrician who could see her immediately, and went for her first checkup. She came out with prenatal vitamins, a stack of literature on what to expect, what to do and not do, and another appointment in five weeks. She made a silent commitment to herself she would tell Pierce, before they got further involved, and this budding friendship that they had developed into something more. There was no future in pursuing him when an extremely high likelihood existed that he would bail on them.

Maggie waited right where she'd left her, sitting smugly in the rocking chair with a warm lap-robe wrapped around her short, fat legs. It was her reading chair, and beside it sat a towering stack of books. She owned a tablet, loved to read fiction while waiting at doctor offices or in the evening when she was too sleepy to concentrate on anything requiring working brain cells, or when she just needed that juicy escape provided by romance novels. But there was something wonderful about holding a book. As a librarian, she appreciated them.

CeeDee had almost been hoping for rain, hoping Pierce would call and cancel, not that he had her phone number or her last name, so how he could officially cancel she had no idea, but a good solid east coast soaking would keep him inside. By the time she exited the physician's, CeeDee realized it was a day stolen from the past, one involving sunshine, and hardwood trees passed the prime of their autumn finery merged with that sparkling, tingling feeling in the air of excitement. Rhode Island had changeable moods. Although small in land mass, the state could never be trusted from week to week or for that matter, from day to day to be what she expected.

And CeeDee loved that. She kept an umbrella in the car, an extra jacket and a bottle of sunscreen, although the first two got far more use than the third. She learned to deal with storms because the Atlantic could be felt over every acre, and the weather bowed to its lead. Rhode Island could be haughty, sophisticated, playful, angry, or any of a dozen emotional extremes.

Today it felt innocent.

CeeDee, anticipating anything, didn't.

The mercury hovered around sixty, pushing past the wimpy fifty forecast, and blazing past the forties, she had woken-up to. The sky was so intensely blue, she wondered if there were a limit to how much of one color the Earth could hold, and if so, then blues from all over the world had been leeched out, so Rhode Island could glisten this one pristine afternoon.

Christmas decorations had been appearing in stores for a month now, but this glorious day didn't feel like Christmas. Instead it felt like something golden, stolen from the depths of time, a Camelot day where anything was possible. She had a child now, and her future had changed dramatically.

CeeDee had wondered if she should go to his house, meet him there, using the weak excuse that she wanted to check on the bulbs, but convinced herself that would be stalking, and the date was to meet here, on the bench. She parked herself early, and she wiggled her toes as she thought about the podiatrist while she watched for him. She found herself startled when he somehow snuck up on her, approached without her being aware.

He looked great and her breath caught as she knew, in her mind at least, he was hers, and hers alone. His hair was windblown, with a professional cut that when wind-styled only made him look far more handsome than any human male had a right. He wore designer sunglasses, but his smile when their glances met nearly had her swooning. She'd never really understood that verb before, never felt the need to swoon with any other man of her acquaintance, wondered if pregnancy hormones had anything to do with it.

She recognized the designer label on his jeans, and the jacket he wore was butter soft black leather. She supposed he'd have no trouble making a house payment if he pawned that watch. It was no wonder the IRS was chasing this fellow. Her only problem was why she found it endearing instead of obnoxious. She really despised men who had no trouble adorning themselves at the expense of others, and wondered what made him the exception.

"Hi, how did your week go?" His voice was lusty, seductive. For some reason, CeeDee realized the sound which wrapped around her heart didn't come as a surprise, although it was far different from the tones he used every other time he had visited this park bench. It was the voice she heard in her dreams, when hugging a fat stuffed bear while she imagined hugging someone far more substantial.

Pierce bent down, kissed her lightly, far less than a kiss of passion, far more than a kiss of friendship. Although there were no teeth involved, no tongue and it took place in broad daylight on a main street, it was one of the most intimate experiences she ever had. She had no idea why. She didn't feel possessed nor assaulted.

When Pierce offered the light pressure of his lips against hers, CeeDee felt somehow cherished. She hadn't quite gotten used to him holding her hand yet, and now she tingled from the sensation of his welcoming kiss.

CeeDee suddenly felt breathless. Being near Pierce always did that to her, as if her heart didn't beat at the same rate when he was around. Actually, she suspected it didn't. He sprawled down beside her, one hand on the back of the bench, to support his efforts as he tickled the soft hair at her neck.

"I can't think when you do that."

"You suppose I want you thinking?" His laugh rang around the street. "No, honestly, I'll stop. Please tell me what you're thinking."

"Thinking?" she swallowed. She wasn't about to confess daydreams and night visions of them entwined on sheets, completing their union in a manner that always left her feeling needy. She wondered if it were pregnancy hormones, and if a good rocking climax would harm her baby. But she decided not. She couldn't possibly be the first pregnant woman in the history of the species to feel the need to engage in mind-blowing sex.

His grin started slowly, encompassed his entire face. "No need for words, darling. I can tell by the color on your cheeks just about all I need to know."

She put her hands to her cheeks, mortified. "I'm blushing, aren't I?"

"It's nothing to be ashamed of."

"Not if you're eleven. It's a curse. I've very expressive skin."

"CeeDee, listen to me. I've got plans for tonight. For the two of us. Do you know what I'm saying?"

"Yes."

"Is there a man in your life? Someone else whose territory I'm encroaching?"

She didn't need to think. The only 'man' in her life at the moment was the 50/50 chance of her child being born male. "No. there's no one else." She hoped she would be forgiven eventually for this lie.

"This is very important. Nothing will happen tonight that you don't want. I'll stop when you say. If you're not ready, I won't start. You're in charge here. I think we've got something developing between the two of us I'd like very much to explore."

He took her hand, pulled her to her feet, wrapping her chilled fingers in his larger, warmer ones. "I'll drive," she said, and strolled with him toward her car. She liked the feeling of him holding her hand. No, she loved it. It was enchanting, almost magical. She experienced an indistinct pull between them which she felt in her heart and in her bones. She'd never felt this magnetism with another human being and wondered if she could blame pregnancy hormones for this as well. Maybe she should start a list.

She thought of her baby and the sin of omission and feared what Pierce would do when he found out.

Pierce settled in the passenger seat, and pulled his seatbelt on. He was so self-controlled, so masculine, she wondered why he didn't insist on driving, but decided he was letting her choose the pace. When they got to the beach she could leave whenever she felt she had to. She would not be dependent on him for a ride back.

"Tell me how your week went."

She checked the mirrors, pulled the car into traffic. It wouldn't be a long drive. "I've been too busy to think. One of the people I work with got the nasty creeping zamboo, and I had to put in some overtime."

"Nasty creeping zamboo?"

"You know, like the flu, but worse. The kind of sickness when you wish you could die and are afraid you won't."

"Nasty creeping zamboo. Got it. Been there, done that. So, you've been working extra hard." He flashed a grin at her, the one that usually turned his dates to jelly. "Then I suppose you need time off for good behavior. Do you want me to tell you what's in the picnic basket?" His eyes twinkled, merriment—or devilment. She found it particularly telling of her current state of mind that she was eager for either.

"No. Today I want to be surprised. And pleased."

He reached out, meshed his fingers with hers, and pulled her hand toward him and gently, possessively, kissed the back of her wrist. Although he hadn't done so before, there was no misinterpreting what the action represented. This wasn't going to be innocent fun like the afternoon they had spent hunting down wild flowers. It wasn't going to be the sedate comradely of getting acquainted while planting the bulbs. And she doubted she would stop him if he wanted to take a kiss further.

CeeDee had a feeling this afternoon was going to be primal, hot and intense. Although Pierce exerted no pressure, she felt trapped, and until she got her confession out in the open, she could not feel comfortable with that emotion.

She pulled in a deep breath, kept her eyes locked on the road ahead. If there was going to be a confession, in the car, driving was a good place. She wouldn't have to watch his expression as he grew sickened or angry at her condition, and she'd be in control when he ordered her to return him to his car.

"There are things you don't know about me."

"There are things you don't know about me," he responded in kind. "We'll take time to get to know each other. And you don't have to tell me all your secrets. You can let me guess some of them."

"Oh, this one you won't have any trouble guessing if you stick around a few months."

He hooted with laughter. "You've already got my Christmas present?"

"No." But she was charmed, for he had so easily diffused the tension growing between them. And she let her thoughts fly and wondered what Christmas would be like, if they would still be together, making love in front of a roaring fire while a six or eight presents rested half-hidden under a decorated tree, or if she would be alone except for Maggie and perhaps a concave silhouette to her stomach where life quickened.

"I've made you sad."

"No."

"Then at least thoughtful."

"Well, yes. My life is in flux at the moment. I am no longer sure I know where up and down are."

He nodded sagely, as if he understood exactly what she meant. "In that case, you can hold off on buying me a present."

At his foolishness she laughed and said, "We're here."

He lifted his sunglasses, only as far as his forehead, but it wasn't the rocky coast of Rhode Island he studied, it was her. And although there was an endless expanse of water beyond the hood of the car, when he looked at her, it wasn't swooning she imagined. It was drowning.

"I'm glad we decided to do this." His stormy, flashing eyes highlighted his pleasure.

She unhooked her seatbelt, exited the car, taking the time to pull in a breath of fresh sea air. It was a perfect day, the sky marred by only a few puffy white clouds, the water clear, lapping at the sand and rocks. Dozens of sea gulls called their welcome overhead. Why, facing the timelessness of the Atlantic, did she suddenly feel pressured? "Really, there's something I need to say."

"Will it change how I feel about you?"

"It might."

Rather than begging for her confession, he regained her hand and dropped a stately, honorable kiss on her knuckles as if he were a knight and she his lady. "Then you don't know me as well as you should. I want to know everything about you that you feel comfortable sharing, but I promise, though I don't quite understand what I'm feeling, I doubt anything you say would change the way I want to feel about you."

CeeDee's knees grew wobbly. "I, um—"

When words failed her, he showed his manners and helped her. "There's no hurry. Whatever your confession is, we've got the whole day, don't we?"

She swallowed, wondered if she were reverting to type, that this would be the dry run, the preparation for telling him. She didn't want to blow this relationship, and she didn't want to lie. But then, was it a lie to postpone, for a few hours, a confession which might have him heading for the hills?

"Yes. We've got the whole day." She understood too, what that agreement meant. She was available for his seduction.

"I'll make sure we have some time to talk."

She didn't take him to a sand-covered, lifeguard watched beach, for which he was grateful, even though it was the first weekend in November, and the lifeguards would have long vanished. He could have handled that, but it would have been just a shade more difficult. Instead she found a private cove, guarded by half the seagull population of the United States, and underfoot a dozen types of crabs, including his favorite, the violin toting, side-walking fiddler crabs. The ocean lapped the shore sedately, nothing more than a dog grooming already immaculate fur. But off in the distance, beyond the blue-on-blue sky, storm clouds that he sensed with a heightened perception were working on changing all that. By tomorrow hell would break loose. Today, however, would be perfect.

*Why don't you make love with her*? Damn. Pierce wondered if he could get away with giving Candy a second raise.

He set the picnic basket down, and she did the same with the small insulated carrier she held. Sinfully rich dessert, CeeDee had promised. Sin definitely fit into his plans for the evening, as did a passion-ridden dessert, but the reward he promised himself would be shared, and it wouldn't come out of a bag.

She wore yellow, the shade of sunflowers, almost blinding in its intensity, and just the fact that the grays had vanished was enough to heat his blood. It was a summer color, although they were deep into autumn, nearly to Christmas. By rights decreed by fashion authorities of shop-online catalogues, she should be in orange and red, wool plaids and tweeds. His mother, he was certain, would rather be dead than wear a clearly summer color in October.

Her hair looked redder, and Pierce tried to decide if it were the sunlight, or if his perceptions were always skewed when he danced around her. He still could recognize and appreciate the soft, comfortable shades of browns, but now her hair sparkled toward a deep auburn.

"Do you dye your hair?" As a question, Pierce was well aware it fell into the broad category of things men were forbidden to ask. But he had to know. Still, he might have blown the whole day, if not the relationship, with that one question.

"Absolutely." She didn't seem upset, for which he was grateful. "My father had red hair. I only remember it as white-gray, to be honest, but people who knew him a long time called him Red, and my mom swears it was true. But I got this boring western European brown hair, I suppose you've heard it called mousy, but I'm not going into that, for I'm sure you don't want to hear my opinion on mouses in any shape or form. But I have the genes for it, and I think my skin tone is just right for a redhead, so about every other month or so, I'm really red."

Since he'd dug himself a hole, the least he could do was start pulling himself out. "It looks fabulous in this light." What he really wanted to do was question her at length, using subtle forms of torture if necessary, to find out what had to be a delightful story regarding her opinion of 'mouses'.

Canary yellow capris split the length of her thighs, modest things which would give him no trouble prior to his removing them. On top she wore a scooped neck yellow print shell knit with patterns of butterflies, covered with a long-sleeved solid jacket of the same hue in linen. All these weeks he'd been thinking about her he hadn't appreciated her breasts, concentrating on her hands or her expressive eyes or even the graceful slender symmetry of her flat stomach, yet now, under a sun hours from setting, he noticed, and they were perfect. Small, firm, he ached to wrap his hands around them. Soon. Very soon. The only virtue he could find in patience, was it eventually gave way to indulgence.

The way his body reacted, he was a man ready to indulge.

While CeeDee had her back turned, fussing while she settled a blanket, Pierce waved his hands, subtle motions she didn't catch, and the mosquito population and that of the other sand-hopping, skin-biting insidious bugs, left them alone. Gulls took to the air, crying a plaintive yell, before settling a hundred yards farther down the beach. He wrapped lethargic bronze powerstrands into a loose geodesic dome which protected them in an invisible shell of privacy. Now NSA spy satellites or the even more invasive paparazzi parked off-shore with long-range lenses on expensive cameras couldn't see them.

CeeDee settled beside him. "You seem nervous."

"Do I?"

She moved her arms back and forth, in exaggerated pantomime of what he had been doing.

He wrapped his arm around her, molding her to his hip. She didn't protest, and the presence of her body, resting against his felt magical.

"What are you doing?"

"Breathing," Pierce answered, his nose nuzzling her hair.

"No, really. You have to be up to something."

"There's a lot going on in my life right now, but I have to say nothing has ever felt so right."

Watching the Atlantic ebb, leaving behind scattered tide pools filled with sea stars, black mussels, anemones and the pokey sea urchins, they shared quiet confidences, traces of her life she'd left behind long ago. In return, Pierce offered pieces of his childhood he didn't mind recalling: how he had climbed a tree reciting a flight spell found in a paperback mystery and broken both legs, totaled a car at sixteen when the ink was still wet on his driver's license and broke three ribs. He related antics of Woof! his pet Irish Wolfhound, Mastodon, his father called it, and how they had been inseparable for years, until old age caught up, and how Pierce was no longer afraid of dying, since he watched Woof! die with dignity and honor.

The walked the shore for an hour, avoiding ubiquitous seaweed, laughing when a squirt of water would disclose the sand-buried hiding place of a razor clam. They stopped for ten minutes watching the awkward, slow moving antics of a fiddler crab. They let it go unmolested, wishing it long life and happiness while they spoke of Alaskan King Crab and drawn butter.

By the time the tide started lapping back, he had built a roaring fire of driftwood; the pieces he found almost works of art in and of themselves. The temperature dropped, and the first bold stars winked into existence. The sunset was probably glorious, but they watched the ocean and the noisy pirouetting gulls circling above, so they missed it. In Rhode Island, the sun doesn't set on the water, so they made a whispered pledge to return before dawn some morning and experience a sunrise.

He hadn't gone all out on the picnic, instead of expensive trendy foods, he chose the common, things they could eat with fingers rather than fine crystal and sterling silver. Cherry tomatoes and boiled shrimp and six different kinds of cheese and hot dogs they roasted on sticks. Hard boiled eggs, stuffed celery and a small jar of olives. If she didn't notice the mosquitoes left them alone, that they were far warmer than the fire itself could account for, it was all the better.

Wordlessly they picked up their trash, leaving not a single crumb behind.

"Storm's coming," she said.

"I know." He'd felt it for some time, around them, and inside, where his desire built. He wanted her, desperately. "Not tonight."

No, the storm exploding around them tonight would not be weather related.

Pierce used magic to set the seduction, which was something of a first. He never before had accessed any of his talents in pursuing, wooing or winning a woman. The two passions of his life had never coincided. He always had money, talent and opportunity. In the past he had used his special abilities for more finely developed pursuits, the battle of good versus evil for example. But this time on the beach with CeeDee meant more than he wanted to admit, on more levels than he cared to analyze.

He inhaled slowly, adsorbing familiar scents of salt and life and the fire. He wanted CeeDee to have a good time. Yes, maybe it was nothing more than that.

"Maybe I should be going," she said. He understood her statement and the underlying reluctance.

"Stay. A few more minutes." He would beg if he had to and decided that thought didn't bother him half as much as it should have. "You don't have to work tomorrow, do you?"

She shook her head. How beautiful her hair looked, bathed only in firelight. What few stars glowed between the increasingly obvious storm clouds were not bold enough this evening to add to the illumination. "No."

"Then you can sleep in." He felt his body tighten in response, for the image that flashed in his brain of her sleeping in, involved his sheets, his pillow, his passion. He reached for the tip of her braid, took the band off the end and slowly, methodically started unweaving the silky strands. He felt only anticipation. He realized he had learned the skill of unraveling hair from undoing powerstrands. It was a heady feeling, for in both he felt power.

"You have such gorgeous hair."

"It's an annoyance. One of these days I'm going to hack it all off."

And that would be one of the great sins of the universe.

Pierce stretched out on a blanket, his ankles crossed, his weight on one elbow. With a look at him which suggested she knew what she was doing, she too lay down, her head resting on her entwined fingers, her eyes open, as if she sought the mysteries of the universe in the stars. Hair cascaded around her shoulders, down her back, puddleing in glorious silken splendor on the blanket.

"Do you know the names of the constellations? Can you find the planets?"

He leaned closer, kissed her lightly, felt her body settle along the length of his. "No. Everything I've ever concentrated on has been here."

"Here?"

"Earth. Let other men explore the other universes. I've always had what I needed here." His magic was earth-based, although when he did travel to other worlds, he doubted they were the types of places astronauts could reach with a gyroscope and a Saturn V rocket.

"Here?" her pulse quickened just a tad and her grin, showing pleasure held just a trace of rising concern. He wondered if he scared her.

Pierce slid into his seduction routine, finding it with her, new, untried. "Here." He traced his finger down the slope of her nose, over her lips, across the smooth, seductive length of her throat.

She watched him intently. In this light there was no green to her eyes, only darkness, secrets, mysteries. He found it very arousing. One corner of her lip quirked, revealing a deep, seductive dimple. "Anywhere else?"

He groaned, then grinned. A wolf, facing Red Riding Hood would understand that grin. "Oh yeah."

He was finished with his single finger exploration. He cupped an easily captured breast in his palm, and lightly, but thoroughly massaged her firm flesh. "Here." He shifted weight, moved so that both his hands were occupied. "Do you want me to go on?"

She'd been watching his fingers work magic on her breasts, but now she looked up, met his glance, looking for questions, or for answers, or perhaps only for reassurance. Her lips parted, and her tongue darted out, moistening her lips, as if she wanted to speak and had forgotten how.

It was in his best interests to keep her off-balanced. He kissed her, deeply, fully, which fed a hunger and made him want her more.

He sat up, unlaced his deck shoes, removed them and the soaking socks beneath. It was not until his hands reached for his belt that she took notice.

"What are you doing?"

"Pants are wet." And they were. They had not walked along the shoreline so much as they had waded in the foamy surf. "Don't worry. I've got swim trunks underneath." He made an elaborate show of hanging the pants beside the fire to dry. Unfortunately, because of her Capri's, the same logic wouldn't work for her.

With gentle pressure against her shoulders, Pierce inched CeeDee back against the blanket, until he leered above her. "Better," he whispered, "much better." His kisses started slowly, testing her resistance, his own restraint. Soon his tongue made immodest forays into her mouth and she met it, and matched it with a rising passion of her own.

"Bikini top?" he asked, hands poised above her breasts.

"What?" She looked slightly dazed, and the clarity of her eyes had dimmed, becoming softer with her passion.

"Bikini top or bra?"

"Bikini. Swim suit," she corrected. A fine line.

"May I?" he asked, hands at the hem of the butterfly laced shell. She nodded approval. The shirt vanished. It was modest, still from the way she lay, her breasts spilled forth, full and intoxicating. He hadn't included any wine with his picnic, in deference to her condition, now was glad he hadn't. He felt drunk watching her.

So very lovely. So perfect. His body responded predictably. It was, for the most part, his favorite time of making love, this anticipatory moment when great things await. He studied her breasts, had to bunch his fingers into a light fist to prevent himself from touching, caressing, tasting.

For a moment he was content to watch her, her eyes, the shyness she exhibited, the—he would not label it shame—although perhaps concern was the more correct term. CeeDee looked away as bright color rose up her neck, highlighted her cheeks. She was blushing. There was a possibility that her blush was the greatest aphrodisiac he'd ever come across.

"Look at me. No, CeeDee, please, look at me." He put his fingers to her chin, but there was no need to turn her cheek, and so he let the movement morph into a gentle caress. "You've beautiful."

"I'm nothing special."

He thought of the fetus, but when he answered, it was the woman he responded to. "I think you're incredible. Beautiful, smart, alluring."

"Alluring?"

"If you take this from my point of view, you certainly are."

"You've been too long without a woman."

"I've been too long without you." Gently he lowered his head, touched his lips to hers, lightly, a prelude or a tease. Pierce was not willing to give into the pressures rising in his bloodstream, to the desperation he was feeling in his loins, but far more strongly in his heart.

She tasted of the fruit she had been eating, apples, he thought, with a hint of the aged cheddar. But in addition to those, he tasted passion. He was certain he had seen passion enough to recognize it; but this was clearly the first time he'd tasted it.

He tightened his fingers again, a painful fist, then relaxed them, laid them on both sides of her breasts, ignoring the temptation of her nipples, the desire to bare her to his gaze.

"We've got all night," Pierce whispered.

"Do we?" she responded, and to prove it, he moved his kiss from her lips to her ear, to the long expanse of her neck, to the enticing collar bone, long and thin, and desperate, he thought, for him to nibble.

Stars popped out, like CeeDee, they were shy at first, but then they grew bolder, brighter. The seagulls settled. Pierce could no longer hear their plaintive cries. Maybe they found the happiness he did.

She lifted her hips, allowed his seduction to continue as the Capris went the way of the top, leaving her in her two piece swim wear. Her stomach was still flat, slightly rounded not from her pregnancy, but from the perfection of her figure. Without touching her he moved his hand, palm down, over the area of her navel, a seductive movement that, to one with his sharp senses, indicated so much more.

He felt it, the tiny, pulsing life that she hadn't ended. And surprisingly, Pierce no longer felt jealousy. That this wasn't his child didn't bother him, and he found himself immensely pleased it still lived. He had no experience with pregnant women, but she was far more feminine in this condition than any he'd ever bedded.

"What?" she asked, raising up on her elbows.

"What?" He refocused his eyes from the life within to the startled expression on her face.

"You're smiling like you know a secret."

He hadn't realized it, but he was smiling. He felt good. Very, very aroused, but on top of that, pleased, delighted, any of a dozen words. When bedding a woman he usually only felt lust—or desperation—now the emotions were gentler, more honest. CeeDee was more woman than he'd ever met before.

"I like this. I like you." He kissed her again, this time on her slender nose. His body throbbed.

He moved his hand back, sensing the health and the vitality of the child. It almost had an awareness, almost responded to him on a level he recognized. The next place he kissed her was on her belly above the secret, hidden life.

"We're forgetting desert."

"No." His grin was lecherous. "I don't think so."

# CHAPTER 12

"I made éclairs."

He nipped her, through the material of the suit, peaking her nipple to hardness. "I am hungry." Pierce rubbed his hands over her stomach, her hips, her shoulders, let his fingers create a cascade of silken auburn hair. He lowered his jaw, met her lips, this time deeper, more intimate. The kiss continued an eternity, his tongue finding warmth battling with hers.

When he broke, she sat up, pulling the straps he had lowered, back up against her shoulders. She reached for the picnic container. "Éclairs," she said, turning her back to him, fishing for the treat.

"Do you mind?" He reached out, tentatively touched the decorative clasp that held the top portion her suit together. The fire danced, sending a parade of glowing embers toward the stars. Because of a few well-placed powerstrands, it wouldn't need replenishing for a while and they were warm, far more comfortable than the blaze was responsible for. She took her time before she answered, before she shook her head.

His hands trembled, anticipation, desire, and yes, male arrogance. He opened the clasp, separated the strap. She lay back down, the material still covering her perfect breasts, but loosely now, without the form fitting contours of the suit. She had taken a bite from her éclair, and thick yellow custard exploded forth. He kissed her, tasted it on her lips, vanilla and woman.

Pierce removed the top, then without quite thinking, dug his finger into the mass of firm custard of her éclair, and dotted the tips of one breast with the pudding. His lips followed immediately.

"So good. So very, very good."

She raised her hips and arched her spine, responding to his caress. No woman had ever been so responsive in his arms before.

"Baby?" He wasn't sure exactly which of the two of them he meant, but she answered.

"My nipples are sensitive."

Of course. Of all the inconsiderate, cloddish— "I'm sorry, I won't do it again."

"No, please, it felt very good."

Pierce reached for her éclair again, removed more of the tantalizing filling, this time anointing both her throbbing nipples. His body hungered.

His mouth responded. She withered beneath him and the pleasure intensified. "I want to remove your bottoms. Do you mind?"

He ran a hand up her thighs, rubbing, adding pressure as he reached the apex of her legs. She tightened her knees together, trapping his hand exactly where he wanted to be. He wiggled, just a little bit. She moaned. She squirmed, throbbed, dropped the rest of her éclair into the sand. Later, when the powerstrands were released, a few lucky sea gulls would share in gluttony.

He dipped his fingers around the elastic at her hips. She responded, lifting the lower half of her body, allowing him access. The swimsuit bottoms inched down her thighs, past her knees, over her ankles.

"CeeDee, listen to me—"

"Pierce, you don't have to ask. I want you to make love to me. Right now. Right here."

Although he had made them invisible to anyone but another practicing wizard, she couldn't know that. She had to believe they were still on a beach, a secluded beach, but one with public access nonetheless.

She reached for the waistband of his trunks, pulled them down, feeding the desperation they both shared. "Pierce," she wrapped warm, clever fingers against his manhood, and he had to finish the task of removing the clothing by himself, even if he were practically paralyzed by her ministrations.

"Pierce—" on her lips his name became, oddly enough, a verb of command. Pierce. He decided not to wait any longer. He would take her up on her offer with pleasure. He moved over her, slid inside as she parted her knees to allow him freedom of access.

She was firm, tight, and he held his breath for a long minute, gathering strength, waiting for her to feel comfortable with his position. With his weight on his hands, and his heart thumping in a rhythm he wasn't sure he recognized, Pierce felt her, with every fiber of his being.

Heaven, he'd found heaven. He pulled out slightly, and she matched him, rocking, swerving, savoring. They united, became one. Time, for an eternity, stopped.

He grew hot, his breathing became ragged as they mated, matched, merged. Pierce felt the pressure of his own release building, almost painful and unbelievably pleasurable. His hips rocked, matching hers, meeting hers. His lips stayed busy, loving her neck, her chin, her ears, her tender breasts.

He wanted, at that moment, forever with this woman: white picket fences, basset hounds, trips to the orthodontist and Disneyland, baseball games in the backyard and later, standing proud at a graduation, and later still wiping tears at a wedding of a child they had created. He saw a future as his climax exploded through him, a future he never realized he wanted.

He held her for a long time, waiting for his pulse to regulate, for his breath to even, for his thoughts to solidify.

"Did I—" he struggled to find the words, never before realizing how important a woman's answer could be at this point, for it had never mattered before. "Was I—"

She cupped his face with her palms, raised up a bit and kissed him lightly, tenderly. "You need words?"

His pulse still raced, but the sweat on his back was starting to dry. "I think I do. I'd like to know what you feel. This is too important to assume."

"Can you wait a month or two until my heart settles? I'm not sure I've got any words."

"But I pleased you?" It bothered him that it meant so much. He was a good lover, knew how to gage his partner, to see to her needs and her enjoyment. This time, because it was so right, he wondered if he had been selfish, had taken, had not shared.

"Did the universe explode?"

"For a while there I thought it might have."

"Yeah, that's what I was thinking. God, I hate clichés but did you see stars?"

He grinned, felt better. Wondered when both of them would have their strength back to try it again. "I think I did."

"Then all I have to say is, Pierce, I swear somehow we probably ripped the time/space continuum."

He laughed, slowly, carefully pulled himself from her body, then inched beside her, until they spooned together, her back to his front, his arm over her waist, caressing her stomach as if he couldn't get enough of her. He could no longer smell the ocean, the wood snapping in his bonfire. He only smelled them, the deep, heady scent of intimacy.

"We must have been sharing a vision." But his hadn't been of a universe exploding, but instead and inexplicably, of a universe suddenly made right. He had never wanted to be a father before, never realized that power could come not from the twisting of magic strands, but from standing back and watching a child fall while trying to ride a two-wheeled bicycle, or attempting to figure out the nearly unexplainable mysteries of multiplying fractions. The power of the universe came not from manipulating forces most humans thought of as magic, but from creating a child, raising it in love, then standing back while he or she learned to live their own life.

The scent of their passion hung heavy and he wanted to ask her to marry him, to make possible this dream he'd seen when their bodies had been intimately joined.

"What is this?" she asked, moving her finger against the ugly scar. "When you were…" she grinned, finished, "busy, I didn't notice it. Now I can't imagine how I didn't. You run into some trouble?"

He rolled over, onto his back, his hands cupping his head, but before that, he pulled her naked body on top of him, her small, firm breasts crushed into the scar. "It ran into me. Someone tried to kill me. I don't know who or why. I don't have any memory of it. Needless to say, physicians in a Brooklyn emergency room are skilled or I wouldn't be here."

He remembered thinking he was glad he was alive because of the explosion of flavors from bean soup and a lush strawberry milkshake. Now he had additional reasons. If he had time, he would start listing them. "It happened—"

"When?"

He had planned to answer 'the day I met you,' and knew that wouldn't work. He was not yet willing to add confusion to the afterglow.

"A few weeks back. The police are working on it, but they don't have any leads either."

"How very frightening. You have no idea?"

"Well, I am a lawyer, and you know the old saying First kill all the lawyers. Beyond that, there's no one I've pissed off enough want to use a gun on me."

"Do you think they were after you, or was it random?"
"There's some comfort thinking it was random, that they weren't after me specifically, but I honestly don't know. There're no jealous husbands with handguns, no disappointed client with a grudge. Most of the disputes I settle don't even make it into a courtroom. We plead a deal or I find some clever reason to have the charges dropped."

"I suppose you're very clever."

"What's the sense in doing a job if you're not good at it?"

She felt exposed, vulnerable, laying there naked, so she sat up, pulled on the swim trunks. "You wear your watch on the wrong hand."

"What?" He was drowsy, sated, wanted nothing more than to fall asleep holding her tightly, and maybe wake up once or twice in the night and try this new facet of their relationship again.

"You're right handed, aren't you?"

"Sure."

"Most right handed men wear their watch on their left hand."

"Yes."

But she was intrigued and she was fast, and his reflexes had abandoned him about the time he felt his own release within her perfect body. So CeeDee removed the watchband and unearthed one of his secrets.

"You've got a tattoo on your wrist."

"It's not a tattoo," Pierce said, rubbing the spot. "It's a birthmark." More than that, it was the emblem of a wizard, a genetic marker showing the wearer was in tune with the forces necessary to create matter from energy only he or she could see. Oddly enough, the fullness of this mark appeared the first time a wizard manipulated a powerstrand, as if it lay hidden beneath the skin, waiting for the opportunity to present itself. The trace of it had been there when he first met Batty Belinda and she told him he was a wizard, but it was not until he mastered his first powerstrand that he felt he'd earned the mark.

Pierce had been honored when his appeared, so flattered that he had passed another hurdle, was recognized by something intrinsic within his blood.

"Are you sure it's not a tattoo?"

"Quite sure." Again, had he been prepared, he could have masked the ensign. Had he been thinking with any other part of his anatomy than the one which had just brought them both pleasure.

"Look, I've got one exactly the same myself."

"What?" All traces of lethargy vanished immediately. He sat up, literally pulling her right wrist toward him. She wore the marker of mage-born.

"Do you know what this is?"

"My father told me it was a tattoo, that he had it placed on my wrist when I was a tiny baby so if I ever got lost he could easily identify me. He had one exactly like it himself."

A mage? She came from a family of mages? What kind of Pandora's Box had he opened now? If Pierce was sure of anything at that moment, he was sure she told the truth as she understood it. Her innocence radiated through her as it had when she had slept cuddled against a large stuffed bear.

From his shock, he released her hand, and as he had, she rubbed her left thumb against the inside of her right wrist. "It's funny, I never noticed it during my childhood."

"When did you notice it? CeeDee, this is vitally important. Answer me."

"I don't know, about half way through my grad program I guess."

"Did you do anything, see anything, touch anything to make it happen?"

"Pierce, it's a tattoo. My father said he put it there and it just showed up as I matured."

"Does that sound normal for a tattoo?"

"No." Her brows lowered and she looked annoyed, equal parts at him and herself, if he had to guess. Nobody liked to have their personal illusions shattered.

The breeze had freshened, and the waves were hitting the shore with just a bit more force. Although full dark, he knew the whitecaps were forming and the storm he sensed drew closer. Pierce shivered although his wards kept them insolated.

"What's your father's name?" He tried to keep the tone of his voice controlled, didn't want to spook her over something that could possibly be well. He knew most if not all the local wizards, if there was a problem maybe it wasn't his.

"Colin Tristan."

"You don't carry his last name."

"My parents divorced when I was young. I took my mother's name. And Pierce, this thing can't be that rare. Harry, the man who's—the guy I dated before you, had one too."

Implications struck him with the force of a charging rhinoceros. "What exactly are you trying to say?"

"Harry, the creep I dated before I found out he was married. He had the exact same mark on his wrist. I wouldn't have noticed, except he wore his watch on his right wrist. I thought it was strange."

He sat up, pulled her with him, his hands wrapped firmly around her arms, in a way he hoped was both comforting and restricting. "CeeDee, this is very, very important. Harry, this guy with this tattoo, is he the father of your child?"

"My child? What are you talking about?"

"I know you're pregnant. I felt it. Is he the father?"

She wasn't surprised as much as disappointed. She had hoped Pierce would be open to her condition, accept that she had a life before she met him, and this child was a part of it.

"Yes. I meant to tell you. I know guys don't like to date women who are pregnant with another man's child."

"What have you done? You've mated with a man of power?"

"Power?" She'd lost the thrust of the conversation. He wasn't asking the questions she expected. "What does this have to do with power?"

"Just answer the question."

She wrapped her dignity around her. She was a strong woman, facing a problem countless other women before her had faced. "I don't see how that's any of your business. I don't need you, and if you just let me go, I'll be on my way, as obviously you find my condition a turn-off."

"CeeDee, this is more important than you could possibly know. I'm not upset about the baby. I was hoping you were still pregnant."

"Hoping I was still pregnant?" It seemed like she added emphasis to each word individually.

"Long story, I'll explain later. Right now we've got other problems. Tell me about the father."

"I thought he was a nice guy. I didn't know he had a wife—"

It wasn't likely. Wizards were notoriously free, and completely trustworthy when it came to avoiding passing on their genes.

"Did he know you carried this mark?"

"Of course. He said it was one of the first things that drew him to me. He said we were probably tattooed at the same parlor, and about the same time. And I didn't see him as a man of power. Not like a politician or a gangster or a CEO. I'm not sure what he did," then she stopped and thought. "He had money and connections, but he didn't have power. I know, because he told me more than once that he wanted to acquire it."

Acquire power, by birthing another mage, and raising him in his thrall. There was a reason wizards were solitary. Power merged was power lost, by the weaker to the stronger, and a child of two mages would be infinitely stronger, but not at first. If he could be raised, trained just a bit, until he showed the promise of his potential, then his power would be there for the taking.

Pierce looked up, caught the movement of powerstrands, knew their idyll had come to an abrupt end. He stood, pulling her up beside him. "CeeDee, get dressed. Right now." He started manipulating powerstrands himself, and seconds later, he was fully dressed, not the casual clothing he had worn while they walked the shore. He was in a suit, tie loose around his throat, with a black robe open down the front, fluttering in the freshening shore breeze. It should have, she decided, looked like a choir robe, or a graduation gown, but it looked like neither. This, she knew, was a robe of power, and she was only just starting to get an inkling of what kind.

"How did you do that?"

"I haven't got time to explain. We're in danger. Take your keys and go. Right now."

The air about ten feet from them rippled, undulated, and through it, a man stepped from chaos into being. Like Pierce, he was dressed in a robe, but his was beige.

"Pierce, I heard you were looking for me."

"Pasco."

Minelli held his hands out, to show he was unarmed, but Pierce had enough experience to know the gesture meant nothing in a practicing wizard.

"Not now. We're not alone."

"She's one of us."

She didn't sound frightened, she sounded angry. "Pierce, what's going on here?"

"So it would seem," he answered. Without turning his head, he spoke to CeeDee. "Go. I'll answer your questions tomorrow."

She had her back to the two men, was dressing as rapidly as she could. "I want to know what's happening."

"Later." Pierce reached out, grabbed a fat red powerstrand. "I've got questions."

"We can talk like gentlemen," Pasco said, still holding his hands out.

"We're neither one gentlemen," Pierce answered. His features were set, tense. The powerstrand coiled around his fist, one end twining up his arm, around his shoulder, to wrap lightly against his neck. He pulled a second strand, a green one, should a hasty retreat be necessary, it was always best to be prepared. He found it amazing that Pasco did not stop him from arming himself.

"Someone shot me."

"I heard. I'd like to explain."

"You don't deny it?"

"I've no reason to lie. For what it's worth, I am glad I didn't succeed in killing you."

"There was a time I called you brother. A time when I worked beside you." As long as Pasco wasn't stopping him, Pierce wrapped a pink powerstrand around CeeDee. It wasn't much protection, since he assumed she hadn't learned how to manipulate them, but it would help. And it would mark her as mage, in case there were others, as foolish as he was, thinking her uninvolved in this battle.

"Those were good years. Funny, after all that miserable work, I can think that."

"Yet you let it all go."

"I couldn't take the tedium."

"So you sought the easy route."

"And regretted it. I understand you're thinking of taking on an apprentice."

"I'm thinking of it. Master spoke with me."

"I am in need of an instructor."

"Is that what this is all about? You want me to teach you the tenets you've already denied? You shoot me, leave me to bleed to death in a back alley and you think I'll have anything to do with your training? I'll not so easily ruin my own reputation and I am no fool. I'll not be dragged down by association with you."

His robe fluttered in the breeze, rippling behind him. There were powerstrands around them, but Pasco held none. He remained unarmed. "Think of it as atonement."

"Atonement? When you should be held to the law? When the Council needs to hear what you've been up to, especially regarding a rather noxious white power?"

The information came as a shock, which he hid quickly. His features were oddly similar to Pierce's, same shaped eyes, nose and ears. Their height was similar too, but the expression each man wore was different, as if while Pierce was going to law school and learning whatever this magic was, this stranger had indulged in hedonistic behavior, pleasing only himself.

"You know of that? Of course you do. I've stopped importing it. And Pierce, over the past few weeks I've gone out of my way to mitigate some of the more serious side effects associated with it."

"Not that I've noticed. I listen to the police broadcasts on the subject."

"I was told it was something else, what doesn't matter now. I allowed myself to be corrupted."

"An easy enough situation to investigate. Tell Master. He's the one you need to present your defense to. He will bring you to the Council, but don't be surprised if he doesn't stand beside you."

"I can't. Not yet. Too much is still unsettled. I'm thinking of the future. I need a Master, and I know I've burned my bridges with Drollard."

"Stop! We're not alone here. No more names. And I'll never teach you. Not and have my reputation go down in infamy too. CeeDee and I are leaving. If you want to talk after I am sure she is safe, I will arrange it. But now is not the time."

"The child is yours, you know."

"CeeDee's child?"

"I hear things. It's yours."

Pierce pulled back his hand, about to release the powerstrand he held as a weapon. "Impossible. The first time I touched her was tonight."

"I'm not the only one the Council will have questions for."

"I've done nothing wrong."

"Someone set you up, Pierce. Someone close to you."

"No. Never. I know who my friends are, and who my enemies are."

"Do what you have to do. Should you need me, seek and I'll make sure you find me."

"When I look for you, it will only be to bring you to justice."

"Watch your back, Pierce. You have an enemy who knows your every move."

"What does that mean? Why am I being targeted?"

"I know you don't believe me, but there's something significant going on, and you've become a focal point. Powerstrands are getting knotted, and I doubt you've got the insight to free them yourself."

"I'm strong. Or have you forgotten?"

"I forget nothing. I use what powers I have."

"To serve evil."

Pasco grinned, and Pierce remembered the years of apprenticeship when his friend often used subtle power to lure women and acquire trinkets for his vanity. Although mostly innocent, the actions were perhaps the first symptoms of Pasco's abuse of power.

"Your woman is attractive. I never thought you'd chase a wizard."

"She has nothing to do with what's between us. You harm her, and there won't be enough of you left to establish identity. That I promise."

"Listen to me, Pierce. Check genetics. It's your child."

"Do you understand the word 'impossibility'? I was wondering if it was yours."

"No. I thought of increasing power through birth, but I doubt I could train a child. As you know, I haven't got the patience. And, though you don't believe it there are tenets I refuse to break."

"Pierce!"

"CeeDee, I need you to do something for me." He shifted closer until their breaths touched, until they could fold in on each other as they had only moments before on the sand. Pierce could feel her shiver, feared she was afraid, and never wanted her to fear in his presence. His whisper was warm, and he hoped it spoke of remembered intimacy when he touched the gold powerstrand he wound around her wrist. "Can you see that?"

"Yes. When you touch me."

Her eyes were very wide, her teeth chattered. He recognized this was a November beach and the wind had freshened off the water and that she had been warm in his arms. "Can you feel it?"

"Yes."

"You're doing great. In case you're wondering, I'm positive you're not just a wizard, you're a very strong one."

She nodded, accepting the compliment.

"Now, I need you to think of your bedroom as clearly and distinctly as you can. Your linens, your pillow, the fat, smiling bear."

"How do you know—"

He tightened the green strand. "CeeDee, can you do it?"

"Yes."

"If you can do this for me, you'll be safe. This I promise. I need you to think that you're there in your bedroom. If there's anything specific about the room as it is at this moment, concentrate on that."

"Specific?"

"Anything. You left your pajamas at the foot of the bed. The duvet has a stain on it, whatever is specific."

"I know what you mean." She grinned, and he had to give her points that she could be terrified and still flirt. "Pierce, I never leave my pajamas at the foot of the bed."

"You will when I take them off you." He touched her gently when she nodded, accepting his statement as a vow. "Are you thinking of your room?"

She didn't answer. Didn't have the time and her focus had shifted from him to a room twenty miles away. For a moment she stood straight, her eyes closed, a look of intense concentration on her features. A second later, she vanished.

During that time, Pasco had not moved. He stood ramrod straight, with his hands facing palms out. "It seems I'm not the only one dealing in the forbidden magicks."

Now that she was safe, Pierce planned his defense in earnest, twisting his weapons into honed readiness. "Do you deny you've killed?"

"No. But I am willing to explain."

"If you are, I'm not the one you need to speak with. Master has put all of us on your trail."

"I know, and you're the only one who's come close."

"Why don't you try telling me what you're doing here?"

He shifted, enough to have Pierce tightening his grasp on his weapons, but he was only moving his feet. "You won't believe me if I tell you, but I have information you need."

"Let me be the judge of what I need."

The wind gusted, Pierce felt his robe dancing around his feet.

"I've gotten myself in a bit of a fix and I've done things I thought were innocent but turned out evil. I tried to make things better, but I only made them worse. I trusted people I should have avoided, and I've denied things Master taught I now know to be true."

Instead of weapons, Pierce considered restraints, and a simple transfer spell, but he was not foolish enough to set aside his advantage. "We really should convene a Council."

"I'm not quite ready to give myself up. There's too much going down I'm caught up in. I would like someone to know my side of the story before this whole thing blows up. I know you're looking for me. I thought I would make it easy for you and appear. Unarmed."

"There's power missing. Lots of power."

"I know. It's important you know I helped capture the strands, under duress. I would have been killed if I refused. I'm no longer as naïve as I was when I got involved. And you're right, there's lots of power missing."

"What's it going to be used for?"

"Think, Pierce, your brain was always the best. What would missing powerstrands be used for?"

"Opening portals." His answer was immediate, and without conscious thought.

"Yes, but there's something else. Something we have to stop. A weapon."

Because he was holding powerstrands as a weapon, he could not deny the possibility. "Come in. Tell Master what you know. Even if a Council punishes you, it won't be nearly as bad as if you let this, whatever it is, get worse."

He shook his head, for the first time that evening showing defiance. "I don't want them to take my powers. I cannot be defenseless."

"Then you should have thought of that long before you got involved in whatever you're doing."

"Pierce, listen. I'm not the one you need to worry about."

Pierce cracked a sardonic grin. "That's not what my Master says."

"I've become the fall guy for everything going wrong and I don't like it."

"Because you've kept yourself so clean."

"No, because I'm not guilty of a fraction of the things I'm accused of. I may have broken some laws but not this. The wizard who is amassing the power is hurting all of us."

"Who is this wizard?"

"If I tell you, here, now, I sign my death warrant. Besides, no one will believe me."

"Make me believe you."

"What can you offer?"

"A fair trial."

"If that's what you think, you are naïve. The Council looks for scapegoats, not evidence. Trust me, Pierce, if the Council is looking for guilt by association, you're in far deeper than I am. I know what I'm talking about. Any evidence I bring now will only seal my fate."

"Then tell me something. Anything I can work with."

"You're looking for a wizard named Andrew. What you want is quite a bit closer to home than that."

"Andrew is not involved?"

"Oh, he's involved up to his black robe, but he's taking orders from someone far more powerful."

"Black robe, then he's a wizard, not a wer-wizard."

"The term wer-wizard suits him well enough. But his mentor is a wer-wizard, one whose power is immeasurable."

"Give me their names. I need something to take to Drollard."

"It's happening in the next few days. I don't know what's going to set it off, but once it begins, there's no stopping it. I've seen how it works."

"How what works? You're talking in riddles."

"Think about what I said, and corroborate it. You'll see I'm not lying." With that Pasco pulled a powerstrand he must have had hidden, opened a transport and vanished.

Frustrated, angry, confused, Pierce released his weapons, and methodically unknotted the shelter he had built earlier. The fire was already burning low, little more than embers. Far to the east, over the choppy Atlantic, the first lightning flashed.

He removed his robe, picked up the scattered remains of their picnic. CeeDee was a wizard. How could he have been so wrong about her? Still, he couldn't believe she was lying about anything. No, he would take all her statements at face value. CeeDee he could trust. He had no reason to trust Pasco.

Pierce drove CeeDee's car and left it outside her condo, and using a powerstrand, made sure the keys were where she could find them, on the floor, just inside the door, as if she dropped them coming in. After that he transferred himself back home. Daniel met him at his front porch. His friend shuffled his feet and refused to meet his eyes.

"You know I don't want to do this."

"Do what?"

Daniel studied his shoes. "There's been a Council called."

"And?"

"And your name is the only one on the agenda. Master ordered me to bring you in."

"Been waiting long?"

"No, a few minutes. I swear I have no idea what this is about. Snyder and Parsons came and got me."

"Since I suppose you won't give me ten minutes to clean up the lair, I'm ready to go."

"Thanks. I didn't want to have to insist. Since you don't look surprised, I figure you know what this is about?"

Pierce shrugged, his mind working feverously to try to understand this latest turn. "To tell you the truth, it could be any number of things."

His grin was a shade uglier than Pierce had ever seen Daniel make. "Dabbling where you don't belong?"

"No. I haven't broken any tenets, but something is seriously out of whack with the power structure. Maybe they are just interested in asking questions about the murder attempt."

"Maybe." Daniel didn't seem convinced, he almost seemed to be relishing the possibility of a witch-hunt.

"By the way, I meant to thank you for whatever it was you did in the emergency room. I know you were there. I know more than the emergency room staff that it was you pulling me back."

Daniel laughed, an odd sound, clearly lacking mirth. "I did what I could."

"Daniel, I meant to ask, when my heart started beating again, was I being strangled?"

He looked aside, as if he'd rather lie. "Yes."

"You did it?"

He swallowed, took some time to consider his answer. "Not me. I pulled it off."

"There was another wizard? Did you see anyone, sense anything?"

"I thought I did, but I wasn't sure it wasn't you, trying to get back on your own. I don't have any information about that."

"But you know something."

"We've got to go. I don't know what kind of trouble you're in with the Council, but I've been looking for a time to confess. Damn, I'd rather not say anything, but—"

Pierce reached out, snagged a gold powerstrand, held it out as a weapon. "You shot me."

"No, but I'm probably responsible."

Pierce held the gold over Daniel's heart. With a thrust, his friend and partner would be dead. That was probably not the best way to approach the Council summons, however.

"What?"

"I broke into your lair. I knew you would be occupied, and I didn't want to check some time when you weren't there, in case I really made a hash of your wards."

Pierce released the powerstrand, put his bare hands around the smaller man's neck, smashing him against the front door. "What the hell are you trying to say?"

"You were the last in our class to see a powerstrand, months after we did, yet you got your robe three years before me. Since then, you've been the Wunderkind, able to do no wrong. And I knew you had a lead. I wanted to see if there was anything in your lair I could use. I've got nothing. I'm not even sure Pasco is involved with this, so I wanted to sniff around, see what you had brewing."

"What did you find?"

"Nothing, or rather nothing I could read. You've changed your code."

"That surprises you?"

"No, but it didn't occur to me I might need to change mine. I know master told us to, but I figured everything I wrote was safe enough."

"And you made a bang entering."

"Yes."

"And?"

"And I didn't lock up. I figured you'd think you'd been too preoccupied to have done it. I didn't suspect someone else would enter, take you out and shoot you."

Two good friends from his apprentice days, and both of them betraying him with their own agenda.

\*\*\*

They kept him waiting for hours, in a room without windows or furniture. No stray powerstrands lapped around the floor or loitered looking for attention. There were spells that could keep them away, and the Council was making sure he would stay where they left him. Pierce waited alone, except for Daniel.

"By the Code I have sworn to, I am forbidden to speak to you," Daniel said by rote.

"I understand," Pierce said, needing the sound, while he filed desperately through his memories looking for some hint of what this could be about. Daniel stayed away from him, motionless.

"It's time."

Pierce had heard the peal, knew by the sound of bells before Daniel spoke. He shivered, wondered why he felt so uneasy. He had done nothing wrong. If this were about the shooting, he doubted a Council would be called. He was the victim here, not the perpetrator.

Before he stepped into the Council room, Daniel stopped him, whispered, "I'm sorry. I want you to know whatever this is about, I'm with you." He gave Pierce no time to respond.

The floors, ceiling and walls of the Council room were rough hewn stone, mortared by hands of wizards long since forgotten, and gave the arena the feeling of a large cavern. A thousand wizards could sit here on the tiered levels, for when a wizard was offered a robe, graduated, he was allowed to bring in one chair. Each wizard chose their own, so there were no benches, no continuity of style. There were overstuffed arm chairs, tall straight back chairs, some modern desk chairs undoubtedly with lower lumbar support. Ideally when a wizard died his chair was removed, but the chatter among apprentices stated that never happened. Most believed there were chairs that had remained empty since before the signing of the Declaration of Independence.

Pierce walked in, head held high, realized while he had been wearing street clothes when he entered, now his robe swished around his ankles. Magic. He hadn't expected that, although he had no idea why it should surprise him.

Daniel whispered something he didn't catch, then scampered toward his own chair while Pierce scanned the seats. There were probably over fifty in attendance, less than a hundred, yet still a good crowd. He doubted that many had been present the last time he had been here, when he was being honored with his Master's robe. Then, there had been laughter, celebration. The tone of the room was considerably different now, although he didn't have enough information to gage what these wizards were anticipating.

He had no idea where his Master's chair was located, since Drollard had stood beside him for the previous ceremony, and he had been out on assignment and unable to attend when Daniel was honored with his robe, but he located Drollard seated on the stand, one of three wizards who would preside over this meeting. Needing some grounding in reality, Pierce checked an upper tier to his right, found his chair, a comfortable upholstered wingback, the sight of it giving him comfort. He belonged here. These were his peers.

"Pierce Billova."

Pierce stepped forward. He bowed deeply, respectfully. He'd never witnessed a disciplinary hearing, understood they were rare. Minelli had never faced charges because he had never 'graduated' to a black robe.

He held his hands up, palms out, the sleeves of his robe folding down to his shoulders, the traditional "I'm unarmed" gesture he had seen just a few hours before.

"Pierce Billova, you are called before this tribunal to answer charges."

He bowed again, formally. As he straightened, he tried to catch Drollard's eye, to see if he could get some idea what this was about by reading facial expression. "I acknowledge the authority of the Council, and place my fate in its hands." His response was rote, memorized lines he never anticipated needing.

Drollard stood, "I am here only as witness that all proceeds normally."

Not as bad as it could have been, Drollard was not an accuser, but the fact that he was not standing beside Pierce, when it was his right as Master spoke volumes. Drollard was not supporting him either.

The chairman glared at Drollard, as if Drollard's statement was tantamount to treason, but then he turned his attention to Pierce. "Is it true you have mated with a woman of power?"

Of all the things they could have hit him with, this was one of the least expected. It happened less than an hour before they had called him in, although obviously this session was called while he waited.

He was not shackled, and no one in the packed courtroom witness section held a powerstrand, but there were none around that he could reach.

"Why do you want to know?"

"There's been a complaint levied," Drollard said. Pierce wished he could read him, but his master had always supported him before.

"I have made love with a woman of power. This evening after the sun set. It is not a crime."

Drollard continued before the wizards in the audience could respond. "And is it not true she is in fact carrying a child of power, the product of both parents bearing our mark?"

Pierce looked around him. He could not lie. To do so would mean immediate loss of his powers, if not death. And he could not extemporize. He stood in front of his Master and must answer the question posed to him, not one he felt more comfortable approaching.

"I did not know—"

"Answer the question."

"It is my belief the child she carries has a man of power for a father. But it is—"

"And do you know the penalty for this breech of decorum?"

"I'm not sure I comprehend what the problem is. I found out myself only this evening. I would have spoken with you Master, but my summons arrived before I could."

"Do you know the penalty?" A second wizard asked. Pierce was not certain he knew him.

As far as he knew there was no problem with wizards making love, if they could trust each other enough to do so. The dilemma arose in that before such a congruence of powers occurred, the council of wizards should know and either approve or disapprove. Wizard birthrates were low and kept that way by strict adherence to this rule. A child born of two wizards was always more powerful than both put together. It was Pierce's belief that most wizards did not want to be responsible for a wizard far more powerful than themselves.

Pierce knew the punishment. Banishment from the company of wizards, but before that, his powers would be stripped, freed into the universe for a two-fold purpose: so he would have no claim on the powers of the child, and so there would be an atonement for the disruption of power. For mortals must never know men and women of such abilities existed.

"Are you prepared to accept your punishment?"

"Whatever you think I have done, I am innocent in this," he shouted, but his words were drowned out by hissing from the stands. A gold powerstrand appeared before him. He had not called it, but obviously someone in the audience supported him by abetting his escape. Pierce wrapped his hands around it, and disappeared. He appeared seconds later, outside CeeDee's apartment. But he knew before he knocked that she wasn't there.

If they would strip his powers, they would take hers, even if she were untrained and unknowledgeable about what her powers entailed. And the child? He had no idea if there were a way to strip it of any power it might possess. He only knew he had to protect that child and its mother until he understood what was going on. Certainly it could not be possible that every time two wizards met for sex a Council would be called. If it were, his Master certainly would have mentioned it during his apprenticeship. Over the years of his apprenticeship there had been three women, girls, for they had been quite young at the time studying with him. Nothing had been said about dating. This he was certain, although he had been too stressed out, too involved with the intricacies of magic to even consider them anything but competition.

He would have to deal with this, find some way to protect CeeDee and the child. How he was to manage that, he had no idea. There was a possibility he was no longer considered a wizard.

# CHAPTER 13

The Rhode Island university library was crowded, all the tables and desks filled with students working on their computers, trying to find that last bit of information they needed for whatever paper they had due. This cyclical madness was to be expected, and CeeDee fed on the panic the students exuded. It was one of the facets of her job she loved best: there were times when the library was so slow and silent that she could read and follow her own trails of interest through the internet, the book database, or the stacks and then, almost without warning, desperation would coil through the campus, full bodied and almost frightening, and she would be caught up in it. Then she would follow the student's trails, pointing them in the right direction, nudging them as they got closer to their hidden, almost camouflaged information.

Although the school year had started only a few weeks before, the first tests were upon them, the first reports due. CeeDee returned to the reference desk, glad to see the line had developed in her absence. She could find things. She supposed that was the single most important thing she liked about being a librarian, the fact that data, even when available, was not always easily accessible, and she could find it.

There was a second benefit. Keeping busy helped her from thinking. Last night something inexplicable happened. It was only a dream. It had to be. Well, two dreams. One after another. For some reason last night, after making love with Pierce, she had found herself in her bedroom, with no idea how she had gotten there, when she was certain she had been at the beach. Oh, she remembered finding pleasure in his arms, but how she got home after that, she had no idea. She knew what she thought happened, remembered the feel of the golden twist he placed around her wrist, but there was no glowing object around her now and to think it caused her to move through space in some sort of transporter action was impossible.

She was a librarian. She knew impossible.

CeeDee shook herself and helped the next student in line. As she moved from behind her desk to show him the computer he needed, something caught her attention. Two men, wearing severe black suits watched her. They stood out in this mass of college students as both too old and too well dressed. Hoping she wasn't adding paranoia to the list of things out of whack this morning, they were clearly watching her.

She moved back behind the reference desk, wanting to catch her friend's eye, ask, "What do you think they want?" but Janelle was busy and apparently hadn't noticed them. CeeDee rolled her eyes and considered herself foolish. It didn't look like anyone else noticed either.

In answer to a student's question, CeeDee typed into her computer, looking up when she heard a commotion. The two men still watched. She doubted they'd removed their gaze from her once, and it didn't look like they so much as blinked. Muttering about spending too much time watching adventure movies, someone pushed through groups of students.

"Pierce?" For a second her mind flashed back to the dream she'd had last night, when she had finally been able to calm down enough to sleep. The dream had struck her forcefully, far more vividly than usual, and she wondered if it were another symptom of pregnancy no one had bothered to warn her about.

Even after a shower, breakfast and a line of students needing help, the vivid images of the nightmare still hadn't left her. There had been bodies, bleeding in the sand. Although, in complete dream-like way, she hadn't seen how Pierce had killed them, she was aware he had. And it occurred to her, at that second, the place the bodies had been stacked was in front of this reference desk.

She spoke his name again, fighting the disorientation she always got when seeing people she knew away from the location in which she knew them: her hairdresser met at the gynecologist's, the guy from her book discussion group she met at the grocery mart. It was almost as if she felt he had no existence beyond waiting for her at the bench, and he was so completely devised by her imagination that now he had no right to appear.

He radiated panic. His hair was out of place. His suit coat was disheveled. He wore it like he had put it on while running, and he hadn't had a minute's spare time to straighten the collar, level the hems, or adjust the lapels. His tie was undone, but more than that, it was as if he wore it like a prisoner, escaped from a hangman would still wear a noose while kicking his get-away horse into a full gallop. CeeDee perceived he had received a shock so great he wore the aftereffects both physically and mentally.

The police were after him, was her first thought. They found clues. But she had no idea why the police would be chasing him. The dream last night had been just that: a dream.

He reached for her, grabbed her arm. He was breathing hard, spoke around gasps of air. "I don't have time to explain. You're in a lot of danger and you have to leave right now."

This was a library, for heaven's sake. No one made a scene in a library. She twisted her wrist, broke his grasp in an action she had learned on her local news about how to avoid an abduction. "Stop it, you're hurting me. Now, I don't know what this is all about—"

"And I haven't got time to explain it to you, but I'm serious. You're in danger. We have to leave now."

"Are you crazy? I don't know what you think the problem is but if you don't calm down, I'm going to have to call campus security."

But she looked at her two strangers and they were alert now, clearly watching both of them. It made sense. It wasn't her they were after, they had stood there, looking out of place, waiting for him.

Pierce noticed too.

"I don't have time for this." He twirled his hands, and a slim purple band of light appeared, glowing at his fingertips. It looked like those magic glow sticks popular at rock concerts and the circus, where the fluid inside glows for several hours. Except there was no tube, and this was a university library, not a stage performance.

As fast as he was, they were faster. Something bright flew, would have grazed her, had he not moved his hand quickly and somehow deflected it. A second and a third came in rapid succession. One student screamed, went down with a bloody sleeve. Something had sliced through his upper arm. Blood flowed freely.

"Pierce, stay down." From behind the desk she grabbed the phone, started dialing the emergency number. Almost all the students had fled, but the two men were still making motions as if throwing things she couldn't see.

"They won't help you." He took the phone from her hand, while she watched him fashioning a weapon from a glowing strand and throwing it toward the two assailants.

"Do you know what's going on?"

"Not everything. But I know we're in trouble."

"We're in trouble or you're in trouble and I'm in trouble because I'm with you?"

"At this point I have no idea."

"I need you to tell me what's going on."

"I promise I will, but you've got to trust me."

"Trust you? I still haven't got any answers from you forcing me to leave the beach."

"What do you remember about that?"

"Only that someone showed up, you were in a black robe and seconds later I was in my bedroom. Something was wrong there, because believe me, I've tried hoping for something with all my might and I never ended up back in my bedroom before. Now, those men are gone, and I'd imagine the police and campus security will be here in the next few seconds. What are we going to tell them? I never saw a gun."

"Is it safe?" Janelle asked, crawling out from behind the stacks.

"For now," CeeDee called back.

"You're just going to have to trust me." He mumbled again under his breath, "And I hope you're going to forgive me," but when he spoke again, it was for her, and his voice was low, and it held an edge to it. "I don't like doing this." With a movement so quick, she barely caught it, Pierce wrapped the purple strand of light around her wrists. She shivered once, then didn't see it, nor feel it, but she knew he had done something to her.

"You are under my control now, and I need you to do exactly what I say. Do you understand?"

"Yes."

Her mind was still her mind, but it was in a different spot now, an observer rather than a participant. It was as if another CeeDee had appeared, this one a trained cocker spaniel, willing to do what he wanted.

"Tell your coworker you're hurt, and I'm driving you to the hospital right now."

Like an automaton, her voice controlled, CeeDee turned to the other woman working at the reference desk. "Janelle, I'm got hurt. I need to go to the hospital. Pierce will drive me."

"What's the matter?"

She looked blankly, as if she couldn't come up with the answer.

"Whatever those weapons were, I think she got hit by one."

"Her color is bad," the other woman said, showing her concern now that CeeDee was no longer acting normally. CeeDee stood there, as if paralyzed.

"I'm sure she'll be fine tomorrow or the next day. I'll have her call you when I get her situated in bed. Does she have a purse or anything? How about a jacket?"

"I'll get it," the woman said. They could hear the sirens as emergency vehicles converged on their location.

Pierce helped CeeDee slip into her jacket, and handed her the purse the woman gave him. "Take this," he said, and blankly, mindlessly she did.

"We're going out to my car now. I need you to walk quietly beside me."

Without a word, and with a blank stare, she followed. "Get your seatbelt on," he ordered, slamming the passenger side door. He ran around the front of the car. He turned the key in the ignition, and the engine started.

"CeeDee, I'd like to release you, but I can't have you making a scene. This is too important..."

She sat there blankly while another CeeDee, an internal CeeDee battled against invisible restraints.

"Ten minutes, I promise, then I'll release you." He twisted his hands a few more times and the engine of the car following them billowed smoke. "That should take care of them. Don't worry, I've got powerful protection spells on this car. We should be safe for a few minutes."

He left Rhode Island, heading for the Massachusetts turnpike. He would have liked to have transferred them directly, but that made too much noise, and he didn't want to leave a trail this early in his escape, especially when there were several other wizards in the vicinity.

He was able to manipulate powerstrands while he drove so traffic moved out of his way, allowing him unlimited access to the left hand passing lane, and no waiting at the toll booths, which he sailed through.

The storm he felt the day before continued to build in intensity. The clouds were low, hulking and the temperature dropped. It felt like the storm too was after them, chasing them through the countryside.

He exited the toll road, and turned the car off, breathing deeply for a few minutes before he removed the control band from around her wrists.

She blinked a few times, felt disorientation which comes from waking up in a strange room from a long, involved dream. Her mouth opened and Pierce understood her initial impulse was to scream. He respected that, even though he wished she wouldn't. They were not totally private where they were, and while he could deal with police, he would rather not.

Tentatively, because he was afraid of her reaction, Pierce reached out and touched her hand. "Are you all right? Would you just answer me that much?"

"All right? I don't know. Was there a rabbit hole or a stargate?"

"Darling, you're thinking along the right lines. I have explanations if you'd like to listen."

"I don't remember getting in the car. I have no idea where we are, or how we got here. And the last thing I remember was there were gunmen in the library."

"Ok, the five cent explanation is that I'm in trouble, and because of that, you are too. I had to move you, and move quickly, so I did something very akin to kidnapping."

"Very akin to kidnapping?" she asked. Her eyes were normal, darting around now studying the inside of the car as if it too had been transported through time and space. She reached up, touched the seatbelt as if it were the only thing keeping her from floating into the cosmos.

"Do you think you could drive? I'd like to put some miles between us and your library. I'd rather not be, physically, where they can find me if they start looking. And before you say anything, I'd like to apologize for what I did. I know that doesn't quite cover what happened, but I don't want anything to happen to the fetus."

"No one is touching this baby."

"I know. I will respect your wishes, and I promise, I will do whatever is in my power to keep you and the baby safe."

"What happened? Where am I?" Her voice, which had been dull, sharpened considerably. "Kidnapping? Is that what you said? I've been kidnapped?"

"CeeDee, please, I'm trying to explain. The child you carry is in danger. People I work for think it's mine."

"What gave them that idea?" She walked around the hood of the car and tightened the seatbelt. "I don't know where we're going."

"I'll give directions," he said, leaning as she took a corner tightly, barely missing an oncoming delivery van.

"Calm down a bit."

"You're bleeding."

"It's not bad, I promise. I'm putting some pressure on it."

"They're going to follow us, aren't they?"

"Yes, while I don't know who they are and what specifically they want, I know they've got a good idea where I'm going, so we've got to keep moving."

"What happened?"

If she were asking about the blood seeping through his pants due to a wound in his thigh, he chose to ignore that. "Last night, after I left the beach, some people I really trust for want of a better word, arrested me. They put me on trial and asked me two questions, if you were pregnant, and if I had made love to you. There was no time to explain that the 'yes' answers to both those questions were unrelated Now if I'm understanding this disaster, they want to strip my power, and take your baby."

"If there's anything I need to make very clear it's that no one is taking this baby. Now I'm not driving any further until I get some answers that make sense." She flipped the turn signal on, started to turn off onto the shoulder.

"CeeDee, I'm not your enemy. I'm trying to protect you. And we really need to keep moving."

She turned the turn signal off, and continued driving. "I want to go on record as saying I will not willingly, peacefully, or pleasantly go with you until I understand what's happening. Let's start with the basics, shall we?" Basics? Was she still breathing? Were the three laws of thermodynamics still functioning? Instead, she tried for a question a little more immediate. "Was everything you told me a lie?"

Pierce had trained as a lawyer, knew how to hide his emotions when a question or answer from a witness on the stand came out of left field. And he was expecting this one.

"Yes. Most of what I told you was a lie."

"For my own protection?" she asked snidely. "Or are you just such a pathological liar that you have less than a passing acquaintance with the truth?"

"I needed to meet you, and I needed to come across as non-threatening. The waitress at the diner told me I needed a crossword puzzle book. I don't know why, but I took it as a sign. After that it occurred to me I needed a reason to be holding the crossword puzzle book. I didn't think you'd start a conversation with a strange man at a bus stop about the transcendental nature of the universe. I don't know where the idea came from to act like I had financial problems, for I have never, and this I swear to you, tried it on any other woman."

"Why did you need to meet me? You seem quite certain of your verb."

"Yes. You're right. I didn't want to meet you so much as I needed to."

"Why?"

He took a deep breath, let it out slowly. "How are you at believing the impossible?"

"Impossible?" She hiked an eyebrow.

"All right, the unlikely, but from your point of view impossible might be the proper noun."

"Tell me your story. I already believed all of your lies. I'd like to try with what you consider truth."

She passed an SUV, leaving about three millimeters of clearance from the bumper. He didn't look at her, but his hands tightened on the bandage he held against his leg. "On October 19th I was shot in the chest three times. I don't remember being shot, but I was found in a back alley in Brooklyn and brought to an emergency room, where I have to say the paramedics and the surgeons were excellent, since obviously I'm still alive. I lost a lot of blood. Apparently it wasn't looking good. I've been told by my mother that during the surgery my heart stopped several times, for varying amounts of time. Here's the part you might have trouble accepting. The first thing I remember after getting shot, was I found myself in the top corner of the emergency room, looking down at my dead body."

"An out of body experience." While the disbelief still remained, some of the snark had disappeared from her tone.

"Yes."

"There is some corroborating evidence such things are possible."

"Trust me, it's possible. From that position I watched for a while. Actually it took me far longer than you'd think to realize the body they worked on was mine. I looked, for want of a better word, dead, and I didn't feel dead."

"And it freaked you out." There might have been the hint of compassion in her statement.

"Big time. So I decided to test my limits. Dead or nearly dead, I no longer knew what the rules were, so I went on a walkabout. I didn't walk through walls, or if I did, I certainly don't remember, but I found myself outside the hospital, in the rain. I didn't feel the rain, or smell it, nor could I feel myself walking, but I could move or travel, where I wanted to go. It was not a good part of town. Graffiti, boarded up buildings, that kind of thing, but I was fascinated and since I didn't feel the rain, I wasn't being inconvenienced, so I kept going. Then, for no reason I've been able to determine, I felt a strong pull in a direction. Since I didn't know where I was, and since as far as I was concerned one direction was as good as any other, I decided to follow what I felt could be considered a prompting."

"And?"

"And I saw you. I think it was you. I'm sure it was you. You're the only one who can tell me if it was."

"What was I doing?" She had gone bloodless, and her hands tightened on the steering wheel, as if she needed to hold onto something.

"You were talking to some creep in a Jag. He wanted you to have an abortion and he wasn't going to pay for it. You wore a raincoat with the hood up, he stayed in the car. I didn't see any faces."

"You were watching us?"

"I was dead! I wasn't spying deliberately or anything subversive like that. I was thinking all kinds of confused things, like how I would react if some woman I had only known for a one night stand dropped that kind of bombshell on me—"

"It was more than a one night stand," she defended.

"I'm not saying it wasn't. I am not trying to judge you at all. I'm trying to show that my feelings were confused, certainly unreliable, and I couldn't see your faces. I couldn't pummel him, which I wanted to, for not even offering you a chance to get out of the rain. Almost immediately after I felt a strong pull back to my body, and the next thing I know I was hooked up to all kinds of life-support and my mother, who lives in Washington DC, was at my bedside weeping. If you knew my mother you'd find it far more likely that I had an out of body experience than the fact that she would be crying at my bedside."

"And?"

"And I recovered. I've got the scar. I can show you again, although you did notice when—"

"Yes, I remember," she said, cutting him off. "So then you found me?"

"Not for a week or so. Frankly I didn't remember, put it down to drug reactions or oxygen deprivation or something along those lines, when I realized I wanted to find you, convince you that creep had no right to tell you to have an abortion, and get his name from you so I could beat him into next Thursday. You looked like too nice a lady to put up with him."

"He does need to be beaten to a bloody pulp, but I've decided I'm going to do it myself." She smirked. "I bought a baseball bat. I told myself it was to teach junior here the things needed for Little League, but if I ever meet the creep in the car again, I'm going to use it on his headlights, his knee caps, and probably his skull."

Pierce laughed. "You should let me. I can do it without leaving a trace."

"Without a trace, like those things those guys were shooting at us."

"Yes."

"I believe that. How did you find me? Wait, before you tell me that, tell me where we're going."

"Our eventual goal is New York."

"What's there?"

"Answers, I hope. There's a dragon and a dead witch and a whole slew of missing powerstrands, and once there was a gargoyle, but I doubt he fits into this crisis."

She started ticking off on her fingers. "A dragon, a dead witch, a gargoyle, obviously a wizard or two."

"Yes, lots of wizards."

She rolled her eyes and started to smirk. "And no vampire?"

"Not yet, but the quest is still in its early stages."

"Fair enough. So eventually we're going to New York. But where to now?"

"My home. There's some things I'd rather those guys from the library and whoever they're working for didn't find. And I've got some spells to stop the bleeding."

"Fair enough. We're almost to Boston."

"A few more minutes. I'll tell you when to turn."

"How did you find me? After the rain and being dead and all, or I suppose even at the library this morning. I never told you where I work."

"I have ways to find things, rather involved, arcane ways, but when I started looking for you after I was shot, I only knew you were not in Brooklyn and but were somehow south of me."

"South of Brooklyn?"

"I believe I mentioned I live in Boston."

"So you said. And the house where we planted bulbs?"

"Bought so I could have a place to plant the bulbs. I might sell it eventually, but I rather like it so I'm holding onto it."

"The vampire can use it."

"If he wants, I'll offer it. I suppose you like vampires?"

"Well in fiction, I have to say a great deal of them are really sexy."

"And how do you feel about wizards?"

"I don't know a lot about them, except the obvious, "Don't pay any attention to the man behind the curtain," type of thing."

"That's our reputation as a fraud, while the vampires get all the attractive women. And we won't even take a drop of your blood."

"Knowing nothing about wizards, I'd say you don't look like you have any trouble attracting dates."

"I do ok. And to set the record straight, you might be untrained, but you're certainly a wizard yourself."

"The mark?" she said, rubbing her left thumb over the mark on the inside of her right wrist.

"Mark of the mageborn. And this is important, it doesn't show until you have accessed your power. You don't have to be trained, but as soon as you start to use magic it appears. So have you been using magic?"

"Maybe." She looked out the windshield, watching the scenery pass. "Does this thing fly?"

"The car?"

"Yeah."

"It could I suppose. I've never tried because the invisibility spells are a bear and at this point it's far easier to drive. A practicing wizard can tell when another wizard is around when lots of magic is used and I'd rather not be easily discovered. I'm using some magic, but not a lot, hopefully not enough to start alarms ringing for those who are looking for us."

"Can we stop?"

"Restroom?"

"No, actually I'm starving."

"I'll get you something to eat. Can you eat and drive?"

"At this pace?"

"At the speed limit, if you wish."

"I'll manage."

"Good. Pull over for a minute." She pulled off onto the shoulder, and he did something by the fuel tank.

"What is that brown thing?"

"What brown thing?"

"Don't play stupid with me. You were shoving a brownish thing into the gas tank."

"You could see that?"

"Well, duh."

"Do you see any more?"

She waited until he got in the passenger seat and locked his seat belt. She flipped her left turn signal on and accelerated, merging back onto the highway. "Right now?"

"Yeah."

"No."

"Have you ever seen a powerstrand before?"

"If that's what it's called, yes. You worked a bunch of them yesterday at the picnic. Brown ones and green ones, and well a bunch of colors."

"Why didn't you say anything?"

"Before we get to that, the gas tank is full. It had to be nearing empty."

"The powerstrand I used was converted to gas."

"Neat trick. And I saw you shooting powerstrands at those two guys at the library."

"But you didn't see them shooting them?"

"No. I assumed it was something like that. Why could I see you and not them using your magic?"

"I don't know. Now answer the question, how long have you been able to see powerstrands?"

"The guy I dated before you could manipulate them, if that's the right verb. I would see him touch them off and on. Then when you did it, I was beginning to think this was some great big conspiracy I knew nothing about."

"Did you tell the guy you dated you could see them?"

"Of course. He got rather weird about it, then told me he was married and dropped me flat."

"And just so we're on the same page, did he drive a Jaguar?"

"Well, yes. That whole rain thing happened the way you said it did. But I didn't see you then."

"It's good to get that corroboration, anyway. And I was probably invisible. I don't know, as they say, I'd never been dead before. You said you were hungry. What would you like?"

"You mean like Chinese, Italian, that kind of thing?"

"No, specifically, what are you hungry for?"

She thought for a minute, her eyes darting back and forth as she considered options. A wide grin slashed across her face. "Foot long chili dog, steaming hot onion rings, and a thick strawberry milk shake."

"Junk food? I wouldn't have pegged you for a junk food addict."

She shrugged, did what any normal healthy pregnant woman with a craving did: passed the buck. "The baby likes junk food."

"Junk food it is. Keep driving."

"You're doing something with your hands again."

"What do you see?"

"You've got a blue one, although I suppose it's more turquoise."

"All powerstrands can be changed into something else. Think of them as unformed raw materials that can literally be anything. Having said that, each color has a strength, something that it is easier to transform into. Some are better at healing, for example, and this turquoise one is readily transformed into biofuel."

"Biofuel?"

"Foot long chili dogs, strawberry milkshakes, sinfully delicious onion rings."

"I should have asked for steak."

"Yeah, but it's hard to eat steak and drive a car."

She concentrated on traffic, which had grown heavy, and turned her head when intense and seductive aromas had her turning her head. "I," she started. "Um—" she finished.

"Takes a while to get used to it."

"No, I think I'm not going to have any trouble getting used to this. Make my day and tell me they have no calories, no fat grams."

"Sorry. I make them as close to the real thing. If they had no calories and no fat grams, I'd have made you celery."

"Mercy, just when I thought I could like this magic."

# CHAPTER 14

He handed her an onion ring, hot enough it burned her fingers and she grinned with unabashed delight as she chewed then swallowed. "Gosh, I haven't had an onion ring in years. Are they always this good?"

"Mine are," he answered with a grin.

"They even come with paper plates?"

"Not much difference between making food and making paper plates. I had to experiment a lot, mostly in college. I got quite adept at making junk food. You should try my pizza."

She struggled, basically holding the steering wheel steady with her knees while she lifted the chili dog and took a bite.

"I didn't ask if you wanted onions."

"Not without breath mints, and I'd hate to put you to all the trouble. Pierce, this stuff is healthy, isn't it?"

"If you wanted healthy—"

"No, I mean it won't hurt the baby. That I will be able to digest it, to use it for energy. That it's not radioactive or poisonous or cause us to glow in the dark, something like that."

"It's as healthy as a chili dog and a strawberry milkshake can be." He took a long pull on the straw of the second milkshake. It was thick enough that he knotted his hands again, came back with to plastic spoons. "Funny, I haven't had a strawberry milkshake probably since I was six or seven, and now this is the second one I've had in about two weeks." He grew hungry for bean soup, decided the chili dog and onion rings made an acceptable substitute.

"We're getting off here," he said, indicating an exit ramp.

"Can you teach me to do that?"

"Make food?" With her nod, he continued. "Yes, that and more. I don't want to leave you defenseless, and until we get this mess straightened out, you're going to be in danger. You're a mage, CeeDee. As long as that mark on your wrist really isn't a tattoo, you can be taught."

"And you can teach me?"

"It's not easy, but yes. I'll be breaking about a dozen of the sacred covenants I've made, but it's my opinion that keeping you and your baby safe take priority over just about anything."

"So what are you doing now?"

"I don't know what we're going to find when we get where we're going. It could be a trap, and the odds are it's going to be dangerous. I'd like to look but I can't. It leaves too many telltales, and as much as possible I'd like to arrive unannounced."

"Look?"

"I can see specific things I'm interested in, equivalent to a closed circuit camera."

"Without being dead."

"Without being dead."

"Did that out of body experience while you were dead have anything to do with you being a wizard?"

"I don't think so. If it did, I'd think someone would have mentioned it to me. No, I can astral travel when I want, and actually I do quite often. It's dangerous, and not something I can do in a moving car."

"But that makes noise too."

"Yes. You're learning."

"Anything you can teach me while I'm driving?"

"Let me see." He found a strand, a thin pink one. "I'd rather a green one, but this one will do." He held it out to her.

"Can you feel it?"

She pulled one hand off the steering wheel. Before she could prepare to concentrate, she grinned radiantly. "Yes."

"What do you feel?"

"Almost soft like fur. Silky, I suppose. It feels, I'm not quite sure I know how to put this into words, but it feels addictive, like it's so wonderful I want to roll around on it."

"Yes. I'm sure I felt exactly that way when I first felt a powerstrand. And in case I haven't mentioned this before, you're amazing. I was almost six years into my apprenticeship by the time I could do what you just did. Are you sure no one's been teaching you?"

"I'm sure." She pet it again, like a cat, realized it had no nap, no right direction to stroke. "It wiggles."

"Yes."

"It feels alive."

"Yes, but don't make the mistake of thinking they are. Take this car for example. It moves, it can make noise to keep you company and it can keep you warm or cool and safe, and it's comfortable, but it's a tool. Something that can be used. Personalize powerstrands all you like, I promise you they're not alive." He thought of the ones that had bowed to him, conveying honor, and the ones that slept, nestled together on his robe or other clothing, and wondered if his master had lied to him, and if he were lying to her. "They seem very life-like, but if they're alive, it's not the type of biology scientists recognize."

He released the strand he had been holding, but instead of vanishing, it coiled up her arm, undulating, snake-like until it rested around her shoulders. CeeDee rolled her head, appreciating this living wrap. "Am I being foolish to think they're alive?"

"My master would say yes, and yell about anthropomorphism, but I want you to know, against all current instruction, I believe you. I think they're alive too." He leaned back in the seat, crossed his feet at the ankles, considered what he had just confessed. He had planned on teaching her, but it seemed it was a two way street. He was learning as well.

"I like the feel of it."

"That's a great start. They're not always this accommodating and not all of them are soft or care to be touched for that matter, but more than anyone I've ever seen, you have an affinity for powerstrands."

"It's almost, and I hate to use this word because it's not quite what I mean, but it's almost sexual, isn't it?"

Sexual. Another aspect of his craft she might have taught him and made a silent vow never to mention that to Drollard. He may have earned his robe, but he'd rather not annoy his master any more than he already had.

Pierce cleared his throat, realized his body was responding to the word on a level that had nothing to do with practicing the tenets of his craft. This would be a really good time to change the subject, or the people seeking them would have no trouble finding them.

"On many levels the working of powerstrands can be considered sexual, but for now, while I have to keep my hands off you, let's call it sensual, meaning, involving all senses."

"It's getting warm in here, isn't it?" she said, fanning her face dramatically and he roared with laughter.

"I'd love to learn more. These things must have incredible applications in almost every area of life. Mercy, if you were actually having money problems, just that little trick with the gas tank would save you hundreds. And the fact that you don't have to buy food—"

He held a hand out, stopped her before she could continue. "Magic comes in handy, but this is an important lesson. Magic should never be used casually or simply for convenience. We're running, so I made food, but I never make food in my normal life."

"It would make too much noise?"

He shrugged, pleased she was adopting the terminology readily. "That kind of noise wouldn't bother anyone, but wizards have to keep a low profile. I have to be seen buying groceries or eating dinner out. I have to put gas in my car like everyone else or people will ask what my secret is."

"And there're too many people you don't want to know what your secret is."

"Right. Believe it or not, the ability to manipulate powerstrands is rare. I know at this point you're probably thinking almost anyone can do it, you can, I can, the guy you dated, the two goons in the library."

"That does seem to indicate a large population."

"On the whole, there probably aren't a thousand wizards practicing in the United States. We tend to die early and not have a lot of children. Add another five hundred or so witches, and you can see, you're odds of running across any of us isn't good."

"Just lucky I guess."

Lucky. His body was interested in getting lucky. He really was going to have to find a cold shower soon. "Slow down, we're turning at the light, and take the next three rights. We're almost where we're going. Ah, here's a red one." Pierce grasped at the powerstrand. As soon as he held it she could see it. "Here's the next lesson after being able to feel a powerstrand. Can you access their power? I know this isn't fair to make you do while you're driving, so I won't hold it against you if you can't concentrate enough to succeed. Really, this should be done in some basement lair where there are no other interruptions and when you can focus."

"Tell me what you want me to do. I'm excited to try." She grinned, looked devious. "And I will get your pizza recipe you know."

"I'm sure. Hold this one, CeeDee, and I want you to make it warmer in here. Imagine it warmer, and try to communicate with the powerstrand what you want."

"No magic phrases?"

"No. Witches use magic phrases. If it makes you feel better you can recite Shakespeare or Latin, or make up haikus but it's your mind and the powerstrand that's going to do all the work."

Although she didn't close her eyes, he could see by the set of her jaw how intensely she concentrated. "Stop, CeeDee, we're roasting in here." She released the powerstrand, and Pierce pushed a button to roll down the window. "You seem to be a natural."

"I was concentrating as hard as I could, but I assure you, I was not imagining a 350 degree oven."

"Ok, so it looks like you won't have any problem accessing their power. In case you're wondering you just shaved about five years off your apprenticeship."

"I'm better than you."

"I'd guess more powerful, since this is coming so naturally to you and I had a miserable time mastering the fundamentals, but let's save the ranking words for another time."

"You don't like me to be better than you are?"

"It's the word I have problems with. If you pick magic up easily, that doesn't make you better. More sensitive perhaps, more in tune with the magic, definitely. No. I don't like the word better."

"Any more instructions?"

"You're ready for another powerstrand?"

"No. I've finished your instructions." The car slowed down. They were in a residential area, the houses huge, well removed from the road.

"Good. Pull over anywhere around here. Since I'm expecting a welcoming committee, I don't want to park in my driveway. My house is that one," he said pointing to a three story mansion complete with gables and gingerbread.

"Historic registry?" she asked, trying not to be impressed.

"No. Not that old or famous."

She stepped from the car, refusing his hand and the psychological help he offered. Dizziness swamped her, and she swayed, holding onto the hood to prevent from falling.

"I've pushed you too far, too fast."

"Is this an expected outcome?"

"Yes and no. I don't feel residuals anymore, but as an apprentice I did. Working powerstrands is second nature to me now. I'd forgotten how it can leave you disoriented. And the fact you're pregnant, and the shock we had earlier today in the library, it's no wonder you're dizzy."

She clutched her stomach. "The baby."

"I promise it's alright. Nothing we did could affect it. I'll check if you want, but I'd rather get inside."

"Thanks. If it doesn't make me sound too needy, I'd like you to check."

"No problem. This is where I live. There are some things we're going to need. Give me five seconds to get some things from my lair, then I can take you somewhere where we both can be safe. Once we're safe, you and me and your child, I promise you explanations. I know you need them, and more than that, you deserve them. Come with me."

Funny, in all that, the only thing that registered was what made the least sense. She looked over the wide expanse of lawn, which, even this late in the season she could tell was professionally manicured. Each bush trimmed precisely, and the flowerbeds were mulched and put to bed for the winter. From there she looked up the four white pillars, the brick façade, the manor which would need more than a single housekeeper to control dust. "That is your house?"

"Yes."

"Then can I say I'm not disappointed you not an impoverished lawyer having trouble with the IRS?"

He exhaled slowly, breathing out a long stream of breath which drained emotions from him. "I told you I needed to meet you."

"Because you were dead."

"Yes."

"Well, you're not now."

"I don't have all the answers yet. Now, I'm going to transfer us inside."

"With a powerstrand."

"Yes, you did it yourself at the beach. I'm going to hold this one, and concentrate, and because I'll be holding you, you can come too. Ok?"

"Ok."

She expected something, an additional wave of dizziness or the feel of wind in her hair or a sensation of squeezing down a rabbit hole, but none of that happened. When she opened her eyes, she was clearly inside. "I was rather stunned when I did this myself."

"I can imagine."

"Now the baby."

"Yes." He pulled a powerstrand, placed it over her. "Everything looks fine."

The powerstrand vanished as soon as he released it, but while the baby had always been real to her, now she felt a fresh wash of possessiveness. "You said Rose Aurora is in danger?"

"The baby?" When she nodded, he said, "I don't have all the facts, but it looks to me like either you or Rose is on someone's hit list. If it were just me they were after, I think they'd attack from another direction. They wouldn't have been waiting at the library, for example, for how would they know I'd go there? Something's happened you're involved with, and I believe it has to do with what I'm involved with. Right now, you and Rose are the victims, and we need answers."

"It's a coincidence that you came into my life?"

"I'm not a big believer in coincidences for any number of reasons. But maybe something or someone wanted me involved with you."

"The universe?"

"As valid an explanation as any, at this point." He shrugged, then took her hand, wrapping her chilled fingers in his warm ones, offering comfort and protection. "We don't have enough facts to narrow down possibilities. It might be I wasn't supposed to get involved, but I did. Or it could be they're only after me, and you're involved as a result. Somehow they anticipated I'd go to the library. I don't know. I promise I'll tell you everything as soon as I get some answers."

"And the answers are in New York with the dragon."

"That's what I'm assuming, although just because upstate New York is where I'm being led, I still can't be certain of anything until I get there."

"Pierce, will you answer one question?"

"Sure."

"If you were me, would you believe anything you're saying?"

His look turned compassionate and he released her fingers, as if he wanted to hold her, but dropped his hand before he touched her. "You know what I'm saying is true. You saw me manipulate the powerstrands. I put gas in the car and made you food. You used power to transfer from the beach to your home. You can feel them, use them. None of that is deception."

"Yes. But there have been so many lies."

"We'll straighten them out, but right now I need you to trust me." He moved quickly through the foyer and she followed. "The stories I told you about Woof! and breaking my legs were true. Everything I felt when I was touching you, everything I said then, was true. I am a lawyer, but that's only part of what I am." He took her hand and pulled her gently, inexorably toward a door. "Ten minutes. Can you wait ten minutes to get your explanations?"

"I'm setting my watch."

"Good. This way," he said. "At the moment I don't have time to be subtle. You'll be safe here, in the hall, if you'd rather not follow me."

"And will I be safe if I follow you?"

He paused, met her eyes, then realized for whatever reason, he couldn't keep his hands off her, so he touched her, rubbing her lightly between her shoulders and her elbows. Safe? Is that what they were talking about? Her scent of coconut and fear and courage clouded his brain, making him feel far more out of control than he ever had.

Pierce kissed her lightly on the nose. "Yes, you'll be safe, I promise, but you might be uncomfortable."

Then miraculously, the gentle kiss changed as his lips met hers.

# CHAPTER 15

CeeDee felt her eyes grow wide, but it wasn't his wealth or lies that had her pulse tripping, had her breath hitching. It was his kiss. His lips were gentle, insistent, invasive. They captured hers as one of his hands cupped her neck the other dug into her hair. His tongue made a foray into her mouth and she matched him, feeding on his passion and his fever.

Her breath became ragged. She could no longer think. She could only want. Her hands were busy, stroking his seductive, muscular back, cupping his firm buttocks. She tried desperately to keep away from his buttons, from his zipper. All evidence to the contrary, she wasn't that kind of girl.

She didn't believe in love at first sight. Couldn't. She was too much a scientist, had too much respect for taking things in proper order, dating to get to know each other better, sharing plans, hopes and dreams while waiting for the Mets to win the National League East, which meant these things took time. But he sat at her bench on what might have been the lowest part of her life and made her laugh and made her realize life was worth living, and without ever noticing when, she had fallen in love.

She didn't understand love. How could she, when so far except for a quiet interlude on a Rhode Island beach it was nothing at all like she anticipated. But love, whatever it was, had invaded her system. She had it bad.

Safety didn't mean as much to her at that second as getting answers to her questions and being near him. Yeah, that was it. The arrows of hell could shoot all around them and the only thing that mattered to her was feeding off his kisses, tasting the salt of his skin, feeling the subtle abrasion of his beard coming in at his neck. Based on that logic, she supposed it was a very good thing Pierce had not kissed her in the library when bullets, or whatever they were, were shattering all around them.

She could see the future, sharing their life together, through good times and bad, raising one child together or perhaps several, with a trampoline in the backyard and one of those elaborate swings-slides-fort play structures beside it. They would have a dog, probably a rescue golden lab to chase Frisbees and go on adventures with, and definitely at least one cat. She'd insist on a cat. He wouldn't put up a fight. It seemed in fiction the wizards always had a cat.

His kisses continued. He had the top three buttons of her blouse undone and was kissing the sensitive, exposed skin of her breasts above her serviceable white bra. She grew embarrassed. No woman liked a man to see her in a plain bra when there were so many other seductive options, but he found her nipple and she moaned her pleasure. That begged the question: did his interest mean he'd be willing to accept another man's child? But then he knew about Rose and it hadn't seemed to bother him.

"Whatever happens," she said, wishing her voice didn't sound so breathless, and hoping she wasn't going to do something as embarrassing as blush again, "we're in this together."

"Together," he said, looking up, taking the time for his eyes to focus, his breathing to regulate. "Sorry. Carried away. In case you're wondering, there's something—"

She wouldn't let him finish. "Something. Yeah, that's what it is. But aren't we in a hurry?"

Obviously he had a lot of practice, for he buttoned her blouse with speed and efficiency, then he squeezed her hand. "There will be a time for us, CeeDee. I guarantee it."

"Time for us. I like the sound of that."

Just like that, the kiss was over, but it felt as if there were invisible powerstrands between them, knotting, no, knitting them together, two pieces of the same whole. Pierce pulled her forward and as she moved, her gaze darted into all the high corners and the low places of his foyer. She didn't want to look at him or meet his gaze, for fear what she was feeling was written all over her face. She hoped to keep her four-letter secret a little while longer, especially since she couldn't trust him to discuss her love, so how could she expect him to feel the same?

"Old family money," he muttered, as if in explanation, and she supposed it was. "I'd be happy with a one room condo or a loft somewhere, but my mother is all about appearances. She seems to think it helps my father, and maybe it does. Besides, I needed the lair. I like having a convenient place to work."

He had a lair. Like the bat cave, she decided. Tickled by the imagery, CeeDee asked, "Does your butler call you master?"

"Anyone who knows I'm a wizard calls me Master. I've earned my robe." He kept moving, limping a bit due to the wound she had all but forgotten about. "But I don't have a butler. There's a cleaning service that comes in. I don't know how often and I don't think I've ever seen them. Does that count?"

She had no idea if it did or not. With him too many things were not adding up to any solution.

This is where he lived. There had to be answers here involving powerstrands that could be turned into hot dogs and high octane gasoline and a man who could kiss her senseless one minute and make her so mad she could spit the next. She planted her feet and stopped rock solid, as if she couldn't move another inch.

"You're still upset I bound you?"

"I'll give you the benefit of the doubt on that one, since obviously we were in danger and you got hurt protecting me." She lowered her gaze, past his hips to his upper thigh where the pants were ripped and stained.

Blood continued to drip from the open wound, but other than a slight limp, it did not seem to bother him. She started moving, but he turned abruptly, so that she gently bumped into him, her breasts rubbing against his chest, her hands reaching out to his arms.

"I promise you I'll never bind you again. By all the tenets I believe in and hold sacred, it was a misuse of power, but I was worried and it was the only way I could keep you safe." He turned, as if to continue through his mausoleum of a home. "And if you'd like to know, I've never done that before, except in training exercises to learn the technique. CeeDee, I don't like to admit this, but I was scared out of my mind for you."

"Pierce—"

He rested his index finger against her lips, and quirked his head. "I know. Trust has to be earned. As you learn more about what we're involved in, I hope you'll learn to trust me."

When he removed his finger, it left her aching. She wanted to kiss it, and more than that, bring his index finger into her mouth, suck it, let it dance around her tongue, showing what even the most casual of his touches did to her. His kiss, if that explosion of emotion could be called something as innocuous as a simple kiss, had left her edgy. Instead she thought of a cold shower, and consciously regulated her breathing.

"I do trust you. I'm following you." She grinned, looked impish. "I suppose here is where you keep your copy of Mud, Muggings and Mayhem?"

It took him a second to catch the reference, an imaginary book he used to describe his reading habits when he was trying to convince her he was having IRS troubles. "God, yes, but it's in the bedroom, and since we have to get out of here, I'd say we'll have to save that for another time."

Dare she be brave? Dare she say, "I'd love to see your bedroom?" Before she could, he darted into an office off the foyer.

"Security system."

CeeDee shook her head, glad she hadn't made that classic blunder and asked for more intimacy than he was willing to provide at the moment. "Don't your magic powerstrands act as security?"

"Of course, but in this neighborhood if I didn't have a security system, the neighbors would wonder." He typed some commands into a computer keyboard and panoramic views of the property appeared.

"Five, no six of them waiting for us."

She saw them, men too focused on his house to be anything but assassins. "Then they didn't see us pop in."

"Apparently not. I can't believe they are all wizards. Most must be hired muscle to drive us toward the wizards."

"Very likely," she said. "They've found the car."

"Then they know we're here." He watched as one by one they touched their ears, apparently receiving new information through some wireless device. "Look, yes, they're going to break in. I've got some nasty surprises for them but it won't keep them occupied for long. We've got to get moving."

"Let's go."

Taking her hand, Pierce started for the kitchen. "This way."

Behind them, thunder rumbled, angry and invasive, loud enough for her to could feel in the soles of her feet. This storm had been building for a long time. She felt it yesterday while waiting on a bench, and while walking in the foamy serf of high tide.

Beside her he shivered, as if remembering another time he could not share with her. "On the bright side, if they try to break in, getting wet is going to be the least of their worries."

As they passed the opening to a formal dining room, she noticed horizontal rain, fed by a ferocious Nor'easter, freezing on contact. Wherever they were going, CeeDee knew, it was going to be tough driving through a good old fashioned New England sleet storm. She hoped he wouldn't ask her to drive again.

She caught a glimpse of a cherry wood dining table which looked like it could seat twenty, and flowers standing tall in vase centerpiece were real: showy carnations, mums, lilies, wrapped in orange and yellows, late fall colors. Thanksgiving was in two weeks. She wondered where they would be by then, how things would turn out. Again she debated if she would have liked him better if he had been the impoverished lawyer with IRS problems. He seemed somehow more human with that vulnerability, and decided to table that internal debate for later.

On a sideboard she saw what appeared to be a silver candelabra and above the table a sparkling crystal chandelier. The artwork displayed on the walls looked like it would be more appropriate at the Louvre. He tugged, preventing her from dawdling and CeeDee passed several other doors, she had no idea where they went, until he took her into a sparkling, ultramodern, large kitchen. The appliances were all gleaming stainless steel, with copper bottom pots hanging from rafters and she heard the muted hum from a refrigerator big enough to walk in. She would have stopped and gawked, but he pulled her along.

"I don't use the kitchen much," he said, passing through. "I'm not much of a cook, at least not on a stove, and I only entertain here when I can't possibly get out of it."

There were appliances on the counters, the ubiquitous toaster, coffee maker, although that was something space-aged, and probably did all kinds of things like grind beans and froth milk. For all she knew it could lift-off and orbit the Earth. She also recognized pasta makers and bread machines, and perhaps ten other gadgets that she would recognize if she had the time. It would be, she decided, the perfect place to cook for a king, should one ever find himself in Boston. And she decided, on a fit of whimsy, should they marry, they wouldn't have to worry about registering for wedding gifts.

Then, as if the house and the kitchen wasn't miraculous enough, Pierce walked up to a solid wall and waved his arms again, and although he used small controlled motions there wasn't even the vestige of subtlety about them. CeeDee watched blue powerstrands separate, and the seams of a door appear. It occurred to her that she was having a lot less trouble seeing his powerstrands. "Neat trick that."

"Not a trick," Pierce said, not bothering to turn around. "If you've got anything mechanical on you, I suggest you leave it here." He held out a small stone box and placed his own watch, his own phone inside.

"Why?"

"Another facet of magic. Where there is a high concentration of powerstrands, mechanical things don't work. I think," he laughed, finger-combed his hair and looked boyish, "I used to think," he corrected, "the powerstrands were jealous. I thought they couldn't stand anything mechanical, anything that worked with a different powersource than they would provide."

"Jealous powerstrands."

"They're not sentient. Don't make the mistake of thinking they are. But if you've got a cell phone, pager, watch, anything along those lines put them here. We'll take this with us."

"Obviously wizards with pacemakers don't do well."

"A wizard who needed a pacemaker would have other options. I'll show you when we get upstairs."

CeeDee considered his words. Did she trust him enough to turn over her phone and her tablet both of which could be considered lifelines?

She tightened her grasp on her purse. "I'll be fine."

"It's your call. But the powerstrands in my lair—"

She wouldn't let him finish. "I know, they're jealous."

His laughter rang around them as he hopped up the narrow stairs, two at a time, in almost complete darkness. About half way up, CeeDee saw a flash coming from the opening of her purse, and heard a large pop. "Cell phone?" he asked.

She rooted through her bag, pulled out two twisted masses of plastics formerly her electronics. "Your explanation better be darn good."

He grinned, shrugged. "It will be unbelievable."

Reaching the top, Pierce waved his hands again, although this time there was a clearly defined door. CeeDee watched the strands separate for him.

"Security?"

"Works most of the time. On the whole, wizards are secretive. Sometimes I think paranoid, other times I think well prepared. I'll reset them. No matter how good those idiots following us are, no non-adept could possibly get up here."

She thought of her exploded cell phone and of a fetus she had witnessed sleeping contentedly deep inside her. "Can you teach me to do that? My life is sort of in flux at the moment and I'd like to be well prepared as well."

He looked over his shoulder, back at her standing several steps below him, a shank of dark hair covering one eye. "The answer to that will come with the explanation. And yes. I could teach you. Whether or not I should will depend on any number of things."

Indignation made the small hairs on the nape of her neck stand on end. "You don't think I can learn? Haven't I proved my affinity?"

He turned back, he was almost completely through the door into his lair and he exhaled like she was holding him back, and he didn't have time for lengthy explanations. "No, exactly the opposite."

While it could be argued that modern women occasionally needed men, they didn't have to like them. "You don't want to teach me because I can learn? Is that what you said?"

She could recognize the look: he wanted to get whatever he came for and get out, but again he paused. Without knowing what he had to say, she felt this was the kindest thing he'd ever done for her, giving her his time and attention when other things pressured him

"The relationship between a master and a student is not easy. It's not supposed to be friendly and learning to be a wizard is excruciating on any number of levels. I don't know if I'm willing to sacrifice what we are building together as a couple to teach you. At this point, I'd rather you went to another master, and fought with and learned from him, and came back to me every evening so we could be develop what's here. CeeDee, our relationship is confusing right now. What we have is new, exciting, and it really might be something we could share over the next five decades, but it's too soon to know. You've got too many questions to make a commitment, and I've got too many powerstrands going off in different directions to take the time an affair needs."

She asked the only question she could. "Affair?"

"I'm sorry. I didn't mean it the way it sounded. Right now I want an affair with you, and if I'm being honest with myself, I am thinking about the next step beyond that, a lifetime commitment." He pulled her down beside him as he sat on the floor, his feet still on the stairs. Pierce entwined his fingers with hers, raised them to his lips and kissed her gently, once, on her knuckles.

"I always thought when I found a woman to marry, I would keep her in the dark about my vocation. I never planned for her to be a part of this world of wizards and dragons and the battle between good and evil. I thought when I returned home to her every night, whoever she was, I would leave the robe and all it entails behind me, and raise our children and share her bed without ever sharing what is most important to me."

He stopped speaking, and the house was silent, no hum from a refrigerator, no gentle purr from an efficient heating system, no bleeping reminders from cell phones. The earlier thunder had traveled north with the brunt of the storm, she knew that intuitively, and the sleet was falling thick, heavy and deadly all around them.

"CeeDee, I don't have all the answers, and right now I don't know what I want, except to say I want you and that little secret you're hiding in your womb in my life. I want you to know about wizards so you become one, and more, I want you to be a partner with me in magic, an equal.

When I put on the robe, here, or wherever we settle, I want to know you're with me."

# CHAPTER 16

Before she could respond, Pierce continued. "You haven't been tested. You have no training, but I don't think I'm going too far out on a limb in saying I believe you have the potential to be an extremely powerful wizard. Whoever teaches you, me or someone else, even if we can't make a relationship work for whatever reason, I sincerely want that for you."

What he was saying should have been hard for her to hear, but instead his words fit inside her, making her whole. Always it seemed there had been something missing, something she was never able to put her finger on, and for a while she thought Rose would be the one to help her find completion, but while Rose would be a part of it, CeeDee wanted the full pot of gold. She wanted Pierce, magic and to understand the arcane secrets of the universe so she could be a wife and a partner. Love, she thought, had to be far more powerful than magic.

She nodded, digesting his words with her emotions. "So, are you going to show me your lair?"

He stood, pulled her to her feet. "You should be flattered. Once a wizard gets a robe, that means graduates to practice on his own, he rarely allows another wizard anywhere near his lair."

She nodded sagely. "So, this is where the bodies are buried?"

Pierce rolled his eyes. "No actual bodies are buried here. Well, except for the moose."

Hanging above the fireplace hung a bull moose head, it's rack probably seven feet across. "It's a rather impressive moose. I suppose there's a story behind it, or is it a mascot, that all wizards have to worship the great and powerful Bullwinkle?"

"No, there's a story. One day when time doesn't pressure us so, I'd be glad to tell you. Except for my master, no one else knows, and even he might not have all the finer details, not that he couldn't ferret them out if he wanted to."

"We'll save the moose story for later."

The attic was large, ran the entire length of the house. While he went to a desk, started doing something with powerstrands, CeeDee looked around. The floor was flagstone, the walls, round river stone, which looked like they had been hand mortared. Along the far wall stood a broad fireplace, and although no flames burned there now, she could tell from the soot and the scarring along the back that Pierce frequently built a fire there. The fireplace was large enough to walk under, and, true-to-form, a large black caldron, rested deep within. Ahh, so the flames were not strictly for ambiance.

CeeDee started mumbling "Double, double, toil and trouble," under her breath, but apparently not silently enough, for he laughed.

"Yeah, you're thinking witches, and that's not what I am. Not what you are."

"What you are remains to be seen," she said. "And remember now that you said I'm not a witch. I understand pregnant women often get hormonal, and their partners often think less than complementary thoughts about them."

"You're not a witch. But I'll introduce you to one, probably tomorrow, depending on how our escape goes."

"I can't wait." The look he returned her was quizzical, but also, she was certain, held more than grudging respect. He approved of her response.

He wrapped a woven mass of different colored powerstrands around his thigh, and she could see how much the wound must have been hurting him, because his face relaxed. Whatever that powerstrand was, it was healing. Then, still wearing his glowing bandage, Pierce darted forward, quickly moving papers and arcane items, the origin of which she couldn't possibly guess. She stepped in, her low heels making clopping sounds against the stone. "So you are not a witch, warlock, or whatever the politically correct term is these days."

"What you need to know is I'm a wizard or sorcerer, or mage. If you want to be a stickler, those three terms have slightly different definitions, and some of us prefer to be associated with one over the others, but that's just terminology."

"For real?"

"For real."

"And the tattoo has something to do with it?"

"Wizardry has something to do with the birthmark. And the guy who gave you that," he inclined his head toward her stomach, and she didn't misunderstand, "was a wizard too."

She breathed in, a mix of scents, not quite banana bread and latte, but not the stench of raw blood and burned flesh either, which, she realized, she had been more than half afraid to discover. Herbs, she thought, incense. Somehow it was both frightening and reassuring that magic existed, a juxtaposition which had her wondering if emotionally she were leaning to one extreme or the other. She should be terrified, or at least queasy about what she was witnessing, but she suspected those emotions would come later. Now, perhaps, the only thing she felt was shock. She rubbed her stomach, spoke to the life there she hadn't yet felt move. "So, what do you think of this? Kinda weird, isn't it?"

She reached out, touched the moose head. It was real, the texture of the fur surprisingly coarse. She was used to petting cats, or large stuffed bears dressed in lace. No wonder they made fur coats out of mink. As odd as it was, it was one of the least odd things about the room. What had he called it, a lair?

He was busy doing something she couldn't see, taking papers and what looked like ancient books, tomes, and shoving them through the solid rock of the walls.

"I think I'd better sit," she mumbled, but couldn't find a chair. The room was starting to spin, and while it wouldn't have surprised her if the room was indeed spinning, she knew the dizziness was her own, her body adjusting to the pregnancy. The shock of this whole scenario wasn't helping much either.

He picked up a bag, similar to a hiker's backpack, and started shoving stuff inside. "Anything else we need, I can conjure," he said. "And everything here should be safe."

She tried leaning against a solid marble table, leaned into it for support, decided she didn't want to be that close to whatever was on it, so pulled herself up, swayed. "In the wall?"

"No. I've had escape routes planned. The, um, things, aren't in the wall, but they aren't here, either, and that's what's important. I can get them when I need them, but I doubt anyone else can."

It struck him that this whole innocent façade of hers might be an act, and she might be a wizard at least as powerful and well trained as he. If so, he had just given all his secrets away, and was a dead man. Still, if she were going to make a move, it would have to be now.

Pierce decided to trust her.

"We've got to go somewhere else. I can take us. Will you go with me?"

"Through this sleet storm? Driving is going to be a nightmare."

"We won't be driving."

"If I told you I wanted to go to the police what would you say?"

"I won't stop you. I promised you I'd never bind you, and I won't. Fiddling with another person's memories is strictly forbidden. Not that it can't be done, but there are rules I've sworn to uphold and one of the most important is, as soon as you start to break what you could call 'little' laws, you're sliding down a slippery slope."

"Toward the dark side?"

"Absolutely."

"You'll answer all my questions."

"Would you trust me?"

"Trust you?"

He wasn't sure if her parroting his question came from the fact the color had leeched out of her face, making her look bloodless, and more than half-way toward passing out, or if she were encouraging him to answer.

"First we go, then the explanations. If, after that, you still feel you need the police, I'll try to bring you back, so you can. Right now, those guys are breaking in. I know you can't hear them up here, but they're making all kinds of noise trying to get through my wards. I would rather you not be anywhere near when they succeed. My security system will call the police, so they'll probably disappear, but I don't think I can trust your life to that eventuality."

"They would have killed us at the library."

"I think so. What they were aiming at me was meant to kill, and CeeDee, since I'm trying to avoid secrets between us, I'm certain I killed one."

"Yes. I think I knew that."

"Your life was in danger. Now will you come?"

"I'm not sure. What does bring me back mean? I assume you don't mean business class tickets at LaGuardia."

He laughed, charmed. "No. But if that's what you want, that's what we'll do. The traveling we will do is part of the explanation. Will you trust me that far?"

She would trust him to the moon and back, but she wasn't certain she was willing to admit that.

"I will protect you. If anything happens to the baby, it will be because of some decision you've made, or over my dead body."

She ignored his reference to his own mortality. "Some decision I've made?"

He had no time to be anything but blunt. "The abortion clinic."

She shook her head, cascading hair, looked stronger than any time since the library. "There was never any chance of that. For better or worse, this one is staying with me."

He nodded, accepting her words, but knowing although he owed her explanations, she owed him the same. "If we're going, we need to go right now. We won't be safe much longer, and I'd like a few moments to hide our trail."

CeeDee nodded, and he took that as permission.

"I, um, have to touch you." Before she could complain, or make any other comment, he took her hand. "Nothing more than this. You need to be linked to me." With his other hand he pulled a fat green strand, twirled his arm so that it was wrapped around his wrist several times. "Off we go."

And before CeeDee thought to scream, they were transferred from the attic to someplace else.

Someplace weird.

The sky shone a blinding sunflower yellow, and the sand under their feet glowed iridescent orange as if were radioactive. The combination of the two colors, and the lack of any other hue was so unexpected it hurt her eyes to look down.

"For a quick explanation, we're not on Earth anymore. This is for want of a better word, a transfer place I use. You can think of it as a train station if you like. From here, we can get to other places far easier than if we weren't here."

"Is that supposed to make sense?" Where was blue? Green? Pierce himself was the only rational thing she saw.

"This is like a hub. Before we go somewhere else, we have to be here. I know that doesn't make any sense."

"If it doesn't make any sense to you, I hate to tell you what I'm thinking. What are you doing with your hands?"

"I don't want to leave any broader trail than I have to. You can think of this as erasing the computer files of any plane reservations associated with this type of travel."

"If this is what you promised me by way of explanation, you've got a long way to go before I'm satisfied." Then she looked at him, gave a startled exclamation. "Your clothing, it's different."

He'd been wearing a wrinkled business suit, as if he'd slept in it, the one leg ripped and blood covered, but now was wearing jeans, a chambray shirt, hiking boots. "We'll be doing a lot of walking, hiking, and I'm more comfortable in this, than the suit. I have clothes for you as well. I can dress you, or you can do it yourself." He held out his left hand, empty except for a yellow and a lilac powerstrand, then raised his right hand, waved it, palm down, about four inches over his left. She thought she saw a flash of color, peach, perhaps, something not quite as garish as the sand they walked on.

Then, as she watched, he held jeans, a comfortable cotton blouse, a sweatshirt with her college logo on it, and thick socks and hiking boots. "Don't worry if nothing looks like it will fit. Just put them on, they will adjust to your body."

She was terrified, but managed to keep her sense of humor. "That's a trick you're really going to have to teach me."

"Sure. After the explanations. Do you want me to dress you?"

"Could you make a changing room as easily?"

"Yes, and no. I don't want to take the time, and this is making quite a bit of noise. Anyone listening, and I assure you, the bad guys are listening, will come right to us."

"I don't want to change in front of you." They'd been intimate only yesterday, but that was before her world went all skiddly-wonkus.

"CeeDee, it will only take a second." He raised his right hand again, and the clothing disappeared, and she screeched, short and abruptly, for when she looked down, the outfit she had on had vanished, and in its place was the clothing he had been holding.

She smiled, her bottom lip quivering. "I think I could get used to this."

"That's my girl. We need to walk. There's no easier way to do this. I could make us transportation, anything from a camel to an F16, but anything I conjure now will—"

"I know," she said, "make noise."

He nodded appreciably. "That's right. Walking doesn't. It will leave a trail in the sand, but I can erase that with almost no sound. Now there's water in your backpack, and food, mostly fruit, since that's easy to carry. I can always make more, but as long as I'm making noise here, I'd rather make all my noise here, if you take my meaning. Anyone who knows me, knows I use this place as a transfer point, so I'm not giving too much away." He handed her a bottle of water, so icy cold that the condensation dripped down the side, and a large yellow delicious apple. "I know we just ate."

"Junior's always hungry."

"I hope you like fruit?"

"I was really hoping for chocolate cake, but this will do for now," she said, biting into the apple.

"For obvious reasons, don't litter, ok?"

"Sure."

"Not even the apple core. It will be a trace."

"I won't. I don't understand any of this, but I won't."

"Good," he said, and started walking, in what she took was a random direction.

"Now, for the explanations. I take it you can talk while you walk?"

"Yes. But if I tell you, you'll never understand normal again."

Never understand normal again. She let his words rumble around the inside of her, let herself chew on them, and it didn't take her long to come to a conclusion. "That's what I'm afraid of," she said.

He stopped so abruptly she had to back up a step to make eye-contact. "CeeDee, are you afraid?"

Following his example she took a second or two to analyze her own emotions. "Shocked, stunned, disorientated, probably disillusioned, definitely enchanted and enthusiastic, but no. Right now I am not frightened."

"Good. I can't promise that you won't be as we go on, for there are some frightening things we're likely to encounter, but this—"

The smile she offered showed more bravery than amusement, for her eyes stayed wide, haunted. And he realized something in this pause between chaos: his feeling of attraction for her was deeper and far more unexpected than anything he could imagine.

Love.

For a long time he thought he would be immune. Because he understood the universe in a different manner than others, he expected so common an emotion would slip by him. Now Pierce realized exactly the opposite. Because he had spent so much time in introspection, because he knew himself, he understood the emotion, and he'd been hit hard.

"What?" CeeDee asked. She put her hand on his forearm.

"What?" Pierce responded. He felt the conflicting emotions of a desire to wrap his arms around her and loving her—and a need to high-tail it out of there.

Her head tilted, her hair swung around her shoulders, making him desperate to dig his fingers deep into its softness and pull her closer. "Your eyes went all funny. Are you hearing something…seeing something?"

Ahh, so she thought his reaction was from his art. If she believed that, it gave him a little more time to understand the repercussions, to come to accept it. Love might be an emotion wedged within the heart, but certain responsive male body organs were also affected. This emotion swirled through him, brain, hands, feet, guts. Every inch of him was attuned to her. Wanted her.

"CeeDee—"

Her eyebrows lowered and she bit her bottom lip. "There's a problem."

He wasn't sure enough of his own control to smile or to hold her, but he had enough control over voluntary movement to shake his head, try to reassure her. "No, not a problem. Actually it's something that might be very good. I'm not sure yet. You'll have to give me a few moments to work through it."

"Pierce, I'd trust you with my life."

Emotions flooded him, molten and overwhelming and without thought, but with a desperation so deep he could not prevent it, he brought her soft, complacent body against him, wrapped his arms around her back and hugged her tightly. He rested his chin against her shoulder, his cheek against hers, breathing deeply the essence that was hers alone. It wasn't nearly enough, but considering where they were, it would have to do.

"Then you're not afraid?"

"Not now and I do apologize again for getting you involved in this."

Although CeeDee slipped from the hug, she kept her fingers entwined with his. "But I was involved with this even before you met me, wasn't I?"

"I don't know. I think so. It's one of the more important things on my list we've got to find out. There're a few things that don't really make sense yet. Now, let me answer one of your questions, if I can, then we've got to get going."

"Well, why the stone around your lair?"

"The obvious reason is tradition. Wrapping a wizard's lair in stone has always been done. There are other things that work, concrete for example, but it's usually stone."

"Iron, steel?"

"No, noise travels easily through both of those. Magic noise doesn't travel through stone, so when I'm working, no other wizard, even one who's listening, can tell exactly what I'm up to. Also, we need the insulation between the lair and electricity. You saw what happened to your phone. I'd hate to have to keep replacing the refrigerator. That would get annoying."

"That I can relate to."

He hadn't realized she had such a fine grasp of sarcasm.

"There's another reason no iron. Most creatures of faerie are deathly allergic to it. There was a time, way in the past when wizards and faeries worked together."

"Faeries?"

"Greater and lesser imps, elves, brownies, any number of bugs that are not insects. Probably over a hundred different species. I had an entire class on creatures of faerie. These days faeries don't have much to do with wizards. I don't know why. My master said there must have been some epic battle or broken accord. On the whole wizards and those of faerie keep their distance, but again, due to tradition, a faerie would be welcome in my lair should I invite him or her."

"Are they evil?"

"Some are, definitely. Many more think only of their own pleasure, but there are some who fight against evil."

"Have you ever met a faerie?"

"Sure. During the course. My master had a few come, and probably fifty showed up. They're interested in us too. Faeries can't manipulate powerstrands, but they can see them. They have magic of their own."

"Could they travel here?"

"I don't think so. I've certainly never heard of a faerie that can use transfer points. Their magic allows them to pop where they want to be without intermediary steps."

"How do I fight one?"

"You want a sword?"

"I think I'd rather an Uzi."

"No, mechanical weapons don't work around the faerie. No guns, no bombs. They either won't work at all, or they'll explode when you least expect it. Although wizards are not creatures of faerie, and neither is the dragon we're going to see, nor the gargoyle I met this past summer, it's always better to fight your battles with no weapon more advanced than a crossbow."

"You fight with a sword?"

"Yes, it's not my strong suit, and faeries can be battled with powerstrands, so that's what most wizards concentrate on. But as for swordsmanship, I had a course."

"I'm sure you did."

"It's important to be prepared. Speaking of that, I should do this, before we get much further." He reached out, grabbed a golden powerstrand and wrapped it around her arm. "You remember how you got back to your room from the beach?"

"Yes. I didn't believe it at the time. I'm still not sure I believe it, but I remember."

"Think of a place you could go where you would be safe. Don't tell me, and don't let it be anywhere someone who has done background on you can find. There shouldn't be too many people around, since you'll look like you've popped out of thin air."

"So the line for Space Mountain in Disneyland is not a good idea. Darn."

"You should be able to find food and water at the place you choose, in case I need to come rescue you when it's safe. Do you have a place you can go to?"

"Yes. But I'm not running away."

"Not now. But there might come a time when I can't defend you. Look at it this way, if you run, Rose will be safe."

"Ok. I know you've said this before, but I have to keep asking, this thing won't hurt my baby, will it?"

"No. They're perfectly safe."

"Of course. That's why you use them as weapons."

"We're not using this one as a weapon. And I never would have let you eat the chili dog if there was danger to the baby."

Passion renewed, flaring sharp and unexpected. Pierce never realized that a stalwart, brave woman could be so unabashedly sexy.

"Good." She decided to accept his explanation.

Pierce continued walking. CeeDee looked back over her shoulder, noticed each time she lifted her foot the footstep vanished, as if some small rodent followed them with an eraser, obliterating every trace of their passage. He watched her, noticed what she studied. "Clean-up spell. It's not much, and it won't pass an in-depth inspection, but sometimes doing the superficial is all that is necessary. It doesn't make too much noise, and I don't want to make it too easy for our pursuers."

"Where are we going?"

"At the moment, someplace else. It doesn't matter where we go, only that we are not where we were."

# CHAPTER 17

She looked around at the landscape, the sameness of it, the blinding yellow sky, the orange sand they had been following for so long it was starting to look fairly natural. No trees, no water, no sign of anything different like a building or an airplane. "Is one place pretty much like the other?"

"Actually, no. That's why we've got to hurry."

She kept walking, then something fabulous and miraculous happened. She felt the first fluttering of movement from her womb. Life. Her baby making her presence known. Immediately Cee Dee was flushed with warm, maternal emotion. She squeaked, and he pivoted, terrified, until he saw the look of rapture on her features, the way she cuddled her gently rounding stomach. "It felt like a butterfly."

They kept moving. She matched him, step for step, although she realized his stride was longer than hers and he could be moving quicker without her. To keep boredom at bay, not an easy task facing this unending sameness, she counted steps, getting to one hundred before starting again. And again. And again.

Seeing no Starbucks, nor even a conveniently placed boulder, CeeDee sat down on the sand, finding it warm but not unpleasant, and oddly enough, soft. She pulled her boot off, raised it until a half cup of the orange sand slithered out. "Lord, but I need a rest."

"We can stop. It's as safe as anywhere else. They didn't follow us here, whether they're waiting for more instructions or reinforcements, I don't know, but I think it's a safe bet they haven't given up, so we can't drop our guard for long. I can't sense them any longer. We should get a few hours' sleep."

"Sleep. Really?" Her response was half sarcastic, half wishful, and half invitation. He smiled, looked down at her, then started pulling the strands of power he would need to make their presence invisible to anyone who came looking, even another necromancer.

"They're really quite beautiful, aren't they?"

"The powerstrands?"

"Yes."

"Yes. By any definition of beauty, they are beautiful."

"How did you feel when you first saw them?"

"Stunned, shocked, grateful. Any number of other words. Elated, certainly."

From nowhere she could determine, although he had his back to her, and was rooting around in his backpack, he handed her a blanket, a pillow, and a tall glass of what looked and tasted like fresh orange juice. When he turned back Pierce held a second pillow. Telling, she supposed, that there was only one blanket.

Pierce settled in the sand, yawned deeply, not even bothering to cover his mouth. There were dark shadows under his eyes, and he wore his exhaustion like a shroud.

A dozen questions flirted around her head, or three or four times that many. However, she wasn't sure she was ready for any great, encompassing confessions he might make, especially involving her and her baby. But she was curious, and she did want some answers before she gave into her own exhaustion. She set her pillow on the sand, stretched out the blanket. "I don't suppose it's going to get any darker?"

"Not here. Not ever."

He looked around like a man who has brought a guest into his home, and then sees the place where he has been living through her eyes, the dirt and the clutter and the lack of amenities.

She wondered too, if she asked, if he could retrieve her teddy bear. She didn't want Maggie to get lonely.

"Are there sand fleas?"

"Sand fleas?"

"I feel so itchy."

"No, it's the sand itself. It gets annoying."

"Ok. I'm annoyed." To take her mind off the sand, she chose a different direction. "When I was in your attic, your lair, there was a moose head."

He dropped his head to his shoulders, mumbled to his chest. "Yes."

"You said you would explain it to me someday."

Pierce opened his mouth, and although she couldn't see him directly, she could read him, and knew he was searching for just the right excuses to put her curiosity on hold for a little while longer. But instead he surprised her. "You're right, I should tell you but I don't think you're going to like it."

CeeDee smiled smugly, settling herself on the sand, stretching her legs out, resting her head on her hand, her elbow on the pillow. She wondered if he knew of the flaw in his personality which didn't allow him to treat her as an equal, and she wondered exactly how long it would take to break him of the habit.

"Just tell me and let me be the one to make value judgments." Her nails were short, bitten, weren't giving her the supreme satisfaction of a good scratch on an itch any self-righteous individual could tell you was the barest of the bare necessities of life. Scratching an itch, finding out what made a man tick. Two sides of the same coin.

Pierce didn't tell her right away. He made her wait while he finished knotting his power bands to create his shield, he provided a meal of berries and some unidentifiable thing which looked like a tree root but tasted like a baked sweet potato and crunched like an apple. She was patient. If she knew anything about him, he had integrity, and if he told her he was going to do something, he would, even if it were in his own time. And she knew, by the length of time it was taking him, he was formulating his words, and if it were hard for her to hear, it would be harder by far for him to tell.

There wasn't any meat, but she was hungry enough to find his food satisfying, even if a thick quarter-pounder would have calmed her stomach better. While they ate, she studied the sky, finding it unremitting, not a cloud, not an eagle or a mountain obstructing her vision. Still, she would have liked to see the stars.

They had finished eating, except for a dozen or so blackberries, the ones not quite ripe, tart enough to pucker her lips and bring a flash of water to her eyes. She took one, bit down, savoring the sensation of it being just a little too much for her. She figured his story would be like that.

"I killed the moose with my own hands, with tools I fashioned myself. That was the first major assignment I was given by my master." He laughed, looked away, closer to looking inward, then turned back to her with those brilliant eyes which looked right through her. "Not the first lesson by any means, not even the first hard lesson. It would be more correct to say it came early in my apprenticeship, before I knew...other ways to accomplish the same thing."

"While you were still willing to jump when your master said jump?"

"In case you're wondering, I'm still willing to jump when my Master says jump. I've got my robe, my—" he thought, rubbed his long fingers over his darkening stubble, "to put it in your terms, my graduate degree, but I owe him too much to ignore him."

He laughed again, picked up a blackberry the way she had, the unripest of the lot and held it in the warmth of his palm for a few seconds. When he uncurled his fingers, it was a peach, large as a baseball, which he offered her, but when she refused, he bit, and the juice dripped down his chin.

"There's a trick I'd like to learn," she said, adding lightness, for although there had been laughter, there had been no lightness. "With this pregnancy I seem to be hungry all the time."

CeeDee was content, for the moment, to let him ruminate. Facing pain is never easy, and hurtful things must be brought to light in their own time if they are true. The air hung stagnant without a trace of breeze, and she almost wished she were frivolous enough to ask have him to make her a bag of marshmallows and a campfire. She had been young once, knew the healing value of campfires and marshmallows, but she held her peace, waited for whatever was to come.

Pierce leaned back, poked his pillow, but made no move to lay down. She could almost see him, dressed in buckskin, riding a paint pony, shouting war cries, brandishing a bow and arrow chasing that stupid moose through the brush. CeeDee flashed the idealized version away, and let him continue with his tale.

"The first assignment. That and so much more."

She waited, licked her lips, decided against another blackberry. There was only so much intensity she could handle.

"I was older than most apprentices when I came to my master, twelve. It's best started at seven or eight. If the children are caught early enough, five is not unheard of. The strongest of us generally start early, because we cannot function as 'normal'. We experiment with noisy things, so we are generally discovered early or we find too many unusual things in what is considered normal existence so we're institutionalized, drugged, not too long ago lobotomized and therefore lost. I'm getting off track here. What matters most is I was older, so I think I had more to prove or something."

Marshmallows, she thought, and a chocolate bar, and a box of graham crackers. Comfort food. For herself, for him. Whatever he had to confess, he would need comfort. She hoped her touch and the soft blanket he'd conjured would be enough.

"Why were you so old? Certainly you sensed your own power earlier?" She didn't mean to distract him, to take him off topic, but she could see Pierce was having trouble finding a place to start, a beginning. CeeDee was only hoping to help him along.

"Oh, yes. I was aware of my power from an early age, probably I hadn't even learned to read yet when I first felt its stirrings. But every time I brought it up to my mother, she'd try to channel it into something hideous, dance lessons, polo, fencing, things appropriate for a wealthy scion of Washington greatness, and when I told my father, he would try to beat me senseless."

She waited, said nothing. These memories were even more painful than his killing the moose. What kind of Pandora's Box had she opened with her simple question?

"I don't know if I told you, but my mother likes soothsayers. Palm readers. Psychics. Most of the people she goes to are complete charlatans, people who know how to spin a tale, turn over a tarot card and talk for an hour about something could mean anything, so when something does happen, they can run the complete "see, I told you so," number on her. So when I stopped telling her about the things I felt, the weird things I saw and told her I wanted magic. That is what she thought I wanted. She basically ignored me while I was growing up. Mom's a card carrying member of the children-should-be-seen-and-not-heard club, but occasionally I could catch her on a good day and she'd indulge my whims, so she introduced me to slight-of-hand books, illusion, card tricks. It almost killed me because it wasn't real and wasn't what I needed. I tried to explain that I wanted real power. So she bought me tarot cards, a crystal ball, the old runes of power her guidance instructors used. This was even worse, since I felt the power could be there, but wasn't, at least in not in any of the people she introduced me to. There was power there they couldn't access and couldn't tell me how to access. I ran from that life like a coward. I couldn't face it."

She reached out, rubbed his knee, not a sexual gesture, but a human one. "No, even in your ignorance you knew the difference between real power and that which is showmanship. So, you went to your father." Here she was just guessing, but by his reaction, she knew she'd hit the nail on the head.

"Oh, god, he was livid. 'You want power, boy, go into politics,' he yelled. 'Making laws, having people under your control, that is real power.'" His voice changed a bit when he used his father's words, was more cultured, but by the same token artificial. Pierce continued. "And he would raise no son who was a sissy, who didn't shine on the athletic field, in the classroom, in the school elections. He understood power all right, Washington power. That's all that ever mattered to him."

She thought of a question, didn't ask it, at least not aloud, but he heard her, whether he read her expression or her mind, she had no idea, but continued with his narrative. "My father is a senator, has been for going on twenty years. He's on all the right committees. When I was young, I often thought he would run for president, and he had the backing. Heaven only knows enough people asked him to, but I later learned the real people holding power are not necessarily the people you think of as the most visibly powerful. He had no interest whatsoever of being that obviously in the limelight, when he could rule from the relative obscurity of committees." Pierce took a deep breath, flexed his shoulders as if remembering a beating at his father's hands. "At any rate, I learned early not to bring my interest in magic to him, which was all things considered, for the best. I had to learn circumspection, it was better I do so when I was younger. Then, one day I got lucky. I met a witch, I didn't know that was what she was until much later, and she told me how to find people of power. I looked for a few weeks, then one afternoon after school, I passed the man who was to become my master on the street, and I knew exactly what he was. I followed him for days, making up all kinds of conversations in my head. He was so mundane. He worked as a high school janitor. I knew I couldn't be wrong, but I didn't understand. Then finally he spoke to me, agreed to take me on as an apprentice."

There was more to the story than that. She'd remember, pull it out of him later. She'd bet here, too, he'd had a battle on his hands, fighting for something he needed as much as he needed to breathe, when he didn't even have the words to explain what he wanted.

"Which brings us to the moose head," she said, to keep him on topic.

He needed to move, and he could tell she had sat long enough, gotten her strength back, so absently he packed up the blanket, the pillows and pulled her to her feet. "Which brings us to the moose head," Pierce agreed.

He started walking in what CeeDee thought was another random direction, could even be the way they had come for all she knew, but since there were no footprints, no landmarks, she couldn't be sure.

"I didn't understand it at first, perhaps I still don't. I've come to the conclusion it was a test on more than one level. First, would I obey. Mastery of this art is hard. Obedience must be complete and instantaneous. Second, how badly did I want to be a mage? Was I willing to kill for it? You've got to understand where I was raised, regardless of what you read about other rich kids with submachine guns in prep school, we didn't even pull weeds. I'd never killed anything in my life. Death was glossed over. When my dog died, I was told he went away to a farm where he could run free all day. I didn't even realize he passed until years later. And camping on my own, heaven forbid, I'd never roughed it worse than a luxury suite at the Marriott. But beyond obedience, there had to be more. In order to begin my apprenticeship I had to want it enough to kill for it. The power I wield, that he would teach me to harness, is dangerous. It was important I learn from the start the consequences of my actions." He spoke to himself now, almost as if forgetting she was even there. "'Before I take you any farther into the art, you must kill,' he said. It didn't matter what. I think I could have brought back a praying mantis or a caterpillar and it might have satisfied him. I don't know. Some of the other apprentices, the younger ones brought insects." Daniel had brought a fish he'd caught with line made from his shoelace. That sacrifice had been accepted as well. I was older. I had more to prove. I was also dumb as dogshit. I didn't really set out to kill a moose. A groundhog or a mole would have sufficed, a field mouse. I fashioned a slingshot first, found some stones, thought to bring down a bird. More than anything, this single act of aggression was a means of cutting away civilized society, taking me from my parents' care into another world. Do you understand?"

"It must have been very difficult for you," she whispered. Support was the only thing she could offer.

"It was damned near impossible. Anyway, the slingshot didn't work. I'd never had any practice, couldn't hit a specific tree, let alone a specific branch. I had no idea what was safe to eat, and being raised by my parents, I knew better than to drink from any stream that didn't have fluorinated water. I never even drank from the garden hose."

Silently, CeeDee made a promise that her child would have a wild and free childhood, and she would drink from a garden hose. For her child too would be mageborn.

As they walked, the monotony of the land was killing her. She wanted thatched huts or skyscrapers and picturesque winding roads with covered bridges and trees as big as redwoods someone had carved a tunnel through so no one had to walk all the way around. And she decided, as long as she wanted all that, some signposts would help, "Oz, 60 kilometers," "Narnia next left!" or even a scarecrow crossing his arms in two different directions saying "Some people do go both ways!"

Instead she found only iridescent puke-orange sand and a blinding yellow sky. There was no sun or sun-equivalent she could see, and no part was any brighter than any other. It was uniformly garish. Their feet made slushing sounds against the sand, and walking was difficult, for the sand kept shifting, and she knew her legs would throb in the morning, for they started to ache already, but he kept a steady pace which had her walking constantly, but not so quickly she was out of breath.

"How much longer?"

"About an hour should do it. Then we can transfer."

"I'd set my watch, but I always used my phone for the time."

"Sorry about that."

When they had first arrived at this miserable transfer point, Pierce had taken his watch and phone from the small stone box he'd put them in. Then he put the box down and it had disappeared. Back to his lair, he told her: it had a return spell on it.

How cool would that be? CeeDee made a silent vow she would force him to teach her the return spell first.

"We were talking about the moose. No slingshot," she said, prompting.

He muttered something she didn't quite catch. "What? Is it so secret?"

"No, but I want you to think favorably of me, and that moose, well, I keep it in my lair to remind me of my major and classic mistake. It humbles me any time I get to thinking I'm, for want of a better phrase, 'the great and powerful Oz.'"

"Now I'm intrigued."

# CHAPTER 18

"You'll have to tell me. It will keep my mind off this nauseating orange sand."

"I agree. I've always felt it rather bilious, myself. I want you to know I think I've learned my lesson, and I don't think I've done anything quite that idiotic in a long time."

"It was a lesson."

"Yes. I hope you still believe that when I finish this ridiculous story. The slingshot wouldn't work. So I sharpened a spear against a rock using a branch I found. I couldn't find stone hard enough to create an arrowhead, so it was simple wood. I had no knife. I was terrified. I'd spent one night alone in the forest, getting eaten by every kind of bug imaginable, and listening to all the night sounds, knowing I was at the bottom of the food chain, vulnerable to all kinds of hungry predators, for all I knew there were bears, bobcats, wolves. I finally drank from a stream, certain my insides would soon be on their way out. I wasn't sure I had the courage to kill anything. If my master had taught me magic I was certain I would have no problem. I'd just zap it with power flowing from my fingertips. I was very young."

"And had been exposed to a lot of science fiction movies as a child."

"Yes," he laughed, "that too. So, I tried to call on my magic. If this was a test, it was probably a magical one. Would the power come when I called? I knew it was there, but latent. Maybe I only lacked need. I sort of prayed, not to god, or to any other power like that, but to the magic itself. Really, I was probably hallucinating from hunger."

She reached out to touch him lightly on the hand. "You did nothing to be ashamed of."

"Yeah, right. Anyway, into this clearing where I'm planning on spending my third night lumbered this bull moose, big as hell. It wasn't quite what I had in mind, but still, it was almost like an answer to a prayer. It came in, knelt, then sat down. This idiot moose. I wanted to shout, 'Go, get outta here! Can't you see there's a lunatic here?' Besides, I was afraid. I only had the spear. You saw the rack didn't you, the antlers?"

"Anyone would have been afraid."

"My parents thought I was at Boy Scout camp. What would they think if I came back gored by a moose with no scout leader in sight, but at this point I had to try. I needed magic in my life. I couldn't give up. I didn't even think to go around, come at it from behind. I just came right up to it, bold as you please, and stuck my idiot spear into its neck, well below the jaw. Not one of the brightest things I've ever done."

"And it died."

"Eventually. So I go back, all puffed up like King Kong, thinking I'm Merlin the magician or something, and does my master thank me, tell the other apprentices how much better my kill was than theirs? No, he just says, 'for your second lesson...'"

"So you had it stuffed to remind you of your own idiocy?"

"Precisely. I never thought you'd understand."

She grinned, rolled her neck on her shoulders to ease the stiffness there. "There's a lot about me you don't know yet. Besides, I think I've got this thing figured out. Put yourself in your master's position. Say you've got five, six apprentices. You know some of them are never going to make it, one or two will finish training and never be more than mediocre, but maybe you know one will be brilliant at what you have to teach, maybe even far more adept than you are. And into this lair comes this cocky young rich boy dripping with potential power and toting a bloody moose head. What would you do?"

He grabbed a powerstrand, scratched it, as she had earlier with her bite, then let it go. He laughed out loud. "I don't even have to think about that one. I'd say, 'for your next lesson.' Mercy, it feels good knowing that."

Pleasure rippled through her for she knew she had healed him slightly, but there were other aches within that would take much more than a cathartic story to make him laugh again.

"Master said the time to know if you could kill was never when you needed to, so we had to have the experience. Death, whether it be a field mouse or a moose, is the same. He wanted us to know killing is taking a life and should never be done idly or for fun."

"You already figured that out."

"Yeah. So I took the head home and had it mounted. Every time I see that head I remember that power should never be abused, and killing, for the most part is wrong. Don't misunderstand me, I'm not a pacifist. I'm just not a gun toting liberal—or whatever the equivalent is for wizards."

"So, do you think you could conjure me some ruby slippers?"

"Do you want to click your heels together three times?" he asked.

"Probably."

"I'll work on ruby slippers. But when did we start walking again?" he asked, as if this moment he realized they were moving.

"I think some things are easier to talk about when you move." The baby, she decided, liked movement too.

"We've come far enough, and we both can use some rest."

He placed his pillow beside hers. While there was enough room around them, since they were in a desert probably as large as the state of California, without a rock or a tree root to get in their way, he could have slept anywhere, it pleased her that he planned to sleep beside her. And while they nestled together, side by side, they were not intimate, at least not sexually. She knew she could get him to make love to her, and that it would take very little effort on her part, but she also knew if she did, although they would both enjoy it, it would be positively and absolutely wrong. Sometimes sex was more involved than physical enjoyment between two people, but concerned commitment and strings from the past.

Sometimes, it even required passing up momentary pleasure for something deeper. CeeDee knew Pierce wasn't ready to take their relationship to the next level, not while they were here, at this transfer point. There was too much unsettled between them to add another complication.

She patted her stomach, in a comforting gesture, and spooning behind her, Pierce tenderly laid his broad palm over her wrist and repeated her motion, so both of them comforted this child huddled in her womb. This was yet another level of intimacy: showing love through a touch, a caress to a baby not yet born.

Although exhausted, she doubted she would sleep. It was too light out and the environment was too strange, but lying next to him, feeling his heartbeat, hearing his even breaths, she drifted off almost immediately. And she was pleased with her analysis and his control, for she could feel the erection he did nothing about.

Having him hold her while she slept was as intimate a gesture as CeeDee had ever experienced.

She woke when he stirred, instantly alert. She waited while he stood, looked around with his eyes and with his senses, trying to see if danger had found them. She had no idea if they had been out eight hours or eight minutes, but she was completely rested, and the aches from her back and her legs she expected from walking on the sand hadn't materialized, for which she was grateful. She wondered if somehow he was responsible for her wellbeing.

Satisfied, he pulled on his hiking boots, and she spoke quickly, knowing they would be moving out soon, and perhaps there would be less time to talk later.

"Pierce, I understand that we're in a lot of trouble, and you're doing the best you can to get us out of it, but is there anything I can do?"

"What do you mean?"

"I don't know. Can I recite incantations while you weave your spells? Can I clean the cauldron?"

He met her eyes directly, a leveling of the playing field between them, he had never done with her before, and which she could easily believe he had never done with another woman. He shrugged, used that as an apology. "I didn't actually bring the cauldron."

"For which I suppose I should be grateful. We won't be safe here much longer, you said so yourself, so rather than being a burden, I'd like to do what I can to help."

She couldn't see the powerstrands when he wasn't touching them, so there might have been none, or there might have been a morass of a hundred thousand, she had no idea, but she knew there was power here he could use as a weapon if need be, power he could use too for tenderness, as he had earlier, when he made her a peach. Like any weapon, the goodness or the evil came from the person wielding the tool, not the tool itself.

He squatted beside her, resting on his heels in a position which looked so painful to her, but which he did so effortlessly. "There is something you can do to help. Or at any rate, I'd like to see if you can."

"Anything, I'm ready."

"Do you know what astral travel is?"

CeeDee wasn't into any form of mysticism, or at least she hadn't been before she met him, but she had a broad education, and insatiable curiosity, enough to put in an acceptable performance should she ever appear on Jeopardy, so she knew what he was talking about. "It is when a person leaves his physical body and travels in spirit form."

"Yes."

"It involves separation of body and soul, which is generally considered synonymous with death."

"I won't be dead, and I will always be connected to my physical body."

"And you need to do this astral travel?"

He rubbed his stomach, and she wondered if it were a mirror image of her own action, before she realized he wasn't caressing his washboard flat abs, he was scratching the unsightly scars from an assassin.

"Before I can make any decision about what needs to be done, I need more information, and I can't get it sitting here in a TPW."

"TPW?"

"Transfer point world. This place is good for very little but as a stop to somewhere else."

"And hiding out."

"Yes, exactly."

"What can I do to help?"

"I would like to have a look around, but when I travel, I leave my body vulnerable. If you could guard my physical body while I'm gone, I'd feel safer."

"Guard how, when you're the one with all the weapons at your disposal?"

"I'll fashion a spear. You could throw rocks."

"But the people who come after you won't be susceptible to spears and rocks. They will be magicians like yourself. I won't even be an annoyance to them."

He scratched his chin, acknowledging her point. "I'll think about it." He pulled her to her feet. "Let's keep walking. They are not close, but it is inconceivable they gave up. We still need more distance."

She looked around at the unvarying scenery, the orange sand, the yellow sky, and grew hungry for Rhode Island and blue. As they walked, he handed her an orange and a small cluster of seedless green grapes, both sweet and rich with moisture. "Sorry about all the fruit. It's the easiest. Tonight I'll work on chilidogs or hamburgers if you like."

If I like, CeeDee thought, filling in what he did not say. If we are not caught, killed by whatever hunters follow. "How are you at chocolate?"

"Complex carbohydrates are not called complex for nothing. But, I'll see what I can do."

She kept walking beside him, uncomplaining, the sands shifting under her feet, making walking hard, as if it fought her, pulling her back. A few minutes later, he stopped, let her catch up, for he had been about ten feet ahead, and in his hands were five round candies. She bit one, found it a chocolate covered cherry.

"I told you, fruit is easiest."

"This is incredible. I may have to keep you around." And he waited patiently while she ate four of the five, consenting to eat one, only when she insisted he needed to keep his strength up.

The walking grew harder, and she grew nauseous, from the infant, the all-fruit diet, from the relentless orange and yellow landscape which had no basis in her own reality, and from the strain on her muscles. As a librarian, she never abused them to quite this extent. "Stop. Sit." It wasn't an order, but compassion, expressed when he realized how much she had fallen behind.

He reached out, twirled a power strand, red and pulsing, and just seeing the color cheered her. "You can see this?"

"Yes, of course."

He moved it away from her questing fingers. "I'd rather not teach you how to manipulate them, not while that baby rests inside you, but can you tell me how this feels?"

He wrapped the red powerstrand around her right leg. At first CeeDee didn't feel anything, not even a change of pressure of her pants against her leg, but then, slowly, she felt the ache from her muscles drain, as if he had opened up a faucet.

"Yes, it feels marvelous."

"Good." He found another red strand, this one he had to grab for, and he wound it around her left leg. "If this makes walking difficult, I'll have to release them."

"How could it do that?"

"Some of these powerstrands don't like being moved from place to place. They'll obey, they have to, for I've bound it, but they can exhibit drag."

"Like a little kid digging in his heels, when he doesn't want to follow his mother."

"Exactly. If I have to take them off, I can put them on again when we rest for the evening."

"Well, even if you can leave them on for five minutes, it will help. Can you do this for yourself?"

"Yes, and no."

"I suppose you're not going to clarify that?"

He sat beside her, taking off his shoes, as she was, releasing the captured sand. She noticed big, open blisters on his feet, raw wounds that had to hurt. Her own blisters were slowly disappearing, replaced by pink, healing flesh.

"I can work the powerstrands. You can see that. But it is forbidden for a wizard to use them on himself."

"Why?"

"Mercy, all the intricacies of this law will take years to explain, and most of them I didn't quite understand until I was taking my master's exams myself." He set aside his shoes, found a green strand, worked it somehow so he produced a large, red delicious apple. "You know power corrupts and absolute power corrupts absolutely?"

"Yes."

"Well, these," he said, indicating the powerstrands at her legs, "are power. Raw power that can be used for anything."

"Yes."

"And a wizard who is using power for himself runs the risk of being corrupted absolutely."

"But you do use the power for yourself. You make food. You make blankets and keep some kind of force field over us."

"Yes. But I do not heal myself, nor increase any of my physical attributes-and before you jump to conclusions, I mean strength, intelligence, endurance."

"And that's different?"

"It's different. A wizard who does not heal himself with powerstrands when he is wounded is a man keeping his humanity. It is a way to keep us humble and mortal."

"But you did heal yourself. I saw you put powerstrands on your leg in your lair. You seem much better now."

"That was a healing charm I bought, kept in a first aid box. I didn't make it."

"Oh. So you can heal me, though. And another wizard?"

"Yes, it is not forbidden to heal another wizard. As a matter of fact, it is encouraged. There are very few who specialize in healing, but all of us have the rudimentary knowledge of how to do it."

"Why could you heal another and not yourself? That seems like nit-picking."

"Healing another wizard requires trust from both. Let's say you were a powerful wizard. You would have to trust me enough to let me near, when I could easily harm you under the guise of easing your pain, and I have to trust you, that when you were feeling better, you wouldn't turn on me. Because we are mortal, we can be killed any way a normal human can."

"And trust between wizards is encouraged."

"Yes. By our very nature we are solitary creatures. Very few ever marry for example, and most of our work is done alone. Still, if we can form alliances, even temporary ones, we can be very strong."

"But you could heal yourself. If you were grievously wounded."

"I have the ability. The powerstrands will obey. They are...mindless...and except for drag, and sometimes being hard to catch, and a hundred other little annoyances. So yes, I could heal myself. But after a while I would seek power for myself, and it becomes addictive."

"Do many wizards become drug addicts?"

"Yes they do. Our training is extensive, and as an apprentice I felt far too much time was devoted to ethics, but now that I have reached this level of expertise, I see why it is necessary."

CeeDee reached over, touched him lightly on his foot, above the biggest and ugliest of his open sores. "I wish I could heal you."

"Time will heal, and should we ever get back to earth, any doctor can. Don't worry about me."

She looked back over her shoulder, at the twisty way they had come. Tiny brown strands worked behind them, erasing the path, but she could still see traces of where they had been. In a land without landmarks, she was confused. "Pierce, how do you know where we're going?"

"I don't. I thought I explained. All that matters is that we move." He took her apple core, and his, and held them in his hand, and a second later, a small green strand slipped through his fingers and vanished, and the cores were gone. "CeeDee, I've been thinking about the astral travel."

"Yes?"

"There might be another way for you to help."

"Another way? Darn. I was so looking forward to the spears," she quipped, and he grinned in acknowledgement.

"When I slip from my body, I leave a tail, a connection between my body and my soul. It is similar to a powerstrand, but without power. I don't know if that makes sense to you—"

"It's the lifeline your soul uses to find your body again."

"That's as good an explanation as any. Now, I'm going to slip from my body for a few minutes. I want you to hunt for the cord. It probably won't be visible at first."

"What do you want me to do with it when I find it?"

"This first time, if you find it, pull it. It will be a test, to see if this will work."

"Sounds good. Let's give it a try."

"There shouldn't be any danger to you, or to your fetus. It will only be a part of me, my life energy, if you will. And you've already felt that."

She blushed, decided his comment deserved none of her own.

"I understand." She chewed a knuckle, thought of a question, hoped it wasn't idiotic to ask such a thing of a major wizard.

"Has anyone ever pulled you back before?"

"No."

"No one ever found your cord and tugged?"

"No."

"Then how do you know it's possible?"

"From reading I've done. Every time I've done astral traveling, I've left my body in a safe spot, or at least what I thought of as a safe spot. We don't have that luxury any longer. It will be easier for me to go without worrying about my body. You do understand that, don't you?"

"Will you stop asking me that? I understand."

"If you can't find it, we're not really out anything. I'll just have to discover another means to find the information I'm looking for. You won't be frightened, will you?"

"I don't think so. I am willing to do what I can."

"I have no sense of time when I'm gone, so although I'm telling you I'll only be a few minutes if you don't find the cord and pull me back, I may be gone quite a while. I won't be dead. Regardless of what you might think."

Standing straight, arms at his sides, feet together, eyes focused on a distant point of his own imagining, Pierce held himself still, then methodically slipped from his body. He would plan be gone a few minutes as he told her, but as long as he was out, he would continue his search.

And, as he rose further from his body, he found something very interesting, and well worth pursuing.

# CHAPTER 19

CeeDee thought she was prepared for what would happen, but as she watched, his body lost animation. She had no idea how she knew, but without a doubt, the person she knew as Pierce was gone, and what was left behind was a shell which only looked like him.

Curious, rather fascinated, she approached him. He lay straight, rigid as a totem pole. His eyes were shut, but with no trace of movement. She trembled, reached out, put her hand to his neck where she pressed against the jugular vein, found a pulse, soft, almost indistinct, but still there. "Alive," she whispered. "He's still alive." Needing further proof, she put her index finger under his nose, felt the slight warmth as he exhaled, the cooler passage of air as his lungs filled with oxygen.

Then, feeling like a voyeur, she continued her exploration of his vacant body. "Pierce, wake up," brought no response, nor did poking him on the arm. She brought his hand to her lips, kissed his knuckles, found the action distasteful, as if she were kissing a fire hydrant or a department store mannequin. He wasn't home, and she was curious.

She placed her palms against his chest, feeling a low level arousal she didn't like. She wanted to explore his body, liked the freedom of touching him, when she didn't have the courage to do so as freely when he was aware. She trailed her fingers up his legs, around his forearms, felt the muscles of his thighs and his shoulders, didn't like how hard they felt, not from use, but from abandonment. She pinched his buttocks, wondered what it would feel like to be so free with him when he could respond, when her touch could be considered a caress and not an invasion.

The power, for all it was heady, was ugly. She could undress him and he wouldn't be the wiser. She could study his chest, and the ugly scars he tried to hide, touch him intimately, explore that male part of him which so held her curiosity. She could wrap her hands around that singular part which had once brought her such pleasure.

But there would be none if he wasn't able to simultaneously enjoy it, wasn't able to respond. No matter what she did to him, he wouldn't know.

Disgusted with herself and the darkness of her thoughts, CeeDee turned her attention to the task at hand. "He said there's a possibility I can see the cord," so, with determination, she set out to look for it.

Without quite knowing why, she walked around to his back, half-suspecting the cord he spoke of would come from the base of his spine, like a tail, but she saw nothing. Nervous, she made several quick circuits, looking for the cord, knowing she would be useless to him if she didn't discover it. Time passed, still he didn't return, and she started to worry.

"You will find it. He has faith you will."

She took a deep breath, steadied herself, as she had seen him do. She whispered "concentrate, concentrate," until she was sure she had her blood pressure under as much control as she could.

Then, for courage, or perhaps because she was superstitious, she rubbed the birthmark on the inside of her wrist, as if looking for her own abilities. "I can do this. I can."

She didn't see it at first. She'd stepped back from him, deciding she would look from a distance, then move closer until, if necessary, she would all put press her eyes against his skin looking for this mystical cord he promised would be there.

She expected it would glow, like a neon colored powerstrand, exhibit power, for his life-force had to be such a source, but it didn't. It was dull, pale and thin, and it reminded her of an umbilical cord. She decided that is exactly what it was, this connection between two distinct parts of him.

She was feeling heady with success, managing to see this lifeline which she suspected would be invisible to most people, when a small sound alerted her she was no longer alone. Checking his vacant body first, she decided the sound did not originate there. They had been walking this transfer point world for what she suspected was close to fifteen hours and in all that time they had been alone. No hulking beasts, no birds in the sky, no insects. Now, as she looked around, saw that condition had changed.

Although none of them were close, a group of what she suspected were monsters approached, running on all fours directly toward her. If they had been silent, she never would have suspected they were there. Over the past day she had grown nauseous scanning the horizon of this orange and yellow bi-colored world and finding nothing to disrupt the monotony, so when she walked she kept her head down, and with Pierce 'traveling' she had concentrated entirely on him. She left herself vulnerable.

The things approaching were black-colored beasts with their heads hanging low, drooling saliva, with their lips pulled back from their long snouts, showing long white, deadly looking teeth. They snarled but

CeeDee recognized it was not in threat, but in anticipation of slaughter. They had broad, well-muscled chests, and what looked like sharply pointed claws. Their teeth would not be their only weapons.

There must have been twenty or thirty, loping toward Pierce and her, black marks against the orange sand. Although from the lack of reference points distance was deceiving in this world, they were close and coming closer.

CeeDee thought perhaps they looked like grizzlies. They bounded, growling and out for blood. She pulled on Pierce's life-cord, and hoped it would be enough to bring him back.

"I've got to go back," he said, annoyed to be drawn from his investigation, but the words were torn from him as he noticed the threat.

"Garntz." Pierce rolled on the sand, coming back to his feet and started fashioning powerstrands into weapons. "I've never seen one before, but I know what they are."

"Monster," she said. As they approached, she knew her comparison to a bear was inaccurate, but she couldn't say how.

They had maybe five, ten seconds before the creatures arrived. "Garntz are supernatural monsters, not from the faerie kingdom, not human, but are considered in the literature more like a golem, a creature made alive by magic."

"I see."

"Fire is about the only thing which frightens them although they can be killed. Decapitation is probably best."

"Well then," CeeDee said, "I'll try to decapitate them."

"Always your best policy."

"Still, fire would be easier."

"There's one significant thing you don't know: wizards can't make fire. Not that it is forbidden, we just can't."

"Bummer."

"My master told me it was because fire was one of the four primal elements: air, fire, water, and earth, but I doubt that's true. I can make air, when I need to breathe, make water when I am thirsty, and what is earth, but any element pure or in compound form found on the periodic table, and there wasn't anything there forbidden."

"Ok."

"I think wizards cannot make fire because fire was matter in transition. Matter turning into energy, heat and light, and because it is in transition, it consumes oxygen, and maybe wizards, no matter how powerful, cannot manage all that all at once."

"Good thing we planned to decapitate them."

"You seem awfully calm about this."

"I thought of screaming, realized it wouldn't do much good.

He grabbed a powerstrand, fashioned it into a long handled spear, caught the boldest one in the chest, as it leaped, seconds away from ripping his throat out. It wouldn't die that way, so the next powerstrand he manipulated he formed into an axe, and drove into battle spewing carnage around him.

He wished he had thought to form a second axe, leave it where CeeDee could reach it, for he didn't like leaving her defenseless, but he was too occupied with the beasts, which had a pack mentality, and they attacked as a single unit.

He hacked, and his axe grew bloody, but their numbers increased, and he knew these were not normal animals, but enchanted, for when one fell victim to his assault, three more appeared, larger and more aggressive than the last.

"CeeDee, to me!" he shouted, and tried to work his way back toward her. She kept her distance, more because of the broad range of his axe, but he lowered the weapon, and pulled powerstrands, and she ran into his arms, and the air shimmered, then pulled apart, and he transferred her from the world they were on to another one.

She fell, on the grass, gasping, shaking, tears running freely down her cheeks, rubbing her stomach, were she felt heaves, and prayed her terror wasn't contagious, and her baby was still safe and unaffected.

"What were they?"

"The short explanation is monsters," he said, releasing the powerstrand, so the axe he held vanished so completely it was as if it were never there.

"Monsters," she said, between gasps, "yes I can see that."

But there was something else he was not telling her. The garntz had no interest in her, they attacked him. They were tools of a master wizard, and they had been seeking him deliberately.

"You're not hurt?"

"No."

She looked around. A few hundred yards in front of her was a two lane road, the traffic sporadic. They were in a tall, untended meadow surrounded on two sides by a massive forest. "Where are we?"

"Upstate New York."

Pierce reached down and gently raised CeeDee to her feet. He knew it wasn't necessary, that she was perfectly capable of getting up on her own, but he wanted to touch her again, and more, he wanted to act chivalrous, show her that beyond being a wizard, he was a man.

"What's here?" The sky was darkening toward night, and the air very cold. Funny she hadn't realized how warm their transfer world was until they came here.

She faced a bonfire about fifteen feet away, and without thinking approached it, needing the heat, the security of something as normal as a well-tended bonfire. The blaze was neatly ringed by round river rocks, the flames almost as high as her shoulders. The fire burned cleanly, without the scent of wood she expected.

"Dragon fire," Pierce whispered, almost in awe.

"Dragon fire? I suppose you mean that literally?"

"Yes. A dragon lit this fire. I've never met a dragon, but I know what this is. It won't easily extinguish, so I have no idea when it was lit."

She held her hands out, appreciating the flames. "The warmth feels good, though, doesn't it?"

"Yes. Dragons are not creatures of Earth, but there are a many who come and go at their own whim."

"Are they dangerous?"

"This one is. He killed a witch I knew and a mortal man. I want to investigate where the battle took place. When I was here before, I was in astral form, so I could do no in-depth analysis."

He looked around. "The inn is right there, can you see it?"

She looked where he pointed. Around them were tall trees, a dozen different kinds, filling in a dense forest. Then as she searched, she saw a house. Not just a house, a massive structure: a mansion or a fortress.

"Yes, I see it. Did it just appear?"

"Yes and no. It's always been there, but it can hide itself. This is the Dragon's Roost Bed and Breakfast."

"This monstrosity is a B&B?"

"Yes. A sanctuary. People who come here are usually in need. I'm not quite sure anyone else can find it."

"Anyone else, normal people on vacation with two children and an itch to see the Adirondacks."

"Exactly."

"I suppose you had a class on this."

"Yes, a couple lessons, anyway. Come on, let's walk around the front."

"The front?"

"When entering someplace where you're not sure of your reception, it's always best to knock on the front door."

"Fair enough."

"Now remember when I asked you to think of a place to transfer to, should you need to escape?"

"Yes."

"Did you pick one?"

"Yes. It's a place I haven't been to in years and no one who knows me now will associate me with it. There won't be a lot of people and I can blend in."

"Good. There's money in your backpack. A lot of it. If you have to leave without me, go to ground as unobtrusively as you can. If you're still talking to me, and I'm still alive, give me a couple days to find you."

"Right now I'll say ok, but if I have to transfer on my own, I doubt I'll be ok."

"Actually, if you have to transfer, you'll be fine. As far as I can tell, you're an extremely strong wizard. You're accepting a lot of this far better than I expected. After your baby is born, try to find someone to teach you the arts. You're old for an apprentice, but you've already mastered all the basics. I don't think you'll have any problems. Now, we're going to the front door. I'm not quite sure what we'll face. Are you ready?"

"Of course. I'm just so happy to get away from this orange sand."

"I promise you, as far as I know there is no orange sand in upstate New York."

He stopped, looked around, sniffing the air. She grabbed his hand, entwined her fingers with his for the slightest of seconds and wondered if she should pull on her transfer powerstrand and disappear to someplace she hadn't seen since she was four years old.

"What do you sense?"

It was growing darker by the second, the sun's rays, which had painted western sky into muted shades of pink and purple, had traveled west so now those in Ohio and Michigan were experiencing sunset. He squeezed her fingers slightly in reassurance. "These woods are loaded with faeries, elves and imps. I've never come across such concentrations."

"Will they bother us?"

"Not at the moment."

"Are they evil?"

"Some, certainly, but mostly they concentrate all their attention on not being caught by humans."

"But wizards are another story, aren't they?"

"Yes. To imps and faeries, wizards are another story."

"Will you think me naive and fanciful, if I said I've always wanted to see a faerie?"

"No, of course not. I would imagine it's another facet of your mage talents. You know instinctively there are other creatures, beings you haven't been trained to see, yet you are perceptive enough to know they exist."

Although fall colors had passed their prime several months ago, she bent down, picked up a branch, maybe three feet long, filled with stunningly beautiful red maple leaves. Then she saw another, this one with yellow leaves, and then another, with orange. Enchanted, she held them together, pleased she had a bouquet.

"How old were you when you first saw a faerie or imp or elf?"

"Twenty-two. I was late in my apprenticeship."

They walked around to the front of the house. Two cars sat in the driveway, and CeeDee laughed to herself, for it looked like they were 'together' by whatever definition.

"We should be able to get a room. And I think there are answers to questions here we're looking for."

"Welcome all who come as friends," CeeDee read a sign beside the front stairs. "Are we friends, do you think?"

"I suppose that remains to be seen."

A dark shadow passed over them, something huge, blocking the sun. "CeeDee, run to the front door. Right now!"

She raised her head, saw what he saw, a creature flying, coming in fast, and although it was still far away, she had no illusions that it was a bird.

It was a dragon.

She started running.

# CHAPTER 20

CeeDee pounded on the door which was opened almost immediately.
"I wasn't expecting anyone—"

"You've got to call the police. There's a dragon, right there—"

"Goodness me, so there is. I wonder what the old worm wants?" The woman who answered was older, maybe in her mid-sixties, with long gray hair woven down her back.

"Are you going to call the police?"

Her eyes sparkled. "Do you think they would do any good? Do you think bullets could get through dragon hide?"

"I have no idea." CeeDee screamed as a molten flow of liquid fire exploded from the dragon, right down into the driveway where Pierce stood. He had fashioned a shield and stood under it, and she could see he held a sword, although for all the fairy tales she'd read knights killing dragons with swords, she didn't see how it was possible, not when the dragon was awing.

*I seek my revenge against you, Wizard,* the dragon said, and it was the most frightening thing CeeDee had ever heard. The words rang like a bell, yet were perfectly understandable.

"Revenge? Revenge for what? You're the one who killed the witch, and a mortal."

*Both were in your employ.* A second bolt of fire flowed.

"No. I did not know the man, and while it could be argued the witch was a friend, I had no dealings with either, and certainly have engaged in no action against you."

*You lie! You kidnapped one of my spawn, intended to slaughter my son when his wings came in, to use in your spells.*

"I and those who stand by me would never commit such an atrocity." Small fires burned around him, but did not seem to be spreading. Nor did Pierce himself look burned.

The dragon settled on the gravel parking lot, settling his wings and blasting Pierce with one final furnace discharge of fire. *You work with Andrew! I know his scent and it is all over you. If you have come to slaughter dragon flesh you will meet your own death first.*

"I seek sanctuary at the Inn."

"Byron," the woman at the door called. "Hear him out."

The dragon shimmered, and a second later it was not a reptile facing Pierce, but a man. "I am not defenseless in this guise. You would be wise to be aware of that."

"If you had just cause to slaughter Belinda and the hunter, then I have no grievance against you. I come seeking answers, nothing more. There is an upset in the power structure I worship. It is severe, and it is centered in this general area. I hold you responsible."

"The wizard you seek is named Andrew. I do know if that is his name or a bastardization of his name of power, but here, we call him Andrew. You are welcome to come in, take tea with the family. I will answer what questions I can."

"There are wizards after me. I would not enter and put your family at risk."

"I can defend myself against wizards. And since I am not certain about you, I have questions I would also like answered."

"I will tell you everything I can." Pierce took the steps to the main door two at a time. As he faced the woman standing at the door he grinned. "I know you. You were a waitress at the diner. Bean soup."

"You could think of me like that. And that's one of my favorite recipes. I turn up where I am needed."

"Jan?"

"You've a good memory. Jan Pikorski."

"Thanks for the idea about the crossword puzzle book. As you can see, it worked."

Jan stood aside, ushering in CeeDee and Pierce. Byron followed on their heels. Chattering about inconsequential things, she led them down a long corridor, through an immaculate kitchen and up a narrow set of stairs.

"One room or two?" Jan asked, as she stood, key in hand on the second floor. "I know you have already started your family, and I don't mean to be rude, it's just in this day and age, it doesn't hurt to ask."

CeeDee fumbled. It was on the tip of her tongue to say "two," when Pierce said, "One will do nicely."

"I know you don't have any luggage, but I suspect you can make what you need. Also, the house is quite adept at providing things like toothbrushes, shampoo and lotion. Anything you cannot find or conjure, let me know. I can generally be found if you call my name in the kitchen downstairs."

"I am sure we'll be fine."

"Also, if you are interested, the family is eating downstairs at eight. You are invited to attend. There's an event planned, so we will all be rather festive."

"Event?" Bryon asked. He had kept quiet, but it was impossible to forget the fire-spewing dragon, even if at the moment he looked like a tall, well-muscled man.

Ignoring him, Jan turned to CeeDee. "You have a wedding bouquet," she said, indicating the colorful fall leaves she held. "Were you just married?"

"No."

"Planning on getting married?"

"No."

"And the dragon?" Pierce asked.

When Byron said nothing, Jan answered. "He lives here. Well, here and there, depending on your ability to grasp definitions. Don't worry about Byron. He and his wife will welcome you. Dress is formal." She turned to leave, then turned back again. "I know your father," she said. "For a moment there, I thought you were him, but I can see you are not."

Pierce inclined his head in acknowledgement of her statement, then with his hand at the small of her back, ushered CeeDee into the room.

"Strange woman," CeeDee said.

"Yes, and you don't know the half of it. There are vortexes all around here, particularly visible in the backyard," he said, looking out the window. "This house stands on the nexus of about a dozen other worlds."

CeeDee ignored the window, concentrating instead on the large, ornate bed, the window hangings, and the room's ambiance. "Did we need one room?" she asked.

"Yes. I don't want you out of my sight while we are within the dragon's jurisdiction."

"Oh," she said, trying to decide if she were pleased or annoyed by his answer. It was said so casually, so matter of fact, and was not at all what she wanted to hear. But before she could continue her internal conversation, Pierce spoke again.

"There is one other reason," Pierce said, inching closer.

CeeDee looked up, expectant. "Yes?"

"I want you all to myself. We are safe here. Not discounting the threat from the dragon, but safe from anything which has been hunting us."

"And you can let your guard down?" she answered, hoping she teased. She still hadn't gotten the statement, the invitation she wanted.

"Yes. We need to regroup, plan a strategy."

"Strategy?" In another moment she was going to strangle him.

He sidled closer, as if he were only interested in powerstrands and tactics for fighting wizards. Then he quirked a half-smile, and when he spoke, it was in a whisper, the words tickling along her neck. "We'll start with your hair," he said.

With clever fingers, he pulled out pins, having her dark hair cascade down her shoulders. His hands dug into the richness there, a prelude, not an attack, and his eyes closed. "The baby won't mind."

She reached out, intending to unfasten the buttons on his shirt. Her hands were not quite steady. She wanted so desperately to love him.

"No," Pierce said, capturing her hands, planting tiny kisses along her fingertips. "Tonight, let me be the one to pleasure you."

"But I want—" she said, pleased when he wouldn't let her finish. How did she know what she wanted, what she needed, when she couldn't think? How could she come up with coherent sentences when his lips traced her neck, when his tongue darted quickly into her ear?

"We'll get to your wants directly," he answered. He made no overt move to remove her clothing, touching her through the material, caressing the tender responsive skin of her cheeks, on the back of her neck. She wanted to be thrown on the bed, to be taken, but her knees were weak, and perhaps she'd let him go slowly this time.

"I like the taste of you. What do you say we skip dinner tonight, and instead I will stay here and feast on you?"

She touched him, how could she not? His hair, his shoulders, the flat enticement of his stomach. Her heart beat faster, thumping, her breath hitched. She was even certain her toes curled, but she felt pleased her voice sounded controlled, reasonable, when she spoke. "I think there is no need to make that decision just yet."

He nibbled on her neck, small, biting kisses, somehow connected to the central heating. For some reason, the room was getting very warm. She felt flushed, knew there was high color on her cheeks, could only imagine what the sensitive skin of her breasts looked like.

"I like it when you do that." Her voice inflection was not quite as controlled as it had been only seconds before.

He laughed, supremely pleased, and she was certain, more than a tad arrogant. "I'm just getting started."

With quiet efficiency, Pierce removed her blouse and her bra. Her eyes were closed, but even had they been open, her sight was unreliable. There seemed to be powerstrands line-dancing or it might have been the conga. Red, yellow, green, a hundred hues all standing straight, watching her, perhaps worshiping.

Her slacks slid down her legs with a motion so quick it had to be magic. Surprised, embarrassed, and a trace insecure, CeeDee put her hands over her exposed breasts and the bump that was her stomach.

The laughter in his eyes died, and now there was only sensitivity, understanding, and passion. "No, don't hide. You are so beautiful, so incredibly beautiful." He placed his palms over her breasts, kneading gently, her nipples puckered tightly, and oh, so very responsive to his ministrations. Seconds later, his lips replaced his hands, laving her tender flesh, his feasting bringing her pleasure. She swayed, her universe unsteady, her eyes clamped shut all the better to absorb all the myriad sensations he evoked deep within her.

Pierce picked her up, carried her to the bed, laid her down gently on sheets which were soft and cool on a bed which was firm, but which gave as he placed his own weight beside hers. His clothing, and whatever remained of hers had vanished. They were not discarded in a heap on the floor; they were not swinging on the chandelier, from being tossed there in a passionate surge of seduction. They had vanished. If she could think later, if she survived this 'now', she would ask what happened to them, and if she could get her clothing back. They had probably been transported to some other universe, and the creatures there were undoubtedly wondering where they came from, what they were.

His kisses continued, the underside of her breasts, the jutting nipples, the hollow where her belly button was. He stopped, and stared deeply, as if reconsidering what he was doing, but she realized he was looking at her stomach, where the bulge from the infant was distinctly visible.

"Do you find that a turn off?" she asked, again wanting to shield herself.

"Exactly the opposite." His face softened, and the intensity of his sexual passion muted, and when he lightly tickled the sensitive skin above her stomach, it was a caress. "I like knowing a child is growing within your body." Pierce kissed her gently, above her belly button, a kiss for a child, a kiss for a woman experiencing for the first time the changes caused by becoming a mother.

"I want to show you something." He left her side, but before she could complain, say that her body ached for the completion she approached but had not reached, he came back with a wiggling powerstrand, a deep blue one, dark and passionate like the Atlantic during a storm. "I don't know if this will work for you, but it might."

He released the strand above where he had kissed her seconds before. She was still sensitive there, her heart throbbed, and her breath was ragged, but as the powerstrand nestled on top of her stomach she felt only softness, like a Persian cat. Pierce took her hand at set it directly on the strand, then put his own larger, warmer hand on hers. "Close your eyes and try to relax."

"You want me to relax? I tell you, relaxing isn't what I want right now."

"We'll finish what we started in a moment. This won't take long. Close your eyes." With his free hand, he gently touched her eyelids, again a caress that had her purring. "Think of your womb, of the perfect life you have growing there."

"Pierce, at the moment, I'd rather think about you."

"I'm sorry. I know my timing is bad. I should have finished what I want too," and her eyes popped open long enough to see the slight of his erection forever in her memory. Yes, he wanted her, and obviously this pause in the lovemaking was not caused by any dysfunction on his part.

"The baby. Think of Rose."

She grinned, felt maternal, whole, complete, and then in the darkness from behind her eyelids, she saw a tiny fetus, sleeping in the waterbed of her love. She saw the placenta attached to the child, the cord that would be cut at birth, but which would remain a tangible reminder between mother and child.

"Is that—"

"That is your child. Our child."

"How?" Her eyes popped open, and the vision vanished, but seeing his expression was the most erotic sight she'd ever seen. His face held rapture as with eyes closed, he looked down through her stomach to a tiny hidden treasure.

"These strands, the royal blue ones, reveal what's hidden. They're sensitive and they don't always answer, and they are very rare, so we were lucky to find this one."

"And I can see my baby."

"I'm not a doctor, and I assure you, this is the first fetus I've ever seen, but CeeDee, the child looks so healthy to me. Growing just right."

"Can you see? Is it a girl?"

He grinned, his hair was all tussled, and he looked boyish. "Do you want to know? Would you rather wait?"

"No, don't tell me. I'll go in for an ultrasound eventually. For now, I'm happy thinking of her as Rose Aurora. Pierce, thank you. And you," her hand still lay between the royal powerstrand and his hand, "thank you for your service."

The strand slipped away, and it looked like it somehow bowed, as if conveying that it had been its honor to show them something so precious.

He leaned over, the distance was slight, and softly, almost reverently settled his lips against hers. A kiss of love, of banked passion, one, then another, then another, and the pulse sped up, between their lips, involving their questing fingers, their dueling tongues. He cupped her breasts, taunting the nipples, which were sensitive from her pregnancy, but which seemed to have a direct connection of the internal feminine workings for that pesky orgasm coiled again.

Pleased with her fevered response, Pierce left her lips, moved lower, kissing her neck, below her ear, working his way down past her stomach and finally parting her intimate lips, the ones at the apex of her thighs. His clever tongue followed suit, and she lost herself while pleasure built, and mounted, growing in intensity.

She had never experienced pleasure this strong and wondered if it were a side effect of pregnancy or if love had anything to do with it, for while she had been intimate with Harry, and tried to convince herself she loved him, she never had. While they were dating, he pursued her, seduced her, made her feel so beautiful and wanton. But making love with Harry always made her a little uncomfortable, and never mindless, like Pierce was making her. The pleasure from Harry, she could admit now, came for the anticipation of making love, not the actual act.

It felt so liberating to finally understand that. Harry was supremely romantic at a candlelight dinner, saying the right things, doing the right things, but in the bedroom, she was always a bit unsatisfied.

But she would not think of Harry any longer, not when there was a man pleasuring her, taking her to heaven. CeeDee coiled her hands around his firm shaft. She stroked him, liking the hardness, the softness, the way Pierce moaned with pleasure.

"Are you going to finish this?" she asked. She licked her lips. "If you don't, I can."

"You'll kill me," he said breathlessly and moved above her so his knees rested on either side of her on the bed, and that marvelous erection approached her. CeeDee removed her hands and reached out, and grasped hold of his hair, pulling so very desperately, trying to get his mouth to mate with hers, so the rest of their bodies could line up. She wanted to be pierced by him. She wanted to be complete with him on her, over her, and in and through her.

"Pierce, I'm dying here," she said, for it felt that way, the ribbons of pleasure coiling, tightening, throbbing. Her body felt hot and cold and needy. She had never felt this degree of desperation before. She needed him buried deep within her, so her body could rock, matching the pace he set, the rhythm they were meant to follow, so she could explode against him.

"My greedy, impatient little wizard," he whispered against her ear, but there was depth to his words, and something that sounded suspiciously like love. He rose on his knees, knelt tall, magnificent, and she reached out, caressed his hard stomach, his chest where this time he had not tried to disguise the ugly scar. "You feel so good to me," she said, wrapping her fingers a bit lower, rubbing and stroking and holding him. "Now I don't want to see anything else. I want to feel."

"Feel?" he asked, feigning outrage as he bent again, continuing his sensual assault of her breasts, his manhood rubbing against her, but not entering, teasing. "Up to this point you haven't felt anything?"

Her hips lowered, rose, high enough that she touched, just barely, the firm part of him to the intimate, desperate part of her. "Right there," she said, as if he couldn't tell, and then, because he seemed to be slow, and she seemed about to collide into a supernova, she said, "Deeper. Right. Now. As. Deep. As. You. Can."

"I fill you," he said and slid home, deep within the wet, welcoming confines of her body.

"You complete me," he bellowed several minutes later as his own pleasure ripped through him.

Naked, sated, cuddled together, Pierce idly rubbed his fingers lightly over her skin. "Would you marry me?" he asked, and was half surprised in himself, for that is not what he meant to say.

"What?"

He could vanish. He had the power. He could lie, although he had sworn to her he never would. Or he could speak his heart.

"I don't know what's going to happen. Powerstrands are vanishing. I've got a dead witch, and a dead wizard who tried to kill either me, or you and me. I've got a baby I've been assured is mine, although I am sure neither of us remembers the moment of its conception. I have wizards I've trusted putting me on trial for something I am certain is not a crime, and never in my life have I wanted anything as much as I want you beside me forever. I'll train you. I'm sure you won't be satisfied until you reach your potential. If I can't teach you because it interferes with our relationship, then I will find someone who can. This I promise. If you marry me I'll never lie to you, and as much as possible as a wizard, a man and a husband, I will put your happiness ahead of my own. I will be faithful to you in my heart and my mind and my soul. Anything you want, you have only to ask. But I want this baby born in a family with a mother and a father. I want no questions when it comes to paternity. Even if he or she," he added with a wink, "can be proven not to be mine biologically, I will claim the child as my own. I can do no less."

"You don't think that."

"Don't think what?"

"That the child is not yours."

"You're right. I don't know how, but this is our baby."

"Magic?"

"I suppose. I never heard of it done before, and it really is an invasion I am glad is not painful to you. I don't even have a clue how I would set about to do it, if I wanted to, which I assure you I didn't. I promise you I don't go donating my biological fluids to other wizards for this purpose."

"Yet another question."

He entwined his fingers with hers, and she grasped him tightly, a sign he hoped that she would not reject his plea.

"Are you sure?"

"I am. Never more so. I cannot deny this connection I feel. Marry me."

"Yes." She laughed and hugged him, and held him tightly. "Yes. I would love to."

"Come, let's go down to dinner and spread our good news."

After a quick shower and ten minutes with the hair dryer, CeeDee twirled in front of the bathroom mirror, watching the way the dress moved with her body. She considered herself only merely passable, she was a librarian for heaven's sake, and she had always felt she fit the stereotype: bookish, spinsterish. Although she was still young, CeeDee always felt she lacked the sparkle that turned men's heads when a woman walked into a room. But this dress made her look incredible.

Sitting on the bathroom counter, stark naked, and more than a little interested, Pierce must have read her mind, for he said, "You look stunning. Every man there won't be able to keep his eyes off you."

She turned again, studying her bare back. The dress was very high in the front, daring in the back, an iridescent material that might have been silk based, or she supposed, moonbeams. He had made it twisting powerstrands while she had foolishly complained she had nothing to wear for a formal dinner. The dress sparkled in a rich midnight blue, interspersed with stars and moons.

"Symbols of wizards since the beginning of antiquity," he told her.

"Then I suppose I need a tall pointed hat."

He coughed politely, into his hand. "Let's not get carried away."

She looked thinner, and, conversely, fuller in all the right places. She never remembered her waist looking so slender and the pregnancy was doing marvelous things to her breasts. They were high, firm, full, and incredibly sensitive. Who knew beyond a child, that a pregnancy could have such a positive effect? That, or his loving earlier. Or his magic.

Like Cinderella's fairy godmother's creation, her dress came with shoes, matching the hue of the dress with heels a height she had never managed before. Perhaps that is why she looked so much taller, more graceful.

She tore her gaze from the looking glass, and stared at him. "Did you do anything?" she asked.

He hiked an eyebrow. "Do anything?" he parroted back. "Could you be a little more specific? I've been doing a lot of things lately. As a matter of fact, if you don't mind arriving to this dinner late, or not at all, there are things I wouldn't mind doing again."

"Stop that!" she said, swatting toward him. The dress had long full sleeves, form-fitting at her shoulders, then spread out with yards of material at her wrist. If she had a tiara, she would have no trouble impersonating a medieval queen. "I am not this..." she said, then broke off, to gaze at her reflection again.

"This?" The idiot was having trouble answering her questions. It seemed all he could do was parrot back some phrase she had just asked.

"This gorgeous."

"You are. That's why I'm having a rather hard time keeping my hands to myself. And CeeDee, although the dress is lovely, it is only because you possess such natural beauty that you look so beautiful."

She decided even that did not detract from her looks, it only made her look more enticing, more of a challenge. She could hear the rate of his breathing change.

"Then you only like attractive women?"

"I only like you."

From her high neckline, the dress cupped her breasts, then swung freely, loosely, both highlighting and concealing her pregnancy.

"Wolfgar and I are starving. You have to feed us."

"You are not to call my child Wolfgar. Do you understand?" he asked, and he growled, but it wasn't nearly as endearing as when she did it.

"I want food. And I want to be fair. If it's a boy, I don't want him to have a complex that I called him Rose for the long gestational months."

"I could tell you."

"And spoil the fun? No, thanks. But I must be satisfied."

"Here?" he asked. "Satisfied? Again?" His eyebrow hiked and there were all kinds of unspoken innuendos involving tubs and showers and marble countertops.

"No. Downstairs. You are going to act civilized, and if the opportunity presents itself, you are going to ask your questions, but most of all, you're going to behave yourself around the dragon. After all, we are his guests."

"I can act civilized. Can I do your hair?" Without waiting for her permission he twisted a powerstrand and her hair coiled and curled and shimmered in a regal-looking up do.

She touched her hair. "I love it. But, are you sure this is me?"

"Darling, it's always been you. And in case you haven't recognized one salient fact, I could be dead and be attracted to you."

"Well," she blew out a deep breath. "I guess that takes care of me for the Ball. Still, there is one other thing."

"You want jewels?"

"No."

"Perfume? I have to tell you that scents are not really my thing."

"No."

"Manicure? Pedicure?"

"No." She sounded exasperated.

"What?"

"I really hate to mention this, because I am enjoying the view, but don't you think you should get dressed?"

# CHAPTER 21

"Oh. Why didn't you say so?" He stood, and in the space of going from sitting to standing, probably less than three seconds, he stood fully dressed in black tie and tails.

"I could put my robe on if you think I need it."

"Tell you what: if I think you need it, you can conjure it."

"It's not actually conjuring, I mean, witches use that word."

"Let's not fight over semantics. Wolfgar and I are hungry."

CeeDee thought Pierce looked rather devastating in his formalwear, especially because he had a rather scruffy looking five o'clock shadow that he left. She liked clean shaven men, had no idea the start of a beard could be so sexy, except as she rubbed her lips, she remembered the slight abrasion from kissing him, and realized she did know why a beard was sexy. It added another texture to their loving. Hard. Soft, bristly, the list of adjectives involved in their lovemaking could go on.

She would have to insist, if they ever married, that he wear a tuxedo and provide the dress. Holding hands, they went down the back staircase to the kitchen and were met by an attractive woman facing four children locked in high chairs. The dress she wore was reminiscent of a formal Japanese kimono, a brilliant yellow with embroidered fire breathing dragons in the fabric. If CeeDee wasn't so entranced with her own dress, she'd be jealous.

"Hi, I'm Lori." She held her hand out, and shook hands first with CeeDee and then with Pierce. "I love that dress. Did the house provide it?"

"The house?"

"I'm not giving away any secrets. You didn't come in with luggage and this house has the occasional habit of supplying exactly what you need."

"How fabulous must that be? But somehow he made it. I try not to ask."

"I understand. There are so many things Byron is involved in I don't want to know about."

"She's the dragon's wife," Pierce said by way of introduction.

"Yes, of course. We met the dragon earlier."

"I can see you don't believe about the house. It took me a long time too, before I could accept that things just showed up."

"Are you, and I don't know how to put this delicately, always tripping over bones?"

Lori's laughter rang through the kitchen. "That's a worry alright, but Byron eats the bones too, or he isn't allowed to bring his kills into the cave."

"Sounds like a good plan for marital bliss. If I haven't said anything yet, let me mention I find your dress stunning. Are you afraid to get it dirty watching the children?"

"This house is loaded with magical spells, but my absolute favorite is nothing stains."

"I'll have to see if I can find that spell for myself, although I'm not much of a klutz."

"And these are our boys." All four were wearing nothing more than diapers, playing patty-cake with their dinners. Seeing their expression, Lori laughed. "I know. They make quite a mess. It is apparently a draconic trait. Their father will bathe them later. He's getting quite expert at it. They are not human children. I know they look it, but they are dragons, so I'm trying desperately to raise them as such."

"I am glad you found this one's chakra," Pierce said, touching one of the children.

"Yes, me too. We're all sleeping easier since he became complete."

Chakra? CeeDee wondered, but decided to table her question for later, for a huge hulking monster entered the dining room, walking toward them. He was greener than any normal flesh color, with huge wings growing out of his shoulder blades. He had a long snout, horns and ferocious looking fangs. CeeDee moved closer to Pierce, giving him room to fight, if he had to. Lori made no move to protect her children.

"It is good to see you again. When Jan told me there was a wizard coming to the celebration tonight, I wondered if it were you."

"My pleasure. We were never formally introduced before. I am Pierce Billova, this is my lady CeeDee Radling."

"Milton St. Caspian. My wife will be joining us soon." He turned and faced Jan, the only other adult in the kitchen. "Your dinner will not be ruined. Her car is pulling into the drive as we speak."

"My dinners are never ruined. Milton, be a dear and pour the wine, will you?"

The monster did not get a chance to carry out his assignment, for an attractive red-haired woman ran into the room, jumping into his arms. "I made detective!" she screamed.

"Then we have another reason to celebrate tonight," he said, nuzzling her neck with his snout.

"If you give me about thirty minutes, I'll run upstairs and change." Brenda said. She was wearing a police uniform, complete with a holstered sidearm.

"With your permission?" Pierce asked.

"What?" Brenda asked, when Milton held his hands out, palm up, indicating he had no objections, that it was her decision.

"I could dress you."

"It's weird," CeeDee said, fingering the material of her dress, "but I think he's got a flair for women's fashion."

"Yes, if this wizarding business doesn't work out, I could always go into dress design," he said dryly.

"I'm game. Will it take long? Jan doesn't like to have her dinners held up, and I know the boys. It is unlikely they'll remain this placid for much longer."

Pierce waved his hands, in an abrupt, exaggerated movement, which CeeDee knew was complete drama. "Mercy," Brenda said. "I've got a fairy godmother. I feel like I should start singing 'bippity, boppety, boo'."

The dress was a deep, rich hunter green, with a wide gold belt and a full, almost floor length skirt. The neck was high, the sleeves of the dress puffed out, then were tight from the elbow to the wrist. She looked like she should have a knight beg a favor from her. "What do you think?" she asked her husband.

"I think you have always been lovely, and the dress enhances your beauty."

"Your uniform and your weapon are on a high shelf in the bathroom CeeDee and I use. I didn't know where else to put it. If you tell me where you want it, I'll have it moved."

She waved her hands in dismissal. "There's no need. Things in this house have a habit of moving to where they're needed. And I do love the dress. Will it turn into my old servant's clothing at midnight?"

"No time limit for this magic. Should you like it, it can be allowed to stay that way."

"Now that we are all here, I would like us all to be seated," Jan said. She sat at the head of the table, Byron at the foot. The seat immediately to her right was empty.

"And look, there's a cake," Brenda said. "Is it for me? Did you already know I made detective before I told you?"

"No. I have not interfered. Jan started making this cake early this morning. She told me it was a wedding cake."

"A wedding cake?" CeeDee asked, her mouth suddenly feeling dry.

Jan shrugged, but made no movement to start bringing food to the table. "This is very hard to explain. Sometimes the tasks I do are for the future. Sometimes they are for the past. And occasionally I do something for the day it is needed. I rarely know from moment to moment what my tasks are going to be, and when they are for, but I do know this wedding cake is for today."

The four tier cake was decorated in a silver ganash and decorated with white roses made of icing. "When I saw the bouquet, I thought it was for you."

"Bouquet?"

"The leaves. They're lovely, aren't they?"

The branches with the brilliantly colored fall leaves were in a vase on the table, serving as a centerpiece.

"That's the front door. If you will excuse me," Byron said. He was back almost immediately. "There are about a hundred elves, imps and faeries at the door, here to bless a wedding. Should I let them in? They brought more food."

"Honey nectar?" Brenda asked. "Since I've been pregnant, I'm starved for honey nectar."

"Yes."

"You're pregnant too?" CeeDee asked.

"There's something in the water," Brenda answered.

"Or the tea," Lori finished.

"I'm relatively certain that's not how it happens," Pierce said.

"Would you like to explain how it does happen, then?" CeeDee asked.

"In your case, no."

"Should I invite the faeries in? I hesitate to leave them unattended at the front door."

"Yes, they can come in. Green living room. If nothing else, they can entertain themselves."

"As for a wedding, I asked CeeDee if she would marry me a few minutes ago."

"And I said yes," CeeDee answered, radiating her happiness.

"So, you're our couple? Do you wish to be married this minute?"

CeeDee's expression turned slightly panicked. "I haven't even had twenty minutes to get used to the idea myself."

"We don't have to rush into anything," Pierce said. "If you want a big, fancy wedding, in the spring or the fall or even next year, it can be arranged."

"No," she said, then finished, "I mean yes," she said. "I'd love to be married right this minute in this fairy tale castle surrounded by dragons and imps and whatever you are."

"Gargoyle," answered Brenda and Milton simultaneously.

"I haven't got a ring," Pierce said, "and I'd rather not make one, although I can, and replace it with gold."

"I've got a set," Byron said, going to a kitchen drawer and coming back with a velvet covered black ring case. "If you don't like these, I've got two dozen or more at the store."

"My husband's a jeweler," Lori said. "I'm sure you know the legends about dragons and their gold. Sadly, all true."

CeeDee pulled the emerald cut diamond engagement ring from the box and held it up beside the matching white gold wedding band. "It's what I've always dreamed of. They're perfect."

Pleased with the quality and the style, Pierce asked, "I suppose you take MasterCard?"

Byron shrugged. "We'll deal with that later."

"If you would rather wait, there is no hurry," Jan said. Lori was taking the leaves from the vase, wrapping the base in paper towels, then covering it in ribbon.

"Today sounds perfect."

"If you've got parents, they'll yell," said Lori, who spoke from experience.

"CeeDee?"

"I want to be married, right this minute. Pierce, I want this baby to have you for a father, no matter who he is genetically linked to."

"It's my child," Pierce said, taking her hand. "Do you want a wedding dress? Something white with a veil?"

"This is perfect," she said, swirling the full skirt. "Moons and stars, like a real wizard."

"Then if we're doing this like a real wizard," he said, and a moment later his tuxedo was covered with his robe. "And you'll get your chance to meet the faeries."

"Make sure you get your piece of cake early," said Brenda. "Trust me, all these faeries have a sweet tooth. There won't be any left. Not even crumbs."

"Do we need a blood test, or a license?"

"I've got the license here," Jan said. "And your marriage will be legal. I should warn you, I officiate at your wedding with the power I was granted as keeper of this Inn. That means there will be no divorce."

"That means we will be happy every day of our lives," CeeDee said.

"She married Byron and me," Lori said. "So far so good."

"And Milton and me," Brenda added. "We couldn't be happier."

"Well, let's not keep the imps waiting."

"Always a good idea," said Jan. "If they feel we've kept them waiting too long, they may eat the curtains."

Brenda rolled her eyes. "And the rug."

"And the books," Lori added.

"And the drywall," Byron added, sharing a look with his wife.

"And sometimes I'm certain we're missing cats," Jan said, "but so far they've always come back, even if days after the imps have gone."

CeeDee linked her fingers with Pierce. "I suppose every little girl dreams of her wedding day, what the venue will be like and the guests, and this is so much more fabulous than anything I imagined."

"I suppose that means we're ready," Pierce said, "although we'll probably have to allow my mother to host a dinner later. We'll tell her we were so totally in love that we couldn't wait another minute."

"Always best to stick with the truth," said Milton, the hulking gargoyle.

"Oh, I'm glad there won't be pictures. The boys are a mess!" Lori said, and Pierce waved his hands again and all four toddlers were dressed in perfect tuxedos, faces clean, hair brushed.

"If I pay you, would you show up every day and do that for me?" Lori asked. Byron, beside her, rolled his eyes.

The green living room had the appearance of a small sports arena with stadium seating for the imps. They were smallish creatures with odd facial features and mostly long ears, who were behaving as if this were a playoff game and their team was the favored. "Do they bite?" she wanted to whisper to Pierce, but seconds before her wedding ceremony didn't seem like the proper time to be voicing such concerns. Milton and Byron spoke to some, but it was sociable, like getting reacquainted with friends not seen in a while. Lori herded her boys, as if the four crawling children were sheep, but the boys giggled, having the time of their lives. They were apparently no strangers to imps.

While the room was huge, CeeDee could see the back wall was filled with tables overflowing with delicious smelling food, which had her stomach juices gurgling. The food was presented like works of art, small pyramids of vegetables or fruits, three dimensional statues of cakes and breads.

The four tier wedding cake had somehow made it in from the kitchen and stood on a table by itself, decorated with flowers, surrounded by a bubbling fountain. If she had thought elves and imps ate mushrooms and bugs in the dark she was sadly mistaken judging by this feast.

She walked deeper into the room, holding Pierce's hand, as if should she let go, this fantasy panorama of wedding extravagance would vanish. They stopped in front where there was fireplace with a roaring fire, the ten foot mantle decorated with cream colored vanilla scented candles and green ivy. Other pillar candles were dispersed throughout the main floor. A wedding arch covered with ivy had been placed a few feet in front of the fireplace, and Jan placed Pierce and CeeDee there. Oddly enough as soon as she handed her vibrant leaf bouquet to Brenda and took Pierce's hand, CeeDee noticed the floor swarmed with powerstrands, most standing tall, sitting on the shortest of tails, as if a dachshund begging. She believed they came to give honor to her marriage, and CeeDee felt more deeply in love, and with a contradictory emotion, she felt should someone pinch her she would wake up and this fantasy would disappear. Sometimes things were just too perfect to be believed.

Jan, who had been wearing a floor length spotless housedress that had obviously seen countless washings, now wore a navy blue embroidered dress, studded with flickering gems that caught the candlelight and sparkled. It looked like something a queen would wear. Her hair, worn a few minutes earlier in a long braid down her back, now circled her head in a crown, with jewels randomly dispersed, adding to the regal image. She held her hands out, and the auditorium grew silent.

"We are joined together in happiness," she started, her face almost as radiant as CeeDee felt her own. "The union of a man and a woman into a husband and wife is a sacred ordinance, initiated with the first humans on this planet, Adam and Eve, and continued through this day with those who hold the power to seal for all eternity. With the vows spoken, the two shall become one: one heart, one voice, one purpose. Neither shall have dominion over the other, for marriage is a joining of equals."

Jan's words were magical, musical, and it felt almost, but not quite like a well-rehearsed ballet performance, with a full orchestra playing in rising crescendo and everyone doing their part while she and Pierce were somehow blessed by this odd mixture of guests.

When asked to speak her vows, CeeDee did so with a firm controlled voice, certain she was doing the exact right thing for precisely the right reason. Standing there beside him, his hand wrapped with hers, her love for Pierce doubled, or perhaps quadrupled. Her heart, thumping, felt near to exploding. She knew she had no understanding of the word 'eternity' but recognized as Pierce slipped the diamond engagement ring and the flawless etched wedding band on her finger that she would have a lifetime and perhaps longer, to hone her definition.

"You may now share your first kiss as husband and wife," Jan said several minutes later.

Pierce tightened his grip on her hand. He hadn't let go since the kitchen, and brought her into his arms. His eyes twinkled and he looked very pleased, as if he had gotten very lucky indeed.

"I may have been dead when I first met you, but I don't believe I started living until then. In front of these witnesses I vow I will do my best to make you happy every day of your life."

Then, not giving her the time to express the same vow, their lips met. The kiss was long, passionate, and every faerie, imp and elf in the place was widely cheering before it finished.

"My husband and I would like to thank you all for witnessing our happiness," CeeDee said. "I've never met any faeries before but I have to say from this day forward when I think of faeries, I will do so with happiness. And I hope I am not breaking any secret wizard covenants when I say if any of you have problems that a lawyer, a librarian or two wizards, one which will be an apprentice for a long time, can solve, we would be honored if you came to us."

"That's a pledge none of them will forget," Jan said, but she rubbed her eyes and looked like the statement moved her deeply.

"Faeries often have problems with humans, witches, wizards and their ilk," said a small bearded man who CeeDee thought she heard was a brownie, but it might have been he was eating a brownie, for the food was brought forward and the reception had everyone in a mood to party.

"We would be most grateful for mediators to hear our grievances."

Pierce bent down, speaking to the diminutive man eye to eye. "On my word I will honor my wife's pledge and add my own. We will offer support and appeal to justice to all who come to us."

"We can pay."

"Good," Pierce said, kissing his wife again, "for I understand raising a child will be expensive."

"Then your life has already been blessed," this from an ethereal woman with fluttering wings who looked like she couldn't weight twenty-five pounds. "Children are our greatest blessings."

"I should like to raise my child to be a friend to all faerie," Pierce said, "but before I exchange promises, I have a quest I must fulfill. Powerstrands are missing and we seek a wizard who goes by the name Andrew, responsible for much evil."

"We have myriad grievances against this wer-wizard ourselves. He is responsible for the slaughter of thousands of imps, elves and other creatures of faerie. We will help you as much as we are able."

"Good, and I offer my thanks in advance. Now, while I am eager to continue with my quest, I should take my bride up to our room. We have much to discuss regarding this change in our relationship. I imagine it will take the whole night. I will meet with those of you who care to offer aid or information tomorrow, say five o'clock in the morning?"

CeeDee rolled her eyes. "To support a new wife, can you make it seven? I don't want to send him out to fight evil when he's exhausted."

Around them, all the faeries cheered.

They stayed for the reception, especially since CeeDee insisted she and Wolfgar were starving. And thanks to Brenda running interference, and what sounded like a very loud roar from the gargoyle, they each managed to get a piece of wedding cake, although seconds after they were offered their piece, true to predictions not even a crumb of the magnificent cake remained. Wine was served as well as a dark bronze colored honey mead, for faeries do like their spirits. Brenda and CeeDee abstained, and in their honor, so did Pierce, who found himself toasting the marriage time and again with tea, which had a rich almost creamy taste of vanilla and perhaps hazelnut, that somehow made him feel invigorated. He had no idea where Byron had gone.

While they were eating and socializing, the faeries had brought a band, ethereal musicians and instruments he did not recognize, but the music was lively and many tunes recognizable. "Do they listen to the top 40?" Pierce asked, although it wasn't pop songs he heard, more like folk music, timeless, familiar. He was relatively certain he had been rocked to sleep as an infant to many of these tunes.

"No. It is entirely possible all human music has roots in faerie lore. Some humans are sensitive and can hear the tunes, often without physically hearing them," said Milton who had been dancing with his wife. For such a large, hulking creature, he appeared very light on his feet.

The song, which had been lively, joyous, ended, and another began, this one eerie, haunting. It left CeeDee with an unnamed ache, and a desire to keep wiping her eyes. All the elves and most of the imps and faeries joined in the singing, a dirge, perhaps, of lost homelands, lost comrades, lost opportunities, the words spoken in a language she could not understand. After several seconds of prolonged silence after the last bar faded, a new tune began, this one again spirited, lively, and all the more jubilant because of the comparison.

"Will you be staying long?" Milton asked. He had been hand feeding his wife who continued to fight him, insisting she could locate her own mouth, while obviously enjoying their joint ministrations.

"I leave in the morning. I don't know how long I'll be gone. With Jan's permission, I would love to return and enjoy the Inn when things no longer pressure us. This place is unique. I would like to get to know the elves and other creatures who roam here, and take time to heal, for I can see there is something here far more relaxing than just good friends and good food can provide."

"This Inn is blessed with healing," Milton said, while Brenda shoved a slice of cake into his snout, apparently feeling she was getting revenge for she laughed, but his tongue was long, and he did not seem to mind cleaning his own face.

Pierce grabbed his bride's hand again, tightening his grip momentarily in love and reassurance, speaking as much to her as to the gargoyle. "I would like CeeDee to stay while I am gone. I have seen the wards on this house and know she will be safe here. There is a wizard who I would like to see die at my hands."

"If we are talking about the same wizard, there are many of us at this table," Lori said, "who feel the same way. Also, although I hate to admit it, there's something I can do that might help. I can close portals."

CeeDee was about to comment something along the lines of "Well, duh, I can shut doors too," when Pierce's mouth dropped open.

"Are you sure?"

"I've done it twice before. This Andrew has an interest in opening them. I don't quite know what he's looking for, but he hasn't found it yet."

"Have you told anyone—"

"No, and I'd appreciate it if you didn't either. My husband is possessive of my time. Maybe later, when the kids are in school or something I'll hire myself out, but right now we're not hurting for money."

"Still, there are about a dozen doors that should be shut, just to make it easier for the people living around them. The one on Mount St. Helens is a good example."

"Mount St. Helens volcano is the result of a wizard's work?" CeeDee asked shaking her head. The more she learned about wizards the more she didn't know about wizards.

"Absolutely. It's been centuries since it was opened but things would be a lot better if someone could find a way to close it permanently."

Before she started fighting the headache she felt growing behind her eyes, CeeDee made a silent pledge to ask Pierce about shutting doors, and whisked him off to the dance floor where they joined imps and perhaps thirty distinctly different species of elves.

The music was just a bit fast, but Pierce held her securely in a slow dance, molding his body to hers. "I thought I'd never get you alone. Do you think wedding festivities were devised solely so the bride and groom couldn't escape easily, and thereby driving them out of their minds?"

She laughed, loving the feel of him, the pleasure of touching, swaying with the music. They both understood they weren't dancing, rather subtly and significantly starting their marriage, determining how they would relate to each other, how they would survive the trials they would face.

CeeDee rubbed her forehead against his. "Is it possible to put the quest on hold for two weeks? I'd like a long vacation here, learning about magic and portals and what certain wizards like in bed."

"You will be safe here."

"That's not what I meant. I'll soon be too pregnant to be seen in public."

"In case you're wondering, I think pregnant women are hot."

"You're turned on by pregnant women?"

His grin was devilish and his hips, as he danced, brushed against her. "Absolutely."

"This a new appreciation, or something you've had for some time now?"

"I'd have to say it started about ten minutes ago, although there were definite symptoms on the Rhode Island beach."

"So, you're going to keep me barefoot and pregnant?"

"We'll take our marriage one day at a time, and discuss how quickly we want our family to grow."

"First we find out who's trying to kill you, me or us."

"Absolutely."

"And get a hold on missing powerstrands."

Sexual arousal before this had always been a hormonal thing for him, response to external stimuli he could act on or ignore. Now, caressing the soft skin of her arms, breathing in the intoxicating scent of her hair, studying the countless expressions of her eyes, he knew how superficial that was. His sexual arousal with this woman was based on ten or twelve different things. Maybe more. And any one of them would have him looking for a bedroom. "What was the question?"

"At least you remember there was a question. I have to give you credit for that. "We have to get control of the missing powerstrands."

"Yeah, it's my assignment." How could he think when holding her?

"And if there is a chance to stop Andrew, we'll do that too."

Pierce rested his lips against hers, again and again, and whispered, "As long as it doesn't interfere with me loving you."

# CHAPTER 22

They were pulled apart when things were just starting to get interesting by three bearded elves, although they might have been dwarves or heaven only knows, brownies. "Hey! Let me show you how faeries drink!"

It was late, probably approaching three or four in the morning when the bride and groom made it back to their room. "CeeDee, just a minute."

"What?"

"I've got a message."

"Message?" She looked for a phone, or a letter shoved under the door.

"Powerstrand," he said. "When one wizard wants to communicate with another. They are not used often, because they can be diverted, and worse, they can be changed, so they are occasionally dangerous." He moved closer. "I recognize my master's hand in this one, so I'm sure it's safe."

"Can I see it?"

"Sure." He reached out, took her hand in his. For a second a deep sense of wellbeing flashed through him, that he could see himself ten years from now, fifty years, working beside her and holding her hand exactly like this.

"What?" she asked.

"What?"

"Your face went all, I don't know soft or confused, or something."

"I don't often see the future, and I'm not sure that's what it was, but CeeDee, I want you to know I'm glad we married, and I'm going to do my best to teach you all I can."

"All that in the message?"

"No. I haven't opened the message yet." Still holding her hand in his left, Pierce used his right to open the message.

COMFORT

"Comfort?" CeeDee asked.

"You got that?"

"Just about hit in the head with it."

"You're going to be a joy to teach. You've got all the basics down. Are you sure no one's been instructing you?"

"I'm sure. What does comfort mean?"

He shrugged, pulled her beside him as he sat on the edge of the bed to remove his shoes. "I'm not sure. Any number of different things, I suppose. It could mean we're safe here, and we don't have to keep running from the wizards who were following us. Or I suppose a more obvious thought might be reassurance. He recently did something to me I could construe as betrayal, I'm not sure I saw it as that, but it left me confused. This might be a sign he was acting in my best interests by not telling me the whole story. Also, I suppose it's not impossible to think he knows about our marriage. I doubt he's watching, but imps and elves have a rather elaborate communication system, or so I've been told, so one of them could have dropped the news. It's entirely possible he speaks with elves."

"Do you? Speak with elves?"

"Besides this evening? They rarely come up in the work I do, but they've been known to throw a party I've been invited to. I'm sure you've noticed they like a good party."

"How come normal people don't know about these parties?"

"Normal people have no trouble coming up with parties on their own. Elves and people don't traditionally get along."

"So, comfort." She sidled against him, slipped into his arms as if to nestle into sleep. "I'm all for comfort."

"Then you're likely to be disappointed, because I'm in the mood for hard and fast."

"Hard and fast?" she said, laughing as he waved his arms and her clothing disappeared. "Yeah, I can do hard and fast."

\*\*\*

After consummating their marriage, Pierce decided there wasn't enough time for sleep before he had to go downstairs and meet with the elves, so pragmatically he decided he needed a shower, and CeeDee did too.

"Are you coming?" he asked, his hand on the doorknob, about to walk into the hallway.

"I'm naked."

"Yeah, I noticed. I kinda like you that way. Do you think we could somehow make a promise to spend most of our time together naked? I mean I understand librarians have this prudish image to maintain—"

"I am not a prude!" she insisted, slipping into a robe.

"You are, but don't worry, I'll break you of that habit soon enough." Before she could respond, he grabbed her and tossed her robe away, held her over his shoulder, butt end high. She squealed and kicked, and pounded his back, but he laughed, and as far as he could tell they made it to the bathroom with no one the wiser, not that it would have mattered.

The well-appointed bathroom had no shower.

Still holding her, and ignoring the pelting he received down his back, Pierce declared the tub perfect and started the taps running.

"Have you ever made love in a bathtub?" he asked. He lowered her slowly from his shoulder making sure her body rubbed against his, hitting all the highlights.

"If you think I'm going to bathe with you after that Neanderthal tactic, you've got another think coming." Her disavowal would have had more force behind it if her nipples hadn't puckered, and her body flush as she studied the effect she had on his anatomy.

"Personal cleanliness is important," he said, wiggling his eyebrows.

"While I'm not a prude I don't think—"

"Don't worry, I've dozens of irritating habits you can break me of, but first we've got to work on this one of yours." He dropped her carefully, although there was a massive splash, into the tub, and then slipped in front of her, so they faced each other, his legs riding above hers. The water was delightfully hot and the tub itself massive. There was no doubt they were not the first couple to put his perfect tub to such intimate use.

CeeDee leaned back against the side, shutting her eyes in faux relaxation while Pierce found some foaming soap and started cleaning her breasts with deep concentration, and after a few minutes replacing the cloth with his lips.

"I think—" she started, and he laughed.

"I stopped thinking during the ceremony. I am just feeling, and if I haven't told you, what I feel for you is love."

She felt effervescent, as if champagne bubbles popped in her bloodstream. "I love you too."

"Good, then come over here, position yourself on my lap." The action came naturally to her, and she lowered her body and with a single purposeful thrust, made them one. He stayed still for a second, letting her get used to his width and length, letting himself adsorb all the tiny tremors he felt pass through her body, faster than the speed of sound. Everything felt so right.

She wrapped her arms around his neck, finger combed his hair while at the same time he held her tightly, raining a thousand small yet powerful kisses along her neck. Laughing, CeeDee raised her hips, enough to separate them slightly, teasing, taunting, and he growled, deep and feral, and plunged back down inside her. "You'll not get away from me that easily."

For long, delightful minutes they rocked and splashed. She only felt passion and love and an explosive completion which came all too quickly. It was, she decided, the very best way to start a marriage.

Keeping his arm wrapped around her, her back now to his chest, Pierce relaxed. "It's getting cold in here. Let me add some more hot water."

"Wait a second." CeeDee closed her eyes, let the sensation of warmth travel through her. A moment later the water warmed.

"You manipulated the powerstrands! I thought you said you couldn't."

"No, I just heated the water. I like to take baths and just soak and after a while, if I think about it hard enough, it gets warmer. I was always sure it was my imagination, but I do like to soak in hot water."

"I'd really like to know how powerful you are, since you are manipulating powerstrands without even being able to see them. We'll start your next lesson right now."

"I don't know much about being a wizard, but I think it doesn't involve the part of you that is growing hard."

"Sorry. Wedding night. And you're right. Making love has nothing to be with being a wizard. It's just I find you so sexy."

She picked up a washcloth, started rubbing his arms. "In that case, how about if we work on the lesson another time?"

Later, in their room with damp blue towels piled in heaps, the ones they had used to dry each other, the ones they had each used on their own hair, CeeDee nestled against her husband. "Pierce, I've got a question." The bed was large but very little was being used. Every inch of her body which could possibly be in contact with his was. The sweat from their exertions had dried, and the air in the room smelled deeply of the passion they had just renewed.

"Only one?" he asked, lightly caressing her breasts.

"All right, at least a hundred. I thought if I said that though, I would scare you off."

"I am so relaxed now, I doubt if the dragon could scare me off," he said with a grin. "And you do know there is a dragon around here somewhere. Please, little wizard, if there is something I can tell you, ask."

Little wizard. She cherished the endearment, now, lying naked in his arms, but she would break him of that soon enough. She was not his 'little' anything.

She was afraid to ask her question, afraid of his reaction, and knowing the answer, so, she asked a banal one. "What time is it?"

"Yes, that is a question which could scare me off. I am glad you warned me before you plundered the depths of my knowledge." She tried to hit him, but he captured her hand, and kissed her knuckles, then placed her palm over her rounding stomach, his own warm hand over hers.

"Is it a bad thing for a wizard to have a child?"

He caressed her tummy, let her know through his actions, if his words were not enough, the truth of his statement. "Yes, and no. Generally, none of us want children. It is not something we are taught, it is something we know. Wizard children are very hard to raise, children of mages are always more powerful than their parents, and what wizard wants to raise a child who will be stronger than he is?"

"But some wizards do have families?"

"Yes, of course, or there wouldn't be any left. But wizard children tend to be willful and dangerous. It's hard to keep a seven or eight year old in public school if he can have instant gratification by manipulating a powerstrand. Keeping a secret isn't easy, especially one that would make you look powerful."

"They tend to be bullies?"

"So I've been told. My own childhood was different, as I knew I was different, knew it with every fiber of my being, and I had no idea how to tap into my heritage. I studied arcane books, but trust me, little to nothing of what is written about witches and wizards is true."

"Or dragons."

"Yes, or dragons. And I suppose if we're feeling magnanimous, we could add elves, imps and the rest of the faerie kingdom as well."

"Do you fear this child?"

"No. We will find some way to raise him so that he gets all of the benefits of his birthright, and none of the detriments. I don't know how. We may have to send him away to someone else to learn discipline, but that decision is years in the future, if ever. CeeDee, this I swear to you: I want to see my son or daughter take his or her place as one of the strongest mages of this century."

"And we won't have to worry about playground bullies picking on him."

Pierce moaned. "We'll work on the definition of the word 'secret'."

"There's something else. I don't want you to leave me here," CeeDee said. "I want to go with you."

"Someone is trying to kill me and I think it's not much of a stretch to say someone is after you too. I wouldn't be able to survive if something happened to you, and I don't want to take the chance of someone hurting you in an effort to best me."

"But this is as much my quest as it is yours. Remember, when you were looking for clues as to who did this to you, you found me."

He kissed her tenderly on top of her head. "You can come. I need you. How or why I don't know, but I think it would be a mistake for us to separate. Yes, you will be protected here, but wizards aren't always known for doing the safe thing."

"We should get dressed. It's time."

"I've never had a night go so quickly. You are a distraction."

"Good. I like that. I like being able to distract you."

They dressed quickly and raced down the stairs to the kitchen.

"Jan had something she had to do," Byron said when they got down to the kitchen, "but there is oatmeal if you're interested. I know it's not much. This kitchen usually runs to fancy breakfasts, omelets, Danish, Belgian waffles, fruit salads, enough food to feed a conquering army."

"Oatmeal is my favorite breakfast," CeeDee said. She scooped a big bowl, and then added toppings, brown sugar, chopped walnuts, raisins, dried apricots. "Eat this, it's good for you," she said handing the bowl to Pierce, then going back and doctoring her bowl the same way. "You've got to keep up your strength."

"Yeah. We have no idea what we're going to find. Is the gargoyle around?"

"No. Milton went to Albany with Brenda. They left earlier this morning. But I can answer any questions you have."

"And I have information. We met last night," said a small, bearded man. At first CeeDee thought he was a midget, but realized from his long nose and pointed ears, that he was an elf.

"I am Elfben. I am leader over a mess of elves in the forest around here. At the moment I speak for the faeries and the good imps too."

"Elfben, it's a pleasure," said CeeDee. "You were at the wedding."

"Yes. Weddings are important to us and should be celebrated. I, like those with me yesterday, offered my blessings. But that is not why I have come this morning. There is an artifact missing and so I have been searching the portals. I haven't found it, but I have some information perhaps you do not, and it is possible this artifact fits into your quest."

"Does it involve Andrew?"

"Yes," Elfben said, but Byron interrupted.

"I'll start that story. When my wife went to school in Arizona, she dated a man named Andrew Westline. She thought he was a normal grad student but it turns out he was a wer-wizard who sought to open portals as a way to increase his own power. He wanted to use Lori to gain access to this Inn and the portals it controls but she grew wise to him and that didn't happen so he decided to open portals elsewhere on the grounds. She found two and closed them. I was able to defeat him, but not kill him, through a portal close to here."

"We should start there. He might go back."

"No need. I keep a close watch on it. A few weeks ago he tried to access the portal and let's just say I discouraged him."

"A full grown dragon can offer a lot of discouragement," said Elfben. "There were elves huddled in their burrows as far away as Vermont. We were pleased it was not us the dragon was after."

"Anyway, when he was trying to open the portals, he collected powerstrands. Lori made sure they were all released. But I am certain they are being collected somewhere else, so I assume he's trying to open another portal."

"What does a portal do?" CeeDee asked. "I hate to be ignorant about these things, but you seem to know what you're talking about and I don't."

"Portals are your rabbit holes, the magic mirrors that you can slip through to get you somewhere else. When we used the transport world we didn't need a portal. We were able to move from one point to another, but it took some work."

"I remember the walking, but I don't think your descriptions are making things better."

"This is high level coursework, if that helps."

"And it is a concept not natural to humans," Byron added. "Dragons understand portals, although we can neither make them nor close them."

"In case you're wondering, I'm not real sure I believe in dragons either. I mean I love the concept of dragons but actual dragons?"

"You should talk to my wife. It took her a long time to be comfortable with my other forms."

"Forms. Can we table that for another time?" CeeDee asked.

"Sure. Anyway, there are seventeen known kingdoms and any number of different worlds. Most of the ways to get to these places are closely guarded. This Inn, for example is attached to any number of portals. Milton and I guard them to keep undesirables from getting through. There's a kind of agreement between the kingdoms and the other worlds. If we do our part to make sure Earth-based undesirables don't go through to create havoc on the other worlds, they will try to do the same for us.

"It's not a hard and fast rule, for no one knows how someone will react when they arrive in one of the kingdoms or lands. Even good people cannot be trusted to act well at all times."

A fat round blue teapot sat on the table and Byron poured steaming liquid into a mug. The kitchen suddenly smelled like peppermint. "I help guard," he said, "mainly because way back, I was one of those things that should have been kept away from portals. As a dragon, I would go to a world, have my fun, leaving devastation in my wake and go find a new world to conquer. Since I've been on Earth, I've a penance of sorts, so I'm behaving myself. I can't stop all evil, but when I can I protect this Inn."

"As we watch for evil," said Elfben. "Elves and all creatures of faerie are vulnerable enough to the dominant creatures that are already here. We do not want anything worse coming or going."

"Dominant creatures?"

"People mostly," Elfben continued, "but also wizards, witches, and other forms of faerie best not named, even in this sanctuary." He pulled himself up on a chair, he was a short creature, with long hairy feet. He started eating the walnuts plain, using his fingers. Since his nails were coiled down, almost like talons, and looked none too clean, CeeDee was glad she didn't want any additional nuts on her cereal.

Byron played with his teacup. "This Inn is a place for any creature with trouble to find safe haven and sometimes redress. I have a score to settle against Andrew but I cannot fight him by myself. My wife is needed with our sons and while the boys are little I cannot leave them vulnerable, but Lori has promised to help if there is a portal that needs shut."

"We thank you both for your offer. That is a great boon she has offered. Now how can we get in touch with you if we need you?"

"Send a powerstrand. I can't manipulate them, but I can see them. Pick a specific color."

"Alright, lime green if we're in trouble. It will direct you to where we are." Pierce had finished his oatmeal. He found it delicious and wondered if his taste buds were reliable. He had never liked oatmeal before, finding it bland. Now, since his near-death experience he had a new appreciation for all foods. He got up, served himself another bowl, adding brown sugar, milk and raisins. He left the few remaining nuts alone.

"Tell us about this missing artifact," Pierce asked the elf.

He stroked his beard, and as if interpreting a signal, Byron poured him a cup of tea. "I don't know how long it's been gone, certainly not more than a week or so. It was given to the elves to keep safe, but we are easily distracted, and sometimes things that should be watched closely get forgotten."

"What does it do?"

He looked down as if ashamed, then met Pierce's gaze directly. "It kills."

Silence surrounded them, and not one of them moved until Pierce asked, "Kills?"

Elfben's face was lined with deeply edged grooves, as if he wore his faults for all to see. "Elves, imps and faeries on the whole are creatures who seek pleasure and run from conflict. Although we often take our fun in ways some label mischievous, there is rarely any evil about us. There are evil factions who have learned to fight and who have come to love the taste of hot blood, but they are rare. Many thousands of these evil imps were killed recently when Andrew tried to take over this Inn."

CeeDee looked around the quiet kitchen, remembered the laughter and the fellowship yesterday at her wedding, where many different species lifted their glasses in toasts to her happiness. She knew if Andrew had succeeded, something wonderful would have been lost.

"They were trying to capture my sons," Byron interjected, "and to create a monster of unquestionable evil when they were stopped."

"So most of the evil imps were destroyed," Pierce said. CeeDee had grasped onto his hand a moment before, interlacing their fingers and their unspoken communion reassured him that they were doing the right thing in listening to these two creatures, and trying to stop this terror.

"Yes. It gave me no pleasure to kill. The imps that survived will no longer answer Andrew's call. His loss, although he was not killed, was devastating. He still craves power, but as far as we can tell he has few remaining allies."

"So, backed into a corner, with no other options, he found out about your artifact and stole it."

Elfben shrugged, lifted his teacup but did not drink. He was a messy eater, with traces of half-chewed walnuts dusting the brown and green outfit he wore. "So it would appear. As soon as the theft was discovered, we went to the Wizard Council and asked for help. We do not willingly go to wizards but we had to in this instance. All we knew was that the artifact was stolen by a wizard new to his robe who had been seen with an untrained woman of power who carried a child of two wizards."

"Me," CeeDee said. "Andrew knows me?"

"So it would appear."

Pierce leaned forward, thought of a creep named Harry who sat in a warm Jaguar one rainy night.

"Andrew and Harry are probably the same person."

"I have an address for him," she said, setting her expression.

"It won't do us any good. I'm sure he covered his tracks. I would have." It was one of the lessons they were taught, how to disappear completely if their secret life were somehow revealed. This Andrew, if he were Harry, would have been planning his escape from the beginning. "We could look for tell-tales, but it would probably be fruitless."

"And then you were seen with me."

"Yes. If all the Council had to go on was that description, it explains why I was questioned, but oddly enough, no one asked me about this device or if I had any part in stealing it."

"Perhaps someone was trying to frame you and not doing a good job."

He shook his head, waving that possibility away. "Or perhaps I had allies where I saw none. Anyway, it's good to know what that was about. I did not think it could be about the child. Now you said this artifact kills?"

"Yes. It kills. It pains me to mention this for it is a secret kept among ourselves that is not even spoken of over dark campfires. I do not lightly speak of it now."

"We are honored you trust us with your information," CeeDee said. She gazed at her new husband as if seeking his approval. Pierce nodded slightly, accepting that she would make a powerful wizard if for no other reason than she always knew the right thing to say.

"Do know that this device was created so many centuries ago even those of us who are immortal have little memory of it. Still, I am a leader and this information was entrusted to me, so I will tell you what I know." Finished with the walnuts, he shoved a large handful of raisins into his mouth. "No elf, imp or faerie can manipulate powerstrands. There are some who can do simple tricks with them, make them dance and float above us during a midsummer festival, but none of us can access their power, turn them into other objects. We can see them, and touch them, and many of us line our beds with them, but powerstrands are something most creatures of faerie ignore. However, with this device powerstrands can turned into weapons of mass destruction."

"There have been such rumors since I've been on this world," Byron said, refreshing his tea.

"Do not think badly of us for it is not of our doing. Again, we are creatures of pleasure, so we have no use for something that slaughters other beings on a broad and almost effortless scale. This device was created centuries ago when the combined races of elves, imps and faeries were in danger of extinction. We have never used it. Just having it was enough to end that ancient war and maintain peace between the races of faerie, wizard and humankind. Even the dragons would think twice about attacking us if there was a hint the device could be used."

Byron humphed. "Even without knowledge of the device, I have learned to give creatures of faerie a wide berth."

"Just so," Elfben said. "This weapon was created centuries ago, and it was in no one's best interest for us to keep information about it current in anyone's mind. We wanted humans, witches and wizards and the other species to forget we had it. There was a peace of sorts no one questioned, and over the decades as I said, we grew lax. There has been no need to maintain a level of alertness over the artifact."

"Someone must have remembered it, or come upon it accidentally."

"There was nothing accidental about it. We discovered much later that almost five hundred elves were killed when it was taken, and before that, some elves were tortured for days by a practicing wizard seeking it."

"A practicing wizard. Again, I assume the Council thinks it was me?"

"We did not encourage that. We have no idea who took it, but know it was a wizard."

"And somehow I'm involved."

"Yes, your trace was left, but it was determined by the faeries and what representatives the wizard council sent your involvement in this was tangential. It was not you we are looking for, but someone who has been with you, a friend or lover."

"But their early investigations led them to me," Pierce said, and wondered why he was allowed to escape so readily, but then he posed a question. "The wizards who are following me, us, are looking for your device?"

"The fact that you so easily evaded their traps indicates you have something to hide."

"I've nothing to hide. I was defending myself and the woman I love. The wizards at the library wanted us dead. I assume the assassins at my house felt the same way. They were not trying to capture us to get us to confess."

"The ones who follow the evil one want you dead too, probably to take suspicion off them. If you are killed, they would say you cannot use the device as a threat any longer."

"We don't have it. We never heard of it until just now. Although my master did give lessons on elf and faerie history, nothing like this was ever mentioned."

Elfben licked his finger then stuck it in the brown sugar. "We have worked hard to keep it a secret."

"Why wasn't it ever destroyed?"

"Because it has always been felt that there might come a time when the threat of its use might be needed. It need not be in current days, but what has happened once is likely to happen again."

"Yes. History is often cyclical," Pierce agreed.

"What does it look like?" CeeDee asked.

"If you will permit me?" Elfben asked. Pierce and CeeDee both nodded, having no idea what they were agreeing to. He took their hands in his, his fingers surprisingly strong, if a bit sticky, the skin rough like tree bark. "Close your eyes. I will send the image."

The darkness behind their eyelids cleared, and as if slipping into a brilliant dream, the image formed. The artifact shown was small, certainly no bigger than a watermelon, and could be lifted by two elves. A wizard or a human would have no trouble carrying it alone. The image did not end there. The two elves carrying device set it down and they forced powerstrands through it. The powerstrands screamed as if they were indeed sentient and being tortured. They squirmed, as if they wanted to escape, but they were forced, unwilling, into the device. Then the image broadened, showed a peaceful valley filled with thatched houses, with children playing and sheep and goats frolicking in a grassy green field. Seconds later the image changed again. All that remained of the valley was an ugly scar, the people, farm animals and their homes gone, disintegrated, eradicated.

CeeDee swallowed slowly, trying to keep her breakfast in her stomach. She was profoundly moved by the destruction. "You said it had never been used."

Elfben said, "Up until recently that statement was true. Whoever stole it wanted to be certain they had the right artifact."

"And the elves and faeries made this?" Pierce demanded. Five hundred elves murdered. They killed their own kind.

"No, indeed not. We have no technology to manipulate powerstrands. We do nothing more devious than ferment our meads and wines, offer the occasional glamour. We seek only to celebrate the phases of the moon and to cherish what few children are granted us by our gods. This device was made by wizards, given to us to protect ourselves from both wizards and mortals."

CeeDee feared she would never get that vision out of her brain. "It is an abomination."

# CHAPTER 23

"And it has been stolen. We know the wizard who took it has no compulsion about using it again."

"That's how your five hundred elves died."

"Yes. We are sure it was a warning, but we are also sure they needed to test it before they brought it out to their main purpose. They did not test it on humans. That would lead to many human authorities getting involved. I don't know what this wizard and those who follow him want with the device, but I fear they mean not simply to threaten, but to use it."

"And you trust us?"

Elfben folded his hands, took a deep breath. "I will not apologize. I do what I have to do."

"What did you do?" CeeDee asked. As she spoke, she reached out, calmly put her hand over Pierce's, where she could see he was silently manipulating a powerstrand.

"I was at your wedding. I and those I brought with me came to destroy you both. We brought food and gifts as a ruse to gain entrance into the Inn, but we were all armed and willing to break the truce with the Innkeeper which stated we would never bring conflict into this edifice to accomplish any goal. We were certain you were the thief and we needed to stop you. But we listened to your vows, and we know the power of the Innkeeper's ceremony. No one who is evil could have withstood it. And there was a gargoyle present. You did not react to his presence, except as a human would react to a creature that appears a monster. You are pregnant. Through our magic we can see it is not an abomination growing within you, but a child that will be cherished. We understood from the vows you spoke, the way that you kissed, and the way you both welcomed us to your celebration you are not those we seek. Were you evil, we would have met guile. We only found love and celebration and the miracle of marriage sealed with the power of both mankind and faerie. After the party I was granted permission to tell you of the device, even though it is our gravest secret and one we do not speak about to outsiders or even among ourselves. I knew if I had read you wrong that I would be killed."

CeeDee bent over, kissed the elf on his forehead. "Thank you for telling us. All information will help. We will add this to our quest. You are very brave. My husband and I will do all we can to keep all peoples of faerie and human safe, and return this object to you. We promise as much as we are able, to never make public the knowledge you shared with us this morning."

"I add my promise to that. I thought this Andrew was stealing powerstrands to open a portal to other worlds, but that does not seem to be the case. He is stockpiling powerstrands to fuel his weapon."

"It is our belief."

"Byron?" Pierce asked the dragon.

He shrugged, placed his hands calmly on the table. "I am forbidden to interfere. I sit here as mediator, should the discussion have turned ugly. I protect the Inn in Jan's absence. You may not count on me to come to your aid, but should things go badly for you, know that this Inn remains a sanctuary and I am allowed to defend it."

"Then we will begin our quest. We thank you both."

"Where do you start? I only ask because Jan is certain to ask."

"I saw something yesterday while I was in astral form that I do not like, but I believe I recognize the area. It is here, on Earth, and close. But before I go there, I need to retrieve something I left at the TPW when we were attacked by garntz."

"What did you leave?" CeeDee asked.

"The backpack I carried. I hope we can find it. Again, thank you for what aid you have been able to offer."

"Whole milk," CeeDee said as they grabbed coats and left the Inn through the front door.

"What?"

"I eat oatmeal almost every single day for breakfast, but I usually use skim milk. That whole milk made it taste incredible."

"The whole milk, yes," said Pierce, "but also the magic."

"There was magic in the oatmeal? I knew it. I've always suspected there was magic in oatmeal."

"Not all oatmeal. Today's oatmeal. Any meal made in that house has at least a trace of magic in it. The oatmeal was practically glowing with it."

"Like the chili dogs you made me?"

"No, not made by magic, infused with magic. It's like adding a double shot of caffeine. The magic gives you energy. Don't worry, it won't harm the baby."

"Magic, huh? I like that."

"Did you try the tea last night?"

"Yes, I toasted with it. I didn't see any soda, and for obvious reasons I didn't drink any of the wine supplied by the faeries."

"Byron told me the tea we drank last night was literal dragon essence. Think of all the things dragons are: brave, strong, resilient. Some of that is inside you too."

"I've had a dragon inside me. And before you go all crazy that wasn't a sexual innuendo."

"I know, because I decided when it comes to you, I'm very possessive. You don't want to make me angry."

"It might be best if we didn't make Lori angry either."

The wind twirled her hair as they walked around the side of the Inn, toward the place where they had witnessed the dragon-fire. "Hold on, here we go."

Pierce grasped her hand and transferred them back to the transfer point world. "I was hoping I would never see this orange sand and yellow sky again."

"I was hoping it would be easy to find the backpack," Pierce said with a sigh of frustration. "There are some things in it I need, and although many can be replaced, I would rather they did not fall into the wrong hands. They would make a potent weapon in the hands of our quarry."

She kicked through the sand, leaving footprints, knowing that his special spell would erase them. "Is there a problem?"

"A big one. It might take us years to find it."

"What do you mean?"

"I erased the trail."

"So?"

"I won't be able to find it. Look around you. All there is for miles is sand. We'll have to develop some kind of grid, and I don't have the luxury of time to do that. Whoever or whatever is after me, probably this Andrew, could find us here, if we leave tracks."

"Pierce, it's that way." She pointed.

"Any way is as likely as any other."

"Pierce, you don't see the trail?"

"No. Do you?"

"As clear as if it were a road in my hometown."

"You can see the trail?"

"Of course. Can't you?"

"No. I erased it. You're a Finder."

"What's that?"

"You can find missing things?"

"Most things. That's why I love being a librarian. I get to hunt things."

"Good. Lead the way."

"Why did you originally bring me here, if you can't find your trail?"

"For exactly that reason. I can transfer in and out, but while I am here I erase the trail, and no one can find me. And while wizards can pop from one place to another it is noisy and leaves a lot of evidence. This world, when we walk in it, makes very little noise and it's hard to track another wizard here."

"Except for me."

"Obviously. Is there a trace of anyone else?"

"Fifteen or twenty other trails. Most look like they were created by the garntz because the way the sand is disturbed, but there footsteps here, which show humans, or wizards," she added with a wink, "have traveled here."

"Show me. Maybe I can see if I hold your hand."

"Sure. I always like holding your hand." Power rippled through her. Two weeks ago she didn't even know what a wizard was, not that she was certain she did now, but already she was honing her talents, learning, and being of assistance to him.

"Before we go any further, please note that this isn't how I wanted to spend our honeymoon."

He did more than hold her hand. He held her heart.

"After we take care of the bad guys, we'll have time for a honeymoon, then we can officially start my apprenticeship and I'll learn to curse your name in the dark."

He rolled his eyes. "Yes, there's always that. I promise I'll work on finding a line we can walk between husband and wife and Master and apprentice."

"Or I'll turn you into a newt."

"Perhaps I won't teach you that talent early in your apprenticeship."

She laughed with his words for she had no idea if she could turn the mighty Pierce Billova into a newt, whether it was possible at all. All she wanted from him was long afternoons with his legs entwined with hers, learning to understand the word passion across the breakfast table for decades to come, and to share the problems of raising a "terrible two" and a know-it-all tween and a feisty tech-savvy, wizard-trained high schooler. Yes, there was a lot she wanted from him and raising a child caused her more fear than anything the bad guys could threaten her with.

With their fingers entwined, Pierce saw the trail she mentioned. "Looks like two wizards and maybe a dozen elves or imps. We'll have to get the backpack later. This is too important to ignore." Keeping hold of her hand, Pierce and CeeDee started running through the sand as quickly as they were able. The shifting surface made real speed impossible. After about twenty minutes Pierce said, "There's someone up ahead."

"Yes." She was glad to stop, try to catch her breath, and rub her aching calves.

"I know you don't like me defending you, but could you stay behind me just this once? I've had a run-in or two with him before."

"That's Pasco, the wizard you spoke with at the beach when you made me disappear."

"Yes. He has not earned his robe yet. He left his apprenticeship years ago looking for an easy life. He's been dealing drugs and I don't know what else." Pierce pulled some powerstrands to him, arming himself. "The police want him, and he will certainly face censure from the wizard community."

Pasco Minelli finally caught sight of them, and faced them, hands up, palms outward, to show he was unarmed. It was the same action he had taken at the beach.

"Hold! I mean you no harm."

Pierce tightened his grip on a powerstrand. "I should kill you now."

"I'm not the one you should kill," Pasco said, still making no move to defend himself.

"I saw you trying to kill my mother."

"What?"

"You deny it?"

"No. I was certain we were alone."

"I was in astral form. You ambushed her, clearly trying to kill her."

"How much more did you see?"

"Nothing. I was pulled back."

Crimson color stained his cheeks, but Pierce could not decide if that indicated Pasco was sincere or just not an accomplished liar.

"She is a wizard, and evil. I trained under her for a few months, but even I am not that depraved."

He saw red of a different sort, as his anger grew, blossomed. He held about a dozen powerstrands now, all formed into weapons. With a thought he could end this insanity. "What are you talking about? My mother knows nothing about wizards. She chairs political fundraising campaigns, and gives talks about supporting the arts."

Pasco spit, ignoring the powerstrands that coiled near him. If he were lying he was taking an incredible chance with Pierce's trust.

"She has fooled you."

Pierce pulled his hand back threw his first weapon, invisible to CeeDee who only saw the result, Pasco thrown back three feet, to lay face up in the sand. Bright red blood spurted from an open wound in his stomach, staining the orange sand. Pasco clutched his gut, but as far as CeeDee could determine, made no move to defend himself.

"You think I wouldn't find out?" Pierce yelled, his hands kitting together in what had to be another weapon.

Obviously in pain, Pasco lifted one blood-stained hand, his voice strained. "Pierce, stop. We need to talk. I will tell you everything. I'm privy to her plan."

"I do not talk with traitors or murderers. And isn't it the oldest, ugliest lie in the world, 'it's your mother?' I'm not falling for a single thing you say."

CeeDee could imagine a dozen powerstrands around him, maybe ten times that many, and Pierce's statement that a wizard could not heal himself. What fool made that rule? Still, he made no move to defend himself.

"You may not believe this, but I was on my way to find you."

"Sure," Pierce scoffed. "And to get to me, you thought to kill my mother?"

Bright red blood dripped from Pasco's nose, his mouth, all the more macabre because of the unnatural orange sand, the yellow sky. He leaned back, strength waning. "She is not who you think."

Pierce tightened muscles, preparatory to tossing another powerstrand lance. "I know who she is. If you want to come at me, then come at me. Leave my family, especially my wife and mother alone."

"Then you support her? Think before you answer."

"Support her? She is my mother."

His head dropped to the sand, his voice went weaker. "She is the evil wizard behind this."

"And I should believe you? Answer one question for me first. Were you the one who shot me? You swore to me at the beach that it wasn't you."

The red pool around Pasco's waist grew wider. "Yes, I swore that. I was trying to get you to listen to me then, and I didn't have time to go into the background. Your mother ordered me to kill you. I didn't want to, but she has ways to make me do things. She was about to make her move, and knew you would be a formidable adversary. Pierce, I'm not the only one she's manipulating. She's forcing you to make moves too."

Pierce stood above him, clutching a weapon in his hands that CeeDee could only imagine. "You confess to trying to murder me in cold blood and I know for a fact you tried to kill my mother and you want me to believe she's manipulating not only you but me as well?"

"Think. You'll know I'm telling the truth."

"Why should I believe you? While I need you alive to stand trial in Brooklyn, that doesn't mean I need to be particularly gentle with you."

Pierce turned his back on Pasco, took CeeDee's hand, was about to ask her to lead the way, when Pasco shouted. "She's behind all this."

"My wife?"

"Your mother."

"Don't you think that's a dead horse you've beat enough?"

"She stole an elf-device of mass slaughter. I watched her use it on an elfish community. I helped her capture the powerstrands to do it. Pierce, the device does more than mass slaughter, it destroys powerstrands. I know our tenets say they cannot be destroyed, but these are used up, burned, vanished. The powerstrands are not transformed, they are gone. That's why she's been stockpiling them. That's why she needs so many. I don't know what her main target is, but you've got to believe me, it's big and she's going to hit it soon."

"I'm sick of listening to him, CeeDee," Pierce said. "Lead me on."

"Five more minutes of your time. I probably don't have that much life left. Please, listen, so when you see her you won't be going into this blind. She has been instructing Andrew, and after I left Drollard, she was my Master. That is how I got involved in illegal drugs."

"You lie so poorly it's not even worth a comment."

"I have no reason to. Consider this a deathbed confession. I've been trying to stop her for the past week but I've made some serious miscalculations. She's more powerful than you could imagine."

"Of course she is, as I know her as only a human." Pierce turned around, started walking away, not even concerned he had chosen a random direction.

"Think about it, a wizard born marked to non-wizard parents is rare," Pasco shouted.

"But not unheard of. Drollard never questioned my legitimacy."

"He doesn't know about your mother."

Pierce turned around, faced him with a sneer. "If she's so powerful, why didn't she make herself known to me? All those years I spent looking for a master I begged her for advice. She gave me charlatans, tarot card readers, psychic frauds. I nearly killed myself I was so desperate for real magic. I made no secret of it."

"I don't know why she didn't train you. That she never told me. She wanted to keep her distance. I don't know. But I know she has been manipulating your father and some of the important votes to serve her own ends. She has no interest in the presidency, but she is the power behind your father, and now she's seeking another arena. I don't know specifically what she wants, but what if she chooses to eradicate the elves and as much of faerie as she can? Then she will be invincible."

"I would lie too if I thought it would keep me alive another minute."

"I know where the device is and I know who has it. Certainly that is enough?"

"A self-confessed assassin? I was in my lair. How did you get in?"

"Andrew broke the seal. He said he knew your work well enough to feel comfortable breaking your wards. You were in astral travel. I pulled the trigger. I admit it, but your mother is behind it all."

"We're leaving this fool, CeeDee. If he's still alive when this is over, we'll take him to stand trial."

"Go then. But remember I warned you. You are not strong enough to defeat her. She will blindside you. And Pierce, almost everything she will tell you will be a lie."

"Why would she lie to me?"

"Because she has kept up her pretense all these years. You've grown used to listening to her lies. Think back. Are there things your parents, or more specifically your mother did that in retrospect didn't make sense? When she came to me, I was flattered. I knew her relationship to you, of course, and I liked to have that to hang over you, that your mother, a powerful wizard, came to me for help, but I also know who she is in the public arena. She helps your father write bills. She is the puppet-master. If he becomes president, or even if he just continues to head the appropriations committee, think of all the power she controls."

"Pierce, is there a chance that any of this makes sense?" CeeDee asked. It was the first time she had spoken in several long minutes.

"No. How could I be that blind? Nothing he says is believable."

"But should we consider it?"

"Do you believe me?" Pasco asked. He hadn't moved since Pierce wounded him, and the orange sand around him was sticky, red.

"I want to keep an open mind," CeeDee said, but knew as soon as she spoke, she was making a mistake. She had been a wife less than twenty-four hours, and was already consigning his mother to mass-murderer status. But she couldn't support her husband, not when there was a chance he was wrong. "Pierce, I don't know your mother, and I don't know this man, and I understand we have no reason to trust him, but what if he's telling the truth?"

"He's not."

"Is there a way to tell for sure?" CeeDee asked. "Could one of your magic strands insure we could believe him?"

"Yes, but the procedure is not always reliable and I'd rather not take the time."

A powerstrand sailed over his head, close enough to act as a warning. Pierce pulled CeeDee down to the sand, protecting her with his body. "Weapons," he whispers, "someone is shooting at us."

Pleased that she stayed down, he looked up and recognized a friend. "Daniel? Stop it! It's me, Pierce."

"I can see you quite well. Sorry to inform you, but I've been working, as they say, for the other side for quite some time. You're surrounded. Put the powerstrands down. Not that we don't appreciate you catching Minelli for us. He made a great patsy for a good long while, but I think his usefulness is coming to an end. And, my dear, it's so good to see you again."

"What's going on here?"

"None of this making sense?" Daniel laughed. "You do have a lot of catching up to do. My master, my real master, has been instructing me for some time, teaching me things that Drollard never mentioned. There's a whole world of magical property out there wizards can affect that he never told us about."

Additional powerstrands flew, and as Pierce dodged, one caught him in the side. He gasped and rolled, and she could see he started bleeding heavily. CeeDee inched over to his side, trying to close the wound.

"We've got to get out of here," but before Pierce could fashion an escape powerstrand, Daniel approached, knotting his hands in a manner CeeDee recognized as him working his magic. Seconds later, she, Pierce and Pasco found themselves restrained.

"Sorry we have to meet like this, but it really was inevitable."

"Has the whole world gone insane?" Pierce demanded. "Pasco, you, my mother—"

"There will be time for explanations soon. I promise you. As a matter of fact, I'm quite looking forward to it. At the moment I'm going to transfer us somewhere we might be more comfortable, because there is a chance the noise you've been making has been heard by other ears."

A second later, Pierce recognized the basement of his parent's New Jersey home. He struggled against his restraints, with no luck, although the wound had been lightly tended, so it no longer bled freely. It still looked like it needed stitches or a good patch of healing powerstrands. CeeDee was tied several feet away, alert and snarling at Daniel. Beyond her lay Pasco, unconscious or dead.

The basement, which had always been boring, now looked sinister, and it took him a moment to figure out why. Powerstrands were stacked in readiness, like weapons of war, against the far side. They were bound in a manner he never considered possible. In Pierce's experience, powerstrands had always roamed freely.

He struggled to sit up, feeling the pull of his wound, starting fresh blood flowing. "What are we doing here?"

Daniel laughed. He wore his robe, but it was no longer black, but closer to tan. "I really thought you would figure it out. There were enough clues."

"Clues?"

"Those bullets did stop you for a while. It is unfortunate they didn't kill you, but that can be easily rectified. How would you feel about heart attack as cause of death? I can make a brain tumor if you'd rather something a bit more exotic."

"We were friends," Pierce said, "are friends."

"No, actually your past tense was correct. We haven't been friends for a good long while. I tried to kill you in the emergency room, did you realize that? That powerstrand choking you was of my manufacture. Death in the ER, no one would have considered it suspicious. You were close enough, but somehow you rebounded."

He thought of the rain and a woman who gave him a reason to live. He hadn't realized that was why he struggled so hard to survive. CeeDee and the baby. His baby. He would survive this too.

# CHAPTER 24

"I've got too much to live for."

"We'll see. Maybe my new master will need you to take the blame for the catastrophe about to occur."

Fire burned through his chest, making thought and speech difficult. He struggled to find the words. "You're insane. Daniel, you were taught better than to get involved with creating and selling drugs."

Daniel's chuckle was evil, grating. "Is that what you think this is all about? You really should get caught up."

"Then you're involved in stealing a machine that has the power to destroy thousands?"

"Well, yeah. Power comes in many forms, and one of the strongest is the ability to destroy. Does that sound familiar?"

"No. Drollard never taught us that. He taught us to build."

"We'll build a new order on the ashes of the old."

"You're working for—"

"For someone so adept at manipulating powerstrands she never left a trace. You always were a little dense, weren't you? Oddly enough back there in the TPW, Pasco was telling you the truth. Your mother is the power behind this little coup. She plans to destroy all the elves and most of the wizards. Those who will pledge allegiance to her she will allow to live."

"Daniel, why are you doing this?"

"My name is Andrew!" he shouted, spittle forming at his mouth. "You may call me that."

"Andrew? You're the wizard who's been causing all this trouble? The dragon and a gargoyle told us about you."

"Well, from their point of view, I guess you could say I've been causing trouble." He smiled, taking the time to rein in the insanity plaguing him as if the idea pleased him. "But like your mother, I crave power. I thought I could get it by opening a portal, but my first attempt failed. My second led me to a viable TPW. I figured I could make a fortune off that, but Lori, an old lover of mine closed the portal."

"The dragon's wife can close portals."

"Indeed. She was mine before he ever got his talons into her. So I needed someone to fund my next attempt. I figured I was one for two, and those are great odds, so I located a wizard to back me. Oddly enough, she happened to be your mother. Oh, how I laughed when I found out. Poor you, searching so long for a master, when your mother could have taught you."

"And why the weapon?"

He shrugged, was restless, roaming the confines of the unfinished basement. "We don't like competition. Now, speaking of my former lovers, aren't you going to say anything my dear?"

"What?" Pierce asked.

"CeeDee, please tell your current lover who I am."

"Pierce, I'd like to introduce you to Harry."

"Harry?" He struggled against his bindings, succeeding only in making them tighter. "You're the one who got her pregnant?"

"Well, the answer is yes and no. It's not my child, for which I am profoundly grateful. It's yours. But your mother did set me up to seduce her."

"What?"

"She wants to start an army of wizards loyal to her. She feels strongly that she needs to breed them. This antiquated notion two wizards shouldn't have children has served its purpose for too many years. In ancient eras, wizards were afraid of the power of their children. Now she thinks it's time to embrace it. Your mother is going to train them when they come of age."

"How does CeeDee fit into this?"

"Your mother has been looking for untrained wizards. There aren't many. Cynthia Diane is perfect for our cause. I was able to seduce her. It was frighteningly easy. All I had to do was spend a little cash, and ooze some charm, after all, my former lover was no longer available."

"I'm sure the oozing gave you no trouble."

"Well, I knew the child wasn't mine. Your mother is rather interested in a grandchild. I'm always careful, well, except around nosy dragons and whatnots, and I wasn't about to claim the bastard, even if he shows great potential."

"Don't worry. You won't get a chance to claim the baby. I claim it."

"Leave us, Andrew."

Pierce struggled against the bindings as a well dressed woman in her mid-fifties entered. "Mom?"

"That's your mother?" CeeDee asked quietly.

"Yes. Mom, what are you doing here? I don't believe any of this."

"Pierce, I'm so sorry all this had to happen."

"Then let me go."

"I would love to. I can't tell you how happy it would make me to work beside you, but you'd have to give me your binding oath you would assist me."

"Of course. Tell me everything they've said is a lie, you're not planning on using a killing device, and you had no role in my getting shot."

"I suppose I can't deny any of that. I have plans only a few hours from fruition. I am seeking power. Pasco is weak, he never showed even a fraction of your innate abilities, and I am growing tired of Andrew. He's, as they say, a little too full of himself. But you were always a natural. Join me."

"Has the entire universe gone insane? You're my mother."

"And in what parallel world did you think I would be content to simply support your father? I had to stay in the background for years, until I got a lead on this elf device. I'd heard of it, once in my childhood, and I spent decades searching for it."

"I must be losing too much blood, because you look like my mother and you act like a lunatic."

"So sorry to destroy your illusions. They were necessary for so long, but I no longer feel constrained to continue with the asinine life I've been living. Oh, I still have use for your father. Actually, for the past several years he's been in my thrall, doing exactly what I tell him."

"Thrall," CeeDee whispered, knowing exactly what she meant, for she could remember Pierce doing the same thing to her.

"I should have noticed."

"Yes. You have been blind, although I never would have suspected you would locate my baby mama."

"She's my wife now. We were sealed by the power of faerie."

"Good for you. That only means she will suffer harder for your death. But not for long. Did you know it's impossible to conceive a child with someone in thrall? That's why she's so useful. I can have two wizard bloodlines, without worrying about her using her powers against me."

"Let CeeDee go. She is untrained. She cannot hurt you."

"I know she's untrained. I've been searching for years for ignorant wizards to give birth to my new army. You see, Pierce, I've plans for her child. How did you find her?"

"She is my match in everything that matters. You'll never understand how I was drawn to her. I'm going to train her, and together we'll destroy you."

"Pierce, you may not realize this, but while I need her for a few more months at least, I don't really need you any longer. I know how to replicate your DNA should I need it for my breeding experiments, and I could make it look like whoever tried to kill you before succeeded after a second attempt."

"You're insane. You would kill your own son?"

"For a chance at the power I am amassing, absolutely. I have to admit, I'm sorry I didn't get a chance to train you myself, but when you were ready, I was not as secure in my profession as I am now. Let's just say a lot of my knowledge has been self-taught. And by the time I was proficient, you had already agreed to apprentice to that dullard."

"Drollard," Pierce insisted. "Master Drollard. He has respect for the forces we worship, and has taught me to honor the code of the wizard."

"Yes, I'm very much aware of that."

"Now, where is the weapon? We'll destroy it together, or take it back to the elves so they can hide it for another millennium."

"I've plans for it. Later today, actually. Right now, I'm rearranging a chess board, taking a few powerful pieces out of play. Then there will be no one to stop me."

"CeeDee and I will. Just tell me where the device is."

"I wish I could. There is so much we could accomplish together."

"What are you doing now?"

"What does it look like? I'm building an escape route. If this thing goes wrong, I don't want to be caught defenseless, but everything is going to go well. Andrew found another TPW and we're trying to get back there. We will need a place to lay low after I commit my next act of treason."

"Why are you doing this?"

"Like he said, I enjoy power. And I am excited about my new grandchild."

"How did you manage that? I never touched CeeDee until long after she conceived."

"I have your DNA all over the house, pieces of hair in the brush for example. It is a simple matter to transform that into sperm. I like the idea of carrying on my line. Your powers are formidable. With Cynthia's genetics too, the child will be powerful indeed. Pasco is my child as well."

"I've got a brother?"

"Yes. I kept a closer eye on him, even sending him to Drollard to keep an eye on you and Andrew. But once he found out what that white powder could do he had little interest in helping me."

Margaret bent over Pasco, made some subtle hand motions and the powerstrands which bound him vanished. A moment later, he did too.

"He got away."

"Not for long. It's all part of the plan. The council will pick him up."

"The council?" CeeDee asked.

"Wizard council. Our justice system."

"Why do you want him under Council scrutiny?"

"I suppose there's no need not to tell you. They will convene a session to try him for treason and while it's being seated, I shall use my weapon, and destroy ninety percent of practicing wizards with one blow. I am sorry, Pierce. I did enjoy being your mother, at least as much as I can enjoy anything. In case you're worried, I promise I'll make a better grandmother. This really has been a conversation we've needed to have for the past decade or so. I wish I had more time to pursue it, but too many things are tugging at me right now. CeeDee, I'll be back for you in about an hour. I've got a place where you'll be safe until the child is born. Andrew!"

He appeared so suddenly, Pierce knew he had been listening through some keyhole somewhere.

"I'll take powerstrands with me. We shouldn't need more than one bunch. Take the rest to your TPW and meet me at the Council chambers. Oh, and Pierce, if you're interested in seeing your brother on trial for crimes against the wizard community, I'm afraid you're going to miss out." She vanished, taking one bundle of powerstrands with her. Seconds later, Andrew took the remaining stacks and vanished as well.

"Pierce, what can we do?"

"Can you move? I'm tied so tightly I can't do anything."

"Yes." Although her hands and knees were bound, she was able to crawl over to Pierce. "I will not let that harridan have anything to do with Rose Aurora."

"Or Wolfgar," he said with a laugh. "Together we'll make sure she doesn't."

"Come here, hold my hands. I want you to see these powerstrands."

"Yes. I see them."

"Try to unknot them."

"It's not working. They're slippery."

"Don't think of them as yarn. Think of them as energy."

"Please," she said, speaking to the powerstrand. "I need help. I don't know how to do this." She wiggled her fingers and Pierce's bindings separated. Quickly he undid hers. "My mother had no idea you could manipulate powerstrands. She never would have left us together if she did."

"What do we do now?"

"We've got to go to the Council room, but I can't make it because I've lost too much blood. I need a fat green powerstrand. Do you see one?"

"I think she's taken almost all of them. Wait, some are traveling through the wall. They must have been hiding from her. I've got the green one."

"Think of the Council chamber. I'll transfer the image to the strand."

"You're sending me alone?"

"CeeDee, you're strong. You can do this. You've transferred before. I don't think I'm going to die, at least not if I get some help, but I haven't got the strength to sit up, let alone take on a raving lunatic or two."

"What can I do to help you? I'm not leaving you here without help."

"Pink ones. Are there pink ones?"

She held the green powerstrand in two hands. She could feel it, but once she released his hand, she could no longer see it. "Please, are there pink strands around here?" she asked it. Pierce lay his eyes closed, his breathing shallow. "I don't know how to talk to powerstrands," she said, "and I promised Pierce I would stop his mother if I could, but I can't leave him like this."

Then it was as if her eyes were opened for the first time. She saw powerstrands. Dozens of them, some undulating toward her, snake-like, some bounding like puppies, some regal and stately. "Help Pierce," she begged, "or if you can't, can you find some way to show me what I need to do?"

But that wasn't necessary. A dozen pink powerstrands wrapped themselves around his wound, becoming translucent, fading as visibly the wound healed. Two even entered his body, one through his nose, one through his mouth and she feared he would choke or suffocate but realized they were healing his lungs, the other internal wounds.

"A wizard can't heal himself," she said, almost joyous, "of course not. It takes powerstrands."

"Pierce, stay here and heal. I'm going to the Council room, that is, if this green one knows where it is."

Seconds later, she was somewhere else, obviously a council chamber, for the tiers were filled with robed wizards, and on the floor stood Pasco, bound with a dozen powerstrands in different colors. A trial of some kind was in progress.

"If you are not a robed wizard, you cannot be here," a passing wizard told her. "If you are a wizard, put your robe on and get to your seat."

"Thanks, I will," she said, quickly traveling in a direction to take her away from the floor. She didn't see Pierce's mother or Andrew.

She was huddled in a hallway, with a partial view of the council chambers when Pierce showed up beside her. She hugged him.

"You're ok."

"You're quite a powerful healer. If you weren't a finder, I'd say that was your vocation."

"I did no healing. I spoke to the powerstrands and they did it. Now, what can we do here?"

"There's a big crowd tonight. It does look like my mother chose the right venue to destroy most of the society of wizards. We police our own, and he is guilty of most of the crimes he's accused of."

"But he's your brother. Is there anything we can do to help him?"

"I'll see. Do you know where the device is?"

She closed her eyes and concentrated for a moment. "Down one level. Is there a basement?"

"Apparently."

"Hold my hand. Let me see if I can show you."

"Got it. They're feeding powerstrands into the device right now. They're almost ready to fire it. We've got to get these wizards out of here if I can't stop it."

"Let me take care of that." CeeDee ran down to the floor, waving her arms and screaming. The distraction worked, as the wizards all stared at her. "I am CeeDee Radling. There is a powerful device being loaded with powerstrands right now, about to destroy us all. You need to get out of here."

"What nonsense is this?"

"You are not a wizard. You have no business being here."

"You must listen to me. Margaret Billova, Pierce Billova's mother is trying to kill all of you. Ask Pasco. He has the information."

"We have allowed him to make a statement. We are about to pass judgment."

"You'll all be dead if you don't move soon."

One of the wizards did. Although she could not see it, she knew by his actions he twisted a powerstrand, and moments later, she felt herself being transported. She gripped desperately, finally locating by feel the powerstrand moving her. "Take me to Pierce," she ordered, and her movement changed. She found herself crashing into a wall in a dank subbasement of the Council room.

"You ok?" Pierce asked. He had a dozen powerstrands beside him, and CeeDee could see clearly through a wall encircled by powerstrands Margaret Billova loading the weapon.

"Yes. They wouldn't listen."

"Fine. We'll do this ourselves." He handed her two of his powerstrands, which she could clearly see as he handed them to her. "Throw them, when you get a chance, ok?"

"I'm with you."

"Come on." Taking her hand, Pierce and CeeDee walked through the wall. "Mom, I'm here to stop you."

"How did you get away?"

"Powerful friends. Don't ever underestimate CeeDee again." With dynamic hand motions Pierce released the bound powerstrands. Without hesitation, they disappeared through the floor and walls. That only left those already locked in the device.

"Help me find a way to destroy this thing."

She looked insane. Whereas in her own home she had been meticulously groomed, now her eyes were too wide, and she spit as she spoke. "I'll never help you. I'm seconds away from succeeding."

She moved her arms and dozens of powerstrands attacked Pierce and CeeDee, restraining them, and more cutting them with a hundred painful slices, wrapping around their necks, and cutting off oxygen.

But it was not his mother he was speaking to, it was the few remaining powerstrands, the ones which did not answer to her. A yellow one coiled around the device, and pointed to a switch. Pierce had no idea what to do, but with the last of his oxygen, he spoke to the yellow strand and a piece moved, then fell off. The powerstrands in the device were able to wiggle free. "There, it's useless now."

Drollard and a dozen other wizards entered the room. Oddly enough, CeeDee had no trouble seeing they were all armed with powerstrands. "Pierce, we'll take it from here."

"Thanks," he said, slipping to the floor, unconscious.

\*\*\*

"CeeDee," he came to and searched for her.

"I'm here. I'm fine. They healed us, and I made them check the baby. Wolfgar is still healthy."

He closed his eyes, leaned against her, resting his right hand against her stomach. "Yes. Healthy and very active. It's a good thing you're a powerful wizard. I get the feeling it's going to take both of us to raise this child." He opened his eyes, realized they were someplace else, a holding chamber for want of a better word. "The weapon?"

"I'm not sure. But it was disarmed. You did that."

"The powerstrands did. And my mother?"

"I don't know. They marched her out just a few seconds ago. I think she's lost her mind."

"Obviously. So, what's happening?"

"I'm not exactly sure. We're not allowed to transfer out. They need us for a trial. There're guards at the door so I don't know if we're here to testify against your mother or stand trial ourselves."

Pierce studied the chamber. There wasn't a single powerstrand loitering they could use for escape. The room was sealed. They weren't going anywhere until this was resolved. "Drollard was here. My master. I'm sure I saw him."

"Yes, he introduced himself. He's one of the ones who healed us, but I think there will be charges against us too. Daniel, or I suppose he prefers Andrew, spread lies about us, made it look like we were engaging in forbidden practices."

"I won't let them hurt you."

"Somehow we'll figure this out."

After keeping them waiting several hours, Pierce and CeeDee were brought to the floor of the council chamber surrounded by black-robed wizards clearly acting as guards. Although they were not bound, when they reached the main floor, Pierce noticed his mother, Pasco and Andrew were.

"This disciplinary hearing is commenced. Margret Billova, you have been found guilty by this Council of gross misuse of power. It is our decision that your wizard powers be stripped."

She wasn't ranting, or foaming at the mouth like someone insane. She stood powerfully, almost regally, and spoke like the trained orator she was, which only made her more frightening. "You can't. I am more powerful than all of you."

"Powerful, perhaps, but your crimes are legendary. You have imported controlled substances that made the mortal world look in our direction for answers. You have tried to create your own wizard army through guile and force. You have stolen an artifact of great danger and attempted to use it to destroy this council of your peers. You murdered hundreds of innocent creatures of faerie, who before this looked to us as comrades, and now see us as potential enemies. You have kidnapped and tortured wizards. The list goes on. This council finds you guilty and you will be stripped of your powers."

Her scream was shrill, piercing and ended abruptly. Whatever the procedure involved, it was painful and immediate. She slumped unconscious, but the powerstrands binding her kept her upright. "She will have no memory of the use of powerstrands and after a short convalescence, will be allowed a normal human life."

"My father—" Pierce said.

The councilmember was seated high above them. He looked down his nose. "You have not been given leave to speak, but the bindings on William Billova have been released and his mind wiped. He will be told his wife suffered a minor stroke and will be fine after some physical and occupational therapy. He will return to his work in the human political arena, although it is unknown now if he will be able to undo some of the damage done under his wife's command."

"He will. He's strong."

"Daniel Andrew Rayock, we have heard testimony today from a gargoyle, an elf, and a dragon in addition to your peers regarding your seditious activities. It is the judgment of this Council that you are to be given a choice. We can strip your powers and you may live a normal human life or we will send you to a penal world to serve out a life sentence without possibility of escape."

"With my powers intact?"

"Yes, but it will avail you nothing, as there no powerstrands which will answer to your call."

"I take the penal colony. I will not have my power removed."

Seconds later Andrew disappeared.

"Pasco Minelli, it is the decision of this Council that you were beguiled by the one you considered your Master. Your knowledge and current abilities will be stripped from you but we do not take your potential. Should you find someone willing to take you on as apprentice, and should you follow the tenets and commandments of our profession, it is the decision of this council you could eventually earn your robe."

"Thank you. I accept the punishment."

"With the Council's blessing, I will take him on as an apprentice," Pierce said.

"Pierce Billova, you are found innocent of any charges that this council sought against you. We give blessing to your marriage. You are allowed to mentor and instruct as you see fit."

"CeeDee Billova, your child will be a wizard. Do you wish to continue with the pregnancy?"

"I am hoping that is a rhetorical question, for I am going to continue to nurture and give birth to my child. We will raise him or her with all the love and understanding my husband and I can muster. And if this child is a wizard, we will instruct it in the laws and commandments necessary."

"Good. It is the decision of this council that no matter the means of your child's conception, the baby will be a blessing and an example to all of the wizarding world that children of two wizards are to be cherished."

"Pierce, then it's over?" she asked.

"It's over." Swiftly he wrapped a powerstrand around her and they vanished, reappearing only seconds later in his Boston home.

\*\*\*

Although still early in the season, snow settled thick and heavy on the ground, fat wet flakes from a warm Atlantic ocean and a powerful nor'easter cold front. It was a quiet fall, persistent, driven by an invasive wind, covering everything. It was almost as if because of its near destruction, the world needed down-time to rest and reset parameters. With wizard sensibilities, Pierce recognized it would be a long, brutal winter, but when spring came again, life would be renewed.

Inside the huge Boston home, warmth prevailed, comfort, and time to heal. Pierce and CeeDee had dropped a line to the Dragon's Roost, to let them know Andrew and his mentor were no longer considered dangerous. The device of mass destruction had been returned to the elves. This he wasn't sure of, for Pierce wanted nothing to do with it. Although he said nothing, he was certain a small yellow piece had broken off, and not been returned with the weapon.

Pierce poured warmed wassail into two mugs, and handed one of the non-alcoholic drinks to his wife. "It's over," he said.

She sipped the sweet, tart, seasoned apple juice, found it to her liking. Inside her womb a baby turned summersaults, getting stronger every day. It was still months from being born. Her eyes sparkled with good health and a radiant pregnancy. "It's only beginning."

"You're right. Whatever happens from now on, we're together."

The fire on the grate burned cheerfully, adding warmth and the comforting scent of pine pitch to the room. Although this one had been lit by a match and judicious application of kindling, Pierce doubted he would ever enjoy a fire again without thinking of a bonfire outside of a bed and breakfast, burning as a beacon and a testimony to dragon power.

Pierce settled in beside her on the couch, but was disturbed only moments later when the doorbell rang.

"Master," Pierce said, letting Drollard in. Once he shut the door, he bowed deeply, showing his respect. "Please come in. CeeDee and I are by the fire."

"I don't wish to disturb you. How are you doing?"

"We are fine. We plan on going to the Dragon's Roost tomorrow. We found peace there, and we'd like a honeymoon."

"You should have gone tonight. It is a restful place."

"You've been there?"

"A time or two. The Inn is a friend to all who thoughtfully deal with magic."

"We needed a few hours of quiet."

"And I've interrupted. Do know, what I've come to say will be an interruption."

"Master, you are always welcome here. And maybe you could help. We're just trying to decide what we want to do with our lives. I'm given it a lot of thought. I am not excited about practicing law any longer. I think I passed the bar to please my parents, placate them into thinking one day I would be interested in politics. That's not going to happen."

"And your wife?"

"CeeDee isn't interested in returning to the library. She will have a long apprenticeship ahead, and we expect the baby will take most of her time and concentration."

"I'm sure something will present itself."

"What is it?" CeeDee asked, slowly rising to her feet, and taking Drollard's hand in hers. "You've got bad news, don't you?"

Pierce recognized his wife's insight. "Would you like a drink?"

"What are you having?"

"Wassail. CeeDee has been craving it. It is a bit unusual, but I have to say it's delicious."

"Certainly." He accepted a small decorative mug from Pierce. "It seems like exactly the right thing on a cold snowy night like tonight. And you're right. There is bad news." He paced, stood in front of the fire. "Pierce, your mother was killed tonight."

"Killed?"

"Obviously a wizard, probably someone she annoyed while she was amassing her power."

"She had no power to fight back."

"The decision was made by the entire council…"

"Yes, I know, and it was the right one. Does my father know?"

"Yes. I suspect he'll be calling you soon. He was told it was a random mugging. From what we can tell, he had no idea how she was manipulating his power base. Before this murder, he had plans to get back to work in Washington. It seems he still believes in the political system."

"And now my mother is dead."

"I wanted you to hear it from me."

Pierce carefully rubbed his stomach. Although it no longer hurt, the scars from his initial bullet wounds remained. "Any leads on the killer?"

"No, but you have my word the council is taking this seriously. Although she was not a wizard when she died, Margaret Billova was considered one of us. This is being handled as an attack against all wizards."

"Good. She would like that, at least."

"And what of the rest of your life?"

"I don't know. We've some hard decisions to make. We're thinking of selling this house. If you know a wizard who would be interested, please let us know. I can dismantle the lair easy enough, but it's a good place to work."

"I think I can find someone without much trouble. No need to destroy your lair. And where will you go?"

"We don't know. Be sure we'll tell you as soon as we have an idea."

"She wasn't always evil," Drollard said.

"I know," Pierce agreed. "I have a lot of happy memories from my early childhood. Times at the beach or at an amusement park, when we could be just a family."

"You must also realize perhaps the reason she didn't train you to be a wizard, was she did not want to corrupt you. She saw in you something too perfect to interfere with."

"That's a good thought. Thanks. I cherish that view of her."

"And CeeDee, for the work you have done for wizards and creatures of faerie, know you have our gratitude. We haven't had a finder in decades. I have no doubt wherever you settle, you will be kept busy."

"Thanks. I think maybe instead of charging money for my services, I'll simply ask for advice. The baby and I are going to need it. I understand raising a powerful wizard isn't easy."

"I have no doubt you two will manage. There's the phone now. It's probably your father. Do know you have my deepest sympathies over the death of your mother. I'll show myself out."

# EPILOGUE

After the funeral, they spent two weeks in upstate New York, at the B&B, honeymooning, playing with the four young dragons, walking paths through the mountains which local rumor stated were made by elves, and learning to snowboard. By mutual agreement they did not officially start her apprenticeship, needing this healing time to concentrate on their marriage while they could be considered equals.

Still, at night while they nestled in one of the living rooms, alone or with others who had also come to the Inn for healing, someone would invariably stop by, needing something vital found, and CeeDee would think for a while, and give directions, some general, but most precise.

While every wizard could seek and find things, like a normal person looking for misplaced car keys, the magical ability of honing in on lost artifacts was not a skill most possessed and could not be taught. She could find things. She certainly had found him. It bothered him that when she accepted her robe in a few years, she might not need him any longer.

As he punched the button on the elevator, Pierce scratched at his abdomen. The scars remained, but he discovered the habit of scratching them comforting.

The elevator door open and Pierce stepped into the floor as he had daily over most of his professional career. The law offices were quiet, professional, most work done behind closed doors or in meetings where deals were discussed or potential jurors evaluated. He had been coming here for years, every workday, staying late in the evenings, working weekends when needed, having no life beyond practicing law and his other more arcane vocation.

He had dated for the appearance of normality. Funny how normal had changed in the past few weeks.

He had been mindless, like a powerstrand. He wondered if he should follow a previous example, and turn tail and run. He should not be here any longer. He would not. He had come too close to death, had lost too much that meant the world to him. Once he turned in his resignation, he would be through.

He took a step toward his office, found he no longer had strength in his feet, his hands. He wondered if he would pass out. Powerstrands undulated around him, although in the room he shared with CeeDee, they seemed more attracted to her. But then, she had an affinity for magic.

He had his resignation in his pocket, fought black spots behind his eyes, struggled to control his breathing, for it seemed he wasn't getting enough air.

"Pierce? Mr. Billova?" Candy stood there, poised, control, confident.

He shook his head. When he could concentrate on her he felt better. "How are things?" he asked, to see if his voice worked. It did. It may have sounded a bit gravely, but he hoped nothing she would notice.

Instead she gave him an odd look and said, "You have visitors waiting for you in your office."

Visitors. Did she mean clients? He wasn't sure he could face either, not that he had any conception what a visitor would be doing in his office. The only person who had ever come to see him on a non-professional level was his mother. She was dead, and looking back he doubted any of her visits had to do with the maternal concern he always believed. She had been a practicing wizard. How could he not know? How could he have been that blind?

He dropped his hands to his side. One had been about to reach into his pocket for the resignation, the other about to scratch his stomach muscles.

"Did I have any appointments scheduled?" It had been almost a month since he had last been here, if he ignored the few days he came back immediately after the shooting when he was present in person only, and no work got done.

Candy flashed a smile, extremely white teeth against her black skin. The smile vanished leaving her looking confused for a split second before she resumed her professional mien. "No. Since I didn't know when you'd be back, I've kept your schedule open. But Mr. Billova—"

"Yes?"

"They're—" she shifted here, foot to foot, as if she hesitated, afraid to say any more.

"What Candy? Are they federal marshals or IRS agents?" Since meeting his wife, he found he had a soft spot for IRS agents.

"They arrived about five minutes ago." She shook herself, as if trying to find a politically correct term. "They're different. I suppose you'll have to find out for yourself."

"Ok. I'll see them, but I may have to ship them off to some of the other lawyers or one of the partners. I'm resigning effective immediately. My wife and I are going to hang out a shingle in a small upstate New York town."

"Wife?"

"I was right. She was pregnant."

"No abortion?"

"No abortion. Apparently there never was any danger of that."

"Well congratulations. And it was your child?"

"Yeah, actually, it turns out it was. I'm going to be a father." The word he preferred was 'daddy' but he supposed he'd have to work to achieve that one. Anyone with a Y chromosome and a bit of luck (or conversely, a lack of it) could be a father, but to be a daddy required hours of training while running beside bicycles with training wheels, selecting healthy snacks when cookies were easier, and winning bedtime negotiations over the desire for yet another story.

"We made it legal a couple weeks ago." CeeDee. Why did he concentrate so hard on all the horrid things that had happened, when obviously the best thing in his life was waiting for him right now? She was amazing.

Pierce pulled in a deep breath. For courage he decided he needed his lungs full. "I don't want to work here any longer. There're other facets of law I'm interested in pursuing. Now let's go see who's in the office."

"Mr. Billova, if you don't take the case, I might be interested in it. I've just taken the Bar, and if I pass, I've been thinking of starting my own firm."

"There will be plenty of work for you in my firm. You'd be welcome, if we can come to terms and you're interested in relocating. If not, you know I'll give you a glowing recommendation."

"Let's just see these visitors."

"Mr. Billova," an elf hopped down from a chair. It was a long jump for him, since he was only about two feet high. "I need a lawyer."

"You can see them, Candy?"

"Yes. He said he was an elf. He didn't take coffee."

Pierce rolled his eyes. "Tell me you didn't offer them chocolate?"

"Well, I didn't have any hot chocolate to offer."

"We'll never be rid of them. They're worse than cockroaches."

"In case you're wondering, I can hear you," the elf said. "It was very good chocolate."

"The stuff I sent from the candy store in upstate New York?"

"I've been hoarding it. It's fabulous."

"Yes, we'll have to stock that at my new office. You do know mortals aren't supposed to be able to see elves. I don't suppose you're a wizard or a witch?"

"No. I'm a lawyer."

"We let any mortal see us we want to. She had chocolate."

"How do you guys keep from being on the front page of every newspaper in the country?"

"Not all chocolate is as good as hers. Besides, you will need help with your new firm," the elf said. "She will be able to assist you. We have a lot of work that needs to be done. The faeries are intruding on our territory. We need an injunction to stop them."

A second elf chirped in, "And my cousin has stolen my mead recipe and claims it is his own."

"And the bumblebees are refusing to pollinate our flowers. They say we've betrayed them, when it was only a small glamour."

"Glamour?" Candy asked.

Pierce could use some of that chocolate himself. "When an elf gives you something, usually in payment for something you've done, it's usually gold. It will look like gold and even assay like gold, and then after a month or so, it will be dried leaves or something."

Another elf spoke up, sounding supremely disappointed. "You know about glamours?"

"Maybe we don't need a lawyer," the second said, shuffling his feet.

"We'll never be able to pay him," another elf muttered.

The first spoke again. "We need a lawyer. We have gold enough. Real gold. It will be worth it if we can get some of these disagreements settled."

The foot-shuffling elf spoke. "There have been many slights unanswered for too long. There is work enough for a hundred lawyers. And we know what your wife's power is. We will have work for her too. All of faerie honor a finder."

Another elf popped up. He had been hiding under the desk. Pierce decided he'd better check under there before he thought to do any work. Elves weren't evil, but releasing a handful of slugs into the carpet was their idea of a friendly joke. "And don't forget the really big thing. We need to sue that cookie company. They are using our image without our permission, even going so far as to say their cookies are baked by elves."

Pierce laughed. "I'd be glad to represent all of you. Candy, are you in?"

"Sure, it sounds like fun."

"And if you want us to treat you nice, you should have chocolate," an elf said with the others agreeing.

Why then did that sound like a threat?

\*\*\*

"You look exhausted," CeeDee said, as Pierce walked in the door of his Boston mansion.

"I am. It's been a tough week. I resigned, and I've got us a bunch of clients, ones my old firm wouldn't be interested in, so I'm not stealing them. It doesn't look like we're going to starve. Are you sure you're ok moving to the Inn?"

She wore maternity clothing for the first time that morning, not that she really needed it, but her regular slacks were feeling more than a tad snug. His appreciation of her wardrobe update and her gravid body was one of the main reasons it took him so long to get to work that morning. "Yes. I liked it there."

"You won't have to do any cooking, and there will be lots of help as you come nearer to your time to deliver the baby."

"Good."

"One other thing. I moved the house."

"The house?" She looked around her as if she should be able to see the wicked witch of the west on a bicycle out one of the windows. "What house?"

"The one I bought. I moved the bulbs and all. It's now on a lot in upstate New York, Au Sable Forks. With some new carpet and furniture, I think it will make a great office."

"Good."

"And it's got a basement, where I am going to train apprentices."

"Then you'll train me?"

He stopped, watched the hope light up her eyes. "How could I not? You're the most brilliant wizard I've ever met." She bounced into his arms, wrapped her legs around his waist, her arms around his neck. "I've also spoken to Pasco. He wants in too. My master, Drollard can send us some more apprentices when we're ready."

She kissed him, deeply, fully, then pulled back a few inches to gage his reaction. "Are you afraid to teach me?"

"We'll have to come to an understanding, so the way I treat you in the lair will have no bearing on our private relationship. I can't react to you any differently than any other apprentice, but when we're alone, I'll try to make it up to you."

"Will you yell?"

"Like my master did? I don't know. I'll try not to, but it might be a part of the learning process."

"And will I have to kill a moose?"

"No. We won't need that lesson. It was just to know if an apprentice could kill and I have no need to know if you or Pasco can kill. Now let's go upstairs. We can start packing in the morning. Our life is going to get interesting really soon, and I'd like a little time to spend with my wife."

"Before the elves take all our time?"

"Then you know about them?"

"There's not a lot about your life these days I don't know. Besides, they said they'd pay in gold."

"Really?" he asked, carrying her up the stairs. "What a surprise."


THE END

# BETSY J. BENNETT'S AUTHOR'S PAGE

My name is Betsy J. Bennett and write fantasy/paranormal romance. I often tell people that I write because my characters are far more interesting than the people I know, and that's true, but there are other reasons. I write because I see these people. I know their stories, their problems, their search for love and I have to tell it so readers can see it. I also write to avoid depression and possible homicide charges. When I write I'm happy with the world around me. I can not always control my worlds, but they always lead me to fascinating places and take unexpected turns which always turns out happily.

# Betsy J. Bennett's Books

**The Dragon's Roost Bed & Breakfast Series**

| | |
|---|---|
| Book 1 | **A Dragon's Tea** |
| Book 2 | **A Gargoyle's Vow** |
| Book 3 | **A Wizard's Spell** |
| **Book 4** | **A Ghost's Chance** |

**Santa Takes a Wife**
**Yes, Virginia.**

**The Frog Kiss**

**Her Puzzle**

**Strangers in the Night**

**Left Star of Orion's Belt**

All books are available on AMAZON.com

www.ingramcontent.com/pod-product-compliance
Lightning Source LLC
Chambersburg PA
CBHW020554180626
46810CB00007B/2506